SUSPECTS

Wright Morris, *Reflection in Oval Mirror, Home Place, Nebraska,* 1947

SUSPECTS

David Thomson

Vintage Books
A Division of Random House
New York

FIRST VINTAGE BOOKS EDITION, October 1986

Copyright © 1985 by David Thomson

All rights reserved under International and Pan-American Copyright
Conventions. Published in the United States by Random House, Inc.,
New York. Published by Alfred A. Knopf, Inc., in 1985.

Library of Congress Cataloging in Publication Data

Thomson, David, 1941—
  Suspects.

Reprint. Originally published: New York: Knopf, © 1985.

I. Title.
PR 6070. H678S8   1986   823'.914   86-40145
ISBN 0-394-74468-3 (pbk.)

Manufactured in the United States of America

For
Tom Luddy

"Each man's life touches so many other lives."
—Clarence the angel, in *It's a Wonderful Life*

"Round up the usual suspects."
—Captain Louis Renault, in *Casablanca*

Jake Gittes	Vivian Sternwood
Noah Cross	L. B. Jeffries
Ilsa Lund	Lars Thorwald
John Clay	Alicia Huberman
Axel Freed	Alexander Sebastian
Eileen Wade	Walker
David Staebler	Chris Rose
Judy Rogers	Ma Jarrett
Kit Carruthers	Cody Jarrett
Waldo Lydecker	Brigid O'Shaughnessy
Laura Hunt	Casper Gutman
Helen Ferguson	Victor Laszlo
Dickson Steele	Richard Blaine
Laurel Gray	Elsa Bannister
Roy Earle	Adeline Loggins
Marie Garson	Jay Landesman Gatsby
Henry Oliver Peterson	Norman Bates
Gwen Chelm	Bruno Anthony
Alma McCain	Dolly Schiller
David John Locke	Bernstein
Maureen Cutter	Susan Alexander Kane
Al	Raymond
Joe Gillis	Mary Kane
Max von Mayerling	Sally Bailey
Guy Haines	Gilda Farrell
Pete Lunn	Hank Quinlan
Kitty Collins	Ramon Miguel Vargas
Amy Jolly	Jeff Bailey
Norma Desmond	Bree Daniels
Julian Kay	John Klute
Walter Neff	Mary Ann Simpson
Phyllis Diedrichson	John Ferguson
Wilson Keyes	Judy Barton
Debby Marsh	Smith Ohlrig
Harry Lime	Howard
Kay Corleone	Evelyn Cross Mulwray
Skip McCoy	Harry Moseby
Cora Papadakis	Paula Iverson
Frank Chambers	Travis Bickle
Jimmy Doyle	Frederick Manion
Francine Evans	Mark McPherson
John Converse	George Bailey
Jack Torrance	

SUSPECTS

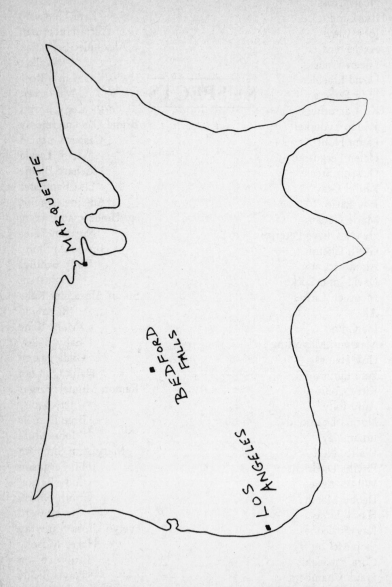

At this time, in the evening, with fifteen hundred miles of moist heat sighing against the house, I let my unsteady heart beat in its paper prison. . . .

JAKE GITTES

Jack Nicholson in Chinatown, *1974,*
directed by Roman Polanski

In November 1901, at the Tulip Tree, a whorehouse on Stockton Street in San Francisco, where she worked, the nineteen-year-old Opal Chong gave birth to Jacob. She was a Eurasian who named her child after Jacob Schwartz, an agreeable policeman whose patrol included that stretch of Stockton. The infant was allowed to live on the premises, and Opal (a star of the house—she was alluded to occasionally, with awe, in the social column of the *San Francisco Chronicle*, written by Herbert Kane) was permitted a second room of her own by the proprietress, Adeline "Lady" Ray. The other girls spoiled Jacob whenever they could, but Opal went from carefree to strict. She was not as imaginative a whore after his birth.

Jacob was acquiring Chinese and pocket money from errands for the house laundry when the Tulip Tree was leveled in the San Francisco earthquake of 1906. Opal perished in that disaster, but only after she and her son had been trapped seven hours in the debris. Later in life, Jake told the story that his mother protected him from the full weight of a collapsed beam, and instructed him in the pleasuring of a woman before she expired. He never made this story plausible, but listeners took it as a sign of his romantic inclination.

The boy's education and welfare were assumed as duties by Mrs. Ray and the policeman Schwartz. They put him in an orphanage in Sacramento and had his name changed to Gittes, apparently after a lawyer who had been disbarred a few years earlier. "Jake" Gittes had few visitors in his years in Sacramento, and he left the orphanage in 1918 with a reputation as a dark schemer, a promising middleweight and the chronic teller of tall stories.

Moving to Los Angeles, and fighting as "Chink" Gittes, he had a three-year ring career that included a bloody but honorable draw with Harry Greb. He gave up the game when he was obliged to "lose" two fights in a row for gambling coups. It was in one of those thrown contests that he suffered a broken nose, leaving him with a somewhat nasal intonation and recurrent respiratory problems, so that he was sometimes known as "Snort."

Jake retired from the ring in 1922 and was then a worker with —soon to be manager of—a swimming-pool construction company that employed mostly Chinese labor. It appears likely that Gittes was personally responsible for some fanciful novelty designs—for instance, the Cobra Pool at Rudolph Valentino's Falcon Lair home. Apparently thriving, the company was driven into liquidation when one of its pools was shown to have a defective chlorination system, as a result of which a Silverlake child had died of cholera. Jake always believed that the "accident" was linked to his refusal to take out insurance with the local police.

Thus, in 1925, having learned fatalism, Jake Gittes joined the Los Angeles Police Department. He was promoted and in 1928 he was assigned to Chinatown as a detective. A distinguished career might have been his but for the Iris Ling case. Another Eurasian, and the owner of a small, prestigious brothel, she and Gittes became lovers. But Ling was under pressure from a Tong gang, and Jake rashly promised police protection—it was LAPD practice to stay aloof from native disputes in Chinatown. Iris was found, wandering and incoherent, in the Santa Monica mountains, blinded and abused. No arrests were ever made, and Jake resigned from the force in helpless disgust.

He next set up the J. J. Gittes Detective Agency, specializing in divorce work. He was experiencing a modest if rather flashy prosperity when, in 1937, he was drawn into the affairs of Evelyn and Hollis Mulwray. This led Jake to investigate the part played by Noah Cross, Evelyn's father, in the manipulation of water in southern California. In love with Evelyn—by then a widow—Jake was there in Chinatown when police shot and killed her after she had wounded her father in an obscure family altercation. In the investigation, Judge Robert Evans said Jake had acted with "disastrous good intentions . . . and culpable naiveté, especially when you recall the clever pug he was."

For a year he did not leave his Los Feliz apartment—a victim of hepatitis and melancholy. He drifted thereafter, but found work farther north in 1942 at an internment camp for the Japanese. He married Aioshi Ichikawa, an internee, and there were allegations after the war that Jake had run a ring of prostitutes in the camp for munitions workers in the area.

By then, however, he was in Japan. In 1946, he and Aioshi went to Tokyo, where Jake returned to the swimming-pool trade with a partner, Alex Dawson. A daughter was born in 1949—Iris—and Jake became rich enough to travel in the East. Rumors spread from Macao to Manila that he was an operative of the CIA, and it is known that in 1960 he was in Saigon supervising the installation of an exotic indoor pool for Madame Nhu.

In 1972, Aioshi (still resident in Tokyo) said she had not seen Jake for four years; she was then in personal charge of the swimming-pool/golf-course design company. Iris, a photographers' model in Hong Kong, said she had met her father in Saigon in 1971, and reported that he was in poor health, suffering from jaundice, but working for a gaming club known as the Red Sash.

Dead or alive, present whereabouts unknown. There can be a lurking poetry in reference-book style: official statements with a hint of suspiciousness, as if one were hard of hearing between the lines. I will never let Jake die.

> *All those movies, hundreds a year for fifty years, with only seven or so story structures in all of them. I can see through the window the street lamp on the corner saying Bedford Falls is safe and civilized. And there is the light in my window that anyone passing by might call tranquil home life, or anxiety's tireless friction. I write by night.*

NOAH CROSS

John Huston in Chinatown, *1974, directed by Roman Polanski*

What follows can be no more than notes waiting for the publication of Gore Vidal's biography of Cross, so often announced and postponed, yet still promised as *Noah's Flood: The Wealth of America.*

Noah Cross was born in 1870 in a prodigious rainstorm that prompted his name. He was the son of Julian Cross (1828–99), a leading Virginian and tobacco farmer, and Minna Russell (1851–91), granddaughter of Lord John Russell, British Prime Minister from 1846 to 1852. That couple met in London in the early 1860s (when the lady was only a child) during a secret mission undertaken by Cross on behalf of the Confederacy. Married in 1868, Minna went with her husband to live in Charlottesville. Her life there was made wretched and abbreviated by an asthma played upon by the rich, humid air, by her husband and by the fatal onset of lung cancer, which she ascribed to "living, willy-nilly, in America's fuming humidor." Her son was her single consolation, and local lore had it that he would sleep in her bed on thundery nights, up to the age of twelve.

Noah studied history at the University of Virginia and graduated in 1892. A noted horseman, he entered the cavalry and, as a colonel, he took part in the 1898 skirmishing in Cuba, where he was wounded in the right thigh. In the aftermath of these hostilities, Cross purchased land in Cuba very cheaply—"for what I had in my pocket"—and this became the basis of the Cross Fruit Company.

With both parents dead, Cross inherited lands in Virginia and Derbyshire, England, as well as the family tobacco interests. Leaving these under wise management, he went west and spent a year riding in the Sierras. In 1901 he built a house for himself near Los Angeles, and in 1902 he married Hester Doheny, the daughter of the oil magnate Edward Doheny. Their daughter, Evelyn, was born in 1905, but Hester died of influenza in 1919. In four generations, no Cross woman lived past forty.

The first decade of this century was a period of vast business expansion for Cross. By the time of America's entry into the First World War, *The Wall Street Journal* estimated, he was growing 8 percent of the cigarettes smoked in the U.S., canning 12 percent of its fruit, and "effectively licensing" the water flushed away by Los Angeles. This last accomplishment was the result of a collaboration between Cross and William Mulholland of the Los Angeles Department of Water and Power that took possession of water from the Owens River Valley for use by the city. Officially an urban policy, it only proceeded after Cross had purchased key acreages, the value of which kept rising in direct proportion to the population of Los Angeles. This enterprise provoked angry controversy (Upton Sinclair called Cross "The Great Rapist"), but Cross repudiated every charge by quoting Mulholland's first estimate of the water in the Owens Valley: "There it is—take it."

What *The Wall Street Journal* of 1917 could not know was that Cross was also a silent partner in the Hughes Tool Company. In 1909, he had gone to the aid of Howard Robard Hughes and Walter Sharp when they needed capital. Cross remained a shareholder in that company until it came under the control of Howard Hughes, Jr., a man Cross could not endure and about whom he said, "In the old days a tycoon was a man who, tastefully I daresay, threatened *other* people. This gray-suit cowboy is perpetually alarmed about his *own* health. No good will come of it."

Also in Los Angeles, it was Noah Cross who had prevailed upon a young "photoplay artist," Cecil B. De Mille, to make his film *The Squaw Man*, in the village of Hollywood. Thus Cross deserves much credit for bringing motion pictures to Los Angeles: he had, in 1910, helped arrange the co-opting of Hollywood into the city of Los Angeles in return for its water supply. Cross and De Mille became fast friends, and it was through that contact, in 1921, that Cross joined the board of Paramount. He is alleged to have told its chairman, Adolph Zukor, on that day, "My life—make that," little guessing that soon after his death the same company would treat parts of his career in *Chinatown*. It was De Mille, also, who introduced Cross to the actress Norma Desmond—their affair resulted in his setting her up in a mansion on Sunset Boulevard which she retained in the fierce suit that followed his boredom with her. Some felt his admission of it drove her mad. (Actresses sit on a narrow ledge, and they are preserved by our response, our loving them.)

When Edward Doheny was implicated in the Teapot Dome scandal (1922–24) it was his son-in-law, Noah Cross, who went out of his way to pay off witnesses and journalists. For those services, Cross gained entry into the oil industry, links that would prove instrumental in the eventual sale of Paramount to Gulf & Western, at which point Cross is reputed to have told his colleague Zukor, "What you have never had to find out, my dear Adolph, is that under compelling conditions a board may do anything."

It was in 1921 that Cross's daughter, the sixteen-year-old Evelyn, married Hollis Mulwray, the diligent head of the Department of Water and Power, when she became pregnant with her father's child. This child was named Katherine. In his nineties, Cross would talk privately about the matter: "Evelyn should not have been so much around that summer," he said. "My wife had died and . . . it was a provocation." By then, however, Cross's longevity had transcended morality: it is the survivors who present history, and for Noah Cross life was always larger than its crimes.

The Depression brought scarcely a pause in Cross's progress. By 1935, he was reckoned to have a personal fortune worth over $500 million. It was in 1937 that his son-in-law, Hollis (salaried at $32,500 a year), began to threaten Cross. As the matter grew uglier and more confused, a private investigator, J. J. Gittes, was involved—both professionally and romantically. Hated by Evelyn, attacked by Hollis and hounded by Gittes, Cross found fresh impetus in his old zest to survive. Evelyn was killed by the police after wounding her father. Katherine went to live with her grandfather. But Katherine Mulwray killed herself when she was eighteen: she was found drowned in the Hollywood Reservoir. Cross had her cremated, without autopsy. He could get things done.

In his last decades, Cross retreated—to Galway, in Ireland, where he bred, rode and talked to horses; and, until 1959, to Cuba. No waning in his faculties was observed, apart from a little arthritis from his several old wounds. His empire swelled still, always under his scrutiny. He dabbled with a volume of memoirs, *Deep Waters Run Still*, never finished. We must wait for Mr. Vidal to find confirmation of whether or not he was a patron of, and advisor to, Gregory Arkadin, Eva Perón or Warren Beatty.

He died, early on the morning of June 18, 1972, in Ireland, of a massive heart attack, while on the phone to Washington, D.C.

> *I will never quite escape the sway of Noah Cross or the urge to imitate him. It would amaze anyone who knows me, but I could have been like him, could still put on a Stetson and drawl away. He was as grand and convincing as an actor. But I am real and splintered. I have hundreds—well, seven or so—to please.*

ILSA LUND

Ingrid Bergman in Casablanca, *1942,*
directed by Michael Curtiz

Although only a hundred miles from Stockholm, Askersund, the country estate where Ilsa Lund was born in 1918, was an idyllic enclave made claustrophobic by the dire feud that prevailed between her parents. The girl could do nothing except hope to outlast its withering effect. We know how valiant her spirit was because, until the moment of her unexpected death, she never backed away from the sincere hope that lives could be improved. But in her last photographs, we see the grave marks of disappointment.

Her father was a count whose small fortune was wiped out by the Kreuger speculations exposed in 1932. Her mother was a determined feminist at war with her husband and horrified to discover her own pregnancy. The country people had a notion that Ilsa was "simple," but that was only the servants' gossipy view of a child who never took sides and was invariably frustrated in her attempts to love two people who hated the sight of each other. The mother died when Ilsa was only eleven, of an illness that seems to have been just the breaking out of unmanageable rage. The girl was left alone with a morose father whose one need for his wife had been as an enemy.

So it was that Ilsa became infatuated with one of the young men servants in the household. They had a clumsy, furtive affair and he told her they would elope. But when the moment came, his nerve failed; Ilsa faced humiliation and misery if she stayed. On her own, and with very little money, she made her way to Germany in the summer of 1937.

In that terrible country, she was like a refugee from another century. But in Munich, and then later in Berlin, she was employed at a school for languages, first in a menial capacity, and then, when her German was more secure, as a teacher of Swedish. It was a bare existence in which her peace of mind was further eroded by the daily persecution of Jews. She intervened once or twice in street brawls and was once detained by the police. It was this incident that made her German pupils persuade her to leave Berlin. The language school had premises in Paris, and she went there late in 1938.

In Paris, she met an American expatriate, Richard Blaine. Not only were they lovers in that time of phony war; Blaine also served as the mentor she had never had. A former labor organizer in America, who also claimed to have fought in the Spanish Civil War, he introduced her to the works of Marx, Trotsky, Victor Serge and John Reed. Their relationship was stormy: he was a heavy drinker and she challenged his brutally despairing attitudes too much for his comfort.

Blaine quit Paris on the eve of the German occupation, but Ilsa remained behind. As a national of a neutral country, she was able to live in Paris teaching languages to German officers. Late in 1940, she was approached by "Octave," a leader in the Resistance, who wanted to exploit her contacts in the enemy high command. She undertook several assignments for Octave—a hungry, lazy, rootless man—and had "Elena" as her code name.

Early in 1941, she was sent through Lyon to the vicinity of the Swiss border to rendezvous with Victor Laszlo, a Hungarian partisan who had escaped from a concentration camp. Together they traveled by way of Biarritz and Lisbon to Casablanca. Unbeknown to Ilsa, Blaine was then established in that city as a café proprietor.

It was widely assumed that Ilsa and Laszlo were married, but that was only a cover which inhibited Ilsa's reawakened feelings for Blaine. In truth, she never warmed to Laszlo and had early misgivings about his genuineness. But thanks to Blaine's assistance, she and Laszlo were able to obtain the scarce letters of credit that permitted departure from Casablanca. And so they made their circuitous way to America.

In New York by the fall of 1941, they were hailed as heroes of the struggle against fascism. But security agencies were not satisfied that Laszlo had indeed been in a concentration camp. Some wondered if he was a Nazi plant; others felt that he was a quixotic opportunist bizarrely touched by good fortune. In the words of the official report, ". . . it was so contrived an escape from German authority that it seems to have required the personal attention of Germany's ace, Major Heinrich Strasser." Later on, it was impossible to measure the balance of truth and masquerade in either Laszlo's boisterous identification with Communism in the years after 1942, or his tearful coming clean to the House Un-American Activities Committee in 1949. In all of this, Ilsa was an unhappy bystander, estranged from Laszlo but under suspicion by association. It was an undoubted relief for her when Laszlo died, of emphysema, in 1952—he had kept up a vulgar society trick of smoking two cigarettes at the same time.

Ilsa's American period was as unsettled as the rest of her life. She again taught languages, being proficient by now in five. She did some work subtitling the early films of Ingmar Bergman, and she was for a while the intimate of writer Delmore Schwartz. He refers to her in his collection *Vaudeville for a Princess*:

> And we shall never be as once we were,
> This life will never be what once it was!
> There is no prospect for tomorrow's thrills,
> Now and Tuesday, I must remember Ilsa.

More recently, research by Gail Levin has suggested that Ilsa may be the tall blonde woman, naked but for a blue sleeveless wrap and red high-heeled shoes, standing in the doorway in the Edward Hopper painting of 1949 *High Noon*. There are other mysteriously austere sexual icons in Hopper's later work that might be Ilsa Lund.

It was in 1955, against the concerned urgings of the FBI (still uncertain of her ideological allegiances), that Dag Hammarskjöld, Secretary General of the U.N., hired her as a personal assistant. True to their very close working relationship, she died with him in 1961 when his plane crashed in West Africa on its way to Kinshasa.

JOHN CLAY

Sterling Hayden in The Killing, *1956,*
directed by Stanley Kubrick

On a windless night, a little after nine p.m., how long would it take the engines on a DC-7, warming up, to disperse the contents of a large suitcase full of notes to the value of two million dollars?

John Clay, Johnny, was born in Oakland, California, in 1920. His father was a railroad conductor and his mother looked after the seven children. Twice a week the father was home with dry accounts of how the train had made its way between Seattle and Los Angeles. There were men who rode the freights then, going up and down the coast looking for work. Mr. Clay tipped them off, awake or not, whenever he found them, in the way he took a toothpick and coaxed shreds of meat from between his teeth after a meal. "Don't you ever let 'em ride?" asked Johnny. "No, sir," said his father, "against the rules."

"You miss some, I bet," reasoned his son. "If I see 'em, I don't miss 'em."

A suitcase forty-six inches long, twenty-eight high and a full fourteen inches deep—18,032 cubic inches. All those numbers, and all the notes with numbers on them. These were the notes taken in at Bay Meadows racetrack that day, small bills, crumpled, torn, some put back together again with Scotch tape in a last hope of a killing.

Johnny Clay was too big for school by the time he was fourteen. So he went away from home and down to the San Joaquin Valley. There were supposed not to be jobs, but Johnny knew where to go and he spent his teens following work between Modesto and Bakersfield. He picked almonds, artichokes and so on, all the way to zucchini. He was picking things he'd never eaten. By the time he was eighteen he was as hard and straight as a pole, and he smelled of onions. No washing could get rid of it. He used to think he was growing in that Valley himself, that strange reformed desert where canals and aqueducts patrol the earth and will not let it die. He counted the vegetables as he picked them, the boxes where he and the other pickers stacked them, the trucks that went out every night, and then all the other operations like the one he was on. It gave him a feeling for the millions in America.

No one ever knew for sure—the beauty of this robbery was that no one ever knew just how much—but about 4,000 fifties, 20,000 twenties, 80,000 tens, 100,000 fives and 60,000 ones. Over a quarter of a million bills, and an estimated total of two million dollars.

Johnny rode the trains in those days, and he still knew which ones his father was on. All the Clays had the timetable by heart. So sometimes he would slip aboard at dusk on a long uphill, and he'd be back home just a few minutes ahead of his father—with dust in his hair still—and he'd look up when his father came in and he'd say, "Still throwing 'em off the freights?"

He boxed a little, he was so impressive physically, but Johnny didn't know how to put another man away, and they said he didn't punch his weight. He looked good in the ring, but no one believed he was going anywhere. In 1941 he went into the navy. He served all the war as a seaman. Torpedoed once, and then again, his ship was sunk at Leyte Gulf. He was in the water once, and a small boat the other time, thirty-one hours and eleven days, seeing sharks all around the first time, and counting out the food and the days the second time. If he had been a prince or a president's son there would have been a book about him.

This case had been purchased at a pawnshop. It was strong, and it had metal corner pieces. But one of the fasteners didn't work; it flapped like a broken wing. And Johnny had no time to get a strap to put around the case. A strap would have made it all right. Johnny thought afterward that he could have used the belt on his pants.

When he came back from the war he was two hundred pounds and only twenty-five, so he fought some more. He wasn't as gentle a man either; anyone could see that the war had hardened him. They called him "Seaman" Clay on the bills, but it wasn't quite right, and though Johnny kept winning he never looked confident. People would always bet against him, no matter that he was the stronger man. Then one hot August night in Stockton in 1948, Ezzard Charles nearly killed him. People relaxed and said they'd always known it was going to happen.

So Johnny got out of boxing. He knew some gangsters, from Tahoe, and he fell in with them. They used him as muscle in the casinos. Johnny heard of jobs they were on, and he asked to be let in, but the others kidded him that he was punchy. So he watched these jobs and worked it out why most of them failed. And then in 1950 he went after one of the casinos in Reno. All on his own, with a plan. He studied the place and saw how at five a.m. on the third Sunday of the month there was a way to take everything. It was over a million, they said. The job worked, and Johnny was free for two months because no one could believe it was just one man. But they caught him, in Eureka, with all the money, except what he'd spent on meals and gas. He could have lived four hundred years on it at the rate he was going.

The case was on the top of two layers of luggage at the outside corner, so when the little motorized cart taking it to the plane swerved, the case fell off and a bump on the concrete broke it open.

They sent Johnny to Alcatraz in 1951. He was mild and patient about it, and he never ate all the heavy foods they gave the cons there. He ate moderately and worked in the yard while the others were up on the top bleachers looking across the Bay at the city, asking themselves how all the people could go about their business every day with the prison only a mile and a half away in the sunshine, and men festering there. But a prisoner is likely to be more philosophical than a free man.

Johnny was in a cell with Kola Kwarian, and Kola taught him chess. It nearly broke Johnny's brain to see how many moves you could figure. But there were just sixty-four squares and just thirty-two pieces to play with. So he worked it all out and got to be a fair player,

11

though he could never beat Kola. One day the Russian told him a story about how an emperor once had held a city to ransom. He'd said he'd take a sack of grain on the first square of the chessboard, two on the next, four on the next, and so on, geometric progression. At first, the people thought that would be easy. But Kola laughed and he told Johnny there would never be that much grain in all the history of the world. Johnny nodded quietly, for he had always known the world must end.

The cart swerved because of a dog. Today, there'd be no chance of a dog getting out there. But in 1956 airports were less formal.

In Alcatraz, Johnny planned the Bay Meadows robbery, and when he got out he went straight ahead with it. It only needed five of them. Marv Unger put up the seed money. George Peatty, the cashier, opened the door to let Johnny in behind the scenes. Mike O'Reilly, the barman, had brought the gun in earlier in the day, and left it in his locker so Johnny could use it for the holdup. Randy Kennan, the cop, would put the bag of money in his car and drive out; who was going to stop a police car? There were two others for smaller things: Nikki Agoglia to shoot Red Lightning on the far turn so everyone was diverted, and Kola to start a fight in the bar to get all the cops' attention.

Two million dollars, and it worked. Except that Johnny could see notes spilling no matter how careful the cashiers were. And then later, out in Daly City, when he transferred the money from the duffel bag to the suitcase, there was some left on the ground. So maybe it was only $1.9 million in the case, going to the plane, warming up to fly to Boston, with Johnny and his girl Fay at the gate. Then the dog and the swerve. When the case opened it still took eleven seconds for all that money to be whirled away by the aircraft engines, and they were only thirty feet from the case. The money had been thrown in like dirty laundry. There were people at the airport for years afterward looking, and you still hear of notes being found. But officially they recovered $632,127.

They sent Johnny back to Alcatraz and he died there in 1960.

> *Is the order of these entries significant? I do them as they come into my head, but my head keeps running back to system. So design and randomness bump together, skirmishing, like lovers.*

AXEL FREED

James Caan in The Gambler, *1974,
directed by Karel Reisz*

"We will see that the boy is brought up nicely," A. R. Lowenthal encouraged his daughter, Naomi, in 1943. She was holding her baby, a foot long, with yards of fine white robes reaching to the floor. The child was born swarthy, with piercing brown eyes and a sensual mouth. No one could remember seeing a baby who paid such attention so early. "He has the stare of a victorious general," said Lowenthal. "Or a painter?" suggested Naomi. Her husband, Lowenthal's son-in-law, a frail man named Rudolf, stood by like a stranger in the three-stage family rapture. He noticed his own weakness in his new son's face, but he was too reticent to say the word *gambler* out loud. Anyway, he died a year later, of a perforated stomach ulcer, with so many things unsaid.

A. R. Lowenthal, Armyan Lowenthal—he added the *R* much later for rhythm—had come to America from Lithuania in 1911, when he was fifteen, with "nothing except wit and balls and will." He had won a reputation as a king of style, and a killer in business. By the middle 1920s he owned a chain of furniture stores in the New York area which he still supervised and for which he remembered every smallest detail. He was an awesome figure for any family, a giant of achievement and appetite, nearly a monster of success. No flaws showed in his castle.

His own wife had dimmed in his light. Their daughter Naomi had elected very early to please him. In bringing forth a son, she had met the wish always uppermost in his mind. A.R. looked on Axel—a name he had urged—as if he were a golden bowl smuggled across a continent for his delight alone. The old man loved to hold his grandson, humming long passages from Mahler and swaying the tiny bundle in time with the sweep of his own romantic longings. Secure, old, and weak in the heart, A.R. dreamed of further glories. Axel's chestnut eyes watched him with intense curiosity, certain somehow, no matter how immature, that he would have a contest of wills with this gray-haired dear. He conceived the urge not to please his grandfather, even if it destroyed him, Axel, in the process.

A dedicated mother and a rich grandfather made a brilliant child.

He was eloquent at five. He could sketch quickly, dance with grace, play the piano by ear, tell stories to his elders, captivate strangers, play games with a skill ahead of his years. He was like a perfect child. But he had a momentous temper that could turn him into a dervish of violence in an instant. It was beyond his control, a passionate anger always directed at playmates or people on the street, but so dramatic it served to put a dark cloud around him in the eyes of others. It was self-destruction, not yet aware of its true target.

He went to Harvard in 1961, becoming best friends with the sons of Latin American dictators and Brahmin families. He wooed the daughter of a branch of the English nobility and married her. He was, for the short duration of the marriage, mentioned in Burke's Peerage. But he moved with equal ease among mobsters, bookmakers and loan sharks. As his father had known, Axel could have been a lord, a poet, a banker or a killer, but gambling became his abiding interest. He would be locked in writing a textual analysis of Donne and Marvell, only to reach out for the phone and put a thousand dollars on Boston College to beat the spread against DePaul. He read every newspaper he could find, but only the sports sections. He loved the games, not for their beauty or the prowess they required but because of the odds and the likelihood that hovered above them, like bees near flowers on a hot day.

This went on for several years, the scale rising. He could be breathtakingly rich one day, and then a week later forced to borrow twenty dollars from Naomi. Sometimes he was a center of cheerful groups; sometimes he hid from his creditors. Not that either state pleased him. The indecision was his greatest gratification, the risk. There was no winning so great, no luck so magical, that he would not bet until it crashed down.

Nineteen seventy-four was the last chance, the last crisis. After that there was no going back. One night at a private casino in Manhattan, he lost $44,000. It was the largest debt he had ever had. Axel got up from the table exhilarated by the magnificent danger, smiling with love and a killer's kiss at the casino management, discussing how he would pay them back. "Soon, Axel, soon," they said. "Sure," he answered, "soon." They were so businesslike; he was such an amateur. His amusement always hurt them and made them feel shabby. They could guarantee an extra slash of the razor when the time came.

Then he went to see Billie, his current girl. She was a model, lithe, thin, blonde, Californian, the most unsuitable sexual prize he could find for a scholar and a Jew. She was butter next to his anchovy. He went to the college classroom and talked about Dostoyevski: he was a part-time professor, a natural at existentialism, a firebrand for *The Idiot*, *The Gambler* and Karamazovian bargains with destiny. He went to his mother for $10,000, a stay against execution. He went to a birthday party for A.R. on the beach. He explained his whole predicament to Naomi. So as not to spoil her father's day, she gave Axel a check for $44,000 along with the advice, "Come to terms with why you're doing this."

He scooped up Billie, and took her to Las Vegas. "I'm hot as a pistol," he assured her, and there in a Nevada casino, at blackjack, with 18 showing, he did not so much ask as tell the croupier, "Give me the 3," with a force so great that the woman was not surprised when she flipped it over for him. He won $90,000, the most he had ever won. But he lost half of it again when Brown beat Harvard at basketball, and another $50,000 went away when, in the last second, Seattle turned it on the Lakers 111–110. He bet all he had left on another game, and won. It was desperate and ecstatic. "If all my bets were safe," he said, "there wouldn't be any juice."

He went back to New York, and the Mob sent men out to catch him, hold him by the ears and bring him in. "You owe us," they said. "Sure," said Axel. "But I'm broke. Stake me again." They said, no more. He would have to do something for them. There was a black kid in his class, Carl Spencer, on the basketball team, the star forward. Get him to fix the spread against Syracuse. "How?" said Axel. Impress him, they said, the kid respects you, genius. And as he was going on this drab mission, one of the mobsters called out, "Hey, Axel, one day you'll be killing someone for us."

He grinned, lustrous with exaltation. The game was fixed. Spencer was ashamed. The debt was canceled. Axel had a clean slate. So he went up to Harlem into a black club, demanding the best whore in the place. He insulted the pimp. "What do I have to do, nigger?" And the whore cut his face with a knife. With the bliss of nearing disaster, Axel looked at his wound in the mirror.

EILEEN WADE

Nina Van Pallandt in The Long Goodbye, *1973,
directed by Robert Altman*

Frederick Gould was an eminent King's Counsel. He specialized in litigation and society divorces, and he acted in England for Mrs. Wallis Simpson in the divorce that freed her to marry King Edward VIII. Eileen, born in London in 1938, was his second child. The family stayed in town, living in the Boltons throughout the Blitz, though Eileen and her brother John, with their mother, were evacuated to Devon for parts of 1941–42.

Eileen grew up a tall, attractive blonde girl, a pupil at St. Paul's School for Girls. She sang at school, and took the part of Ado Annie in a production of *Oklahoma!* Her father wanted her to go on to Cambridge, but an unfortunate misunderstanding over her entrance exams sent her instead to a finishing school in Switzerland. While there, she added several foreign languages to her education and perfected the straightfaced lie, a ploy that some had noted in her at an early age. It was while in Switzerland, in 1957, that she became the mistress of the American business tycoon J. J. Cord. The affair lasted only one summer, but through Cord's graces she was able to go back and forth between Europe and America for the next few years, an assured resident alien.

She did this and that: she managed an antiques store on Wilshire Boulevard in Los Angeles, she had a stud farm in Galway, and she was a literary agent in Paris. But in 1962, in London, she set up the first of a small chain of health-food shops—Nuts—that were known during the sixties as a trendsetter. Eileen herself traveled in the Mediterranean and North Africa, obtaining the best possible supply of grains, nuts and pulses, raisins, dates and other dried fruits. In 1966, she wrote her *Health Food Cookbook*, which was a big success when published by Penguin.

In London, in the mid-sixties, Eileen Gould was a frequent figure in the gossip columns: she was alleged to be a close friend of Albert Finney, Andrew Oldham and Tony Godwin, then the editorial director of Penguin Books. She also spent several summers on the island of Ibiza, and it was rumored that she had acted as a middleman in the sale to major galleries of paintings done by Elmyr de

Hory—who had a studio on the island—but "signed" by Dufy, Matisse or Utrillo.

Late in 1967, the British Customs and Excise confiscated a consignment of dried apricots sent from Morocco to London for Nuts. The barrels were found to contain several pounds of high-grade hashish. Eileen Gould protested that she had no knowledge of this secret ingredient; and the police could find no clinching evidence that she had been involved in the illegal importation of drugs. However, the affairs of Nuts came under close scrutiny, and in 1968 Eileen sold the company for £1.1 million to the Trust House Forte group.

With the proceeds, she traveled—to the Mediterranean and to America—and farther afield, to Africa and the South Seas. It was in Tahiti, in 1970, that she met Roger Wade, the novelist. Wade (1918–73)—real name Billy Joe Smith—had been a soldier captured at Bataan and a prisoner of the Japanese. A wanderer and a sailor, after the war he had lived in Sausalito, and started to write—*A Man Cannot Stand Confinement* (1949), *Vienna and Johnny and Old Nick* (1957) and *Undertow* (1964). These were all best-sellers, and they allowed Wade—his adopted name as a writer—to buy a series of sailboats. However, by the time he met Eileen, Wade was an alcoholic, more inclined to talk about his next novel than get on with it.

They were married in 1970, on board his schooner, the *Aquavit*, in Pailolo Channel, off the island of Maui. The couple sailed back to California and took a house in the Malibu Colony. Wade struggled to write a new book and Eileen opened a health-food store in Santa Barbara. It was not a happy marriage for very long, and Eileen started an affair with Terry Lennox, a Malibu neighbor and a former baseball player.

It was in 1973 that Lennox's wife, Sylvia, was found beaten to death and Terry Lennox disappeared. In fact, he had been driven to Mexico by an old friend, Philip Marlowe. Eileen stayed behind and hired Marlowe to look for her husband when he disappeared on one of his drunken binges. This was only a way of making gambler and gangster Marty Augustine, as well as the police, believe that Terry had killed himself in Mexico from remorse. Eileen flirted with Marlowe, and one night at Malibu, as they were becoming intimate, the drunken Roger Wade walked out of the house and into the Pacific, where he drowned.

Not long after that, Eileen sold the Malibu house and went away. Marlowe played a hunch. He went to Mexico, to the small town where Terry Lennox had been certified dead and buried. He talked to the local authorities, and guessed that they had been bribed. So he waited and explored, and he talked to kids in the sunny squares and to old men in the sleepy bars. He met a drunk named Firmin who told him he had seen a blonde woman, nearly six feet tall, with hair the color of sunrise. Tequila sunrise, thought Marlowe, but he checked it out.

Marlowe found the villa where Lennox and Eileen were living, and he went there one day when Eileen was at the market. Marlowe had liked Wade; they had sat on the beach one afternoon seeing how much they could drink. Lennox laughed when Marlowe told him the story. Nobody cares, he said. Nobody cares but me, said Marlowe. You're a born loser, sighed Lennox. So Marlowe shot him, and when Eileen got back she had food for two with her lover floating on top of the pool.

There has been no word of Eileen Wade since then, nothing to pin her down. She had money, but she was the kind of woman people notice. There are no charges against her anywhere. Marlowe never put in a report. Maybe Eileen went farther south. There was a story in 1980 about a white woman running a resort hotel in Sulaco. And that's where Frederick Gould retired in 1974, the law set aside.

DAVID STAEBLER

Jack Nicholson in The King of Marvin Gardens, *1972, directed by Bob Rafelson*

Four times in ten years, different doctors have suggested he try reducing the dose. David Staebler doesn't welcome the thought, but he has always been obedient and self-pitying enough to suffer under the system. It's important that he treat this warning about scaling down the drug as if it came from the IRS, or some other arrangement of initials stamped into the spine of the state, an authority not to be denied or questioned. David has always expected to be taken and exploited; his tender sadness is waiting for it, and his flat, ironic voice was trained not to give any sign of the pain. You'd never know about the pain, if you didn't notice the unalleviated morbid song in that famous voice. "This has been '*Etcetera*,' I am your host, David Staebler . . . "—a calm accountant, describing disasters in the early morning hours, making them up, sometimes slipping in true horror, but no longer sure which pills kick and which are clever placebos.

David and Jason Staebler were born in Philadelphia, in 1936 and 1938—"in that order," Jason added for years. He was so much more convinced than David, so much more worldly, that everyone took him for the older. Yet Jason wanted to be spoiled; he wanted to cling onto the chance of being the "kid" brother. David looked at him with the gloomy awe of an innocent who has met a wizard. While they were still boys, a kind of deferential slowness overtook David so that Jason was always beating him—to the punch, the dinner table, or the dream. It was Jason who lived on the spur of moments, deciding what they were going to do; while David, with eyes like a dark pond in shadow, waited to be ruffled by the wind. David had only two advantages. He remembered everything and then gradually, over the years, he retold it all as stories. He built Jason into a legend on the radio, and it did for the poor guy, long before that set of bullets ripped him apart in Atlantic City.

Their parents were both killed in 1938, on Sunday, October 30, when their car was in a collision just outside Grovers Mill, New Jersey. They were on their way back from New York to Philadelphia, two happy young people, not long delivered of their second child, returning from what they called "another honeymoon" in the city. They had everything to look forward to; they were listening to the car radio, spellbound in the dark, a fragile cabin buzzing along the road, touching, their hands held on the ledge of their two thighs . . . when a panic-stricken truck came out onto the highway. Their hands were still locked, and the radio was still playing . . . or so it went, according to David's bewitched account of how radio came to be his metier.

The boys were brought up by their grandfather, a movie projectionist in Philadelphia. He was a dour, conscientious man, ruined by the death of his daughter, their mother, who gave the boys a steady-paced routine for life, stable to a point of emphasis, that had not the least effect on them. Both Staeblers grew up crazy. They were intelligent and they could pass, but they were out of their minds and into that night in which young married lovers met their death. Jason was supposed to be the wild and reckless one; after all, he got himself killed for a reason no one could ever quite put into words. But it was David, and it is David, who has already told five different stories about how his parents died. All on "*Etcetera*," all heart-rending and as arresting as a vision in moving headlights. Not one person in Philadelphia has ever called up to say, "But a year ago, you said that . . ." David Staebler's fleeing from the truth holds sway in the night airwaves of that city. People may raise their eyebrows, but they let the storyteller go on. It lets David suppose that no one's listening—one more nail to put in the coffin of himself, his arms reaching up and tapping it into his wooden top.

David went to Temple: he studied literature and ran the campus radio station. By his senior year, he had seven separate voices and characters on the air, he was always on the radio, those eyes so planed away of their own shining, always craving the red light, "On Air." Jason left school at sixteen, and by the time he was twenty he was running a chain of grocery stores in the Poconos. There are still those in the area who say that Jason Staebler was a merchandising genius, that he could have been an emperor in supermarkets. But he got bored easily, he was always changing his plans, always talking about Hawaii, or Alaska, or South America. He may never have read a book, but he couldn't abide hard facts. He wanted the melting life of fiction, and he lived out scenarios in the way David let them creep into the night air, like fog.

Anyway, by the late 1960s, the brothers were apart. They didn't "know" where the other one was—except that David still lived at home with his grandfather, and always worked for the same radio station in Philadelphia. So Jason knew, just as David could count on it that his brother was somewhere close but unexpected. They went years without a word or a call, always expecting to bump into each other. Jason had made a promise that they would both be big, kings of Marvin Gardens, by the time they were forty.

David was thirty-six when the call came. He was on the air, telling a story about how he and Jason had once watched their grandfather choke to death on a fishbone. "My brother and I became accomplices forever. 'Don't ever say a word about this,' said my brother." David was drawling the story into the microphone, and the city and the grandfather were absorbing it in the same mood of stoic wondering. Then the call came from Jason: come to Atlantic City, right away.

David went, always available for disaster, always punctual and giving of himself. Anxious to please, horrified by the possibility of not being liked. It was his need for company, his fear of being alone, that made for so much trouble. Yet he was a retiring fellow, drifting into the bathroom in the middle of the night to practice a soliloquy, a gaunt loner sufficient to inspire a young woman's fervent insistence that he should have the john and all the time he needed—"I know you're an artist." So she peed out of the window, and David didn't ever get to screw the fabulously pretty Jessica, the stepdaughter of Sally, to whom Jason, in Atlantic City, seemed precariously married. Though the gloomy David was sure his brother was fucking Jessica too. He only had to look at Sally's burnt-out eyes, and see how she hacked off her hair on the wintry beach, letting the copper hanks burn in a fire that was the best reason for being out there on so cold a morning.

Jason had this plan for a casino and a hotel in Hawaii—he had Hawaiian shirts already packed. David was to direct entertainments there: seances, charades and wakes, presumably. They were going to make their fortune. It was 96 percent finalized. But it was all bullshit. Jessica had looked to David once amid the buzz of Jason's plans, and said, "I wish you didn't really think I was part of all this." "Well, aren't you?" David had asked. And Jessica nodded and grinned, "Of course I am. We all are."

And just to stop him talking, just to halt the inane momentum of packing and the gravitational absurdity of "going to Hawaii," Sally shot Jason. She sobbed in Jessica's arms afterward—it never had much to do with betrayal. Jason's pitching had to be stopped.

But David went on. He took the body back to Philadelphia, he organized the funeral, and so on. And he went back on the radio, not a whit more or less fatalistic than he had been before. But friends told him he was depressed, and so he made depression his new brother. He went on drugs that slowed and blurred him, but he got used to them and he can still spin those infinitely sad myths into the night, like a kid lying on his bed tossing curve balls at the ceiling so that they bend round the light bulb, never hitting it, always missing explosion.

JUDY ROGERS

Natalie Wood in Rebel Without a Cause, *1955,*
directed by Nicholas Ray

They lived in a four-bedroom house in Altadena, after Ed Hopper came out of the army. He got a job as a salesman for an ice-cream company, and in the years between 1946 and 1955 he won salesman-of-the-year three times. Judy, the elder child, was born in 1937, a pretty girl whose looks had turned angry and suspicious by the time she entered high school in 1951. No longer did she go to her dancing lessons; on weekends, she never went riding; and she had given up her suitable circle of friends. In high school, she went with the rougher boys. She was interested in cars, movies and being out late. The happy Hopper home was filled with recrimination. Ed Hopper took to slapping his daughter's face when roused. There was a perpetual flush of disgust on Judy's cheeks mixed in with those ignominious pimples. With a bottomless supply of ice cream, she had always been beset by baby fat and acne, and she loathed her own weakness.

By the time of her senior year, Judy was going with a bunch of hard-faced kids—Buzz, Goon, Crunch, Moose and so on—who looked too old for high school. That's when Jim Stark came to the school: his family had arrived from back east somewhere. He was a weird kid, shy but bold. He made friends with Plato, the fruit; but he gave Judy a glance that let her know he was straight. And he got into a chicken-run with Buzz his first week at school after the two of them started a fight outside the planetarium.

Judy was Buzz's girl, not that she'd gone all the way with him yet. But others kept off. Still, just before the race began and she was giving both the guys some dust, she didn't know which one she wanted to win. Then Buzz sailed over the cliff, like a car in a movie, and before he hit the rocks and the water she thought that she didn't really know him. Jim looked after her then, and the two of them took Plato into L.A. to an empty mansion off Sunset Boulevard. That's where the other kids came after them, and Plato got out this gun and shot Crunch. Then he took off and got into the planetarium. The cops came and Jim went in to try and get the gun off Plato. He borrowed the gun for a while and took out the clip, so it was empty when he gave it back. But Plato got scared when the cops put the lights on and he ran out waving the gun, so they blasted him. It was the worst thing Judy ever saw. She hated the cops more than she felt for Jim.

But Plato's death brought them closer together. She saw later that it was a pressure from which they were too vulnerable to escape. So when they graduated, they married. Both eighteen. A marriage with four worried smiles from the parents.

Jim enrolled at UCLA. They lived in a tiny apartment on Gayley Drive, and Judy worked as a waitress in Westwood while Jim drove a cab four nights a week. They didn't see too much of each other, but a son, Caleb, was born in 1958. They were hard-pressed then. Judy couldn't work as much. The costs of child-care were high. And in his junior year Jim was put on academic probation. They fought whenever they were in together. It was plain to Judy that their teenage romance had been a brief passion encumbered by marriage. Jim had a circle of friends he never talked about. He was secretive. If Judy heard any of their names he became angry.

In 1959, she moved out. They both called it a trial separation, because they were too hurt to face the truth. Judy moved to Anaheim, where her father had got her the manageress job at a fast-food outlet. Within three months, Jim had stopped calling. She lived with Caleb in an apartment, helped out by some money from her parents and some from Jim's father. She vowed she'd never marry again. But in 1962 she met a doctor, Herbert Rogers. He was forty-four, divorced, with two teenage daughters who lived with him most of the time. He wooed Judy, and he talked to her about psychology in a way that impressed her.

He offered her his house in Menlo Park, a large family and no need to work. He seemed like a good man, kind but disciplinary with Caleb. So in 1963, she married him and moved north. Three years later she walked out, sick of his greedy daughters, worn out by his tiredness and the terror with which he viewed the failure of a second marriage. Moreover, he was very conservative, critical of young people and mocking of the antiwar movement.

The rebellion in Judy was rekindled. She took Caleb and moved into a Haight-Ashbury commune. Once there, she became active in the antiwar movement. One day in April 1966, she got a call from a voice she knew:

"Hey," it said. "Anniversary."

"Jim?"

"Good guess."

"What anniversary?"

"Day Plato got it."

She had forgotten. Jim wouldn't tell her where he was, or how he had found her. Judy mentioned it to a woman in the house, and she wasn't surprised at all, so Judy worked it out that Jim was known to the group. As time went by, she reckoned that it was a kind of anarchists' cell, and Jim was something of a leader. He came by one day in the summer with an Oriental woman who didn't speak English. He talked to Judy and they took Caleb to Golden Gate Park. He asked her what she thought about the war. After that, Judy got trusted with more important jobs.

On October 11, 1968, she was killed, driving over the Bay Bridge when a homemade bomb she was carrying exploded.

KIT CARRUTHERS

Martin Sheen in Badlands, *1973,
directed by Terrence Malick*

It was only as I came to write this piece, and thought to study the map of all the small places Carruthers passed, that I had a surprise. There on the Rand-McNally Road Atlas, page 77 in my edition, about fifteen miles in from the western edge of South Dakota and on a line with the Montana-Wyoming border, there is a small red square and "Geographical Center of the U.S." It's in there near Antelope Butte and Haystack Buttes, just to the west of a line you could draw between Rapid City and the Slim Buttes battle site. Carruthers must have gone right by it, but I doubt if he stopped to notice or think about it.

If you consider the map of the whole country, then I don't see how it can be called the "Geographical Center." For a start, it's a whole lot closer to Canada than to Mexico, and maybe only half as far from the Pacific as it is to the Atlantic. I always heard it said that Kansas City was the middle of America, or the nearest large place, and that Bedford Falls, Nebraska, was the heart of the country, the mathematical midpoint. So it came as a shock to see this red square in South Dakota. It makes me wonder whether there may be others all vying for the honor. Not that it's much once you've said it. It reminds me of a book I read about the race to the South Pole between Captain Scott and Amundsen. When they got there, both of them, they couldn't be sure they were there. No red markers—just white as far as they could see. So they marched around for miles just to be sure that they'd stood on the damned pole itself. As for the center of America, you might have to do the same, unless you have a sure feeling where it is.

This Carruthers was an old-time desperado, some said; I thought he was a new breed of disgrace. I knew the country was in trouble when it celebrated him so. These are the facts:

Kit Carruthers, b. Birdeye, Arkansas, 1933, never knew his father; his mother did laundry and went in to Memphis at night

1938–47: some schooling, yet he could barely read

1947–50: went with a traveling preacher, named Powell, who worked the roads between Fort Smith and Nashville. Carruthers was his assistant and his advertising manager, and he often played the part of a country boy who had been struck blind, so that Powell could cure him. He was also abused sexually by Powell, until one day Carruthers beat him to a standstill and quit

1950–54: on the road, Carruthers would say he was a wounded veteran of the Korean War. He tried to join the Army, the Texas Rangers and the state police of both Oklahoma and Kansas, but he was rejected for lack of education and psychological instability

1954: ninety-day sentence in Amarillo, Texas, for shoplifting

1955: occasional disc-jockey and raconteur on Arkansas radio station, but he was fired for persistent use of obscenities on the air. He said he just couldn't eliminate them

1955–56: worked for a chain of supermarkets as manager for stunts and promotions

1956–57: arrested for brawling in Wichita, Kansas; assigned to State Mental Hospital for observation, and released

1957: drifted north; time in McCook, Nebraska, as railroad maintenance man

1957–58: into South Dakota; barman in Rapid City, fired for haranguing customers; to Fort Dupree, worked as member of a garbage crew.

On June 8, 1958, Carruthers went into the offices of the local newspaper and demanded to be interviewed. A reporter sat with him, to humor him, and the young man said that as "a decent, enterprising American who liked to listen to the other man's point of view, I have got nowhere." He added that he was about ready to do something. A week later, he supposed that the paper was not going to run his story. On June 17, he met Holly Sargis, and June 29 he shot and killed her father, set fire to the Sargis house, and he and Holly drove away, toward the buttes. She was an impressionable girl, and all agreed he was a rousing talker.

They led the life of hideaways that summer, living in the forests and then beating out across open country into Montana. The thing that tickled him was stopping off in small towns to take a look at how he was doing in the newspapers. In that summer he shot Sargis, and two, three, four, some hunters that stumbled on their tree house, then five, an old friend of his, six, seven, the two kids who happened by—he shut them in a shelter and fired into it—and then a policeman who came after them, that's eight.

He was stopped finally on a back road in Rosebud County, not far from the Little Bighorn battleground. He was taken back to Rapid City in South Dakota to be tried. He gave interviews and pleaded guilty, and when the judge asked if he had anything to say, he talked for twenty minutes, saying that Holly Sargis hadn't been old enough to know what was happening, and how he'd started to get respect after he killed some people. Then he said he hoped he'd get the juice, and he did, in the state prison, January 23, 1959. In his last interview, he asked to be known as "The Dakota Kid" after he had died, and if he didn't rise again. But he had donated his body to science, and they cut him in pieces.

WALDO LYDECKER

Clifton Webb in Laura, *1944,*
directed by Otto Preminger

In 1935, at the peak of his fame, and just before the scandal that ensured this would be his only honorary degree, Waldo Lydecker was dressed in an academic gown at Pembroke College and asked to speak to the senior class. He surprised the occasion by offering not some barbed remarks on how young ladies should behave, but a heartfelt tribute to the example set by Charles Dickens. Among his few intimates, it was remembered that he sometimes quoted from the English novelist, did own a set of first editions, and may have inspired a passion for Dickens in the young Welsh actor Emlyn Williams.

The journals of Waldo Lydecker cannot yet be published: too many mentioned and mocked there are still alive. But I have had an opportunity to examine them (my thanks to the Steffensen Collection at Wesleyan University) and I believe that this will be the first public revelation that "Waldo Lydecker" was born Walter Little, in 1893, in Portsmouth, the English south-coast port, where Dickens had been born, eighty-one years earlier.

He was the son of Elsie, a boardinghouse keeper in the Fratton district, and of a sailor, Arthur Little, who was lost at sea in what we must now call the first Battle of the Falkland Islands (in 1914). Young Walter, an only child, grew up with few advantages and poor schooling, earning coppers collecting glasses in Portsmouth public houses and being an errand boy for sailors on shore leave. Fond of horses and always slight, he was an apprentice jockey in the years 1908–11, familiar at the various stables and racecourses in southern England. However, a controversy over his rough riding at the

Goodwood meeting of 1911 put an end to his career, and it was noted that, thereafter, he went into employment with bookmakers.

At around the same time, he fell in with traveling theatrical companies, working as an actor and a writer of romantic lyrics. This seems to have been a happy time, in and out of scrapes, as Walter roamed that lovely, gentle part of England, playing Malvolio at Haslemere one evening, and taking bets at Plumpton races the following afternoon. There is some evidence that Walter appeared a few times on Fred Karno's houseboat at Tagg's Island, on the Thames, and the possibility that he had shared the homemade limelight there with the young Chaplin. More intriguing still, although no text survives, it is clear that Walter adapted a stage version of *Nicholas Nickleby* that played in Brighton, Bournemouth and Portsmouth in 1914—"the last summer of enchantment" Waldo once called it in his New York column.

He was conscripted into the British army in 1916, shortly after the death in Rye, Sussex, of Henry James. Walter had been employed in the James household, to read to the dying novelist, a task that may have accounted for the rather stilted grace of his speech. Whatever, he went from reading *Dombey and Son* to James to khaki and drill in a few weeks, and he might have died in the Flanders mud but for an emotional involvement with a lieutenant (Walter was only a private) from one of the nation's most distinguished families (the de Winters). No action was taken by the authorities, and no evidence preserved. However, in 1917, Walter Little was discharged, without comment, and sent back to England. The country had changed, and Walter was not the same blithe young man. He had influenza in 1919, and was never strong again. There were incidents with the police and a squalid business with a canon at Chichester Cathedral.

Escape came in the form of work as a steward on the Cunard line, and so Walter Little arrived in New York in 1920. The city and the prospect of a fresh start there thrilled him, and a year later he quit his ship at the docks and hailed a cab.

The next few years are vague: the journal ceases, as if its author were busy transforming himself. It is certain that Walter Little went to Los Angeles, to the new picture business. While there, he became Wallace Lydell, an extra and a stringer for gossip columns. But in 1928 he surfaced as Waldo Lydecker, running a salon in Santa Monica that never let its own notoriety detract from the verve with which it pronounced on the stupidity or iniquity of others in that city. Waldo started a column for a Hearst paper, rose quickly to syndication, and appeared to relish the fear and loathing of many film stars. Without stooping to sensation, let me just say that he was by then a promiscuous homosexual who ran the dangerous gauntlet of reporting on liaisons and human mishaps observed among his own circle of associates. Attacked once or twice, he adopted a walking stick and did nothing to discourage rumors that it sheathed a weapon.

It was in 1931 that Waldo moved to New York to make the nation as a whole his target. In an interview given at that time, he indulged the legend that he was Hungarian and of noble birth. This was the foundation of his reputation as a model of Manhattan manners, correcting speech and table arrangements, advising on dress and deportment, but always, somehow, remaining a law unto himself. It was the Lydecker secret that while he intimidated others with etiquette, he behaved like a libertine of insult, deploring, criticizing and making himself a fountain of sarcastic rebuke, all in the name of politeness.

In addition to his column, he had a regular radio program on CBS, a potpourri, in which he wearied of current affairs, recommended restaurants and designers, and read from Dowson, Swinburne and Tennyson. There were books—*How to Be Insulting but Forgiven* (1934) and *The Caustic Christmas Book* (1937)—overly mannered, to be sure, but amusing still and forever spiked by the nervy line drawings of Norman Clyde, Waldo's close friend in those years.

Lydeckerism was characteristic of the smartest American cities of the 1930s—glamorous, heartless and addicted to fads and cults. In fact, Waldo had a healthy streak of ordinariness: he enjoyed Laurel and Hardy; at home he fed on rice pudding and blancmange; and even when he posed in his marble bath, at the typewriter, for Cecil Beaton, he took care to wear shorts in the water, of what looks like a very garish plaid. He lived on Park Avenue in two apartments knocked into one and furnished with ostentatious "taste": "It's lavish, but I call it home." He was fond of bogus antiques that deceived guests, and he was a silent partner in the company of "Lejon Fils, Paris" (to be found in Hoboken), specializing in Louis XV reproductions.

By this stage he was too prominent to escape the public censure that followed his arrest in Central Park for soliciting a sailor. He was fined $5,000, and he "retired" from his column for over a year. He came back eventually, for Kane papers, but never with the same space or brio. His nerve had been shaken; there was a new edge of jittery malice in his talk and writing.

No longer feared, sometimes laughed at, he was lunching at the

Algonquin one day in 1942 when Laura Hunt, fresh in advertising, approached him to endorse a pen for which her agency, Bullitt's, had the account. That he accepted impressed Miss Hunt as a testament to her winningness. Waldo's diary says simply that he appreciated how a young actor in the restaurant noticed him only when the "glaringly luscious" Laura appeared.

The entire patronage of Laura Hunt was for ulterior motives: she was bait in a time when he feared his own looks were fading, not much helped by a new mustache. He made her, "if it counts for anything to make this city notice a selfish sexpot from Nebraska who will give as much head as it takes to get ahead." He would say anything for a laugh. Behind her creamy back he ridiculed her—especially to Tavorian Jacoby, the painter he coaxed into doing what he regarded as a swooningly vulgar portrait of Laura. In time, Miss Hunt discovered his real scorn and did anything she could to oppose him. "My dear," he said to her one night, "if you only had real intelligence I would have to kill you."

Laura threatened to expose him, and he urged her to do her worst. He felt his life was a bore, marginally alleviated by a teenage protégé named Falco. Perhaps Waldo meant to murder Laura that sweltering weekend in August 1944; perhaps he knew that Diane Redfern, a model, was staying in Laura's apartment and put both barrels of buckshot in her face as a warning. Whatever the answer, self-destructiveness had set in, and his fate was fixed when—in the course of the investigation—Waldo made an erudite pass at the detective in charge, Mark McPherson, and then explained its raw meaning. Forty-eight hours later Waldo was dead, shot by McPherson's assistant in Laura's apartment, as he lunged theatrically at the heart-shaped face he had made famous.

> *I cannot write that without flinching—my arm jumps out—to protect her, or is it because I have imagined myself aiming at her? In the years since, I have sometimes cursed Laura and supposed her desire accounted for my action. We imagine others with so much more zeal than we ever see ourselves. We are like close-ups in a movie, staring into the dark so that we do not have to face the camera or the discipline of being seen.*

> *Am I jealous of Waldo, because he discovered*
> *Laura when I wanted to be her auteur? We*
> *watch in a crowd, sure the picture is ours alone.*

LAURA HUNT

Gene Tierney in Laura, 1944,
directed by Otto Preminger

"Only prettiness," I say out loud in the quiet house, flipping through the packet of photographs in Laura's file. The prints fall like rubber leaves, preserved but unnatural. I put them in order long ago to trace her life. There is always the same body—from when she had a career as a model—a promontory of bare shoulder and the taut slopes of her breasts, arising from this or that cast-satin evening gown, or the season's most tastefully risqué swimsuit. There are painted clouds behind her, ghosts of sky. But what was risqué in the 1940s only makes her smile naive now; unless you were young then and grew up with her.

Her body has a hundred heads on it, all turning to be seen, to catch some fleeting lens or lover, to monopolize a nightclub flashbulb. In every picture, the face wants to gobble up its watchers. But look at twenty pictures and you notice it is those "pretty" eyes that are at bay, and her face that is being eaten. The mouth is open, and the teeth are polished tablets. Her tongue, in the dark slit of her lips, is as blatant as 1942 or 1943 allowed, and sometimes there is a saucer of saliva in her mouth, ice to skate on in December.

I would as soon do without these photographs; there will be no illustrations. The sharp corners and the clammy sheen of these prints feel dangerous. They make anyone they "take" the viewer's slave, an unfree being, a woman "taken in photography." The movement in movies is redemption for the death in photography.

To look at Laura's glossiness here I could despise her. Put the stills away and I can recall the trembling white woman who took me to her cool body at the Pierre and let an afternoon swell with unspoken healing. It must have been a very sudden, chaste love we made; there was nothing expert about it. I have kept her pictures, but I seldom look at them. I do not want to make a shrine of her or what we shared. If we did share. Two people can come away from such an afternoon in love, or in love with love, but strangers in their sense of the words. And if I ever felt, leaving the Pierre, that knowledge or wisdom had come down on me like grace to save me—even now I say "healing," pouring the word into the wound—I had to learn that the brief touching had ensured all the rest of the damage. The afternoon had prepared me for the night.

Laura Hunt was born in Omaha, Nebraska, in 1920, the younger of two daughters, the Hunt girls teenage Omaha called them in the 1930s, when it seemed possible that their parents, two tall worriers, might have in one characterless home the best actress and the prettiest girl in America. Their father was in insurance and their mother was the maker of some forty-five thousand wholesome and lacklustre meals in a scheme of regularity which never quite blanked out the speck of a visiting madness. Once a year, when the prairie wind stirred her nerves, their mother went domestically crazy, taking apart clothes she had made or snapping the handles off every cup in the house. Then she was sensible again, and her life resumed its level, grounded stretch. Every few years, their father bought sets of new crockery at a sale.

The other sister, Mary Frances, was three years older than Laura. She was not unappealing, not unappealing, but she deferred to her younger, more accessible sister; she was somber in her expressions and outlook, except when on the stage. There, and only there, Mary Frances Hunt came to life. People who had seen her acting sometimes passed her by backstage, no matter that they were on their way to give her flowers and to tell her she had a remarkable future. But I married her.

"Muffy," said Laura one day, "if you looked like me you would be Margaret Sullavan, but if I acted like you I would only be . . . Hedy Lamarr. As it is . . . " I know, I heard it, and winced at the smart, three-quarter accuracy. The true dilemma was much stranger. On stage, Mary Frances was beautiful, but she had not one spark of Laura's lust for getting ahead and pretending. Laura could worm her way in anywhere, she was slippery and convincing. But Mary Frances waited to be asked, and stood back from crowded elevators. It was called timidity by most people, but there was an iron door of suppressed vanity there, a fearful pride too great to speak. She was a great actress, but too shy or too ashamed to talk about it.

Laura was a poor actress, fussy and overdone: in one gesture on

31

stage she became blurred. So she drifted, from regret, into being a liar and a user. There was no plan or malice to it; it was the sign of how much her prettiness troubled her. But so close in age, they grew up together, Laura with beaux and secrets, Mary Frances with Electra, Hedda Gabler, Perdita in *The Winter's Tale* and an implacably closed-off inner self. Which I once thought I could free. For, in 1938, rather than risk New York and the theater, Mary Frances Hunt had a breakdown: it was called marriage, to put the theater out of bounds. She is alive today, alive tonight, upstairs like a threat, but she has never got over it. Laura found herself alone, all the more determined to leave Nebraska and impress the world, but guilty because she was a mere pretender, untouched by acting's genius.

She started east in 1939, and in Iowa she entered a beauty contest under the name of Mitzi Glass. It was a hysterical adventure to disprove her own reputation. But, mortified, she won and had to smile for the slow photographers of Des Moines. One of her prizes was a ticket to Hollywood—"Good God!" raged Mary Frances—but Laura went steadily east, out of love with herself, yet wooed twice on the train. In retaliation, she surrendered to a traveling salesman who called her "doll" and roughed her up when he was satisfied. "My lovers are always disappointed," she said years later at the Pierre Hotel. "They expect me to be Cleopatra, but I am as plain as Nebraska!" Did she think I was let down?

For two years in New York she was a photographers' model, kept by several men, indulged, idealized and then dropped so often that she became brittle if not breakable. She might have been more in the city, but she was too hostile to herself to try hard, and too attractive to want for much. She lifted herself out of this dismal hole in 1942 for nothing but money. Laura went into advertising, so that she could sometimes send a check back to Nebraska. The challenge reminded her of her old ability to get whatever she wanted.

And so, in 1942, she broke in on Waldo Lydecker's solitary lunch at the Algonquin and asked his austere celebrity to endorse a fountain pen for an advertisement.

"Does it work?" he asked her, signing the menu.

"Does it matter?" she replied, dipping a breadstick in his hollandaise and sucking it clean.

They neither of them appreciated it, but Waldo and Laura were two "personalities" yearning to escape their base selves. He schooled her, and did not think of touching her. She learned about fame, imposing herself, and how the means of mass communication told the dreamy public what to think. "I am always addressing the vast unknown," said Waldo, "just as you in your photos are looking out at those you will never meet. We are both of us without private character." She met influential people, and she found that she enjoyed advertising just because she saw through it: it was a way of bringing prettiness to any cause or commodity, spreading the joke. It was a language not spoiled by aging or lack of substance. Laura Hunt was one of the first in America to guess that people bought magazines for the legendary prospect conspired in by all the advertisements. It was a new culture, movies in your lap.

Murder altered Laura's outlook. It brought a defeatist respect for violence that lasted all her life. It introduced her to Mark McPherson; and it helped her see that someone else, Waldo, might think less of her than her own estimate. She had been with men who disparaged their manliness: Waldo and Shelby Carpenter, the whimsical Kentucky cad who had not outgrown the wish to please everyone. McPherson reminded Laura of Mary Frances: he was haunted, he blamed those who flinched from his darkness, and there was that same hunched intelligence that expected rejection. McPherson made love to Laura as if she were his prisoner, a suspect he could grill for his pleasure. She liked that. She felt aroused when he put her in a small, stale interrogation room, turned the light on her and began to whip at her with questions from the shadows. "I'd reached a point where I needed official surroundings," he said. And there, on the small scuffed table where confessions were signed, Laura arranged her voluptuousness and dragged his ungiving force into her. "Slut," he whispered when she came, and her eyes leapt in appreciation.

They were married in 1945: one daughter, Paula, was born in 1946; and then a year later Mark beat Laura so badly that no careful surgery could hide disfigurement. She never charged him, but the city threw him off the force. There was a divorce, and he went away with nothing much except that portrait of her—the thing he had fallen in love with and which no one else liked—and her last present to him. (Or last but one—there was that other cruel gift.) Mark McPherson went away, as if unfit for the world. Laura was sure he would not be back—as if she had disposed of him. He went away, but I never forgot him. It may sound foolish or conceited, but I trusted I would find him.

Laura was finished as a model. But she had a daughter to support, and she guessed that television advertising was the coming rage. She made Bullitt's, her agency, the leader in that field for fifteen years. She produced commercials, bringing the product together with visualizers, directors and actors, and foreseeing that commercials could be as beautiful and suggestive as small movies.

She married Shelby Carpenter in the 1950s, but it was a marriage that barely disturbed the lives of the two people. A few years later they divorced, though remaining at the same level of frosted amiability. She moved to Los Angeles, consumed by work and Paula's education. She sent the girl to Smith, and she saw in 1969 that Paula got a job at the ICM agency in Los Angeles. From that start, Paula Hunt became a powerful young packager in the entertainment industry. I saw her at the funeral, and we talked a little. It was not comfortable because I could not forget the rumors, after Laura's suicide, that Paula had outmaneuvered her mother in an agency deal in 1971, taking a batch of clients Laura had regarded as hers.

But when we buried Laura, Paula turned to everyone there, let her brown eyes swell with love and told us, "The modern awareness of personality would not be as it is without the career of my mother. She gave meaning to the old American dream that a nobody could be someone, and she did it with flair, with style, and with love." The little speech appeared next day in the trades, like a handout. There is a frenzy from Nebraska, it is the mania of being in the middle, without seabreezes, of being unknown, and I have sometimes felt it in silk sheets on a hotel bed or in PR prose, a tremor in the smoothness.

I am not cut out for this—God help me.

> *I have always called her and thought of her as "Mary Frances." Yet I never use anyone else's middle name. It sounds a declaratory but conflicting name, or is that only because I know her? I wonder how different it would be if she were only one or the other?*

HELEN FERGUSON

Barbara Stanwyck in No Man of Her Own, 1950, directed by Mitchell Leisen

There are two Americas. I know you have heard this before; there are countless two Americas: north and south, Atlantic and Pacific, straight and crazy, National League and American League, the rising and the falling, blue cheese or creamy Italian. Let me suggest one more—I know it, because I have crossed over a few times.

There is the America of the Interstates. This is a land like an airline map, of major cities held in place by straight lines, a grid of business, population and the certainty of being in the mainstream. Then there are the old back roads and places where no one would go except to live quietly in a small town with a main street and one of everything a town requires—a school, a church, a bank, a cemetery, a hotel verandah for the old-timers and a scarlet woman about whom they can make up stories. Take any state in the Union. Look at its map and find the green lines of the Interstates; then look away at the "empty" holes the green lines contain. Imagine the life there, with so many content to be unknown, and others who hope to get away and be recognized. This is the America torn between refuge and prison.

Helen Ann Ferguson was born in one of the holes, at Bridgeport, California, in 1921. It's sixty-five hundred feet up, in the Sierras, between Yosemite and the Nevada border. There are sparser holes. Bridgeport has skiing, extravagant scenery; it's not far from Mono Lake, on a road to Bishop in the south and Carson City to the north. But it's not on a main route; the Sierras are closed in winter, and Bridgeport is left to itself. The passable highway, 80, goes from Reno to San Francisco; and beyond Reno 80 is Salt Lake City, Cheyenne, Omaha and Chicago. Bridgeport, California, and Caulfield, Illinois, must be about the same distance from the rush and throb of 80.

Ann Ferguson, as she liked to be known, was the daughter of Bridgeport's dentist, an only child who became a capable housekeeper when her mother died in 1936. Ann made her father proud: she brushed her teeth, she studied and she led an active, uneventful life. She did well in school, but never disputed her father's opinion that it was foolish to send a girl to college. She took a short course that qualified her as a dental nurse, to help her father. She enjoyed cross-country skiing, and in the summer she was part of the swimming-and-tennis gang. She had boyfriends, and her father was mild to all of them, hoping that would avert seriousness.

Ann was twenty-five when, suddenly, an upper front tooth went rotten. Her father pulled it and made the replacement. He took every care to make it fit, but he never saw that her full confidence in him had gone. Then Ann got involved with Jeff Bailey, who had taken over the filling station in Bridgeport. He was a mysterious figure, from far away, a man who paid his bills and never sought acceptance. In retaliation, the town called him a loner; but he was most alone in his own mind, and that was a little eased by the friendship of Ann and Dickie, a deaf-mute boy who helped at the station.

Bailey—it is an old name—had been a detective, mixed up in New York gambling. There had been a woman and a killing, and Bailey had ended up feeling used. He had removed himself as far as he could, to a hole in the country; but then he had decided to make his living at the roadside so he could see who passed by. One day in 1947 someone recognized him, someone lost, on a back road, stumbling on a find. The old associations closed in, unsettled business, with debts to be paid and old attractions awakened with a glance or a forgotten perfume. Ann did whatever she could—no matter that her father and the town warned her about Bailey—but Jeff was found dead in a crashed car, along with the other woman from out of the past.

Ann left Bridgeport. She went to San Francisco and met a man, Stephen Morley, whom she had encountered in the last frantic days of the Bailey episode. Morley had been an operative for a lawyer named Eels; he was a gambler, too, a ladies' man, adept at the smaller forms of fraud and extortion. He seduced Helen Ferguson (she had made a small change in her name to get Bridgeport out of her system), and he made her pregnant. When she went to tell him, she discovered that he had left for New York. There was a note telling her not to be upset.

She waited awhile, and then she followed him east. He was living in a cheap apartment on the Lower East Side with a blonde, Carol Mather. When Helen showed up, he laughed at her and said how did she know he was the father of the child? Helen believed he would relent. He did see her from time to time, when Carol was working; he slept with her again, and though she despised him Helen could not appreciate that she did not need him. One day she called on him, knocked on the door to the apartment, and felt the horror of subterfuge and indifference when at last an envelope was slipped underneath the silent door. It contained some money and a rail ticket back to San Francisco. It all smelled of a gardenia scent she knew as Carol's.

On the train, she met a friendly couple, the Harknesses, Patrice and Hugh, not long married. They started talking for a simple reason: Helen and Patrice were both pregnant, and due at about the same time. Hugh Harkness had been in Europe on government work, and he had met Patrice there. She was an orphan: her only family was his, and she was on her way to meet them for the first time. They would get off at Chicago, and thence to Caulfield, Illinois (between Moline and Normal), where the Harknesses lived.

But the train crashed in Ohio—the Maumee disaster of July 3, 1948. Helen and Patrice had been in the ladies' room at the moment of impact; they were laughing and talking, and Patrice had asked Helen to hold her wedding ring while she scrubbed her hands (the smell of oysters from dinner). Helen slipped it on for safety, and was thinking of life's ironies when the crash occurred. In the hospital, she was known as Patrice Harkness. The real Patrice had been killed, as well as Hugh. But the shock had started Helen's baby, who had come into the world—delivered amid mud, flashlights and the groans of distress —as the son of Mrs. Harkness, the woman wearing the ring.

She hated the dishonesty, but she was on a slope of providential force; and she had envied the couple on the train their future as rich as her warmest memory of small towns. Helen Ferguson went to Caulfield as Patrice Harkness, delivering a grandson and a hope for the future to Donald and Grace Harkness, who had lived there all their lives, consistent, quiet and attentive, like readers. As she met them, Helen felt fake, stepping into a myth. Her son was christened Hugh, and the dead Hugh's brother, Bill, came home for the event. Helen liked him, but she knew he looked at her in a quizzical way; he noticed her false tooth.

Helen slipped into happiness. The Christmas holiday was the best she had known, even if the fear of betraying herself never went away. She guessed that Bill was falling in love with her; she thought of her own son as Hugh Harkness. When she looked at him in a grandmother's arms, her thoughts were no longer framed by the deception. And then Stephen Morley appeared, a blackmailer now.

He had read of the crash, and gone to identify the body. He had looked at Patrice Harkness in the morgue and smiled. Yes, he said, poor Helen Ferguson, and the unborn child, too. But he had heard the story of two pregnant women in the ladies' room and seen where the other one, Harkness, had her address. It's the Irish in me, he chuckled, as he reconstructed the chance plot.

He came to Caulfield and learned that Helen would be rich when Donald and Grace Harkness died. So he extorted money from Helen, and he compelled her to marry him: they drove to Iowa to do it. Helen wanted him dead. Grace, who learned enough of the story, planned to get a gun and shoot him; her own heart was bad, and she might as well do something bold and useful before she died. And then, one morning, in the rooming house in Caulfield, Morley was found shot.

The two women were ready to own up, for they both suspected Bill had done it. But the police smelled gardenia. Carol Mather had shot her lover after learning he had married someone else, and put on extra perfume to be more herself.

The shock killed Grace; Donald died fifteen months later. Caulfield was agog when the story came out, and in 1951 Bill and Helen, married now, moved away with their son, Hugh, determined to give him a happy home in one of the quiet, secret places in America. Let them go, there are perils enough in those quiet holes.

DICKSON STEELE

Humphrey Bogart in In a Lonely Place, *1949,*
directed by Nicholas Ray

"The king sits in Dunfermline town, drinking the blood red wine." That line is set in my mind, like a stain in wood. I must have learned it in school, in Bedford Falls, on a winter day when the heating system clanked and grumbled and I wanted to be out skating, with Violet winking across the classroom, so sure she knew what I was thinking. The line has come back to me over the years, whenever I hear the word *blood*. Sometimes I get a little more of the poem; it goes on for pages, I think, about a sea captain sent on a mission by the king, Sir Patrick something or other. I think I recall that he has to find a woman—at sea? or on land? I don't know. I can hear the class reciting a line about the king's daughter and Noroway. What does it mean? Lines you can't get out of your head, and the notion of a woman you search for but never quite find?

I never knew that Dunfermline could bring it all back, too; it's rarer than blood, I suppose, and so it might be more piercing. But I didn't know that Dix Steele's people had come from there, a town in Scotland. Two brothers, Andrew and Fergus, left there as young men in 1907, to come to America. They settled in Trenton, New Jersey. They had a hardware store and they started a mechanical repair shop; they were sure that the automobile was going to be big, but trouble. They worked every hour they could find, and they bought themselves a good old house on Spruce Street. Then one day, in 1912, Andrew was called to look at a bus that had broken down. It carried a traveling theatrical company, on its way to Philadelphia, and there was a dancer in the group, a Spanish woman, Adele Santana. As Fergus tells it, she took one look at Andrew and decided to have him. He had barely talked to a woman in his life, and here was this one, just as bright and noisy as a parrot. I asked Fergus why she snapped up his brother, and he answered, "Oh, there had been a wishing in Andy all along. She knew it. She touched it." He may have meant that literally; somehow this tango dancer put her hot skin against his, and he was done for.

They were married, and there was the boy, John Dickson Steele, born in 1914. Adele left them all when the child was two. She took off for the West, saying she had to be dancing again. Andrew died three years later, technically of the influenza that was so grim in Jersey. But he was a broken man before that. So Fergus became the boy's guardian as well as uncle. He brought him up without a mention of Adele and Dix, I suppose, studied Fergus's milky skin and sawdust hair and wondered about his own carbon looks. But there are things we can never tell our young, matters of shame and pride that we long for them to find out, but that are past our telling.

Dickson Steele grew up clever and strange. He had no close friends, but he was always in demand. He could mend anything, or take it apart and explain how it worked. By 1930 or so, he was learning to fly, and he spent a lot of his time at the airfield in Trenton working on planes. Fergus wanted him to go to Princeton, and he was rich enough then to pay. But Dickson put it off several times, and he didn't go to the university until 1934, when he was twenty.

At the end of his freshman year he dropped out. He had done well enough, with distinction in engineering and literature. But he was bored, or displeased, and he took off for Manhattan. He knocked around there in 1935 and 1936, and somehow the hawk on *Time*'s cover, Jed Harris, took a shine to him. Harris was about the best known stage director in the city—he did *The Front Page* and *The Green Bay Tree*—and possibly the wickedest man in America. If you can go by reputation. You can't, but there's no harm in warning people. Harris had a genius for cruelty: it excited as much admiration as horror. He was like a fictitious villain, but alive and breathing and doing it to someone you knew. It was power that really attracted him. As a director, he let a story out slowly on stage so that you felt *his* control. It dripped on you.

It was Dickson Steele who drove Harris across America in the fitful spring of 1938, when Harris was preparing *Our Town* and wanted to say he'd studied small places. That's when they came to Nebraska, and Harris had his infernal night of talk with Mary Frances. I don't call that Steele's fault, or even proof of evil in Harris. It was understandable, what he said. She *was* an actress, still desperate to do it and just as desperate not to. They moved on, with Harris surer how to put on the play, and wreckage behind him.

Harris, I believe, told Dickson to get back to Princeton, and wrote a letter for him to the university saying he was not to be overlooked just because he was odd. So in the fall of 1939, he was a twenty-five-year-old sophomore, who got a name for cutting up professors in crosstalk. He had learned from Harris and given up all thought of hiding his difficult nature. But he was out again in 1940, and off to McGuire Field where he enlisted. They loved him. He had his license already, he knew engines and he was a natural killer.

Dickson Steele rose to colonel in the air force. He was in combat in Europe, flying fighters in the Mediterranean, and thereafter he was stationed in Britain, a leader of the big bombing raids sent against Germany in 1944 and 1945. He was a fine officer, hard but inspiring, adored by his men. The war excited him; it gave liberty to all his hostile feelings. Pilots were encouraged to paint signs on their planes to show how many "kills" they had.

He came back with a novel, *Brucie and the Spider*, published in 1946. Such an unnerving tale, about an American flier in Scotland during the war who meets a girl, Katriona Bruce, falls in love with her, begins to think she is a witch, and hears she has been murdered after he has gone away to win the war. The pilot remembers then all the little things that made him think there was another man, another darker lover, in her life. It was a short book full of rock and cold, harshness and tenderness. The novel was a critical success, and it did well enough to get Dixon Steele—he had made that his working name—out to Hollywood.

He did scripts, but none of them was produced. He drank on the money and he grew quarrelsome. There were stories of fights with producers, and once he took a plane out at Santa Monica and buzzed a studio executive's house at Malibu.

It was in 1949, while he was struggling to do another novel and sell a script, that Dix got involved in the Mildred Atkinson case. She was a hatcheck girl at a restaurant. He saw her reading the very novel that he had been hired to turn into a script. Rather than read the book—a fat bore of a thing—he took her back to his place at the Virginibus Arms on Camden. Later that night she was found strangled. Laurel Gray, who also lived at the Arms, said she had seen Atkinson leave, seldom seen in public

alone, but then Laurel fell in love with Dix. Brub Nicolai, one of the
detectives on the case, had flown with Dix. He hated having to
investigate his old commander; but he could never forget the com-
pleteness of Dix's nature as a killer. In the end, they decided that
Atkinson's fiancé had killed her. But Dix's nerves snapped along the
way, and he even threatened to strangle Laurel once when he thought
she doubted him.

She left him. Dix wrote another novel, *The Evening of the Day*
(1952), about a man who is suspected of a string of rapes and killings.
There were people who couldn't finish the book, it was so disturbing
and true. But it was a hit, and the movie was a triumph for
Montgomery Clift. Dix worked less; he remained friends with
Nicolai; and he knew Laura Hunt when she was in Los Angeles.

I corresponded with Nicolai, but there was not much he wanted to
say. Was the LAPD ever satisfied about the Atkinson case? There
were other, similar murders in the fifties and once or twice Dix came
under suspicion. "He would laugh at me," Nicolai wrote. "And he'd
taunt me: 'Just because I write mystery stories, you think I'm fit to be
a killer.'"

His last novel was *Beneath Suspicion* (1964), about a police chief
who plays a game with the world. He kills his mistress, knowing that
he will be called upon to investigate the crime. When the trail goes
cold, the man commits other murders to rekindle interest. The book
was a sensation: the more so because Dix had given up company by
then, living in Topanga Canyon, seldom seen in public. He died up
there in 1970, wealthy, a man of letters, a distinguished soldier. But
there were some sure he was a killer.

There was a new book, three-quarters done at his death. Laura was
his agent then, and she told me it tells everything—even without an
ending. I don't know. An ending is important; it can say the writer
has been pretending, or not. The book was locked away in her safe,
and, as I said, she is dead.

*I don't know where that safe is. It might be
untouched in the office still, or waiting on some
L.A. dump, battered and rotting, about to fall
apart, so the pages can scatter with the ash and
the seagulls. Or be found by a red-hot
publisher?*

LAUREL GRAY

Gloria Grahame in In a Lonely Place, *1949,*
directed by Nicholas Ray

I wonder why incest is such an American fascination? Is it because of our superstition about coincidence bringing the proper strangers together in the new desert land so that their magical coupling wipes away the loss and separation of leaving Europe? But if we believe in Mr. and Miss Right, then we must suppose an author who made them but deliberately flung them in opposite directions. It takes something like storying to crisscross the emptiness. We have formed a taste for lucky encounter, for intersection and unrecognized coincidence, for the story turning round to examine the storyteller's face. And because we aspire so much to love, we think of this instinct as incest. Yet the chance of coincidence makes us suspicious, too, nervous that the narrator is sleeping with the story, that nice girl who seems to be ours in the daytime. Don't we know when we see the lovely lady on the screen that the very camera has had her?

If she had been less famous or less rich when she died, in 1970, Laurel Gray might have been in an asylum. But that is how we are, here; we buy or talk our way to freedom, and our craziness lays claim to all the visible world. Laurel Gray had rights on the invisible, as well. She was a celebrated seer, who had virtually no contact with other people. Her house in Laurel Canyon was arranged so that she could live as fully in the spirit realm as possible. Perhaps she died from lack of substance, forgetting to breathe in her desire to feel out the future.

Who could have imagined that ending when she was born, in Grosse Pointe, Michigan, in 1926? She was a granddaughter of the man who had funded Henry Ford's first company in 1903. It was said as she grew up that if Grandfather had been more resolute, why, all those cars would be Grays. But he had only invested his money (and it was only a little of his money), watched it grow and then let Ford buy him out in 1917. Laurel was born in a crowd of Grays sure of their place in the century, nearly neutralized by comfort and unaware of the foolishness in being so rich but remaining in Detroit.

Old Gray is the only man I ever heard of who really lost it all in 1929. For all those stories of suicides on Wall Street and families ruined, Gray is the one case that checks out. He lost an eight-figure sum: Laurel was three then. Of course, there was six-figure money left, the loose change, as well as a house, cars and a skeleton crew of servants. Laurel grew up plump, pretty and spoiled; she wore silk underclothes as a child, and there were Maine lobsters brought in twice a week. But the mood of the family was crushed. She lived in the shadow of a greater past, in a family that began to see how Detroit society now looked down on them.

Laurel didn't much care. She took it as it came, tutors, private schools in the East, and the wartime summers at home and at Charlevoix. She moved with military men and older people; she used to sing at supper parties at the Chicago Club; there were stories of an abortion in 1944. In 1945, she went to Hollywood, on the say-so of a producer she had met.

She was in a few pictures: you can see her in *The Harvey Girls*, in the chorus on "The Atchison, Topeka and the Santa Fe" number. For a year, 1946–47, she was married to Henry St. Andrews, a real-estate dealer from Santa Barbara. He had a ten-year-old son from another marriage, Lindsay, and the 20-year-old stepmother was always moved by the beautiful, timid child. They were better company than ever Laurel and St. Andrews managed to be. Even after the divorce, she would call the boy and take him to museums and movies. Lindsay was never robust, and he had an analyst who said Laurel was good for him. As for Laurel, she moved into an apartment at the Virginibus Arms, she had a good settlement from St. Andrews so long as she never remarried, and she tried out for movies sometimes. She had a masseuse come to the place three times a week, a woman who had been a theosophist and met Krishnamurti at Ojai. She went by the professional name "Miss Adele." She talked to Laurel about the handsome young Indian who was supposed to be the reincarnation of Madame Blavatsky, and about his teachings as she worked the oil into Laurel's bare back to the beat of samba music on the radio.

Laurel always sensed something about Dickson Steele; but she was sensing things about most people. Lindsay St. Andrews was off at St. Paul's and, time after time, they used to write to each other on the same days. There wasn't a plan about it. Maybe they had a rhythm. But Laurel suspected it was something deeper. And she thought Steele was dangerous, all through their affair. That was what attracted her—the aura of violence, and the mystery too, the feeling that there was a story there waiting to be read. She guessed he was a murderer, and she told Brub Nicolai what she felt.

Nothing was ever proved. Laurel went in fear for several years, yet it was not just fear. When she heard footsteps following her, or when the phone rang at night and then stopped without a word when she answered, she thought this was it, coming true. She was thrilled. She called Lindsay one night—he was at Yale then—and she had picked on a moment of great crisis for him. Laurel drifted into spiritualism as a business, carried along by this knack. She never advertised, but word got out that she was good. Once or twice, Nicolai consulted her on police matters; he never made it official, he never said where the hunch came from, but he got a reputation for instinct.

It was in 1959 that Laurel and Lindsay married. They were only ten years apart, with no blood ties. But what were blood ties compared to the way they thought of things at the same time? It made news, and there was gossip; some people talked about incest. Laurel replied that while they might have been stepson and stepmother in this world, it was likely they had been brother and sister in another. But she didn't sleep with him, and she took lovers to disperse what she called "those distracting impulses"—this said with a comical shiver. Lindsay sold fine art in Beverly Hills, and they had an intricate double act, bringing paintings and spiritual solace to several homes.

They moved into Laurel Canyon, and there were people in the sixties who spoke of "Laurel," meaning her *and* the place, with hints of magic or danger there. Then Lindsay walked out, calling her a sick, grotesque woman who didn't wash enough and sat in trances in front of daytime television. He was killed in a car crash in 1966, a year after the divorce. Laurel was reported to have murmured, "A Ford, of course," closing the door on reporters. But it had been a Mercedes, on Highland.

To be a spiritualist, I suppose, you must be very selective. When you're wrong, you forget it. When you're right, it verifies the system. Gamblers work the same way. So most people decided Laurel was a charlatan, and a handful believed in her. But she stayed up in the house, with servants to look after her. People saw her by private consultation, except for Joan Didion, who wrote a piece on her for the *Saturday Evening Post*. It was a good article, funny, dry and touching, as if Didion knew this was a deluded woman yet an actress with her own odd poetry. The article contained some of Laurel's predictions—most of them wrong and forgotten now. But everyone remembers the one about an appointed outrage coming, killers and wolves slipping down out of the hills, "retribution . . . somewhere like Beverly Glen or Cielo Drive," Laurel had opined. That was published nine weeks before Manson. A year later, Laurel died, of cancer. She hadn't seen a doctor in fourteen years. She was forty-four, and I suppose in that long a time most of us will experience one astonishing coincidence or premonition. Or did the Manson gang read the *Saturday Evening Post* and believe in destiny?

ROY EARLE

Humphrey Bogart in High Sierra, *1941,*
directed by Raoul Walsh

All these people going west, have they got names to be blessed? It's like being way off from a line of trees, toward sunset, watching people walking through them, all going in the same direction. While the sun beats on your eyes, you study the people, and then you start to feel that the trees are moving too, just ebbing out toward the west, like stick people staggering into the fire.

It's all one motion, I think, the way so many people came west from Europe, and then west again across the country. And these were not nomads. They were the members of families who had lived in one tight place for centuries. And then in the space of a couple of hundred years, they cut off their own heritage, because they were persecuted, because they were poor and always would be, or because they were angry and difficult, and they headed west. But where do they go when they have got as far as they can go, and when they see the kingfisher color of the sea? Can they ever stop?

The great-grandfather of Roy Earle was a cider farmer in the Calvados region, in Normandy, France. The name then was Oeul. He was a Huguenot, and he came to Boston in 1836, though he'd never once in his life seen Paris. There must have been some commotion or upset, something that urged him to get away; no one knows what it was now. You can see the birds go south in August, but don't ask them if they know why they're doing it.

Roy Earle was born in Rush Creek Valley, Indiana, in 1902, in lush farming country, with a creek and a hole where the catfish basked on afternoons. His father grew corn and vegetables, and kept pigs and chickens. In the Great War, as Roy was growing up, his father got enough money selling corn to buy the farm. But he remembered how hard it had been, for him and *his* father, and he expected Roy to work after school without asking for anything. Roy loved the farm and the country, but there was a knot of anger in him.

When he was seventeen, he went to Indianapolis and worked in a factory making parts for cars. But he never got on with the boss, and one day he attacked him and beat him up. The boss pressed charges and in 1920 Roy got a six-month sentence in the city jail.

So, after that, he went back to the farm, no matter that his father treated him like an outcast. That passed away a while, but Roy had a friend in the next town whose brother had been a bank robber. They all hung out together in 1921 and 1922, and Roy got talked into joining them. There were small towns in the south of the state, and the young men held up a couple of stores and a bank without ever alarming or hurting anyone. But no one they robbed was ever going to take them on. Then, in 1924, with some help from Chicago, they went after a bank in Lafayette, and the three of them were caught. Roy got three years in the state penitentiary.

When he came out in 1927, he moved on to Chicago and he was a part of the Mob there, whether he knew it or not. In 1931, he held up the biggest bank in South Bend, and a lady was killed in the shooting. There was a manhunt, and they got Roy and he was sentenced to life in Mossmoor in 1932. He was thirty, and "life" then meant another thirty years before anyone would remember he was there.

But something happened. Some of the old Chicago people put in a word for him. They must have put some money in too, because they got Roy out of jail in 1940 on a pardon. There was noise about it in the papers, but the authorities said that Earle was a sick man. He'd been ill at Mossmoor and he looked thin and gray when he got out.

Of course, the money that had sprung him didn't forget. The Chicago organization told Roy to make his way to California; he could pay his dues there. They gave him a car and in the spring of 1940 Roy drove out by way of Des Moines and Denver to Los Angeles.

He had never seen mountains, or known air as clear. Some days, he reckoned anyone could make a fresh start there. He met a girl, Velma Goodhue, who had a bad leg. Roy thought that maybe if he could raise the money for her to have an operation, she might think of marrying him. So that's how he got drawn in on the Palm Springs Hotel job, along with Red Hattery and Babe Kozak, and Louis Mendoza, a clerk at the hotel. There was a woman with them too, Marie Garson, a dance-hall girl.

They did the hotel, and got away with $500,000 worth of jewels and cash—or so the hotel claimed. Velma had the operation, but once she could dance with anyone who asked, she saw Roy as a sad-looking, middle-aged guy. Roy had trouble fencing the stuff. He knew he was being double-crossed by the Mob, and he killed a man named Kranmer, who tried to take the jewels from him.

So Earle was on the run, with Marie Garson, who was in love with him. He went into the Sierras, around Mount Whitney, and the manhunt closed in on him—"Mad-Dog Earle," as they called him by then. He clawed his way up into the rocks, but it was cold at night, and he had nowhere to go. A sharpshooter got him on the second day, from half a mile away. The press said what a wretched end it was, but Roy really loved the mountains and the views and the streaks of iron and copper color in the rock as the sun went down.

MARIE GARSON

Ida Lupino in High Sierra, *1941,*
directed by Raoul Walsh

Before the two bridges were built in the 1930s, the Golden Gate and the Bay, San Francisco was an island city that relied on ferries to Oakland and Sausalito. The city was made so that the Ferry Building could be seen all the way down Market Street. That point was the eye and ear of the city, and Marie Garson was born a shout away, at Mission and Beale. Her father was a seaman on the ferry, and her mother had been a housemaid in one of the big mansions on Russian Hill. Marie was born in 1919, and the ferry boat hooted its way home through the fog on that November night.

The father was a big, boastful man, a tyrant in the house, and a boyo in the bars. But in the 1930s, as the new bridges felt their way across the water, spelling the end of the ferries, he drank more. He became morose and brutal, and he beat Marie and her mother. In 1936, Marie packed a bag and hitched a ride on a truck going south. Two days later, she was in Los Angeles.

She met a young writer, John Fante, and lived with him on Bunker Hill. It was her first gasp of happiness. She worked as a waitress and read his stories and they made each other feel good. Sometimes they took a bus down to the beach in the evening and swam in the darkness.

He told her great stories, and she loved to keep warm in his arms. But he grew gloomy over his poverty and one day another man flirted with her when she served him. His name was Kozak, and Marie could not get his tough face out of her head.

She moved in with him, and he put her to work at a dance hall: she was an available partner for anyone with a dime. Marie hated it, but she was in awe of Kozak and she slept with some of his cronies if he suggested it. They were small-time crooks too, and it was when they got involved in the Palm Springs Hotel job in 1940 that she met Roy Earle. She liked his rueful eyes, and the scorn he had for Kozak: one glance of his taught her what to see. Marie could tell that Earle was soft on someone else, but she stuck with Roy, hoping that if she stayed loyal and patient he would come round. They had only a summer together, but Roy loved her and trusted her, and she thought of him as a father.

When Roy was shot, in the Sierras, Marie took his dog, Pard. She realized later that the ring he had given her—from the spoils of the hotel robbery—was enough to get her a small place in Culver City. She had a job on the assembly line with the Hughes Company, and that was how she met several fliers. There was even a weekend when Hughes himself noticed her, flew her down to Mexico and had dinner with her. He didn't speak to her again, but he never treated her badly and he had her made a supervisor.

After the war, Marie heard about a "club" being run near Muroc Air Force Base by a woman known as "Poncho" Barnes. She had been a flier herself and had taken over a desert property for the rest and relaxation of the men at Muroc, many of them test pilots. Poncho put in a pool, there were horses, and a bar with a row of bungalows next to the main building, where private parties could be held. Poncho was hiring young women, and she naturally favored anyone with aeronautical connections.

So Marie moved up there to the Mojave Desert, and she started to have a good time. Poncho was the law on her property: the air force let her be, and the pilots had nowhere else to go in the vicinity. Marie took Pard with her, and somehow out in the desert she began to collect stray dogs. Poncho called them "the hounds" and some nights a group would go out hunting rattlesnakes with flashlights. Marie fell in love with one of the pilots, a kid named Bobby Kaufman. They had been married four months when he crashed, out in the desert, in 1948. Killed.

Marie stayed on at the club until 1954, when it closed down. She moved into the nearby town of Lancaster; she liked the desert, and she had plenty of friends on the base—the name of which was changed to Edwards in 1948, after another pilot who was killed. Marie opened a kennel in Lancaster, a way of making a business out of her dogs. And she settled to the life there. She died in her house in the summer of 1969. She lived alone, with only the dogs, and her body was not found for a week. The dogs had begun to eat her, but I don't think the worse of them for that.

> *Yet in a movie, dogs are pals or killers, never unknown. In movies, this garden path and that picture on the wall are all poised with meaning. Everything in the frame seems chosen, asking us to work out why it is there. Is there nothing spontaneous?*

HENRY OLIVER PETERSON

Robert Morley in Beat the Devil, *1954, directed by John Huston*

"I was, I fancy, thirty years or so ahead of my time," H.O. told Michael Parkinson on British television in a merry interview of 1973, the year before his death. "Until the age of about fifty, you see, my life was as spotty as your handkerchief—no offense, I trust. But after that I became quite respectable, and I am pleased to feel today that a modest amount of affection and gratitude flows towards me from people I have never met and who—should that be whom?—I daresay would be thoroughly dismayed if they did meet me. This little talk of ours will probably blow my cover for good. Still, I have enjoyed myself, and that's the thing, isn't it?"

He had been born in 1908 in an upstairs room of the Leg of Mutton and Cauliflowers, a public house in Leatherhead, Surrey, run by his parents. He grew up there, amid the smell of beer, a fat little boy too much accustomed to finishing others' meals. He was, apparently, a natural, fluent liar from an early age. "My father thought I was a scoundrel, but my mother was fond of me and I took gross advantage

49

of everyone. That sounds horrible, doesn't it?" he said to Parkinson. "But such candor seems to be expected of one nowadays. Shady characters are so much more popular now."

The boy was sent to Whitgift School and expelled in 1925 for cheating. His father had an interest in a garage on the A24, and as a young man, H. O. Peterson built up a secondhand car business on its premises. "I never knew the first thing about motors, but neither did the customers. I could sell with style and, in those days, you know, most people thought it was such a serious thing to have a car that they became very solemn in the selling. I treated a car like a new hat, and people liked it."

The business flourished, but in 1932 Peterson was given a six-month sentence in Brixton for petty fraud: "Checks or something, I can't remember. It could have been any one of a dozen naughtinesses." He was a cheerful prisoner who spent the time learning contract bridge—"Best thing that ever happened to me." The day of his release, he saw a vacant property at the top of Brixton Hill—"I saw that the hill was a very hard pull for cars, and I twigged"—he bought it and opened H. O. Motors. Success again: "Streatham was getting very posh then, and I had a special thing—colored cars, pretty ones. They'd all been black or gray before. There were gangsters then in the flats by Streatham Hill, and I did very well."

But in 1937, the Inland Revenue called for an audit, and eventually the business was wiped out by fines and confiscations. "Seemed a shame at the time, but I really should have gone to jug for it. I had to sweeten a few pots to stay out."

In 1938, he took a steamer to Rio de Janeiro, having recently been hired by Sebastian, the coffee merchant. "South America then was heaven. I stayed there all the war years, happy as a sandboy." He dabbled in coffee and beef, in minerals—"all manner of minerals" —and he resided in Santiago, Chile, where he once more went into the business of cars. He also made friends with St. John O'Hara. The couple were All-Chile Bridge Champions in 1942 and 1944: "We'd have had forty-three too, but O'Hara was on cocaine the entire time. He opened three spades once on a hand you could have played *misère ouverte*. Dear fellow, though."

After the war, it was bridge that brought Peterson back to Europe. He and O'Hara were defeated only in the semifinals at the Lisbon Competition of 1948, on a hand that is regarded as a classic. Their opponents were Gutman and Cairo:

O'Hara

♠A6
♥Q10
◆Q965
♣Q10532

Cairo

♠1097
♥J97653
◆J84
♣A

W   N   E

S

Gutman

♠KJ85432
♥K2
◆1073
♣K

Peterson

♠Q
♥A84
◆AK2
♣J98764

The bidding went to 6♣, with Peterson playing the contract. (On the very first round, West had ventured 2♥—unjustifiable, but a shot in the dark that would prove effective.) West led the 10♠ and Declarer won with the ace. He then led a low club from dummy and was not surprised to see the ace and the king collapse on it together. At this point, West led a small heart. Peterson recalled the earlier bid and decided that West had the king. He therefore played the queen from dummy. That disclosed the king with East, won in hand with the ace. But now there was a heart loser—whereas, if he had played the ten from dummy the queen was still a winner. One down. "That's what makes the game a joy," said Peterson, as Gutman and Cairo advanced to the finals.

His reputation in competition bridge brought forth an invitation from the *Daily Telegraph* to be their bridge correspondent. Peterson accepted, and he became known for his astute analyses derived from fictitious and sometimes fanciful hands that were being played amid some Agatha Christie-like intrigue—"It was all done in the space of a column, taxing sometimes, but such fun." This approach was regarded as showy and frivolous by many cognoscenti, who noted that Peterson's own prowess at the tables had suffered accordingly. "Bridge is a very strict regimen if you mean to succeed. Too grim for me, I fear."

Nevertheless, Peterson and O'Hara still played in Europe, and it was shortly after the Trieste tourney of 1953 that they found themselves in Ravello, near Naples. Peterson claimed later that the

British East Africa Uranium Company had been meant as a jest and that the death of Paul Vanmeer had had nothing to do with him. "There was this major, you see, Ross he called himself. And he simply had to be killing people. I think it was brain damage." The ugly voyage of the *Nianga*, the ordeal in north Africa—"too sadly true," sighed H.O.—and their eventual arrest by the Italian authorities were fit for a romance. The charges were eventually dismissed, but Peterson was left at a low ebb, especially when the final, piteous disintegration of O'Hara—long anticipated—occurred in Ravello prison. "He was a sweet little fellow, but unless he had drugs and a few women before lunch there was nothing you could do with him."

Peterson wandered unhappily for a few years, dismissed by the *Telegraph* and shunned by old friends. Then, one summer, he was laid up in the Dordogne with gout and, in the space of six weeks, all from memory or imagination, he wrote *Some Pleasant Hotels on the Continent*—casual but shrewd, and an unexpected hit when published by Constable in 1958. Another publisher approached H.O. to do a more thorough work, and so in 1962 there appeared the first edition of *Peterson's Guide to Touring in Europe*. So far the book has had eighteen revised editions, it has survived H.O.'s death, and it continues to be researched and compiled from offices in Fetter Lane. Reliable, courteous and opinionated, "A book for ladies, gentlemen and their vehicles on the loose with a low budget and higher hopes"—to quote from H.O.'s first foreword.

GWEN CHELM

Jennifer Jones in Beat the Devil, *1954,*
directed by John Huston

There is a statue of Gwen Chelm on the northern plains of Zimbabwe, striding toward the west. It is larger than lifesize. Her hand is arced above her eyes so that she can look toward the sunset. Sometimes the tall wiry grass waves around the plinth, but the statue is itself windswept or agitated by her own romantic ardor. The stone folds of her skirt are blown back, and the fine intricacy of her hair stands out from her head like the depiction of electricity in a comic book. She would have loved the statue, and although the woman is forty or so—Gwen Chelm's age when she died—it is a statue of a girl ablaze with eagerness and hope.

Gwen Perkins was born in Budleigh Salterton, in Devon, in 1928, the daughter of a clergyman. It was a quiet, industrious upbringing, with Gwen a faithful follower of the Allied war effort: there were maps in her bedroom, with flags to show the progress of every campaign. In 1944, her last year in school, she put on a pageant that traced the events of D-Day, as if it were a miracle play. She herself played a Joan of Arc of the Resistance who heard the voices of saints and turned the tide of battle in Normandy by crossing enemy lines.

It was in 1946 that Gwen went to London, to work in a team of young women who composed verses for greeting cards. She was known for her notices of bereavement. But the limits of the job became oppressive and in 1949 she joined the magazine *Picturegoer*, writing the synopses of films and reviewing them. It was in this capacity that she met Harry Chelm, a buyer for W. H. Smith's. He was the son of a newsagent in Earl's Court. The couple became engaged in 1950, and married in 1951, the year of the Festival of Britain.

Harry Chelm was a decent, straightforward man, stupid and reliable. But he did all he could to keep up with his young wife's romantic inclination, and he felt excited by the rapture with which she told and lived out entirely false stories about themselves. He supposed this process was dangerous, but he never denied the stories in public, and blushed if they seemed to require a nobler Harry than he could be.

It was in 1953 that the Chelms set out for Africa. Harry had an uncle in Kenya who was too old to run his small farm, and he had written to England asking if the young couple would care to take it over. It was in Italy that the Chelms encountered Billy Dannreuther, H. O. Peterson *et al*. Gwen insisted on an affair with Billy, and she furnished every evidence of illicit carnal relations despite her own determination to remain virtuous. It was only later, in Africa, that she regretted her abstinence. Harry loyally believed that she had been unfaithful, and that she was passionate and impetuous.

In fact, Gwen never shook off her sensible approach to all matters. Her vivid fantasy life deceived others, but it did not convince her. The days in Africa were long, hard and tedious, but Gwen worked on the farm and took care of the accounts. Harry became more caught up in politics—this was the process that led to him being knighted in 1967 and being called "the obliging Chelm" by Jomo Kenyatta.

The farm spread; it became prosperous. Managers were hired, and

Gwen Chelm was freer to travel. She went to visit a cousin in Rhodesia in 1961 and became fired with that country's political dilemma. Secretly, she worked as a friend to the freedom fighters, a fund raiser and the author of several of their pamphlets. This work led first to her affair with Winston Ntali (assassinated in 1969) and then to her own death in 1971 on a guerrilla raid in the rolling grasslands where her statue now stands with this inscription: "Gwen Chelm, a great believer and a citizen of Zimbabwe." There is a small plaque in the church at Budleigh Salterton and, sadly, there is the six-hundred-page life, *My Wife*, by Sir Harry Chelm, which nearly smothers her gentle turbulence in detail.

> *I read about a young woman photographer. She had a face like a hook. The more she pictured others the more her pale face begged, "Know me. Remember me." She killed herself. Someone in the book said there are two kinds of people—voyeurs or exhibitionists. Suppose we can be both at the same time? Show-people and watchers.*

ALMA McCAIN

Tuesday Weld in I Walk the Line, *1970, directed by John Frankenheimer*

You may come upon a young woman sometimes in the Tennessee hills who has a sly beauty, one you recognize a second or so after you've looked. She's outside a store, wearing sneakers in the mud, and you wonder, Is that something rare or just a flat, dull sensuality, with the look of a battered fifteen-year-old who has never washed properly? Then she notices you looking. A slow smile creeps up in her face and you see green eyes and lips that look swollen. There's a real beauty, you think, a flower in the backwoods. But while you're thinking, her face has sunk back into wariness. Oh, she'll go for anything you dream up, but she won't give you the pleasure of thinking with you. She's hostile to sharing. Whatever happens, you'll see her alligator eyes watching you do it. Her last retreat is not joining you, letting it be done to her, so you do it alone. You could go mad trying to catch the spirit of that nymph; it's like a fish. But you will not scrape her image from your eyes.

Alma McCain was likely born in 1951, around Frankfurt, which is between Cookeville and Knoxville in eastern Tennessee. No one knows where or when for sure. Alma was ripe at eleven, so there could be plus or minus a year. She would have been born in a cabin up a dirt road, without a doctor. Her mother would look too old already and she had had seven children, and three of them lived, Alma and her brothers, Clay and Buddy. The mother died in 1962, along with the last baby. The McCains roamed the back country, doing a little work and some second-nature thieving, following the old local art of moonshining.

That's how Alma met Henry Tawse, sheriff of a town called Nameless in Jenkins County. She and Buddy had gone into town for twenty pounds of sugar which their father needed in the still. On the way back, she let Buddy drive—he was eleven—and the pickup was going all over the road. So Tawse put on his siren and went after them. Buddy took off and hid in the long grass, but Alma said she'd been driving, and oh no there hadn't been a boy, certainly wasn't a boy. That look then, I'm sure. And he saw it because he was moldy in his own dead life. But he saw all the sugar too, and he wondered. He let her off: he was a kind man, not yet aware that he would have kissed her bare, cut feet if she had asked.

A few days later she comes to his office and says she and Clay were going to the fair, but she had suddenly thought why not call in and say thank you to Sheriff Tawse, and Clay and his temper had said do it, you bitch, and put her out on the road by herself. So there she was, and she really was obliged to him for not making a thing about Buddy driving, and that's all. It was getting dark, and he said he'd take her home. She let him kiss her in the police car, and she slithered over onto its big back seat, drawing him after her and just marveling to find what a load he had on him for her. He wept with gratitude on her old dress when he was done. She had a soft spot for him, whatever happened.

Tawse lived with his wife, his daughter and his father in the sheriff's house. But he used to haunt the derelict country place where he had lived as a boy. He took Alma there and told her how his mother and his two sisters had been killed in a crash on the Nashville road. Alma never asked him about his wife. She had never seen a marriage that worked, and she didn't want to embarrass him. He seemed so happy playing in the deserted house with her.

There was a federal agent in Nameless out to make a reputation bagging stills. He had Honeycutt, Tawse's deputy, on his side. But the sheriff was not eager to disturb the McCains. He had a dream of going away with Alma, to Chicago in a plane, maybe. She had never flown. Or to California. But Honeycutt was pushing Tawse. He reckoned the McCains were up to something, and he had seen Tawse and Alma sitting together on the slope of the reservoir. He just casually let it out that Alma had a husband in the penitentiary. "Oh, that's nothing," said Alma, when Tawse hit her and raged at her. She had forgotten Clem, a dumb kid who had married her when she was fourteen or fifteen and had been caught driving illegal whiskey to Chattanooga. After all, crazy lovers like her and Henry forgot their old attachments.

Then Honeycutt went out to the McCain place. He shot their dog and was going after their still when Alma's father came up and clubbed him to death. The family was burying the deputy when Tawse found them. He told them to get out of town, dumped Honeycutt in the river, and went to the old house, where he was expecting to find Alma waiting for him.

But she'd gone on with her family: in danger, the animal goes back into the lair. Tawse went after them. He found them on the road and stopped them. He told Alma to come with him—he was desperate—and she said no just as blunt and factual as she'd ever said yes. He wouldn't have touched her, but he wanted to kill her. As if she guessed his confusion, she put a bailing hook in his upper arm, his gun arm, and ripped it. He lost his job; a sheriff takes a shooting test every year, and Tawse could hardly hold a cigarette, let alone a gun.

Alma went with the family, but she'd been upset. After a while she set off to see her uncle, her mother's brother, in Waco, Texas. He had a barbecue restaurant, and he hired her as a waitress. But she got confused in the busy times, and he took her off the job. He made love to her one night, in his trailer, but when he told her to give him a blow job, Alma set her uneven teeth and bit off the end of his penis. She just left him there, howling and bleeding, and spat out the last shred of family.

She went to Arkansas, to Fort Smith. Honeycutt, the deputy, had told her once that he thought she could have been Miss Knoxville. So she entered the Miss Arkansas contest in 1972, and she placed fourth. There was a young man in the audience, Lionel Leonard, and he wrote her poems, and asked to be allowed to see her. She dated him for a while, but then she left for Nashville and got a position there in a House of Pancakes as a hostess.

A soldier came into the place where she worked, Glenn Kelly. He had been in Vietnam, and he was discharged. But he kept in training and wore a laundered uniform every day. They lived together in Nashville until Kelly went out one day and shot and killed Barbara Jean, the singer. Kelly was tried and put away for life. The whole thing got Alma's picture in the papers. Lionel Leonard came to reclaim her. He was sure they were made for each other. He found her in her apartment one night and begged her to marry him. Alma was tired, laughing and screaming at him to get out. But he wouldn't go, so she herself ran out to the verandah straight onto the butcher knife in the strong left hand of Henry Tawse, a vagrant with a last mission. She gasped and fell, so that her falling made the wound wider. Then Henry thrust the knife into his chest and collapsed on her.

> *I shudder at the violence I am writing, as if I were inflicting it on myself. I can become these people, or let them fill my emptiness. In a sentence, I can change my voice and my life.*

DAVID JOHN LOCKE

Jack Nicholson in The Passenger, *1975, directed by Michelangelo Antonioni*

He was in a small hotel in Chad, in northern Africa, in the desert, in the heat. David John Locke—profession: reporter. He had forgotten what he was looking for—guerrillas, no doubt, but if the urbane French-speaking President had happened by, on a tour of hotels, why not find the casual way to ask whether this civilized man had indeed killed thousands of his opponents? A reporter will ask anyone the old questions that everyone has learned to answer. So the world goes on. The expected interrogation hovers over it like flies above a corpse.

He was thirty-three, born in London; to America, age two, when his father was attached to the embassy in Washington. In America,

1944 to 1960, when his father retired with a commendation and a dinner from Eisenhower. What had his father done? Intelligence. He was one of the few British the Americans trusted. Nineteen sixty to 1963, back in England, at Oxford, reading history. In 1964, he began as a journalist for the *Sunday Times* and the BBC, then the *Washington Post*, and so on, working on projects like Insight, Focus or Survey. A gang of bosses sent him to trouble spots to bring back fresh reports with the tang of danger and impudence—Beirut, Vietnam, Cuba, Djakarta, Bangladesh, Chad, Chad, Chad—he had become an expert there, despite broken French and frosted insight.

There was a wife in Dawson Place, in Bayswater; the wife in a desirable, three-story Victorian house, narrow but deep, newly painted white, a house to keep up, with an attic room called Chad; the wife named Rachel, a tawny, angry wasp in the house, buzzing against him and the walls; a reason to be away and something to come home to; in and out, for how many more years, dark fingermarks always having to be sponged away from the doorjambs. While he had stayed in five hundred hotels.

There was Delamere in London, his blind friend from Oxford who took pleasure in David's American voice. Then, at forty, Delamere's blindness became operable. The operation succeeded. He was elated. But the feeling did not last. The world looked drabber than he had imagined. With his white stick he had tapped out the world. Now he stood on street corners paralyzed by information. He stayed indoors, in the dark. David Locke guessed that Delamere might do away with himself.

The previous night in a Chad hotel, before one more day of futile leads, David Locke met another Englishman, David Robertson. They were alike: same height, same age, same receding hair, same sinking stance, weighed down by a forgotten danger. They drank together. But when David Locke went in to see him a second night David Robertson was dead on the hotel bed, as if crept up on by the sinister peace while taking a rest. No trace of pain or regret: siesta. It was as if his vehicle had taken a turning and David Robertson had been borne off on another trip without bump or sway. Sometimes the dead die where they are sitting.

David Locke worked out what he would have to say at the hotel desk: "Il y a un homme mort. . . . " It was too complicated. He studied the corpse, how much it was like him. He never noticed the idea, but he acted on it, taking the body to his room, putting it on his bed, dressing it in his clothes, a decent fit after all. A lot alike. He steamed their two pictures from their passports. It was a small, magical exchange, like lifting the film of tiredness from a soul. Robertson was an international businessman, that's all he had said. David Locke looked in the dead man's bag; he was curious. He found an air ticket for London and Munich, a key and a diary with a few jottings: appointments, women's names—Melina, Lucy, Daisy, Zelie—and a hotel like another name, Hotel de la Gloria.

Feeling excited, he went down to the desk and said that the man in 17 appeared to be dead. That must be David Locke, said the black man. "Ah," sighed the fresh Robertson.

He went back to London and from the pavement outside the white house he saw Rachel watching David Locke's obituary on television. But Robertson was thinking of the dark-haired girl he had seen sitting on a bench in Bloomsbury. He had always felt a lack of attachment or conviction in himself that could let a friend fade from his life while he followed a stranger. Strangers are more beckoning; they offer new lives. After I had written that, I heard Mary Frances's scolding voice, trying to keep me in Nebraska. "But I never leave the house," I said, and she looked at me helplessly, so that I couldn't stand her eyes. I need to be in the dark, unseen.

Then to Munich. The key opened the locker at the airport. A slender black case stood in the locker, and in the case he found an inventory of weapons. The men who followed him to the Zimmermann church—be a tourist, he had decided—gave him an enormous fifty thousand dollars for the inventory. They all had a friendly chat, agreeing not to cry over the spilled milk of the anti-aircraft guns. Robertson was a gunrunner.

He went on to Barcelona in a hired car. He picked the place from the list of Avis offices. Why there, though? If anyone had known his love of Orwell, and his month in Catalonia in 1962, it might have been surmised. Was the Avis list printed with Barcelona in bold? Or was it chance, a stroke that obviates all this circumstantial speculation?

He found the girl in Barcelona, at the Palacio Guell by Gaudi; there she was on another bench, reading the same book, *Architecture Without Architects.* She could have been the perpetual student. It could have been anticipated that a tourist in that city would seek out Gaudi.

It was not awkward picking up this girl; perhaps she was as ready to take him from his track to hers. They went together, pursued by a Rachel anxious to hear from Robertson about Locke's last hours. They shared hotel rooms and Locke imagined how Robertson would have made love—secretly, so as not to break the package, for he had a weak heart.

Locke and the girl went by way of Almeria toward Algeciras—the rendezvous in the diary was set for there, at the Hotel de la Gloria. They found the place, a white building by the road, with a large open space behind it. He and the girl were in adjoining rooms.

Locke lay down to rest and the girl went to her room. He could feel the steady motion of time, like the hurtle of the earth. There must be an engine or an author carrying it all along. From the bed he could imagine a part of him going up to the window and out into the courtyard where cars came and black men got out to talk and look at the hotel. He could imagine his senses reaching farther out into the yard, leaving muffled noises behind in his room, a door opening, a bump in the air. And left there like an old shell, behind his senses, Locke-Robertson, David, was quietly shot. By whom? The senses were too far away to know. When Rachel arrived, the men, the black men, had gone. The girl was still there, loyal . . . or appointed? Night fell on the Hotel de la Gloria and the lights burning in its windows were like the sad but accepting guitar played within. All the senses of Locke, free but lost, gathered in the warm night air and looked at the girl with love and suspicion, like a reader following a story, saying, "Where next?"

MAUREEN CUTTER

Lisa Eichhorn in Cutter's Way, *1981,
directed by Ivan Passer*

There were two movie houses in Bedford Falls then, in the summers when Harry's child Mo stayed with us. It was three summers she came, in the middle fifties, years as long as the cars, and they were the Dream and the Circle, each pretty in its way, the Dream built in 'twenty-one and the Circle going much further back. It had been a proper theater and an opera house, and it had the old painted curtain with a view of a fine house across a lake at evening.

"Will the film be about the people in the house?" I remember Mo asked me one afternoon.

I was taken aback: she asked with such a weight of need. I would have made up some story about that house, but she seemed too earnest to mislead. "Maybe them," I surmised. "Maybe." But she thought my vagueness was a touch of mystery. You can never put hunters off if they are determined. Even silence entices them.

"It must be," she said, fixing her dark eyes on the house. The curtain shivered at times in some stage draft, and Mo wanted to see if the curtains stirred in the windows of the house. It would have been proof that someone there was watching us.

My brother Harry had married a realtor, Ruth, and they lived in Seattle, where Harry worked for a car dealer. He made money in the fifties and in the summers he'd take Ruth off to Mexico, putting Mo on a plane to Omaha. Nineteen fifty-five, 'fifty-six and 'fifty-seven it was, until she was ten. What a solitary, thoughtful child, tired-looking so you wanted to take care of her. Maybe as she got older and became a woman she learned about that look, and used it. But the Mo I knew was artless and implacable in all she did or imagined.

By looking in my list of pictures seen I can discover what I took her to: *The Trouble with Harry* (we laughed to think it might be her daddy); *The Night of the Hunter* (her hard, hot hand held on to me for most of that; I could count the beat of her alarm); *Picnic* (she was bored, she couldn't know yet the appeal to a provincial girl of doing something awful); and *The Searchers* (we saw that twice—like a view you circle round on so you can look at it again before you have to move on—and you know it's still there, years later, eroded a little, if only you would go back. But you can't, you never do).

Mo liked the pictures, but Travis would never go with us. It wasn't that he didn't enjoy particular movies; he couldn't accept their being stories, not real and true. He cried so much you had to take him away from the place. But Mo took the pretense for granted, the way some children can sit on a horse and not be afraid. As soon as she arrived in the summer, she'd say, "Anything playing, Uncle George?" and I'd make a fuss about being caught unprepared. "Well, I don't know, Mo. I hadn't thought about that. . . ." Then she'd frown at me, trying not to smile. You never forget the light in a child if you've helped put it there. Or it's going out.

"Do you have to spoil her with pictures?" Mary Frances would ask, the dust of bread-making up to her elbows. It was her unsteady humor, and she'd wink at Mo, to grab an ally. But then it turned to rancor and Mo learned not to respond. She'd study her shoes solemnly, counting the cutout holes in the pattern of her sandals while I soaked up Mary Frances's discontent. Anger in others will silence a child, until the quiet makes anger more suspicious. "Well, Miss Tight-Lips?" Mary Frances would demand, and Mo sank into passivity.

The summers came to an end. I had letters from her sometimes: Harry must have told her to write. But when she was fifteen or so, their tone changed and then the letters stopped. She went to the University of Washington for a couple of years but dropped out in 1968, when she was twenty, and then drifted down to Berkeley to live, saying she was going to finish her degree. But she never did.

She sent me a long letter in 1971, nine pages, typed, done over a span of three months, in installments. She apologized for getting out of touch, and said she remembered me well and still liked to go to the movies. When she got to Berkeley, she found a job at the Pacific Film Archive. She was friendly with a man there named Luddy who'd given her books to read on film. But she thought the books spoiled the pleasure, and she didn't persevere with them.

At the time she wrote, she was working in a bookstore for an Elmer Bender and his daughter, Marge, who was married to the writer John Converse. I used to read him in *The New Republic*, and I'd thought he was fair then. You can never tell enough from reading. She sent me his photograph, and that put me off. He had dead eyes, and a level, dishonest face, like a face in a mirror. Mo was in love with him, and they were having an affair without Marge knowing—or speaking. Converse and Marge had a little girl, but he had promised Mo he was going to marry her, told her time and again, and she got used to deceiving herself about it. Until he went off to Vietnam to be a reporter, and she had to recognize that he was more interested in testing himself.

So Mo moved across the Bay. She worked with the Elster Corporation, and then she was taken on at San Francisco General as an orderly. She met Alex Cutter there. He was back from Vietnam, without an arm. I learned this later, from Harry, when I determined to put the bits and pieces of her life together. Cutter was luckier than many veterans, but filled with anger and self-pity, and looking for someone to be his one to blame. By then, perhaps, Mo was prepared to be a victim: it becomes a way of life for so many of us. You can count the broken faces wherever you look.

They were married. I have a picture of the wedding: Cutter in a bow tie, all askew, his black patch slipping off a drunken eye—I have never established whether that eye was damaged, or the patch swagger. Mo is next to him, on his sound arm, but looking alone, staring at the photographer as if he had just offered to shoot her. There's a handsome man on her other side—he seems asleep, propped up—Richard Bone, Cutter's one friend. His drowsy eyes are looking down at Mo's dark hair, as fine as chocolate lace. Is he smelling her?

They went to live in Santa Barbara, the three of them. There must have been good times, but Harry said it was always a wonder Mo stayed. He told her he'd have her back at home. But she didn't budge. She drank more year by year, vodka or rum, while Cutter talked about his loathsomeness. The police said she was drunk and had dropped a cigarette which set light to the house and she'd been burned to blackened bone. It was dry timber, with straw rugs, the house: it was consumed in fifteen minutes, and no one was there to drag her out. They knew her by the teeth.

I fretted over her years before that, and Mary Frances would look at me in disbelief. "Can't you ever care for your own children?" she said. "You dreadful fool."

"They don't want it," I explained.

"How would you know?"

"They hold me off."

"You'd do anything for a stranger." She was crying. "Those films. They make the strange so attractive."

This could be so. They are so full of hope and change. I remember, though, in 'fifty-six how Mo took me for an ice cream after *The Searchers* and recounted the story we'd just seen, about a search for a niece who did not know her uncle anymore. I have done what I can with Mo's life. Cutter died not long after her. He had needed her too much. He had gone to the house of this man named Cord, and become abusive. Bone was with him. It was some stupid quarrel: Cutter was always looking for grievances. I wrote to Bone asking him for information. But all I got was a handwritten page saying, "I let her down, like everyone else let her down. She was depressed that night, and for all I know she shut the door after I had gone and built a bonfire in the living room. We will never know for sure; she kept it her secret. She did not mention you."

How does anyone read that and not imagine more?

AL

Charles McGraw in The Killers, *1946,*
directed by Robert Siodmak

There's no more than "Al" to go on, the one surprised word uttered by his companion as the two men were shot by a policeman named Lubinsky and James Reardon, an insurance agent, in a bar in Philadelphia. There were no marks of identification on this Al, no family pictures, no driver's license, no names or initials sewn into his clothes. He was a man of about forty-five, in a dark suit, a white shirt and a plain black tie, with shoes that someone polished every day. He wore a gray hat with a black band, and the face beneath it was cut out of rock. There was a frown above and between his eyes, cold, hard eyes, but sensitive, or worried, too. He looked like someone who took care, yet he handed out pain without any weakening. Al was a professional killer. Or so they said. They said he had killed a man, "Swede" Lunn, in Brentwood, New Jersey, and that he had done it for money. He was a contract killer. You wouldn't reach him directly. If you wanted someone killed, you need never meet Al or ponder over his eyes. You put in a call, and a few more calls got to Al. The sum of money you had agreed would go down by maybe 60 percent by the time it reached him. Those are the eyes of someone who suspects he's being chiseled.

This was in 1946—I wonder if Als still work in the same way. This Al and the other one came into Harry's Diner in Brentwood just before six, just before dinner. They took over the place, they closed it up, they had Nick Adams stay where he was, and they waited for Lunn. They said they would be killing him for a friend. The other one was fat, aggressive and theatrical, but Al was lean and restrained. He said no more than he had to, and you could have fancied that he was bored by the other one's caustic and unnecessary talk. It was as if Al was the real thing, while the other was an actor horning in on a contract to get material for a picture. The other one was already thinking aloud in script lines—"They all come here and eat the big dinner." But Al saw no act in what he was doing; he did not enjoy the lip-smacking talk. He was worrying whether he could shoot Lunn correctly and get away without a trace.

Al hoped not to be noticed. Real hired killers must not look dangerous. They need a kind of meekness, a gray availability that no one remembers. There were no marks and no identification: in taking other lives safely, Als must surrender much of their own. They live in boardinghouses, moving on, their lack of Social Security, credit rating, tax base and driver's license excused by the propriety of their lives and the steady call for killings.

From my world of law-abiding wallets full of identity, I wonder how one contacts Al and buys the assurance of his unobtrusive craft? I have a job and I do not think I can do it myself. So I am on the lookout for him, patiently examining shamefaced men.

JOE GILLIS

William Holden in Sunset Boulevard, *1950,
directed by Billy Wilder*

Like many who made long journeys to Los Angeles, Joe Gillis had once meant to be a movie star. He never owned up to it; he sneered at actors and their emptiness. When he met them, he was reassured to find his superiority justified. None of this altered how as a youth in Ohio he had longed to be on the screen. It was not exactly that he wanted to be a picture actor. He wanted his life to take place *on* a screen, with all the enhancements of close-ups, dissolves and hushed music.

But one day in the house off Sunset Boulevard Joe Gillis looked at the empty pool and thought what a hole it was, where a drunken slip could smash a face. He thought of those movie moments when tuxedo pomp walks backward into the water, and hilarity soars on the splash. Feeling blue, and trying to organize good times, he told Max to have it filled with water. Should it be cleaned first? Max had wondered. What did Joe know about pools? He said he guessed not. Wouldn't the water clean it? A few days later, he toppled gracefully into that pool—it was his best moment, his starry fall—and, drowning and dying, he swallowed water and spewed out his story.

He had been born in Dayton, Ohio, in 1918. His father had a drugstore. Joe served ice cream and floats in summer and put out the magazines. He admired their pictures, and he had a collection in his room above the drugstore of *Photoplay* and the other picture papers. He sensed that the stories were less accurate than the pictures. The stories were so torrid, so sweet, so full of mood, like advertisements or letters of persuasion. When he grew older, Joe recognized that these stories about the stars' lovers and their pets had the same drama and atmosphere as the stars' movies. He could not be sure whether this was a trick, something no one else had noticed, or whether in Hollywood people did live out motion picture stories. He could believe the latter, for when he went to the movies himself he always wanted to be up there, moving, turning, waiting, watching, smiling on the screen. He practiced those faces in the mirror and he lived with the blessed momentariness of someone always being just noticed.

It hurt his face. He had been a good-looking boy, but in adolescence his features took on the folds and ghostly inside-outness of one of those paper toys that children fold. There were so many instants in Joe Gillis's face it was all he could do to hold the thing together. When he smiled, you felt the parts were going to come apart. So he had to settle for a grin, and that turned mean and sour. By the time he was twenty, he looked and felt unreliable. He could never do a thing without imagining he was being written. Joe did not like writing or reading, but he had announced that as his calling because he could not get the inward scrutiny out of his rattled, dishonest head.

He studied English at the University of Dayton, and he wrote a story in 1939, about a kid who helped the Wright brothers in their first attempt to fly. It was fiction, but it was carefully researched, and it soared on Joe's own wish to mingle with the famous. Paramount read the story—it was sent to them by Joe's professor—and they bought it for five hundred dollars. The studio told him it had been "an invaluable, background contribution" to the 1941 picture *I Wanted Wings*. Joe saw that movie three times, but he never found a trace of his story beyond the common theme of flight and the general emotional yearning for transformation.

He went into the army, determined to use all the idle time he had heard about to write more stories. But within a week of landing in Europe, he had been captured. No shots were fired. His detachment simply walked down a road and found itself among Germans. No one struggled or argued; it was like a journey reaching its appointed end. So Joe Gillis was sent to a prisoner-of-war camp, and there his face became gaunt but his fingers grew calluses as he wrote story after story in lead pencil on the gray paper that he managed to save. There was not one war story. They were all about happiness and success.

When he was released, Joe went back to Ohio, got his stories typed up, and sent them to Paramount with a letter of explanation that was already like a magazine article on how this young writer became a movie scenarist in a harsh, unfriendly stalag. A few days later he followed the registered package on the train, confident he would never see Dayton again.

From 1946 to 1950, Joe Gillis worked on seventeen pictures. He was on staff at Paramount for two years; he got a credit for the shared original story on *My Wife the Mailman* (which claimed to be set in Dayton) and another for a script on a quickie Western, *Canyon Fire*. Other scripts were bought and shelved, or passed on to other writers. He was paid for treatments. He lived well enough, but the insecurity and the lack of glamor sapped him. Studios got to know him, they anticipated his jaded face and anxious calls, and his reputation became that of a has-been. He hated stories now. He regarded the elements of fiction as the cards in a pack. They were always all there. There was no surprise; solitaire always came out if you cheated. He was a hack, and he hit the typewriter with the violence of self-loathing. Back in Dayton his condition would have been recognized as a mental breakdown. But this is harder to discern in Los Angeles.

Then one hot day he tried to get his car out of reach of the repossession men, and he drove it into that unexplained driveway off Sunset Boulevard. It could have been the beginning of a lane up into the hills, or the mouth of oblivion. It beckoned, just as if art directors and gardeners had plotted all morning over its open, sleepy abandon. The mansion was something out of a fairy tale, Joe told himself, and then Norma Desmond called to him from the balcony, the voice like a fingernail dragged across glass.

She took him in; she would not let him go. For she had never lost her love of stories, and she regarded him as a pilgrim, a pen and a fan sent by providence. She lavished clothes, love and her script upon him. He wore the clothes all the time—when they went out, when they stayed at home; he was her male model, with the whisper "gigolo" in his ear and sticking out in exactly the way an ivory-colored silk handkerchief protruded from his top pocket. He suffered her love—he let her clamber all over him, her fearful, sinewy heat and her precipitate orgasms, she was always so in love with love. And he took her pages and folders of script and hacked them down into a polished, lifeless work.

She shot him. He fell into the pool. The script had not sold. He had wanted to leave. And she had never told him that in all those love-stews he had put a child in her. It was as if she regarded the conception as hers alone. But if he had known, he might have shot himself. Joe

Gillis was a coward who was horrified easily. And he had ordered the pool filled so that the Chinese tiles on its floor shone and smiled.

MAX VON MAYERLING

Erich von Stroheim in Sunset Boulevard, *1950, directed by Billy Wilder*

Born in 1894 in Vienna, Max Meck; died in 1964 in Pasadena, Max von Mayerling. A man of many parts—military spy, fraud, illegal immigrant, military costume advisor to motion pictures, director, husband, failure, the humiliated one, guardian of unlocked doors, chauffeur and magician. If every previous generation of the Meck family had felt itself advancing with seriousness, then Max is the augury of modern times, forever stepping into greater implausibility but never losing his balance. As we drag our history forward, we seem able only to find more unbelievable lives. Yet Max never gave up the ghost. He dressed impeccably, and his pained eyes spoke of duty, honor and expectation. Just by glancing at chaos, he could convince his stepson, Julian, that there was still a notion of order, and a gulf between it and reality, a loss, the prevailing message of Max von Mayerling's eyes.

The Meck family was very poor. What did you expect? The father worked in a bottle-making factory in Vienna; the mother had seven children, all in three rooms on the third floor with only one window that admitted daylight. The others were trapped by wells, backs and the gloomy overlay of the bottling factory. All those nineteenth-century cities, filled with children and the memory of others who died in infancy; kids hungry and thin, with eyes burning in their scrappy faces; their heavy shoes clattering on the stone steps, their pale legs striving to carry the leadlike shoes; an era that seemed like a dingy, overcrowded tenement building where there was always someone ill, or dying, or being born.

The most natural mood of the tenement is a jittery, cheerful anxiety—like someone who expects bad luck. But at the age of twenty, Max Meck was already possessed of the grace that could have lived on a country estate. He alone knew how he had acquired it: he may have worked as a valet or groom; he may have read novels and visited the theater. But at twenty he knew accoutrements. He spoke like an aristocrat, and behaved toward women with that curt Britishness that was in fashion with gentlemen. As the war came along, so Max was the picture of a young Prussian officer, thoroughly versed in the history of battles, sentimentally drawn to the cavalry but up to date on artillery statistics.

When he joined the Austrian army, his superiors noticed this authority and extricated him from the ranks. They had his birth certificate, and they could measure how far his presence belied it. Some wise adjutant realized he had an actor on his hands, and so Max was drafted into espionage. He posed as a German flier, was shot down over France and imprisoned, but was taken into the confidence of his French brother-officers. When he had had his fill of their information, he escaped and hiked back to Germany. Of course, the information was trivial. But it delighted the Germans and the Austrians to hug such a trick to their hearts. Max could have been shot in the process, for those tricked must respond severely if they ever detect the trick. He took extravagant risks so his superiors could enjoy a sense of advantage. Espionage is a state of mind, like unfaithfulness; it is more a treasure to the imagination than a concrete advantage.

As the war ended, Max Meck took a ship to Mexico from Lisbon, hired as the ship's doctor. Thus, he came over the border to the south of San Diego, a sturdy, resolute man, dressed in rags he had purchased as adornment to the tan and the scars he had won to make up his peon look. Six weeks later, Max von Mayerling was working as an extra in pictures, and as a military costume expert on films showing the wickedness of the Hun. He watched the making of these movies and saw nothing he could not understand. The realization of plots was second nature to a spy.

He was a director by 1921—*Speckled Hens and Cockerels*, a sardonic portrait of the marriage-market in Granada, about which the legend endures of pornographic scenes shot for the delectation of a studio boss. In 1925, a mangled version of his *Death Valley Days* was all that Hollywood could divulge of an extravagant masterpiece. *The Honeymoon* was withheld; its symbolism was deemed too flagrant. And *Princess of the Micks*, with Norma Desmond, was so immediate a commercial failure that Miss Desmond, its spent owner, withdrew the picture and herself from public gaze.

Max was by then her husband, so she did not prevent his following her to Europe. She had forgotten how they came to be married. But her aberration was his tragedy, for he loved her. She teased him and said he had fallen in love with her only to inspire masochistic ecstasy, a pressing strain in all his films. He replied that love was always absurd; the choice of whom one loved should be perverse. She hired him as her butler when she had divorced him. He could get no more work in pictures, so she kept him on an allowance. Max watched two other husbands come and go. The first was too proud to speak to a predecessor, but the second recognized tradition and liked to chat with Max.

Years passed. Back in America, living on Sunset Boulevard, Norma became more erratic. She tried to kill herself in 1940, and Max removed the locks from the doors so she could not isolate herself from rescue. And so he lived, with a beloved who did not consider him, and who sometimes beat on his chest with wrath. He did not sleep from imagining a suicidal leap in her. He was caught in a trap of frustration. Max wept for an hour every day until his black eyes had the luster of velvet.

Then Joe Gillis came along, offering the phantoms of a comeback and another lover to Norma. Max did all he could for Gillis; being polite to this jerk was a refined self-abuse. And at the time of the shooting, it was Max, a director still, who coaxed Norma downstairs and into the loony bin by conjuring up a camera to track back in front of her languid advance. It was as lovely as an Arab dance, he thought.

He visited Norma, and never mentioned the pregnancy that the star and killer ignored. She had no anesthetics in labor, but screamed at the mysterious pain. The son was born and Norma went back to eight years of asylum hours.

Max petitioned the state of California to be appointed the boy's guardian. He was accepted. He had the boy named: Julian Kay, he told the registrar, the first name that came into his head; he was an effortless inventor.

He took the boy to two rooms in Inglewood. Max worked as a chauffeur and as a magician who hired out for children's parties. He cared for the child in a doting and grim way. He looked after him physically so that he grew up soft and babylike. But he allowed his mind no innocence, and he taught the boy the proper spartan caress that a man must bring to women. So Julian grew up with an odd, unemotional expertise, as appealing and perverse as a mustache.

Max died in 1964. He was returning from a party where he had made pigeons fly in and out of reality. He had a heart attack at the wheel, and his car collided with a truck carrying beer. He was killed instantly, as he had always hoped he would be.

GUY HAINES

Farley Granger in Strangers on a Train, *1951,
directed by Alfred Hitchcock*

Perhaps it is all those gleaming whites stooping to the cunning of lobs and drop shots, not to mention the paranoia of disputed line calls, with smudged chalk, elderly judges set in cherry-colored silence, and the horror of a bad call marring the purity of the game. Still, tennis players are not easily trusted. Their elegant lines of movement succumb to forced errors or double faults. Tennis is a game for flawed saints. Its arrangement of white and green is like a cucumber sandwich in which, somehow, a virulent mustard has been smeared. "Anyone for tennis?" they are supposed to sing out in polite, middle-class theater; it seems an innocent game, a prelude to marriage, what with mixed doubles and the hints of love in the scoring. But it is often the tennis player who is the killer in that land of Agatha Christie.

Guy Haines was never quite in the front rank of players. He looked a little frail next to Savitt, Sedgeman and Schroeder. His backhand was unsound, not so much weak as snatched and evasive—a smile hoping to conceal a cavity. He had never spent a summer driving three hundred backhands every afternoon against an unbeatable wall; he never took his weakness and pounded it flat. Perhaps he admired his own little kink, and so his backhand was a wicked shot—sliced, cut, spun, dropping over the net and twisting back into the netting—but something that broke under pressure. At Wimbledon in 1949, Budge Patty so repeatedly attacked his backhand that Haines lived in the shaded corners of the court, a suspect under interrogation.

But Guy Haines was welcome on the court and in the clubhouse. He was the best-looking tennis player on the circuit. He had a gracious way of losing and a shy acceptance of victory that won sentimental support. He smiled a lot; he was courteous to umpires and pally with ballboys.

He was born in 1926 in Manchester, New Hampshire, with the real name George Hank, of German descent. The father had a laboring job in one of the mills in a town losing its eminence in that industry. Young George had no special talent, except for nimbleness at ball games. His schoolwork was always interrupted by practice. But he was slight and hurt easily. He liked the notion of being safe on his side of the net—no matter that he was one of those who perfected the winner's easy hurdling of the net to land in the loser's lap with consolation and bravos.

During the war, Guy worked summers on Long Island as a ballboy, helping the pros and making himself available as a partner at country clubs. He was not drafted because of flat feet—marching would have crippled him. But he kept the lightest tread on the court, where he was known as a retriever.

He won some worthwhile competitions in New England in 1945 and 1946. Tennis was still an amateur game, accessible only to players of some means. Guy Haines (his *nom de raquet*) was eager to play in Europe, but he needed a patron. In Huntington, Long Island, he found and married Miriam Chitty, who had inherited money from her parents. She was willing to put these funds toward Guy's expenses, and she did understand that it would impede his plans if she accompanied him on the tour. So she kept a scrapbook at home, rejoicing when he won the Italian Open in 1948, and made the Wimbledon semifinals in 'forty-nine.

The marriage drifted. Absences grew into separation. Guy met Ann Morton, the daughter of Senator Morton of Pennsylvania. He was moving in society circles, telling the Mortons that Miriam was a spoilsport, one of the sluts of Long Island, waiting to be bought off with a good divorce settlement. "I could kill her," hissed Ann Morton one day, though never having met her. "Me too," said Guy, always eager to agree.

Their marriage conjured up a strange genie: Bruno Anthony, a tennis fan, who set out to meet Guy on the train from New York to Washington. This was achieved with the full effect of chance and surprise, and Bruno introduced the motif of "crisscross"—lines of force that meet and feel the knot of intersection. "Why sure," said Guy, almost to himself, "your father and my wife." "Exactly," said Bruno. Or something like that. Who can ever remember conversations on trains, with all the rattling of the machinery? Guy was a skilled player, and Bruno an overemotional fan, quick to jump to conclusions, and so touchingly ready to do something, to be as active as a tennis player.

So Bruno killed Miriam, strangling her on an island at a fairground in the town where she lived. And then, like anyone who believes in fair play, he looked to Guy to dispose of his own hated father. Crisscross? One good turn deserves another, the spirit of doubles—one at the net, the other taking the baseline.

Guy was embarrassed. The police could see how he had been freed by the death of Miriam; he had no satisfactory alibi; he did not tell the story of Bruno, that charming maniac, because he was afraid it would not be believed, or because he was guilty about a real pact. Had there been a moment when he had grinned at Bruno, said "Okay, pal!" and told himself, why not, if this idiot feels like it? He did not report Bruno; it was his backhand again, tensing and shrinking under pressure.

But it all worked out. Bruno was too unstable to make a case against Guy: he became obsessed with incriminating clues and some final fairground disaster. He died. Guy was cleared. He married Ann Morton and became an assistant to her father. He was himself elected to the Senate in 1964, representing Delaware, and he was not seriously damaged when Ann Morton divorced him, charging adultery with a woman or women on trains between the capital and the Haines home in Westchester.

Senator Haines became a confidant of President Nixon in the late 1960s, and so it was—crisscross, everything in meetings—that he was charged in the aftermath of Watergate with attempts to obstruct justice, convicted, and stripped of his office. He served eight months, and now runs a tennis school on Long Island where whites are obligatory. He has not temporized with the recent taste for colored shirts. Guy Haines wears long white trousers as he runs around his backhand.

PETE "SWEDE" LUNN

Burt Lancaster in The Killers, *1946,
directed by Robert Siodmak*

Peter Lunn was born in Bemidji, Minnesota, in 1908. His parents were both Swedish—his father from near Askersund—and they had made their way to America in the early years of the century. The mother had been married once before, but her husband fell sick and died in the terrible northern Minnesota winter of 1905. A year later she married Olf Lund, a dairy farmer on land to the north of Leech Lake. The family went by the names of Lund or Lunn, slowly yielding to American usage, not noticing as the lilt in their voices went flat.

Peter was the largest in the family, a runner in summer and a football player in winter. He would have gone from school to the farm, but for the illness of his father in 1926–27. An uncle, Lars, came over from Sweden to help with the farm, and Peter reckoned that he was being edged out. So he left Minnesota and drifted down to Chicago. He was working in the stockyards when he read a notice in the paper inviting strong young men to come to a gymnasium. A fight manager was looking for new talent. Peter had grown up a gentle kid, extreme only in his taste for romantic gestures. He was amused at the idea of putting on boxing gloves and hitting another man, but in his trial he knocked out his opponent in the first round, and he was signed up on the spot. He took it as it came, reckoning that if he made some money he would send it back to his parents. The manager said he was going to change his name for fights to Ole Anderson—it sounded more Swedish—but he called Peter "Swede," and that stuck.

From 1928 to 1935 he had seventy-six bouts as a light-heavyweight; he won fifty-five, lost nineteen, with two draws. All the losses came in the first and last years of his career. In the times between, for five years, he went unbeaten, with twenty KOs. With better backing and promotion, he might have been a contender. But his manager was a mediocre guy, and Swede learned that Scandinavians were not a draw in the big Eastern cities where title fights were held. So he never got his chance, and that hurt him for, once he had been beaten five times as a novice, he stopped laughing at boxing and learned the craft. He wanted to be champion as much as he had ever wanted anything. In 1934, he beat Gunboat Smith in Detroit and fought a twelve-round draw with the Englishman Len Harvey.

He was making as much as two thousand dollars a fight, but he lost half of that to his handlers, and he never managed to control the costs of training and travel. Somehow he had the idea that a potential champion should be extravagant. He bought rounds of drinks and then watched the fun around him as he sipped a soda. Naturally shy with women, he would invite a couple of girls to have dinner with him and his gang. Then he'd see the girls go off with a sparring partner and a second, while he got to pick up the check.

Nineteen thirty-five was the bad year. In January he had promised himself he'd have a title fight that year. Then he lost six in a row, and in Philadelphia in October he broke his right hand on Tiger Lewis's head and stood up like a dumb Swede while Tiger beat him. His corner and the crowd were telling Swede to go down, but it went the full ten, and he was never the same young man again. One fight can age a boxer. If Peter Lunn had lived, chances are he'd have been punchy by the time he was fifty.

So he retired. He still had money and clothes enough in those years. Boxers and gangsters are drawn together. Boxers have grown up more than they know with gamblers and their most obvious chance of reemployment is as bouncers or muscle. For their part, gangsters like to tame tough men who have taken and handed out punishment without notice or much profit. They regard fighters as idiots, and gangsters are so insecure they keep themselves surrounded by foolish strength.

Lunn had known Jim Colfax, and he hung around with him without understanding what Colfax was up to. He had a detective friend, Sam Lubinsky, who warned him off Colfax, but by then Peter was crazy about Kitty Collins, Colfax's mistress. The Swede wasn't as smart as Colfax had been. He believed Kitty when she said she wasn't anything more than a friend of Colfax's; and he was impressed when she told him, "I hate brutality. I could never bear to see a man I really care for being hurt." That one comment finished boxing for Lunn; he saw how ugly he had been for eight years. He was madly in love, but he said nothing to anyone and he thought no one noticed.

Then one day in 1938, Peter Lunn was there when his old friend Lubinsky came into a Philadelphia restaurant and made to arrest Kitty because she was wearing some stolen jewelry. "Don't do that, Sam," said Swede, casual as could be. "I gave it to her. She don't know nothing about it." Kitty went along with the gallantry, Lubinsky had no option, and despite his years in jail Peter never asked himself how the stuff came to be around Kitty's neck and pinned to her sweet bosom. It had been a grand moment, stepping forward, like raising his arms and having the announcer call him the new champion.

Colfax and Kitty were still friendly in 1940 when Peter Lunn got out of jail, and he came back to the gang. Maybe Kitty was touched by him. Maybe Colfax got irritated. In any event, the two men fought over her, and Colfax learned just how hard you can be hit in real life by a hand that was broken so that its owner had to give up boxing. They made a sort of peace, and they got on with robbing the payroll from the Prentiss Hat Company in Hackensack. That was July 20, 1940—a quarter of a million. A champion's lifetime in a few minutes.

Colfax had planned to double-cross Peter, but Kitty warned him and the two of them went off to Atlantic City with all the money. She said of course she loved him, and the Swede was in glory and heaven. But she left him inside a week, took all the money and went back to

Colfax. Lunn was so sad he tried to throw himself out of the hotel window, and only a devout chambermaid stopped him and told him to be a man.

He went away, but not far, to Brentwood, New Jersey, where he worked at a gas station and lived in a room at Ma Hirt's on Spruce Street. He led an uneventful life, plain and straight, and he waited. One day in 1946 Colfax happened to drive by and stop for gas. They had a friendly talk, never mentioning the job. Then a few weeks later two men came to the diner just before six when the Swede normally ate. They waited, and then they went up to Ma Hirt's, found him in his darkened room and put eight shots in him where he lay. Swede must have heard them coming, big men on an outside wooden staircase, all creaks and their repressed breathing, but he never made a move to save himself.

> *I would like to be like Harry Dean Stanton in* Paris, Texas, *calling up the characters on a telephone. Yet I have never met him, and he seems utterly unmeetable. "How pitifully absurd!" Mary Frances said once when I told her I thought, perhaps, I resembled James Stewart in* Harvey. *She was right, is right, like a rope around my neck.*

KITTY COLLINS

Ava Gardner in The Killers, *1946, directed by Robert Siodmak*

"My word, sir, that's a lovely child you've got there," said the gunman to Christopher Collins, a while before he shot him. This was one night in August 1924, hot and humid, in a tenement house in the South End of Boston. Collins was a policeman home by eight for his dinner. Ten minutes later there was a knock at the door and three of them came in, leaving a fourth on the doorstep. Mrs. Collins was indignant and scared, the two feelings coming in rapid flushes, so she hardly knew what she was saying. But her Chris was not surprised, and that shocked her—he a policeman, apparently seeing nothing outrageous in three men coming in, in jackets too on that night, and shooting him. Without a protest. And a fond-faced smile when the man remarked on little Kitty's looks, as if the father had not noticed it before for himself.

This Collins had come out of Ireland in 1919, landed in Boston and joined the police. In 1920, he married Kathleen Carroll, whose father was in the railways. A year later, Kitty was born, and Donal, the next, and Cliona in 1923. Their house was noisy with argument, and because Collins had trouble sleeping he got a habit of cheap white wine. He didn't notice much, which no one found odd in a Boston cop. But it affected those near him. He might have Kitty on his lap, dark with lustrous eyes already at the age of three, yet her father wouldn't reckon he had more than the cat asleep there, something to stroke once in a while.

A week after the shooting, the *Globe* said aha, this Collins was a black-and-tan; and that explained why years later a party would come to his house and shoot off his face in front of the wife and kiddies. It was assumed that he'd done something bad in Ireland, and his colleagues in the police came to the realization that, why, yes, surely he'd been an anxious man. There was a police pension, and a collection in the city (which might have tripled but for the hints that Collins had deserved what he got). So the family lived on in the South End, looked after by the police, and once a year the recipients of a banker's order, out of Philadelphia, for three hundred dollars, never explained, but somebody's way of remembering Kitty's eyes, and allowing they shouldn't have had to see the blasting of her daddy.

Kitty grew up tall, slender and gorgeous, but always fighting with her mother. The mother had formed the opinion that her Chris had been a no-good—hadn't he let her down and ruined her life?—and she said Kitty was like her father, and a liar too. And just to show her mother, Kitty by the age of sixteen could tell sweet, polite lies to anyone with the look of a young nun on her face, and then a wink that was a startling thing, like the Virgin Mary giving you the eye.

She gave up school around then, and in 1937 she found a job as a waitress on the trains between Montreal and Washington. She liked the crowds of men on business, and she got nice tips. But best of all, after dinner, she went to the observation car at the back of the train to count her money. One night there she met a glib fellow, Dickie McCoy, who sat with her and picked her pocket without her feeling a thing. Then, on the spur of the moment, instead of going off with the money, he told her what he had done and won her with the magic of it. She laughed, and later that night he took her maidenhood with the same light touch. He was years older than Kitty, but she woke enchanted and in love. The lying had made her romantic.

McCoy taught her to be a dip, and she was fair at it. The railroad company got complaints, but they never thought it might be a woman. By Christmas 1937, Kitty was rich and happy. Then, one day, between Philadelphia and Baltimore, a man named Jim Colfax caught her hand inside his coat and said she was a wicked girl. He talked about turning her in, but he took her off the train with him and made her his woman in his house in Philadelphia. Colfax was big in the rackets, and he needed a pretty young thing around to impress people.

After she'd got over the humiliation of it, Kitty saw that Colfax was a dull man. She was bored without the motion of the trains and meeting all sorts of new people, joking with them and flirting, bringing them a Reuben and lifting the wallets from their inside pockets. Colfax took her to nightclubs and places but he was always leaving her on her own while he chatted with some men. Once or twice she asked about his business, but he was hard on women knowing anything.

One night at a club in Baltimore, she was on her own when Pete Lunn came over to ask her to dance. He had a hold like a bear, and she thought he was grand. They got close, but then Colfax turned nasty. Kitty liked having the two men growling at each other over her, and she led them both on. It was a change from getting up late and trying on all the expensive clothes Colfax bought for her. But boredom made her reckless. Without any need but sport, Kitty had taken to stealing again. She took some jewelry one night in a Philly hotel, and she was wearing a fancy brooch in a restaurant when a cop arrested her. But Lunn was there, and he knew the cop. With a radiant grin on his face he said *he* had stolen the stuff, and given the one piece to Kitty out of sentiment. So Lunn went to prison instead, and Kitty thought he was the sweetest dope she'd ever met.

Lunn was away two years, and Kitty sent him a few postcards in jail with harmless messages. Colfax never knew about it, and so when Lunn got out of prison in 1940 he was taken back into the gang as someone who was owed a turn. But by the time they did the Prentiss Hat job in July, the three of them were all suspicious of one another. Maybe Kitty never knew which side she was on: it was a lot for a nineteen-year-old, in love with Lunn perhaps, but softened by

Colfax's money, and still a liar. So she went off with Lunn and the money, and then back to Colfax. It had one result: everyone else on the job was cut out. Colfax and Kitty kept all the money—$200,000 to split, said Kitty with a grin.

It was 'forty-six when Lunn was found and shot. But that was the end for Colfax, for an insurance man named Reardon got interested in the case and he worked it all out and stirred up the members of the old gang so they came down on Colfax and shot him. There's always someone whose sole purpose in life seems to be to work everything out—geniuses with no lives of their own to live.

Kitty learned from it all. She decided the gangster life was exaggerated. She called herself Grace Devlin and dyed her hair blonde. So she went to Atlantic City—where she and Lunn had gone on the lam—because she had liked the air and the slow roll of the gray sea. In the summer of 1947 she came in second in a Betty Grable look-alike contest, and she met a handsome man who was bodyguard to all the girls, Lou Guarini, a swell talker. They had a fling and Kitty got a job as a receptionist in one of the hotels. She met Tim Reid, the house dick, and they were married in 1949. They lived in a set of rooms at the hotel until 1963, when Tim died. Grace enjoyed the hotel business, and she got to be an undermanager, friendly with all the people, making sure that Tim was one-up on the dips and grifters.

In 1965, she moved into a place of her own and went back to seeing Lou. Her health was going, or so she said, so Lou would go out for her medicine and her sherry. He moved in with her and they're there still, a well-known couple, devoted and bickering. Grace let her hair go back bit by bit, until she found it was quite white. She never looked better, and she'd had some money put aside, so they manage and feel superior to the way things aren't what they were.

AMY JOLLY

Marlene Dietrich in Morocco, *1930,
directed by Josef von Sternberg*

The child christened Elise Rissient was born in Courbevoie, a suburb on the northwestern side of Paris, in 1905. Her father was a projectionist of moving pictures. As this man extended his influence—to the ownership of theaters, the publishing of film magazines, and at last the production of movies—the family became more prosperous, acquiring a summer house in Rozven, in Brittany. It was there, in the summer of 1922, when Elise was seventeen, that her intense love affair with a young man, Francis de Pene, was observed fondly but inquisitively by a neighbor, Colette, who took it as the inspiration for *Le Blé en herbe*.

Yet Colette was not just a voyeuse, feeding off the girl and the rapid flow of her enthusiasm and wretchedness. The novelist became her character's friend, taking her on picnics, showing her the wild flowers on the cliffs, describing the trial of Landru to her, and teaching her Burgundian cooking. The two women spent a summer in love and fragrance, celandines and garlic, exchanging confidences as if there were no difference in their ages. "Ma belle," Colette exclaimed one August evening, "quand t'es aimé, si jolie." The cascade of open vowels, in Colette's rough voice, was like the first drops of rain before a thunderstorm—Elise Rissient never forgot the sentence, and so it presaged her own next name.

It was Colette who encouraged her singing, and gave her lessons in how modesty could command a stage as surely as nakedness. In 1924, at nineteen, Elise left Courbevoie and took a room on the rue Jacob which Colette helped her find. She worked hard at her singing lessons and began to build an audience in the small left bank cabarets. She sang sweet songs, full of sentiment in a simple, child's way. Yet her modesty sometimes seemed to crack—like the shell of an egg as a fledgling stirs—and the glimpses of a darker wisdom were intriguing to men in the audience. Elise had several short affairs in 1925 and 1926, and in that time she grew into a mysteriously detached young woman, a little teasing toward men and love. In a way she never understood, but which was related to her spreading fame as the model for *Le Blé en herbe*, Elise was called a temptress and a femme fatale. This reputation, however she resisted it, did harden her a little. As a singer, she offered a sexual mischief resting within the fripperies of romantic convention, like a sword wreathed in tissue paper. She won a following whose cheers grew louder and more urgent as Elise declined to notice or be warmed by them.

This quality of perversity drew invitations from Berlin in 1927. Learning enough German for some songs, Elise went there. Whether stunned or indifferent, she responded to the greater salaciousness of German cabarets with a coolness that was all the more inflaming. She seemed untouchable, so corrupt she could resist every man's desire;

there was a clamor to lay hands on her. If she gave herself to no one man in particular, all of them felt her denial. In 1929, a distinguished official in the Ministry of Education named Janrath shot himself beneath a large photograph of Elise on which he had stuck feathers giving an extra sensual texture to her filmy skirt.

There was an ugly noise in the Berlin papers: Elise's foreignness was held to blame; she was called "a depraved nymph" and so on. Pictures of the Janrath wife and children—rather like a soccer team, so many and so glum—were printed in silent accusation, next to Elise's knife of a smile. She did not bother to defend herself. She went by train to Santander, and took a boat for Morocco. During that voyage, she changed her name to Amy Jolly, and elected to be as sinister as the world wanted to believe.

She had come to the land of the Foreign Legion with the same need as many of its soldiers—a new name, a chance to escape, and hardship of service to stand as a rebuke for the guilt she was too proud to acknowledge. The self-respect of the silent and ungiving made a pact between her and the legionnaires. For the first time in her life she was acclaimed but not pursued. The soldiers regarded her as a true myth, someone who would fade into ordinariness if one of them actually had her in love. She guessed this reasoning, and smiled through the loneliness it entailed.

But one soldier struck her. Tom Brown, an American apparently, was a laconic, long-limbed man, secretive yet mocking his own discretion. She felt weak whenever she saw him, grinning back at his grin, and wondering if she would faint. Her desire made her feel she would die without him. There was a dispassionate curiosity in her aware how mad she was for him. She was sensible, of course, at all times, never a hair out of place. But what fuller proof was there of madness when she was really wild with longing?

Brown may have thought of killing this woman: his bleak calm was so close to being ruined by her. He loved her, too, no matter that he had given up on that notion, and its concession to women. But he was not as resolute or hard as he wanted. Feeling would creep in: we cannot look at things, and see them, without giving vulnerability and surprise a chance. So he had to defend himself against her impact. He had an elaborate, insolent salute for her, a deprecating wave of the hand to indicate playfulness. Yet her straight glance cut through the ornate gesture so that he felt pierced.

He gave in to love. He said he would go with her, be with her. Then, out of some horror of the weakness it meant, he picked up a stick of her greasepaint and wrote on her mirror, "I changed my mind. Good luck"—with a slash and a scroll beneath the message, reasserting his salute. She read it, and when the day came for Brown's regiment to march south into the desert, she followed him through the ace-of-spades archway in the wall, kicking off her high-heeled shoes, pleased by the heat of the sand. It was 1930.

Amy Jolly grew dark from the sun. Tom Brown watched her become a Legion whore, taken by other men. He never protested or touched her himself, and he no longer saluted her. She believed their love could only be expressed by frustration; they never dulled in each other's eyes. Amy looked like an Arab, but the nomadic life did not spoil her. She was loved, and nothing else does so much for appearance.

A kind of mysticism settled on her, mixed with hashish and superstition learned from the other camp women. They had seemed impossible companions once, but Amy knew them now, especially Tanya, a Bedouin who taught her fortune-telling. Tanya told her she had innate feeling for the art—she only gave her timing and confidence, just as Colette had shown her how to hold a stage.

They traveled together in Africa and came to Cairo, where they opened a club in 1936. It was a haunt of Allied officers during the war. When Tanya died, Amy took her name and became sole owner of the club. She dyed her hair black, wore kohl and smoked cheroots. She kept girls for the soldiers, but no longer sold herself. In 1946, she took a boat to Mexico, anticipating disturbances in Egypt.

By 1950 she had reached Robles, where she opened her newest premises. It was a small place, but discerning customers sought her out. She served drink and chili, and she slowly acquired a few very young, outrageous girls. Tanya ran the club with a disdain that had become her public persona. She liked another American, a sheriff named Quinlan from over the border. He was a heartfelt detective, who could often tell her her own thoughts. Yet he was not afraid of asking Tanya's occult advice. They were lovers for a time, wearied by their own appetite. They watched their orgies with far-off, amused sympathy. She knew he was a dead man in whom talent was turning sour and fat. He gave her up and then a few years later came back on a case that was already ruining him. Tanya watched him die, like a weighted balloon, in the trash of the border. It didn't surprise her; she guessed Quinlan had chosen her as the person to utter his epitaph.

She closed her place and drank herself to death in a year. It was not hard for someone who still had the inner delicacy of the young Elise.

The most raddled whore can have the self-esteem of a child collecting wild flowers in Brittany, noticed by an author and set down in a freshness that never ages.

I am old, but I can still see myself as a loner not tired by the road and its endless motels. To this day, I would rather think of something out of reach than be emperor of what I know.

NORMA DESMOND

Gloria Swanson in Sunset Boulevard, *1950, directed by Billy Wilder*

You can look at movie magazines from the early 1920s, amazed at the faces of beautiful young actresses, stars then, but so little known now that their euphonious names sound concocted—Barbara La Marr, Lupe Velez, Agnes Ayres, Alexandra Laguna, Leatrice Joy, Norma Desmond, and so on. All brunettes, with black lips, curls stuck on their brows and eyes like bulletholes: they seem to cherish the pain of sexual exploitation by men. There is implacability in the faces, like a ship's figurehead battling into the elements. It comes from signaling feelings; those silent women are stranded in the impossibility of utterance. A few years later, after sound, women's faces softened. The loveliness grew quiet and intriguing. Words were put out, like bait on the threshold of their being. They smiled, where silent faces had had trumpeting frowns.

It must have been maddening. Not many of them lasted more than a few years; the business was exhausting, and that kind of beauty is our endless American resource. It was only will that made any of them famous, or put forbidding strength in their faces. Somehow, they all seemed overdone; no matter how hard they tried, they must have known the shame of feeling coarse or clumsy. You can imagine them killing even, at the end of their tether, laughing if the gun went off and there was only a small puff of light to show explosion. But the man aimed at was staggering, stupefied, his hands clutched to the hole where life was leaking out. The ladies could make you believe.

So many of their names were false. Norma Desmond was born May Svensson in Milwaukee in 1899. She was the daughter of Swedish immigrants, the youngest of five children. Years later, some version of Miss Desmond told *Photoplay*: "I had picked a good time and place to be born. The automobile was not much older than I was, so there weren't many of them. Trolleys and wagons were pulled by horses, and none of them went too fast. It was a safe, clean time. When you were thirsty in the summer, your mother made a pitcher of lemonade. And everyone did the family wash on Monday and hung it out in the fresh air to dry."

Charming, don't you think? But actresses are in love with such crystal-clear happiness. May Svensson's early life was not a pitcher of homemade lemonade or the bouquet of fresh laundry. Instead, she was taken by her father on his tours of Wisconsin and Minnesota, selling Bibles and being driven by penury into increasingly reckless confidence tricks in which the daughter was often the decoy. They lived in cheap hotels, or on the run: there were a few nights in town jails, the child in a cot next to the sheriff's desk waiting for her father to be released.

And so it was, in 1911, that May saw her father shot down by a man named Gregson, the victim of a small enough fraud, a God-fearing but choleric man who had pursued Svensson for seven months. May was holding her father's hand, and talking to him, coming out of a diner in Kenosha, when a pistol blast met them. She felt the pressure in the air and was dragged sideways by her father's fall, his dead grip on her growing tighter.

She had her picture in the Chicago papers, wide-eyed, floridly becurled and stricken. A manager at the Essanay studios noticed it, and his flabby head was so touched by her plight that he saw a way of making money. He found her and devised a series of one-reelers about a waif, "Sweedie" she was called, an orphan and an outcast who got into sentimental scrapes and comic adventures. The films were poorly made, but the child bloomed in them. The camera breathed in time with the rising beat of puberty; in a year of those short movies she became an object of furtive lust, her picture pinned in lockers. The movies learned early how to fashion an arousing innocence that inspires its own spoiling.

"Norma Desmond," as Essanay had called her, was married at fifteen to Wallace Beery, twice her age and the robust exponent of his own ugliness. It was like a virgin princess being taken by a barbarian. The public was thrilled with alarm. In reality, Norma scolded him incessantly, until he left her with the beach house, all but one of their cars and the vases filled with his cash. This was 1917.

She had an extraordinary career in silent pictures, earning as much as $15,000 a week, to say nothing of bonuses. She worked for Marshall Neilan, Cecil B. De Mille, Harry D'Abbadie D'Arrast and Allan Dwan. Her burning gaze played on audiences like the light of the screen. The industry romanticized her and her "enchanted" life. Perhaps she believed those stories herself—her image was over-powering. She had gone so swiftly from the sordid to the luxurious, from being abused to being worshipped. She was a Cinderella who became a tyrant queen, without time to clean the coal dust from her fingernails. An aura of transformation surrounded her. There was a famous portrait of her face staring through an embroidered veil, a celebration of beauty as a fatal delusion. She met the tycoon Noah Cross and he mounted a play with her as Salome, discarding hundreds of veils, while he sat on a stool in the wings to see her body emerge through the misty gauze.

Perhaps her conviction was too intense for the naturalism of sound pictures? Or were her demands for money more than the industry could endure? *Princess of the Micks*, her film for Max von Mayerling, her husband, was a disaster in which she sank one million dollars of her own money. And so she went to France, marrying a marquis whose name she never learned to spell. She made a film there, *Une Jeune Fille de campagne*, about Charlotte Corday, in which the character will not speak—to protect her excessive expressiveness or the actress's lack of French.

While in Europe, she married the German Baron von Rauffenstein. Mayerling had never really been given up during these other mar-riages. He simply went from being husband to personal manager; it meant he dressed earlier in the day. There was consternation in the press, but the three figures handled the "ménage" without dismay. Moreover, in 1931–32, Norma Desmond had an affair with Serge Alexandre, also known as Stavisky. To this day there is a rumor in France that she had a child by the swindler, a daughter, who was passed on to a simple farming couple on the estate of Baron Raoul, a friend of Alexandre's. (An unexpectedly striking face in an out-of-the-way place will often inspire such fancies. But suppose real foundlings are not especially pretty, what then?)

In 1934, she returned to the mansion on Sunset Boulevard (bought for her by Noah Cross), where she would remain until her removal, at the hands of the police, in 1950. Mayerling came back to America in

1939 and became her butler. Norma Desmond slipped from glory to oblivion, unaware in her retreat of any change in her power or her looks. She was so removed from public contact now, she may have thought herself divine.

She had only a monkey as an intimate until Joe Gillis strayed into her life. He seemed to offer the means of a comeback, but he was also a lover and a slave. When he thought to leave her, she shot him, in the belly, as yet unaware that her own body nurtured his child. In the asylum hospital, she never deigned to notice her swelling or the birth of the boy. She was officially insane, lecturing the other inmates and shooting them with imaginary guns when they ignored her. She died in 1959, still firing.

JULIAN KAY

Richard Gere in American Gigolo, *1980,
directed by Paul Schrader*

Critics of our educational system would appreciate Julian Kay, if they could stomach the squalid aspects of his success. They say schools are organized stagnation, where inept teachers confront the brutal young with dread and contempt. They say teaching is brainwashing; only learning counts, and in most of our schools those charged with education are indifferent to whether that occurs. And so, the claim goes, a growing body of young waste forms, overcast and unaware, with no role in society except to infect the educated with their resentment.

I don't know the answer. Some say all children should stay at home and learn from their parents. But isn't that a way of ensuring narrowness and the excess of shelter that leaves us tender? What would happen to business if parents were at home, practising cottage instruction? Yet I wonder, if I had had the time, whether I couldn't have kept my children in what I believed. They might have understood me, and Mary Frances, and that might have helped them in the world. As it was, they went out there and they suffered for it. People talk of change, and faster change too, as if to say parents must be resigned to a kind of knowledge redundant to their children. But I read to them, and all their later pain seemed to have the atmosphere of stories.

Julian Kay is a model of self-education, and survival. In all the gallery presented here, I doubt if another person has overcome such handicaps, or made so much of himself. Out of a tangle of grossness, he has grown smooth, acceptable and negotiable. There is already some talk of a political future for him. After all, he is rich, good-looking, well-spoken, and he has come from the world of the misbegotten. He has great appeal to a voter seeking miracles.

He was born in 1951, in an asylum hospital, taken with forceps from the small, irate body of his mother, Norma Desmond, the onetime movie actress. The father was Joe Gillis, a screenwriter who had become Miss Desmond's companion and paramour and then her victim. Even so, the birth certificate says "not known" in the matter of a father. And since the mother was a certified incompetent, Max von Mayerling, one of Miss Desmond's former husbands, was listed as guardian to the infant.

Julian never spoke to or was spoken to by his parents. Max von Mayerling told him that he was an orphan. Norma Desmond was dead by 1959; Max died in 1964, when Julian was thirteen. But Max left a letter of explanation with a lawyer in Santa Monica, to be given to Julian on his twenty-first birthday. That letter was sent to the last known address of Julian Kay; sent and not returned. Only Julian knows whether he saw and understood it, and his face is still lovely and unlined in its public appearances.

Mayerling took a small apartment in Inglewood, and lived there with the child he called Julian Kay. Long before Max's death, Julian had fallen into a pattern of truancy. Whenever Max had an engagement as a magician at a children's party, he would enlist Julian as his assistant. It was Julian he vanished from closed trunks and Julian he sometimes sawed in sections, only for the little boy, in mauve tights, to reappear as whole and bouncy as a rubber ball.

On other days, Julian was inclined to set out for school, then take some wrong turning and head north to explore Los Angeles. At ten and eleven, having purposefully grubbied himself beforehand, he collected quarters whistling up taxis for people outside big hotels. His special charm in this was his line of chatter to the ladies as they waited for the cab. Without ever being dirty, he was a sophisticated urchin, passing on the ornate words and saturnine wisdom he had picked up from Max. One or two of the ladies gave him presents or called him honey. One, on her own, asked him to ride out to Pasadena with her, and on the way she manipulated him and collected his first pearly semen in an Yves St. Laurent scarf. Julian had to walk back from Pasadena, fulfilled, striding on love's air.

Max von Mayerling had a collection of erotica, which he never hid from the boy. The old man would tell Julian stories at night about his own sexual adventures in Vienna, Budapest, Monte Carlo, and so on. He taught Julian French and German; he told him how to play servant or master; he gave him jokes, gestures, tricks and touches. He made an adroit gentleman out of him.

When Max died, Julian arranged the funeral and went on with his life as usual. There were no relatives to rescue him; no inspectors to make sure he was still cared for. He went to school no more often than before. He kept the apartment up, selling some of the more ponderous furniture Max had collected. As for money, he set out to offer himself and a taxi to single ladies. He was a strong youth, and he got a reputation. Women went in search of him.

One day in 1969, he was picked up by Anne Alexander, a resident of Malibu and the impresario for a ring of call girls. She had heard of this taxi stud, and she was impressed by his agility and courtliness in the confines of the cab. She took him home and questioned him about his life. Nearly twenty years his senior, she was more attracted to him than she could understand. Born in France, she was surprised by his fluent French, albeit in a slightly dated idiom that marked Max's days in Paris. Anne told him he was wasting his talent. Taxi trade was bound to be quick and cheap. Once she slept with him in the greater ease of a bed, she added that a cab could not let his range and diversity show. She proposed to manage his career. She would advertise him discreetly, and then send him out on assignments. She would take 20 percent of his earnings, and she would provide a new wardrobe for him. For the next three years they were lovers. On those rare nights when Julian needed anything like a home, he stayed with her in Malibu.

But in 1973, they ended their personal ties and settled for business. Julian had enough money to buy an apartment in Westwood. He branched out, and worked for other agents. His reputation as a hired lover increased. He took on a few missions in New York, and one in Rome. But he preferred L.A. He knew its attitudes and the spiritual bliss in skin and pleasure; and he had the California patter by heart.

Then in 1979, he drove out to the Palm Springs home of a couple named Rheiman. He relaxed the tense wife, and brought her to seven

climaxes as her husband watched from behind an ivory-hued net curtain. But Judy Rheiman was found butchered, sexually abused, and Rheiman himself had an impregnable alibi. Just as Julian met Michelle Stratton, lovelorn wife of the California senator, just as he thought of marriage and happiness, he found himself under suspicion of murder.

The stress finished the Stratton marriage: Michelle could only save Julian by giving him an alibi—that they had been together. The scandal raged, but Julian acted like its press spokesman. He never hid or scurried; he let the cameras see his face. He gave short, lucid statements to reporters and he thanked them. By the time he was cleared, he was famous.

He and Michelle married. They live in Laurel Canyon and they run the Kincaid Gallery on Doheny—one of the most reputable purveyors of art objects for the home. They own a restaurant and a small art-movie house, the Dissolve on La Cienega, where they specialize in foreign films and do a Bresson festival every winter. They are a favorite couple around the town, and there is every prospect of their interests and power rising.

Is there no sure way of raising our young? Is parenting the tragedy that tears us from our hopes? "I am your father," you nag, talking to yourself.

WALTER NEFF

Fred MacMurray in Double Indemnity, 1944,
directed by Billy Wilder

He was an easygoing kid, liked by most people, a boy strangers were ready to give a nickel to if he had any small talk. Walter Huff had all kinds of talk, and everyone agreed he would go far. "Out of Moline, anyway," said Walter one day when he was eleven. He spent a lot of his time watching the river's inexhaustible flow southward, imagining the places it led to. He put any bit of wood or paper on the water just to see it being carried away from Moline. He thought of the

Mississippi as a glossy, gray road on which he might glide into his future.

He had been born in Moline in 1901, his father a doctor, his mother a music teacher. She taught him piano, and he took to the banjo and the cornet of his own accord. When he was in his teens he used to go over the river to Davenport where he knew a younger kid, Leon Beiderbecke. They both played cornet, and Leon was the better of the two. But Walter didn't mind that. He learned from the kid, and he got into the habit of slurring notes together. It was lazy but it made the girls look up. Leon called him "Skid" because of it, and the name stuck.

In 1919, he got a job on a riverboat, and after a year he made it all the way to New Orleans. That had been his dream. He listened to all the jazz he could find, and he bummed around when he was out of work. Then, in 1922, he got a job on a liner going around the Caribbean, to Panama, and on to San Francisco. He was a year playing dance music on the boat when he dropped off in Panama for a vacation. Music began to bore him on the boat, and so on a whim in Panama he joined the Army and did a three-year hitch there as a sentry on the Canal.

The very day he got out of the service he met a blonde, Maggie King, a hairdresser on a liner. He showed her around and they got talking so that she missed her boat and moved in with Skid and a pal of his, a piano player named Harry Butterworth. They were soft on each other, and Maggie told Skid he should work as a musician again. She said she was a singer and that encouraged him. And she had a fair voice, soft and clear, but sultry. Together they got work at Murphy's, the best club in Panama, and they did a number together that was a sensation, she standing inside the curl of his arm, singing to his muted accompaniment.

They got married, and most of 1928 was as good as it gets. But Skid caught fire with happiness: agents from New York came down to check on him, and other women kept after him. There was a dancer at Murphy's, Anita Alvarez, who was hot for him, and first she took a New York offer and then six weeks later Skid got the call. It was what Maggie wanted for him, and they agreed that he could save money until they had enough for her passage.

It was a reasonable plan, but there are marriages that may need the remoteness of a Panama. Skid was a hit in the city. Everyone wanted to buy him a drink, and Anita slid into the empty place in his arm. Maggie came to New York on her own money, and she found that

Alvarez answered Skid's phone. They broke up. Once they got back together for a radio show, when Skid's lip was going—he had given up practicing. They did their old number that once, and it was a heartbreaker, but Skid kept slipping. By 1932 he was on the street, selling pretzels.

Then, instead of folding up, Walter Huff realized that he was back where he started—no worse than that. His ease returned. He hitched west, and as he went he read a book about insurance. It seemed like a snap, and he knew he was good with people. So he went all the way to California, to Los Angeles, and the General Fidelity offices with Keyes, head of the claims department.

"You look used up," said Keyes.

"Yeah, but I'm resilient," Walter told him.

"What's your name?"

"Huff. Walter Huff."

"Huff? That's no kind of a name."

"No one told me."

"Makes people think you're in a bad mood."

"But I come as a pleasant surprise."

"Have to change it."

"Do I get the job?"

"Who do you want to be?"

"I kinda like the two *f*'s."

"I can see you might. Griffith?"

"That's a park. Cuff?"

"Could be ragged. Neff?"

"You got it."

"No, you've got it."

Keyes could tell he could talk, and he liked his quick grin—it was amiable, but it knew insurance was a play on weak nerves. Walter Neff was hired, and he worked hard to please Keyes. The two men never had a conversation when they weren't telling each other off, but they took it for granted they were friends and the point didn't need to be stated directly. Walter got in the habit of having vestas for Keyes's pipe whenever he seemed to have mislaid his. Walter rented a little bungalow in the Los Feliz hills.

It was February 1935 when he drove over to the Spanish-style house in Hollywoodland about a renewal and met Phyllis Diedrichson. She was wearing blue pajamas, and she kept him talking. She asked if Walter handled accident insurance, too—her husband was at the office—and that's when Walter started to get the chills from her sidelong look. That was the start. Walter was always impressionable, and Phyllis Diedrichson got to him in ten minutes.

They fell into this torrid affair. Walter set up life insurance for the husband, with a double indemnity—twice the coverage if the death was by accident—and Phyllis knew already how it was going to be accidental. The husband signed it one night with a mass of papers. And they killed him; Walter was in the back of the car and he broke the guy's neck. Walter, a gentle man, agreeable too: that was the measure of Phyllis Diedrichson and what she could make you imagine.

Walter got on the train to San Francisco, pretending to be Diedrichson. Then he jumped off the train, and together they put the body on the tracks, as if the man had had a drink or two and fallen off the observation platform. It worked out fine, and General Fidelity was set to pay up. But Keyes knew it smelled wrong. He asked Walter what he thought, and Walter had to give back his ordinary professional skepticism. "Could be," he said.

Keyes worked it out. But Walter was shuffling snakes by then: that was Phyllis for you. He got scared of her, and he fell for Lola, Diedrichson's daughter. Then there was Lola's Italian boyfriend. Then there was the rendezvous in Griffith Park, and Walter picking up a bullet. He'd meant to get rid of Phyllis, but he'd never thought that you could spell Phyllis with two *f*'s.

Walter spilled the whole story to Keyes. He assumed that he and Phyllis were set for the death house. But General Fidelity was cautious. They didn't like the idea of double indemnities getting so much publicity, so they let the two killers go. But they got them tickets on the same boat, going to Mexico. And Walter and Phyllis met on the deck, and it wasn't so romantic. For the first time in his life, Walter felt ruin. Phyllis was full of death, the same as always. They heard there was a shark following the boat and they waited till they saw its fin in the moonlight and they went over the side. With Walter's unhealed wound bleeding. Begging the shark to hurry.

PHYLLIS DIEDRICHSON

Barbara Stanwyck in Double Indemnity, *1944,*
directed by Billy Wilder

I cannot better the last paragraph of Diane Johnson's fascinating *Phyllis* (Knopf, 1983), an investigation carried out nearly fifty years after the event, in which the author was regularly waylaid by intimations of hitherto unheard-of iniquity. The paragraph in question concludes a postscript in which Ms. Johnson reports the discovery that a Phyllis Nirdlinger was registered at the St. Francis Hotel, in San Francisco, over the Labor Day weekend of 1921—the time and place of the prolonged party which brought about the death of Virginia Rappe, and the downfall of silent clown Fatty Arbuckle. This knowledge came in an anonymous letter delivered while Ms. Johnson was correcting the proofs of *Phyllis*, but when there was still time to give her book a last, prescient shadow:

"So we are supposed to believe that Phyllis slipped over the side of a steamer bound from San Pedro to Balboa—this ship was called the *Miranda*—fifty miles or so off Quinones. It would be comfortable to think so. But isn't it more likely that that was the legend Phyllis wished to establish before she started up as someone else? She was a thirty-two-year-old mass murderess, in her prime. What reason is there to take her sudden remorse and its impetuous suicide on trust? Isn't it more credible that she let Walter Neff go first and then turned away to a new alias and a fresh man already scouted out? She would be eighty now, a little deaf, perhaps forgetful, but hardly less than dangerous. Even allow that she took to the water, had she forgotten how to swim? The suggestion is that a shark claimed her and the already wounded Walter. I prefer to pity the fish."

The woman who officially met this watery death was Mrs. Phyllis Diedrichson, widow and co-slayer of her husband, H. S. Diedrichson. She was on the *Miranda* with Walter Neff, after they had both been trapped in an investigation spearheaded by Wilson Keyes of General Fidelity's Los Angeles office.

His report described how, in 1929, Phyllis Nirdlinger was hired as assistant head nurse at Dr. Bruno Sachetti's Verdugo Hills Sanatorium. Her credentials were borne out by scrupulous attention to duties. No wonder, then, in 1930, when the head nurse died in an automobile accident—a vacation mishap, in Salt Lake City, so for once Phyllis cannot be implicated—that she was promoted.

However, in the years 1930 to 1932 there were five deaths at the sanatorium in which Phyllis did appear to have had a part. All five involved elderly victims of pneumonia. Re-investigation traced the hand of the head nurse in every case, and disclosed the modest but touching legacies that went to her from two of the deceased. Of course, people die in clinics and hospitals, and head nurses have the authority of good first officers on ships with captains looking forward to retirement. Too many patients in sanatoriums have no relatives to ask awkward questions or act as likely heirs.

Dr. Sachetti was neither lazy nor inept. He had an excellent reputation, but it was shattered in 1933 when three children died of pneumonia in one week. In hindsight, we must conclude grimly that two of those deaths—Georgie Trescher and Cara Chacon—were extras to aid the impression of an epidemic, and to crowd the death of Dickie Graff, only four, whose one living relative was a Mrs. Lita Diedrichson. It speaks to the cunning of Phyllis that this Mrs. Diedrichson was so won over by the head nurse at Verdugo Hills that the two struck up a friendship.

The sanatorium had to close: child mortality knows no public relations. Phyllis Nirdlinger looked around for a new position and spent time with Lita and H. S. Diedrichson. The strain had been too much. The two ladies became so close that they went off to Lake Arrowhead in December 1933 for a vacation to plan the coming Christmas break. It was an early and severe winter at Lake Arrowhead. Lita, already suffering from lung trouble, caught cold in the high chilled air. Phyllis Nirdlinger went for help, but she took the long way, trudging twelve miles through snow around the lake. Locals wondered why she had not gone the mile and a half on the ice over the lake. It was strong enough to support a truck. But Phyllis said she had not known the ice was thick enough; she had meant to be safe rather than sorry. Yet she had to be both: Lita Diedrichson was found dead by the rescue party.

Christmas was a mourning feast, and Phyllis was the natural comforter for H.S. when he collapsed. Used to being looked after and having a comfortable home, Diedrichson proposed to Phyllis in April 1934. The former head nurse accepted, less for herself, she said, than for Lola, Lita's daughter, so much in need of a mother figure. And so Phyllis Nirdlinger changed her name and moved into the house clinging to the steep hillside beneath the Hollywoodland sign. She may not have been sure what she was waiting for, but Walter Neff decided her.

Because there was no trial, no one bothered about the facts of Phyllis Nirdlinger's life before 1929. Not until Diane Johnson undertook her research. She established that Phyllis Nirdlinger was born in Anaheim in 1903, the child of a German manufacturer of ice skates and an American, Anne Belden, who had been a high-school swimming champion. Kurt Nirdlinger died when Phyllis was eleven—of a fit of coughing brought on when a cod bone caught in his throat. Nothing Phyllis had done in the way of offering him bread to chew had averted the tragedy. The mother was away that day, swimming across San Pedro Bay to raise money for the Belgian atrocity victims.

Phyllis herself was such a swimmer that she became a member of the Mack Sennett Bathing Beauties. It was there she befriended Norma Desmond and Mabel Normand. Dry, too, in one or two one-reelers, Phyllis took on the roles of confidante and cocaine supplier to Miss Desmond. The details are still clouded, but the persevering Diane Johnson has made it clear that the long-held belief in Mabel Normand's part in the death of director William Desmond Taylor in 1922 might be opened up to include Phyllis Nirdlinger. Phyllis was a demure drug connection for the film community, an active agent in the decline of Taylor, and the last person known to have been with him at 404½ Alvarado Street, where he was found shot to death.

The case was confused. At Taylor's funeral, another movie queen, Mary Miles Minter, declared undying love for him. And Ms. Minter is alive still, a recluse, eighty-one or so as I write.

> *I can understand the wish to solve these old mysteries. Over the years, I have lain awake, a supine detective, sorting through the details. It is so like the approach of a killer planning a crime. But then Mary Miles died yesterday, fat and afraid, I hear, to leave her house. Now there is only the picture of her youth left, as white and frilled as a flower, and forever transient.*

WILSON KEYES

Edward G. Robinson in Double Indemnity, *1944,*
directed by Billy Wilder

In 1981 in Omaha there was a retrospective of the paintings of Wilson Keyes. It brought satisfaction to those who remembered him. The catalogue with the exhibit spoke of "this unhindered naive, a primitive from the American heartland who had a career of order and prosperity, except for one disaster and the passion evident in these pictures."

Odd to think of WK as a naive: he was our model of common sense and the deductive process. Harder still to call him primitive: none of us ever saw a discourteous act, or heard a reckless expression. In Omaha, he was regarded as sophisticated, as clever as anyone we had. But I suppose that's what the writer meant. There was something he could never let us see, nothing ugly, but an eye for danger. It's there in the portraits of women, wild smiles resting on folded, blatant legs; California houses with fire-colored roofs and snake-green cypress trees; and the drawings done at Belsen. It's there in the colors, blues that never dry, bloody skies and screaming yellows; and in the signature on all the canvases, the *X*, a flourish like crossed swords.

Keyes was born in Omaha, Nebraska, in 1890, one of five children, the son of the city's civil engineer. Young Wilson excelled in math and science at school, and from the age of ten he was helping his father in the execution of technical drawings. Indeed, Arthur Keyes's classic *The Building of Bridges* (University of Nebraska Press, 1905) contains a note of thanks to "my son, Wilson . . . for his splendid illustrations." In 1908, Wilson Keyes entered the university to study mathematics. He also involved himself in student dramatics, executing backdrops for *The Way of the World* (a production banned by the authorities after its bawdy opening—and still a legend twenty years later).

He graduated in 1912 and was sent to Stanford by his proud father to study business. With what seemed to everyone an equable temperament, Wilson Keyes adapted to his first experiences of California and maintained his high academic standards—but for the spring of 1913, when he suffered a breakdown of indeterminate nature. However, his recovery was as thorough and convincing as all of his performances, and no one had reason to worry about him. "All the worry goes inside with Nebraskans," as my father used to say. "Goes inside and builds, like a twister with no way out." I have seen Mary Frances, standing straight and thin against the sky, just leaning perhaps, and known she was curled and tortured, unable to cry out.

Keyes took his Master's at Stanford in the summer of 1915, by which time he had had several offers from San Francisco businesses. Instead, he took a trip to Paris. It was true to his sensible nature to admit the need for some relaxation, and a part of his conscientiousness to want to visit a city whose treasures were threatened by war. During the fall of 1915, Keyes explored the museums and galleries of the city, while renting a small room in Montmartre close to the Moulin de la Galette. He saw wonders and wounded soldiers, but Bonnard was his greatest discovery.

Not long after he returned to America, Keyes enlisted in the army, and in May 1916 he was commissioned as a lieutenant. Fourteen months later Keyes was in France, a captain. For five months he was in the front lines, playing a prominent part in the design and construction of trenches. The American claim to have drainage superior to that of the French or the British owed much to the resourcefulness of Wilson Keyes. Lives must have been saved in that more hospitable dryness. Elsewhere, some drowned in mud. They are still digging up skulls and bullets.

From 1919 to 1923, Keyes was restored to Nebraska, and to the university, where he taught Introduction to Business, Insurance and Actuarial Theory. He made some of those courses into institutions. Though his time at Lincoln was short, his influence there both as teacher and as friend to those not much younger was considerable. He was loved there, and it was hurtful when he moved away, to Los Angeles, to take up a position in the General Fidelity Insurance Company. People couldn't understand how he was not satisfied by teaching.

He served General Fidelity until 1940, becoming head of the claims department, famous for his instinct in detecting frauds. The Diedrichson case may have been his most secret success, for General Fidelity chose not to take legal action. It may also have been a crisis in Keyes's own life.

He was forty-five, he had been married ten years, he had a home in Glendale and two children. All seemed settled and normal. His co-workers assumed he was content. But Keyes worked hard. He had too little time for his family or his hobby of painting. Moreover, the realization that his trust in Walter Neff had been misplaced was a greater blow than Keyes ever indicated. Perhaps the last angry words of Phyllis Diedrichson lodged in his excellent memory and turned bad there:

"So what's in it for you, Mr. Keyes? You're not an empty man. You're not a machine. You go pale when I attack you. Your damned pipe goes out, and your mouth clamps down on it. So you caught our trick. You saved General Fidelity money. Does that satisfy you? Or tell me, Wilson Keyes, do you sometimes wonder what it's like to step out of line, to give up the rules for someone like me? Don't you wonder, Keyes, you liar? Know how you're a liar? Because you've such a busy little imagination locked in your briefcase. And someday it'll have to come out. Or kill you."

In 1940, Keyes was fifty. He had served his country well. Yet he heeded the invitation from Washington to serve again. Going east ended his marriage, but Wilson Keyes accepted a post in the secret service. He had an aptitude for decoding and his old skill as a detective. By 1944, he was attached to that section of the service tracing war criminals. He was in Europe late that year, and present at the liberation of Belsen in 1945. Keyes did not return to America until 1947, so extensive was his work for the Nuremberg trials.

It was no easy retirement. He came back a roundabout way, chasing Franz Kindler, one of the more brilliant of Hitler's young disciples. Under the name Charles Rankin, Kindler had begun a new life at Harper College in Connecticut where he was masquerading as a teacher and had married the daughter of Judge Philip Longstreet. Keyes was dogged in unearthing Rankin's true identity and in saving his new wife, Mary. Rankin/Kindler died, falling from the tower of the town church, and Keyes's mission was concluded.

Nearing sixty now, divorced in 1945, Keyes found that General Fidelity had no more use for him. A new generation had risen to power. And so he went to New York with a small government pension. He found work as a cashier, and he was picked up by a widow. Remarried, humiliated in his job, he resumed painting: his smothered life spilled out on the canvases.

Then, in 1950, he fell in with a floozy, Kitty Bennett, the kind of woman the insurance investigator had once recognized in an instant. He embezzled for her, he gave up everything for a night or so, and then he learned she was betraying him with her pimp. He painted her and killed her. Yet the pimp was executed, and Keyes became a derelict. He died on the Bowery in 1953, the first year in which his paintings began to climb in value. Today, a good Keyes—of Kitty or Phyllis, lounging in exultant carelessness—can sell for fifty thousand dollars.

DEBBY MARSH

Gloria Grahame in The Big Heat, *1953,*
directed by Fritz Lang

Kenport was the only world Debby Marsh knew. It was like so many of the cities in Ohio—dark gray in winter, pale gray in summer, solid by day, glamorous at night. Then the windows in the tower buildings could sparkle; the streets had a rosy wash, with traffic lights going red and green at every intersection. The night sky was an old mauve cloth draped over the buildings. In the dark, the towers and the streets seemed illusory. You did not have to feel the layer of scum waiting on every touch; you could believe the city was a creature from the lake, still damp and alive. Debby preferred the romance of the night, and she settled for it whenever she could, along with several other lies and half-truths.

She was born in the city in 1930, in the Woodland section. That was a joke, because there were no trees, just block after block of housing for the workers in the auto industry. Debby's father was a fitter and there were six children in the three-bedroom house, built to one of the two patterns available in Woodland—the two- and the three-bedroom units. There were houses where couples lived, without kids, who had a spare room and no use for it. And others where three kids had to share one room, growing up without privacy. Debby pretended to be sick a lot, so she could have days at home and be alone in the room, dreaming in the quiet and the space. Neither her parents nor the school took the illnesses or the truancy it veiled seriously. There wasn't time, or the hope. In the thirties, her father was out of work a lot, waiting around the house, getting drunk. To Debby's mind, it just showed you that people couldn't get along without money. Didn't it follow that they'd manage better with more money?

Then, in the war, Kenport grew rich again. There were military contracts. The factories needed more men, and as the city became more popular there were new, cheap apartment buildings out beyond

Woodland. They went up so fast that one of them fell down. So they built it back up again. The feeling of war brought energy back. A lot of gangsters came into the city. They seemed to have a great life, going out every night, eating at the Lakeside Manor, having cars in pretty colors. The women with them wore fur coats, even on warm nights. Debby liked to be out at night to watch them all go by.

That's how she got to know them. One night in 1948, outside the Blue Gardenia, a nightclub on Wisconsin Avenue, she talked to a group of them. There was one called Vince. He had a girl with him, but he just let go of her, and came over to Debby and asked how old she was. She lied, and he grinned. He gave her a pair of nylons right there on the street, and asked her if she knew how to put them on. Then he pinched her cheek, real hard, and went on into the Gardenia. The woman who'd been with him looked at Debby as if she were a rainy day.

His name was Vince Stone, and he worked for Mike Lagana, one of the most important people in Kenport. Vince took Debby over. He bought her new clothes and sent her to a hairdresser's where they made her look older. He took it for granted she was moving into his apartment, and he fucked her all the time like she was a heavy box he was moving upstairs. It was all right. Her mother had told her to expect this, and the clothes were more than she could have dreamed of.

One night Vince told her to go over to Lagana's house.

"What for?"

"Whatever he wants."

"What does that mean?"

"I don't know. Go on. Hurry."

So she went over to the house, and Lagana introduced her to his mother—who only spoke Italian—and then he took her upstairs and made love to her. "Very nice," he said. "Really quite nice." And he told her if she ever wanted a little more just to give him a call. When she got back, Vince beat her up, as if he'd never guessed. So the next day she called Lagana, but he reminded her that he was very fond of Vince and couldn't take her away. Loyalty was everything.

It could have been worse. Vince hit her some, and he had these foul tempers when he'd curse Lagana—until Mr. Mike phoned, and then he was sweetness, which was not pleasant in Vince. Debby shopped a lot. Sometimes she got to go to Chicago on business, and stay in the hotels. She preferred that: it was nice to stay in, order up cocktails and pastries, instead of having to cook, or go out the way they always did.

She got her mink, though, and she liked to snuggle in it. Vince liked her best naked beneath the coat, so she had a struggle watching it didn't get torn or stained.

Then all you heard from Vince was Bannion, some detective who was trying to shake up the world. It had to do with Tom Duncan's suicide, and how Bannion kept pestering the widow because maybe there was more to it. Then Bannion's wife got blown up in the family car. Debby ignored things like that. It was the only way.

But one night in the Retreat, Bannion was there when Vince put his cigarette out on the hand of the girl who was shaking dice at the bar. Bannion took her side and Vince backed down like a coward. He left the Retreat without Debby and on the spur of the moment she offered to buy Bannion a drink. But he said not on Vince Stone's money, and that stung. Debby never liked to realize none of the money was hers. So she went after Bannion, to be friendly. She knew straightaway she'd got to him. Because he stopped and grinned, a guilty grin. Why? His wife was dead, wasn't she?

They went back to his hotel, and Debby sat on the bed in case he was shy. But all he did was give her a drink and ask questions. So after a while she called it a night and returned to Vince's place.

He was there playing cards with a gang, including Higgins the police commissioner. She had blown him one night out of boredom. But Vince came after her about her being friendly with Bannion, and before she knew it he picks up a pot and throws scalding coffee in her face.

Higgins took her to the hospital. The doctors gave her something for the pain, but they said it would get worse. What about the scars? she asked. Some, they said, but not bad, and plastic surgery would handle it. So they put a bandage on half her face and the neck, which looked cool. So she went back to Bannion's hotel, since she'd got it for him. The two things throbbing in her mind were dread of the damage in her own face and desire for Bannion.

The detective took her in, and got another room in the hotel for her. So much for the allure of half a face! He talked about the case, how he'd realized that Duncan's widow had her husband's last letter—the dirt on Lagana—and how she had it in a safe deposit, where it stayed as long as she was alive, getting $500 a month from Mr. Mike.

Debby worked it all out. She took the gun Bannion had left her as protection. She went over to the Duncan house. Mrs. Duncan was about to go shopping. She was wearing a fur coat just like Debby's—"We're sisters under the mink, Bertha." Debby liked that line and then she shot Bertha. She went back to Vince's place and put a pot of coffee on. By the time he got back she had watched two pots boil away. But the third was ready to go. It slapped him in his ugly face, and he screamed. She had never known him so moved.

She told him about Bertha being dead, about how the heat was going to start. And he took out his gun and shot her. It surprised her. She reckoned that he would only whine and collapse. There had always been something more to Vince. Hadn't he noticed her and liked her on the silky street?

HARRY LIME

Orson Welles in The Third Man, *1949,*
directed by Carol Reed

For someone shot in a sewer, there has been such romancing of Harry Lime. I can never hear the name without thinking of that caustic compound in which English domestic murderers reckoned to have corpses devoured. But if you look at the Harry Lime stories—in their magazine originals, or in the long-running television series —why, Rollo Martins, their author, has made our urbane Lime out of the green fruit.

In fiction, he is tart but refreshing. Whereas, in life, he was poison. How are such tricks worked? It must be that we are fascinated by evil. The most horrible thing is how the world has turned out so close to Harry's cynicism about the ghost of decency having been given up some time ago. "In these days, old man, nobody thinks in terms of human beings." Always with an "old man," the lie in his own bland council. Maybe Harry wanted to think he was lying, so he pushed that fake bonhomie into every other sentence.

He was born in Balham in 1916, the only child of Constance Lime, the widow of George Lime, killed on the first day of the Somme, twelve weeks earlier. George was a subaltern from a well-to-do Streatham family that owned a number of electrical shops in South London. Married in 1914, George and Constance had been able to buy a small house in Balham thanks to money from his father. When George died, the Limes assumed that Constance and the child would move into the large house on Tooting Bec Common. But Constance was the daughter of a bus inspector from Brixton, convinced she would be uncomfortable in the big house with people whose distaste for her was allied to the condescension that falls on poor relatives. With a friend, she opened a ladies' hairdressing shop, Conita, at the top of Brixton Hill, and made a go of it.

It was a brave stand, by a cheerful young woman, so brisk at business that she was able to send Harry to Dulwich College in 1927. Some sons would have been proud. But Harry tended to side with his grandparents in thinking that a mistake had been made. He preferred the large house, the maid who brought him tea and the chauffeur outside the college in the afternoon to run him back to Streatham. He deferred to his grandmother, a petite snob with only three fingers on one of her hands, abhorred by his mother and cold to the child, but a model of odd learning, superior diction and polite sarcasm. Although a small woman, she did everything as if from a height.

Harry and his grandmother played a game in his childhood with a large collection of toy soldiers. It had belonged to his father, and his grandmother had kept it when George grew up. With Harry, she restaged the battles of Marlborough and Wellington. They deployed troops on the Persian carpets, and Harry marveled at how she would tip over the killed lead creatures with the cane she carried. Conferring death seemed so easy. Harry was left to guess how the Battle of the Somme had been managed.

He had too little of his mother's energy, and too much of his own cunning to need it. At school he got by, cheating or stealing others' knowledge, so glib in class it was hard for many masters to recognize his ignorance. He disdained his mother's shop; at least until he was fourteen, when he suddenly seemed to appreciate the bantering girls his mother employed who were always comparing themselves to pictures of Myrna Loy or Constance Bennett. Often with them, he put on fatherly airs, and talked to impress them.

Harry's strength at Dulwich was in theater. He seemed to lose his puppy fat on stage; he came to life, and gave his voice a walnut resonance. In truth, it was a very mannered way of speaking, as if his mother had tried to imitate his grandmother. But it carried in a theater; its bogusness seemed mellifluous. He played Romeo (with Rollo Martins, a pet crony, as his Juliet), the Chorus in *Henry V* and, in his last year at school, a Falstaff who seemed to have the genuine dropsy of alcoholic old age. Never quite a child, Harry was fascinated by the elderly; at the time no one realized how far this bred in him a premature insight into death and decay.

At eighteen, he was a hypnotic hulk: his charm matched his size. He was flat-footed and clumsy physically, but a hummingbird in chat and badinage. He liked to hide the one with the other, so he was often at Conita after school, slumped in a velvet-covered armchair, flirting with the girls or the customers in that languid, elaborate way of his that thrilled anyone with an insecure education.

His grandparents said he could go to Oxford. But armchair talk had made him lazy, and he needed underlings, people easily impressed with him. So he hung around the area and got a job as a salesman for H. O. Motors. He was very winning. He could rattle off a fine line of pastiche poetry about the cars, while his pinched breathless girth was a subtle suggestion that all movement should be by way of limousine.

This was 1935. Harry got a reputation in South London. He became a wrestling impresario—he discovered and promoted "Man-Mountain" Dean. He had a hand in the automobile business and he advised his mother and several other people in hairdressing. The police kept an eye on him, and Harry watched their attention with a mixture of pride and wonder just as, when on the stage, he had paused in a speech and felt suspense and need in the audience running like lucre into the palm of his hand. He knew some bad elements: he mixed with the Elephant & Castle gang, and he was on drinking terms with Moseley's assistant, Hamm. He was what was known as a "wide boy," and no one was a more amused model for the term, opening his fine coats to show that stretch of white shirt. He dressed fastidiously, and he usually had some dolled-up sharpie on his arm, a working girl to whom he was giving his quick shampoo-and-set Svengali act.

It was the war that Harry had been waiting for. He did fire-watch duty and he started up a salvage business during the Blitz that made him £100,000 in one year. It was not pretty: he and his gang cleaned out bombed houses for the survivors or the faraway relatives. He had an estate agency as a sideline, buying wrecked sites and reselling them. He learned fast and he knew as much about shattered structures as anyone around.

The London papers got on to him. He was attacked. And then, in a disarming gesture, he formed the International Refugee Office. It was a private organization, but it had several illustrious patrons on the letterhead—the Duke of Abercorn, Bud Flanagan, Roland Northover. It became an ideal way of absorbing money from the other businesses and it allowed Harry to present himself as a Santa Claus for bombsites and broken lives.

He became an international figure. For much of 1944, he was in

America, speaking about the plight of refugees, filling large halls with his orotund voice, moved by suffering he had never seen. I heard him speak in Omaha, and he spent a weekend with us, in the course of which he tempted my wife into a reading of part of *The Country Wife* that was too much for her. He had been traveling, and he was worn down, as lean and urgent as a tightrope. He was always watching her with his soulful eyes, and Mary Frances was flustered the whole weekend. "What an actress!" Lime said to me. "How can you ever trust her?" You can want to kill a man on Saturday, and be beaten down by Sunday, overcome by his awfulness, aware that you are not what killers are made of, not yet.

Harry Lime went to Europe in 1945. He was in Vienna soon after it was relieved, setting up his International Refugee Office. It was a tidy front for his rackets, the most lucrative of which involved medicines. He invited Rollo Martins over—it was Rollo who had done the press pieces on Harry when the IRO was formed, "little bits of rehabilitation," Harry called them. Now he wanted Rollo again, to polish up his image. But the police were on to him and Harry faked his own death. Only for the foolish Martins to appoint himself detective. It all came out, and Harry died in the sewers, larger than ever in a winter coat, sunk in the dark flow of sewage.

I nearly told Mary Frances, to reassure her. But she could have thought I did it.

KAY CORLEONE

Diane Keaton in The Godfather, *1971,
and* The Godfather Part II, *1974,
directed by Francis Ford Coppola*

A wife in the Corleone family had tasks and duties: to be available for her husband's lovemaking and to bear children; to suckle these children in plain view of the family so as to foster the fullest reverence for motherhood; and then to pass the care of the young children to nurses and maids, but to be an ultimate court of appeal and a source of intimate advice for the children; to lead visits to church, and to ensure that the children were nicely dressed and making progress toward first communion; to deal with the cooks in the choice and preparation of family meals; to know the names of retainers and associates and greet them warmly; to shop and look decent; and to know when to speak and when to leave the room. In return for an exact performance of this role, the wife and mother received the unstinting adoration of all the men in the family. She should never remark on the inadequacy of the arrangement; she should not get drunk or curse in public; she should have no affairs; she should not have a loose tongue or inquisitive ears; she should never question her man; she should accept adoration modestly and wear dark and plain colors. And be above suspicion, like Don Vito's wife.

Kay Adams was born in Concord, New Hampshire, in 1921. Her father, Lawrence, was a lawyer; it was a family of four children, all close in age, in their quarrels and their firm affection. In the long winters they skated and tobogganed, and in the spring Kay developed as a track athlete. She was state champion at 220 yards in 1938, and there was some talk in the *Monitor* about her as an Olympic prospect. But no one knew then that there would be no more Olympiads for ten years.

She entered the University of New Hampshire at Durham in the fall of 1940, at which time she wanted to study law and then perhaps join her father in his practice. But in February 1941, she went up to Dartmouth with a gang of UNH girls for the Winter Carnival. During that weekend of parties she first met Michael Corleone, a pale-faced boy with eyes like black olives, a senior majoring in classics, yet seeming younger than she was. He was so hesitant Kay noticed her own moderate voice dropping to a hush when she talked to him. He had a dark aura that enchanted her. She fell in love with him in a quarter of an hour.

He graduated that spring, and went back to his home in Long Beach, Long Island. But they corresponded, he in his beautiful black script, she in her sprinting hand. He wrote to her in grave sentiments, and she answered as fittingly as she could. She feared that a real declaration of her feelings would have alarmed him. So she curbed her passion, and made herself a cheery girl, full of fun and optimism. From the outset she felt herself responding to him, never taking a lead.

In the summer of 1942, he took her on a trip to Nantucket, telling her he was going to join the army. He added that he loved her, and wanted to tell her as much. Kay was sure he would ask her to sleep with him; she was eager to be asked. But they only held hands and kissed. She noticed how cool his hands stayed and she wept in the certainty that someone so meek would be killed in the war.

But he came back a hero, returning in time to attend her graduation at Durham in 1945—not late despite an illness the doctors could not specify, but which she knew was Michael's absence. They spent that summer together here and there, and in August Michael took her to the Corleone house for the marriage of his sister, Connie, to Carlo Rizzi. Kay understood they were in the olive-oil and groceries business. She was amazed by the scale of the wedding, and the old-fashioned affluence in the house.

Michael was changed. Still slight and reticent, when he did speak there was a new assurance, nearly an insolence. It was as if in disproving fear he had gained an edge of arrogance. This was there when he told her how his father had once freed Johnny Fontane from a contract—asking the bandleader for his signature or his brains on the legal document—so that she could not tell whether he was boasting or joking with her. But Michael introduced her to his parents in a formal way that bespoke his intentions. She was made welcome. Don Vito took her for a stroll on the beach the next day to ascertain she was not Catholic, but would convert. "Oh yes, of course," she said, wondering at her own hurry, knowing once and for all that she was a godless slut.

Then Michael's father was shot in the street: she had always hated New York. A little while later there were stories in the papers that Michael had avenged Don Vito, killing men called Sollozzo and McCluskey. Then there was no word of him. She went to the Long Beach house, and it was a grove of men in dark coats just hanging around. Tom Hagen, Michael's adopted brother, said he couldn't tell her where Michael was or whether he was alive. The only smile on his face was one of irrelevant, distant kindness.

Kay went back to New Hampshire and she taught school in Concord for two years. Then one day, as she was walking some of her children home, a black limousine stopped and a man in a black coat and a black Homburg got out. It was Michael, and he asked her to marry him.

He told her he had been away, but it was safe and necessary now to be back. She asked him about the killings. He said he would tell her one thing, one thing only, and then she was not to raise such matters again. Yes, he had killed them: he was proud to say as much about anyone who meant harm to his father. Would she marry him?

They were married in 1948, and their son Anthony was born ten months later, in 1949. Kay had never seen such contentment in Michael's eyes. They had another child, a daughter, two years later.

Kay had whatever she wanted. The wealth so hurt her New England soul that she taught herself never to want, like a visitor to Arab countries. She had a driver for trips to Manhattan, but she saw how she was never free. Michael had quietly discouraged all her old friends; and there were more men to make up for it; and the family, so often gabbing in Italian. She tried to learn the language, but Michael told her, "Kay, I don't want you ever to talk in Italian." So he whispered Italian to Anthony, like a hot, private joke.

She learned the family business, and realized that the houses—on Long Island, and then at Lake Tahoe—were havens that held her in the same mud, fed by corpses. The children were never close enough to her. All those intermediaries had bred a cold in Anthony such as she had felt early in Michael. There was nothing to do but brood. When she got pregnant again, she managed her own abortion—so badly that she could have no more children.

Michael was solicitous, like a medieval envoy. She knew as he bent over her in bed that she would have to tell him about the abortion. She reckoned he would likely kill her; or have her killed—he would stay impersonal. But he was crueller. He sent her away, keeping the children for himself. It was only later that her father explained how, technically, she had deserted him. Refusing a divorce, Michael could probably keep the children.

That was in 1960. For over a year Kay drank. Michael sent her money to live, but not enough to come to Tahoe more than twice a year to see the children. On every visit, Anthony was grimmer toward her. She thought of killing herself; she would never throw off Michael's baleful authority otherwise.

Then, in 1962, she was visited in her small New York apartment by George Locke. He was retired, he said, acting for friends. He seemed to know so much about the Corleones already. It was he who told Kay that Michael had been married once before, to a Sicilian girl, in the years he was away. She had been blown up in their car. Locke asked Kay how she felt about her children. Had she thought of seeking custody?

She said she had been told it was useless. Yet, their father's character was such that . . . who knows? said Locke. He went away, but he came back often. He let her guess that he was acting for the Justice Department, for Robert Kennedy. Would Mrs. Corleone sue for custody? For divorce? Her chances might be good, even in Nevada, if she could make the character of her husband an issue. What did she know? The administration was ready to help in any way, provide every protection, if only Michael Corleone might be nailed. What did she know?

So little, Kay cried. Michael had things done, at second or third hand. Locke told her they were certain he had had Hyman Roth shot. She told him that she was sure Fredo had not drowned in the lake. Kay searched her memory: it was like going through analysis. She laughed out loud when she remembered, Michael had owned up to killing Sollozzo and McCluskey. It might be enough, said Locke.

The hearings were eventually set for December 1963: Michael's lawyers managed so many delays. But before then John Kennedy was shot in Dallas. Locke came to her and explained Robert's distress and his suspicion that organized crime had been behind the assassination. "Going on will be harder," he advised. "The attorney general is not sure of his position. After all, we do not count on winning in Nevada. It is the appeals process that interests us. But now . . . we have to consider the danger, and the ordeal, for you." Kay looked at his kind eyes but knew such prospects were hers alone, like her thoughts of the children.

She went to live at a military establishment. She was escorted to Nevada, in and out of the courtroom. Michael's lawyers assailed her time and again, but charges were made in court and newspaper coverage spread as the media realized what was happening. The court awarded Michael custody. But he was already fearful of the appeals process and his lawyers met Kay's to propose a compromise—Anthony, now fifteen, should live with her half the year, and the daughter the other six months, her settlement to be generous.

Locke was very tactful. This proposal was in her best interests, he said. Fight on, and she might get far less. Stop the fight and Michael Corleone would escape the larger charges. He supported Kay's wish to accept the compromise without disappointment.

And so, in the fall of 1964, Anthony came to live with Kay. She was surprised that he was friendly, so devoid of bitterness. In the last two years, he had grown more antagonistic, but now he was sweet, obliging and considerate. At Christmas, he had his bodyguard rape his mother, saying she was a disgrace, not fit for the family. Then he told the man to beat her.

She woke up the next day, sure Anthony would be gone. But he brought her breakfast, and chatted with her, until he had her raped once more. He would not do it himself, but saw the rarer disdain in watching it performed. Kay began to drink again and died in June 1965, at which time Anthony told the press he was indeed grateful for

the belated opportunity to get to know his mother. Then he closed up
the apartment and went back to Tahoe.

SKIP McCOY

Richard Widmark in Pickup on South Street, *1953,
directed by Samuel Fuller*

There she was, her face twelve inches away from his, their bodies
bumping and swaying together, all those little enforced touchings
—total strangers, so strange they didn't even need to talk or admit
they had noticed each other. Touching, but not noticing, it was what
he liked about city life and subway work.

There she was, this dame, this broad, in a white sleeveless dress. He
could smell the cheap powder under her arms and see the stubble of
black hair there, shaved in a hurry a day, two days ago. Her hair grew
quickly. He could feel it stirring when he let the car's curve take him
into her thigh. Her dress was made there so that it had a flap folded
down like a lapel on her hip. She had one hand there resting on it with
a noisy bracelet on the wrist, saying look, here it is, come and get it.
You were meant to want to unpeel the flap, but he just wondered how
he could slip his wafer of a clever hand inside it without her knowing
or wanting it to stop.

So he looked at the flap on her right hip, and she noticed and looked
at him watching and made sure he'd seen the sneer. She had big plum-
colored lips he wanted to mash with a fork. Her eyelashes moved
slowly because of the black gunk on them. He could smell the greasy
cosmetics and he could smell her last meal—something with pickles.
She had that sort of statuesque tasty look, the bracelet, earrings the
size of spoons, her hair off to one side and all done, like a football, the
touching flap and the big white plastic shoulder bag resting on her left
hip.

As he looked at the flap and at the *Post* folded in his left hand, his
right felt the bag. It was smooth but sticky with a cinch of a catch made
like two big balls. The noise in the train ate up the click when he
opened it. The girl sighed, as if she was thinking about her guy eating
her pussy. She was a long way away.

He knew it: her handbag was a mess. There was a handkerchief and several crumpled tissues floating on top of the deeper junk. He went farther and touched something moist and yielding. He looked at her, his hand between this alive thing and the sateen lining of her bag. Her sleepy eyes picked up his look and used him as a voyeur watching her get off on her lover's licks. It was a sandwich, half out of cellophane. She was eating again. Pastrami on his fingers. He smiled at her thick arms and their glossy pimples.

Deeper. There it was, a wallet flat and old like a used shoe. He held it in two fingers like tweezers. His one hand lowered the *Post*, held her pouty look in an insolent stare and lifted out the wallet until the *Post* covered it. The dip and the lift, fucking her in her sleep. He put the wallet inside the folded paper and shut her bag for her. Again, her features moved, smug and settled, taking a goodbye kiss, looking forward to a snack.

That was Skip McCoy, also known as Joseph McCoy, the son of Irish immigrants. Limerick people, born in New York City in 1923, raised in the Bronx between 169th Street and Cortona Park. Father a pickpocket, died inside. Mother an ironer and presser in a laundry. Skip one of five kids, taught the trade by his father. A natural for it, which is to say not just good at it technically, but fulfilled by it. Thieving is a sport of the soul, and a dip can only touch anyone without them knowing.

1938, the year his father died, Joseph "Skip" was sent to juvenile hall for three months. 1939, first conviction, sent to reform school. Refused for military service. 1942, for stealing on the subway, three years in Sing Sing. Out in 1944, after more lessons inside. For three years, then, no one could pin a thing on him, but Skip got rich and took himself a room in a Manhattan hotel for living in. 1947, police framed him on another job, five years in Sing Sing. Got out in 1951, went to live in a shack on the waterfront, Lower West Side. Always lived alone. Two-time loser, next time for keeps.

So, that day in April 1952, on the Lexington Avenue line, grinding against the broad, giving her the dead-eyed stare. Candy it turned out she was called: perfect! What he would have guessed. Into the shoulder bag, one shithole of a cunt. The wallet had nineteen dollars, old photographs, the cards of a pack of businessmen, and the pieces of film in a little yellow envelope. The film was pictures of pages in a book, as far as he could tell, full of printing and diagrams.

That was what it was all about. This Candy had been carrying pictures of secrets, atom-bomb stuff, getting it to the Reds. There'd been two FBI guys in the car following her. They'd seen what Skip was doing, but they didn't want to disturb anything and they couldn't lay a hand on Skip in the crush.

So Skip had the cops after him, this Candy *and* the Reds, all hot for the pictures. A dip had got himself into the spying business! But Candy hadn't known what she was doing, that dumb shit. She was just doing a favor for her creep Joey, and he slapped her around and told her to find the artist who had lifted her wallet. Cops knew it was Skip, but they were told to lay off. FBI wanted to get the foreign agents, too, big stuff. Which put Mr. McCoy in the best seat. They pay heroes, don't they?

Candy came around and Skip slugged her and felt her up while she was out. But he hated touching broads, so he hit her some more. And then Joey got into it, and wasted Moe, the tie lady, just to show he was serious. In the end, Skip played it out fine. He got off for handing back the photos. The FBI snatched the Reds and Skip got Candy to pour his beers. But she went all gushy for love on him. So he sent her out to work—hostess in a restaurant (so the slut could eat)—and then the second week he lifted her wages while they was lovey-dovey. And that taught her.

1954, beginning of the end, Skip McCoy arrested on the Seventh Avenue line. Twenty years for Skip. He laughs; this kid won't break. Up in Sing Sing his mind started to go. That's what they say—can't see Skip is out-thinking them. They let him out in '69. Skip still acting. He was simple by then, talking to himself. Losing his touch too, hands shaky. Hang in there, Skip! Died 1971, pneumonia, sleeping out. Never complained, though, not Skip. Happy thinking of the fine work he'd done. Champion.

> *This trashy monologue creeps up on me, just from thinking of Skip's snicker. I have been able to talk like movie people after one look at a picture. But I have had so little to say for myself. Even now I might slip upstairs to Mary Frances and be as gruff and as loved as Tracy in* Adam's Rib. *But my sincerity went to the movies, leaving a bereft mimic behind.*

CORA PAPADAKIS

Lana Turner in The Postman Always Rings Twice,
*1946, directed by Tay Garnett; and Jessica Lange, 1981,
directed by Bob Rafelson*

By the time she was fourteen, there wasn't a man didn't notice her. And almost before they knew it, or felt the new pressure in the air around them, she knew they were looking at her. Out in the street, she recognized the way they dawdled and maneuvered to get a clear view of her. She'd be headed for the store, and two guys half as far from it would suddenly see a butterfly on the ground, or something that they had to study, and she'd have to walk on past them with both of them crouched down admiring the butterfly and just happening to look up as she came by so they could imagine the airy glow under her dress. Cora put on an extra sway to make her skirts move.

This was in Des Moines, Iowa, where she was born Cora Smith in 1913. Her mother was a cook at a hotel, and her father was a farm laborer. He was a big, handsome man, as dark as Cora but more tanned from being out in the sun so much. He was a quiet, resolute man until he understood how other men were studying Cora. Then he got angry and uneasy, and he sneered at his wife, who hadn't let him sleep with her since the birth of Cora. She had been horrified by lovemaking and she turned all her attention to cooking for people she never met or knew. She grew fat, less from eating than from the idea of food and its steady company. Her husband went off every day on foot with a bottle of lemonade and a loaf of bread. But after Cora came of age he took wine instead, and he came home flushed and sour, too tired to play horseshoes.

For Cora, her father felt like other men, except that he looked at her with bitterness. Several times he'd blunder in on her in the bathroom, or while she was putting on her stockings, and he'd scowl as if it had been her fault. So she got casual. She let him see her dressing a few times and she left her clothes around the house. The kindliness in her father had vanished. He was a stranger to her, but he seemed to hate her for causing the new distance.

Cora was fifteen when she went all the way. She was itching to find out. There were boys in school who had felt her all over while they were kissing, and some who'd had their hands in her and even for a

113

second or two their things. But she knew they were ignorant. She wanted someone older who could take all the worry away and teach her. There was a stockman on one of the farms, one where her father worked sometimes, a big man with hands as rough as bark. He'd watched her for a year, until one summer evening she went into a barn with him and got it all over with. He was a demon lover and she was like a soft pillow for him, or like an empty barrel tossed in the air on a bull's horns. Cora got to be an expert that first time. She came five times before supper, every way he worked on her. She was soaked and battered and only wanted more.

But the stockman got bored after that. She would try to cross his path, but he was never there; and once she saw him start a conversation with someone just to avoid meeting her. Cora couldn't understand his caution. She'd have done it on Euclid Avenue at Sunday lunchtime if he'd wanted to. Yet he didn't, so she hunted for others and got the worst reputation in the school. All this while, her father's dark face took on a violent tinge, like smoke. Cora told him, "You're sickening for something. Ought to see a doctor."

Then, in 1930, she entered a beauty contest for all the high schools in Iowa. Which she won, with Cora herself the only one surprised or pleased at that. The prize was a trip on the Chief to Hollywood. When she got there, there were photographers to take her picture, and they all whistled at her, which made her feel happy. She was given a screen test, and apparently the studio people liked her looks. But she had to say some lines and it felt peculiar saying these emotional things without feeling them. So they told her no use. She could have gone back home, she had the ticket. But she stayed and she got a job as a waitress in a hash house near the railroad station.

It was a lousy job. The tips were small, and the men who came in thought they could wipe their hands on her. Some of them were good-looking, and she'd go with them to what they called parties but turned out to be her with two or three of them in a room with a lot of beer. Then one day a big guy came in, tanned like her father, and he told another guy off for feeling Cora's leg.

"You're a gentleman," she told him when she took his order.

"Golly," was all he said, big eyes stupid over her.

So he asked her to marry him. Said he had a diner and a filling station, the Twin Oaks Tavern. He needed help there, and he surely liked her. His name was Nick Papadakis: he was Greek and his hair was like crude oil, heavy and shiny. What decided her was when he said his place was in the country, a long way away, in the hills. She missed the country, so she said, sure, she'd marry him, but she didn't get off till six.

At the Twin Oaks Tavern, she cooked, she served and she pumped gas when he was away. There was just him and the cat, and the cat was a better lover. Nick was the clumsiest man she'd ever met, full of shame and respect for his own size and her "tenderness." Also people thought he was Mexican, and just because she had black hair they took it for granted she was too. She hadn't gotten married to be a Mex.

Then one day this bum came by, Frank Chambers, and he conned a meal out of Nick, and then as a topper Nick gives him a job helping out, mechanic and so on, which Frank says he's expert at. That made Cora laugh, but when she saw Frank noticing her she felt glad he was staying and she got wet watching his mean black eyes. A few days later, they made it and it was the best yet. He was like an animal and he kept up with her good. He'd known what to do from the look in her eyes. Cora never liked to talk while she was doing it.

He was all for them leaving, but Cora said what about the three years she'd put in? She said what was the point of going if it was only to another hash house? What then? he said. She never had to spell it out. He knew from her not having the words, and he was kissing her breasts all the time, working out how they'd kill Nick.

Which they did, in a fake car accident. Only Frank had cracked the Greek's skull first and they drove the car over a cliff. Then Frank messed her up so she'd look hurt too. Rip me, she told him. So he tore open her blouse from the throat to her stomach, and he slugged her in the face. She went down and looked at him and he jumped on her and fucked her once before the alarm. It was all neat, but the car went too far down the cliff, and with Frank pushing it he went too so Cora thought maybe he was dead.

In the hospital, he signed a confession to this eagle lawyer, Katz, who then proceeded to get Cora off but wanted half the insurance because of the confession. What an operation. Just a look at them both and he'd known. Cora wouldn't have minded making it with Katz. And she felt sick that Frank had betrayed her at the first pressure.

So they ran the tavern for a while, and business was good because people came by to get a look at the couple from the papers. But Frank stayed and he was good for her still. Then she got the telegram saying her mother was sick, so she went back to Des Moines and watched her mother die, with her father watching both of them. After she died, he told Cora how lonely he was going to be, and she said sure, she knew, and he cried and she had to comfort him, and then just the once they

115

were in bed and he was amazing. She told him she was proud of him, and he should get remarried quick.

Then Cora went back to California, and there was Frank to meet her, wide-eyed about her mother dying. She found out he'd been with a woman in a circus while she was away, and he was so miserable about it she wanted to laugh. It made her think he really loved her, and so they got married. There were a few weeks when it was fine, and she told him she was pregnant and he was chipper as a kid. They went to a beach up by Topanga, and it was all deserted. They swam and she thought, So, this is love—okay. But she strained herself: she could feel the load in her stomach shift. Frank got her in to shore, and carried her up the sand to the car. And he started to drive to Santa Monica on the coast road with all the curves and he was so worried that he never saw the truck coming.

FRANK CHAMBERS

John Garfield in The Postman Always Rings Twice,
*1946, directed by Tay Garnett; and Jack Nicholson, 1981,
directed by Bob Rafelson*

At Slapout, in Oklahoma, where the two panhandles bang together in the wind and sun, in 1911, the birth of Frank Chambers. (How many different sentences are there to set down the facts of beginning?) He was illegitimate. His mother, Eileen, nineteen when he was born, worked in a hardware store, and lived in an upstairs room. A lot of men, Slapout people and some passing through, got to go up Eileen's stairs, so Frank never bothered to wonder who his father was. But when he was a boy there were jokes that maybe it had been a nigger, which cut him hard because he didn't want it said his mother would have gone with a black.

His mother was a wild-eyed woman. She didn't seem to know if there was a smudge on her face or a rip in her dress. And if she discovered it, she had a high, what-the-hell laugh that troubled a lot of people. She told Frank she didn't know where she'd come from. When she was only a little girl, her parents had taken her to Oklahoma City and she'd gotten lost, as simple as that, and never found them. Nor they her. So she'd been put in an orphanage till she was sixteen, and all she'd known for sure was her name.

As Frank grew up, his mother made a separate part of the room for him out of packing cases, so she could have company at night. Frank's bedroom was dark and dry-smelling, and he kept a candle there to light when the wind was howling outside. His mother never treated him like a child. She would talk to him just as she did anyone else—offhandedly, laughing for no apparent reason, and quarrelsome with just the same suddenness. It made Frank alert, being with her. He never knew when she might whip her hand out and slap him, or draw him against her warm, shaking body. People in Slapout laughed at her, and they made out she was weird in the head.

Once, when Frank was ten, he woke up in the middle of the night. There was burning in the packing-case wall. He cried out for his mother and got out of bed. The fire was creeping across the floor of the large room, like honey spreading. His mother was nowhere. He ran down the stairs out on the street, shouting for help. But it was late, and the wind had gotten up. The hardware store was gutted before the firemen came. There was old wood in the building, and a supply of kerosene in the basement.

Frank watched the firemen, waiting for his mother. She never came, so the Moodys, the people who owned the store, took him to their place. Next day, it seemed Eileen had been out at a ranch all night. Frank couldn't understand how the town reckoned she had started the fire. Just the same, she was sent to the asylum in Norman, and Frank was looked after by the Moodys, who built a new store. Twice a year they took him to see his mother, but the hospital was no good. In a year she didn't know Frank, and she was scratching all the time.

He stayed in Slapout till he was seventeen and all the Moodys saw was that he should work in the store all his life. So he went down into Texas, to Pampa, and for a year he hung out with a kid, Woody Guthrie. Frank played washboard while Woody sang and played guitar. They made a little money, and they knew some girls. But Frank got into fights with them. He never knew how, but all at once he'd punch at the woman and she'd look at him like he was a monster.

So he took to the road in 1929 and became a regular bum. He passed through Bedford Falls in 'thirty-one and I gave him work painting the office. It was badly done; his lunch breaks got longer; and he didn't put sheets down, so he ruined the floors with drops of paint. I had to talk to him, but he blamed the poor paint and the customers being in and out. That downright angered me and I told him, "Just remember, fellow, I never needed this painting done."

117

"Never needed it?"

"Not really."

"I ain't working for no idiot, then." And he threw the brush on my desk.

He hitched to Los Angeles and started to ride up and down the coast on freights. He would stop off, do a few days' work, steal, get into the small jails on vagrancy charges, fight the rail police, pick fruit. He got hard and mean, hating the straight life of homes and jobs. He had a slingshot, and he liked to roam at night, find a window lit up, with a family inside, like an advertisement, and put a stone through the window.

In 1933, he tried Mexico; he'd heard it was easier there. But it was hot, the food sickened him, and he never trusted Mexicans. He came back and hustled tourists in Los Robles. Then he got on a hay truck and rode as far as Twin Oaks before they threw him off.

There was a diner and Frank tried the old free-lunch scam—some guy in a car who was to meet him and pay for the meal. But the dumb Greek served him enchiladas and swallowed the check. The guy even offered him a job, and Frank was trying not to laugh when he saw the woman in the kitchen. He wanted to work her face over then and there.

Cora liked it that way. The Greek husband did nothing for her. The first time, Frank bit her lip and tasted blood like thick sweat. She was a treat, and he got tired for the first time in his life humping her. Frank wanted the Greek to notice and fight him; he wanted to split his stupid skull. So he didn't need pushing when Cora walked around the idea.

"I don't care if I fry for it," Frank told himself. "It'll make trouble for them." *Them* meant that straight world in painted houses. He ended up in the death house, not for putting the wrench through the Greek's skull, but for killing Cora, faking a crash so she went through the screen and her blood fell on the hood like she was taking a leak. There was a priest in the prison, and Frank said for sure he hadn't done it. Then Frank talked to another prisoner, who said it was his subconscious. There were two people in him. It made Frank shiver to think about that. Cora was the only one he'd ever liked as much as he wanted to rip into her.

JIMMY DOYLE

Robert De Niro in New York, New York, *1977,*
directed by Martin Scorsese

"What sort of thing is that then?" asked Jimmy Doyle. He was eleven, but he had that Irish edge in the way he talked, like a chipped curbstone, that was never young.

"That's a saxophone," said Martin Dougherty. "Tenor saxophone. You seen Billy today?"

Jimmy whistled in perplexity, "Saxo—? What kinda name's that? Billy Phelan?"

"That's the one. Named after Adolphe Sax. He invented it."

"Pretty thing."

"It has a glorious tone, too. Billy playing tonight?"

"I reckon. So . . . do you use it?"

"The saxophone?"

"Yeah."

"Do you want it, Jimmy?"

"I might. I might."

That's how Jimmy Doyle got his first saxophone. He was born in Albany in 1920, and this was in 1931, the first year Billy Phelan got a name for himself in Louie's poolhall. Jimmy used to hang around Billy. He liked the snappy way he dressed and the way he got with the cue in his hands—like its long hard line was his gaze and his poking the balls this way and that was sorting out the world. Jimmy loved to sit on a high stool outside the light listening to the click of the balls: it was like tough talk jazzing away while pages of print bored the world.

Jimmy wasn't reading. It was a wonder, his teachers said, when he talked so well and when he could knock out any tune on a piano, the way some one-finger typists can race along. But Jimmy was afraid of the silence in reading, and he couldn't see how the shapes on paper stood for things, not when any shout or tune made everyone look up, as if Billy'd just walked in for a match.

After a couple of months with the saxophone, Martin Dougherty heard Jimmy playing. He said, "You should take lessons, Jim. You're not bad."

"Lessons!" scoffed Jimmy. "I worked it out."

That was that. For better or worse, Jimmy puzzled out a way himself, or he gave up on a thing. He couldn't sit still while anyone told him something for his own good. He learned to play well, but who knows if he might not have been better if he'd listened to Martin Dougherty?

"Won't be told," said Martin.

"Cold little fellow," said Billy Phelan. "Watches me play, but never says a word."

"Because you're better than he is," said Martin.

"Has a great respect for excellence, our Jim."

"Cut your throat if he could get it off you."

So Jimmy grew up proud, lonely and mean-tempered, a lean stick of a young man, hands full of the saxophone, like a priest holding a trollop—that's what Martin said once, and Jimmy flashed him that shark's grin, all teeth and hunger. But he got a job playing in a place on Clinton Avenue, in 1938, and they only threw him out because he played so hectic.

He went down to the city in 1940 and tried to hang out with musicians, but he wasn't relaxed enough. So he went into the army, and in 1942 he heard about a vacancy in the Glenn Miller band which he got for two months before Miller told him he had to go because he was a disruptive influence. "It's this sweet shit you play," said Jimmy on his way out.

So he went back to the infantry and he went to France in 1944, where he got a medal for taking a German machine-gun post outside Caen, all on his own. Still, the army sent him home later that year because he was against taking orders and got into a lot of fights. They sent him back to Fort Benning and he worked there on the camp radio station. He had a two-hour show in the early hours of the morning and he played a lot of jazz records. He got fired when he played Charlie Parker's "Tiny's Tempo" over and over for two hours.

He got out of the army in January 1945 and went back to New York, to Monroe's and Minton's, to listen to Parker, Monk and Gillespie in person. He tried to sit in with them but they wouldn't have anything to do with him. Some said it was because Jimmy seemed so hostile, but he thought it was because he was white. Still, his head was full of the spilling phrases played by Parker and the abrupt harmonic leaps. Once, just once, Parker sat back and listened to ten minutes or so of Jimmy saying why he should be allowed to play. "So?" said Jimmy, exhausted. "I just heard you, man," said Parker. "You can't be better on that horn."

On VJ day, Jimmy dropped by the Moonlight Terrace, where the Dorsey band was playing. He slid in and out of conversations, trying to pick up women. That's how he met Francine Evans, the singer. She thought he was crazy, but she couldn't stop him or stop listening to his tirades of wooing. The storm rushed past her ears, frightening and entrancing. She never got rid of him and next day he took her along to his audition at the Palm Club. He played so hard and fast, the manager there was ready to turn him off. But then Francine got up and started to sing and Jimmy fell in behind her, just like Lester Young's velvet cushion for Billie to loll on. The guy hired them both.

But Francine had to leave town with the Frankie Harte band, her real job. So when Jimmy finds out about this he follows her all the way to Asheville, North Carolina. They got married down there: she knew she'd never escape him. And Harte hired Jimmy so long as he'd keep it down a little.

They toured for a year until Harte decided to give it up and asked Jimmy if he wanted to take over the band. For a while it was a hit, but when Francine knew she was pregnant she decided to go back to New York. She had had an offer to do cover records and the traveling was too much for her. So Jimmy stayed on with the band for a while, just to prove it was his. But without Francine they soon lost their following.

Jimmy got back to the city furious. He laughed at Francine's records and dragged her out to Harlem every night when he sat in with Cecil Powell, the one black musician who took him seriously, even if Cecil had turned him on to marijuana. Also, Jimmy had the hots for this black girl singer, Lucy Wiley. The baby was born Jimmy, Jr., in 1948, but the marriage was coming apart to the sound of Jimmy's frenzied talk.

In the next few years, Francine took Jimmy, Jr. to California, where she was getting into pictures. Jimmy stuck it out in New York and he got some notice fronting a group with Miles Davis for a year until they had a fistfight on the stand. Jimmy was doing heroin by 1951, and he talked less. But his stuff was popular with college kids, and in 1953 he was set up in his own club, the Major Chord. People said they'd heard there was gang money in the club.

He lived alone, more reclusive. He didn't see his son for years at a time, but stayed in a room at the Carlyle Hotel, a room he had painted black. By 1960, he was in bad shape from the heroin, and he went into a clinic for a cure. It worked, but he was dead in 1966. There was a memorial concert where a lot of good players came out for him. When

Thelonious Monk played the finale—Jimmy's "Taxi Cab Blues"—he shouted out into the hall, "Fuck you, Jimmy!"

> *I might kill a man if the right music was*
> *playing, or carry Mary Frances over a snow-*
> *capped mountain, to happiness, sure thing. But*
> *stealthy strings hold sway in these narrow,*
> *italic passages, dark corridors where the*
> *storyteller lurks.*

FRANCINE EVANS

Liza Minnelli in New York, New York, *1977,*
directed by Martin Scorsese

If not quite born in a trunk, Francine Evans had a childhood in which it was her responsibility to keep her parents' dancing shoes bright and shiny. She was the daughter of the Mendozas, one of the best-known Latin dance couples in the West. Felipe was Mexican, and he had a brief career in movies around 1920 before he married Wilma Schuyler, a young dancer he met at Universal. They moved away from Los Angeles and went into business together as teachers of Latin dance. They had studios up and down the California coast, and they boosted their trade by winning several national contests. Wilma, of Dutch extraction, dyed her creamy hair black in order to enhance the image of Latin synchronicity. Francine (born Frances) came into the world in Santa Barbara (where the Mendozas had their home) in 1923. She had magnificent black hair of her own.

Always close to music, the young Frances began to sing as she watched her parents gliding or stamping their way across all the polished floors. She played the leads in several high-school shows —*The Pirates of Penzance*, *The Merry Widow*, *The Girl from Tijuana*. Her parents encouraged her musical aspirations, ensured that she had good technical training, and had the foresight to provide for proper orthodontry when she was still in her teens. It was in 1942 that Frances went to New York, with several letters of introduction to friends and colleagues of the Mendozas. One of these was Tony

Harwell, who became her agent, and came up with the new name Francine Evans. As such she made her first impact, winning a Carmen Miranda impersonation contest on the radio.

She was for a year one of the Peters Sisters, a backup group with a lot of studio work. In 1944, she toured with the Jimmy Dorsey band, and in 1945 she got a position as featured vocalist with Frankie Harte—it was then she had an affair with the band saxophonist, Georgie Auld, and made her first hit record, a song they wrote together, "Got a Thing for the Sax Man," a torch classic.

Then on VJ-night, not long after she and Auld had broken up, Francine was at the Moonlight Terrace when Jimmy Doyle approached her and started talking her to death. She knew inside the first hour everything that was going to happen. He had a nagging energy that was going to free her own repressed need to be a star. But he couldn't stand competition; he wouldn't want to see anyone else's fame. And while she knew that everyone had always liked her, she guessed that the streak of self-destructiveness in Doyle would keep him a minor figure. She would be transformed by him; he would barely notice her. But they fell in love like people going over a cliff hand-in-hand. It was the first time in her happy life Francine had felt the drive of compulsion. The new note of desperation in her singing voice came from Jimmy.

Touring with Jimmy was a nightmare. He lived only to be on the stand, and once there he would cut anyone, steal solos and scold the other players for any mistake. Francine tried to make every passing hotel room a version of home. But Jimmy regarded such rooms as anonymous, transitory bases. He passed through them, unaware and chaotic. But they married, she got pregnant and their music improved. For both of them, uneasy as it was, so full of arguments and silence, this period came to stand for "what it could have been like."

Francine knew the marriage wouldn't survive when she went back to New York to have Jimmy, Jr. She guessed that Jimmy had had an affair with Bernice Kay in her absence. When Jimmy saw his son, he looked at him with the amused superiority he put on when sitting through a drum solo. In two months, he moved out and was living in Harlem.

In 1949, they got a divorce and Francine moved with Jimmy, Jr. back to California. There had been movie offers. Her father had done a lot of talking with her and, together with Tony Harwell, he had been working for a year on Arthur Freed to consider Francine. She tested better than anyone suspected; the rather forceful nose photographed cute. Francine had only one song and fifteen minutes in *Would You Believe It?* (1950, Charles Walters), but it was enough. Metro put her straight into *The Girl from Hot Coffee* (1951, Stanley Donen) as a replacement for Garland.

Her movie career was established. She made *Shore Leave* (1952, Donen); *Vaudeville Family* (1953, George Sidney); and then the enormously successful *Happy Endings* (1954, George Cukor). Francine took Jimmy, Jr., east for the New York opening, and she met Jimmy again. He talked about seeing her another time, and they made an appointment. She was all ready to go when a premonition fell on her. She actually saw the tense figure of Jimmy waiting for her on a street corner, and she remembered the grinning scorn with which he'd warded off all her new success. She decided not to see him.

But ever afterward, she got calls in the night. Sometimes he said nothing; sometimes he blew a breathing tone on a mouthpiece; sometimes he started a huge speech, imploring yet blaming her. Jimmy, Jr., was troubled by the strange irregularity of his father's presence, and Francine sent him away to a private school. She made *Lady Love* (1956, Rouben Mamoulian), and then that adventurous failure, *A Virtuoso Personality* (1957, Vincente Minnelli).

In 1957, she married her longtime accompanist, Paul Wilson. It was a comfortable, unexciting marriage for two years, until the mutilated body of Wilson was found in their Holmby Hills mansion pool when Francine was on location in New England for *Labor Day Picnic* (1959, Nicholas Ray), her last film.

Francine was terrified by the murder. She refused to consider any more pictures; she sold the house without ever setting eyes on it again; and she moved to Santa Barbara.

She lives there still, in her early sixties now, seldom seen, one of the true reclusives of showbiz. Until his death in 1966, she was pestered by Jimmy, and she often gave him money to support his heroin addiction. All offers of a comeback were refused, though she did make one TV spectacular, "Francine," in 1963, remarkable for her undimmed vitality and the promise of Bob Fosse.

So optimistic in her films, so settled in her early life, Francine Evans has accepted tragedy. Still adored by the masses—her films are played more now than in the 1950s—she exists in a state of torment, unable to stop or deter the drive of her son to remind her of his father.

JOHN CONVERSE

Michael Moriarty in Who'll Stop the Rain, *1978,*
directed by Karel Reisz

Would it have occurred to me to pursue Converse if I had not been at the dentist's with one old copy of *Time* to help me wait? It was Mo's teeth that proved she had been burned down to the bone, and now mine guided me to a sleeping clue. The eyes, the mouth—our histories are stored there.

In a *Time* silky with use I found a review of a book, *Wounded Soldiers* by John Converse. It was a 1975 issue, and the book was an account of Vietnam veterans disabled by the war. It was based on interviews, and the review picked out one with "Alex Cutter, intent on finding an incident in his American milieu that will answer for his injury." I remembered Converse as Mo's half-hearted lover. But I had not imagined he would have seen her again, not after her marriage to Cutter.

Wounded Soldiers was in the library. It had been borrowed many times, yet it seemed to me meretricious. The material was full of pain, but the writing was artfully noncommittal: horror built up while the book assured itself that there was nothing else to do but recount these lurid events as meticulously as possible. A photographer who recorded them would have been called cold, but Converse was praised for what *Time* termed "cool lucidity." He could make his emptiness seem like helpless wisdom. Sometimes the book was mere unsentenced lists: ". . . Gangrene. Stench. Flowers by the roadside. Maggots in the flesh. . . ." In shedding grammar he had taken on the role of a torturer. The acid words dripped in my head; it was not reading, but being beaten, quietly, so that one would not cry out.

So I learned about Converse: born in 1941, the only child of a surgeon who moved every three or four years to a richer hospital, taking his son with him. The mother died when the boy was four—I could find no cause of death. "Oh, quite simply, she detested my father. She was worn out by him," Converse told me. His casual hands turned over in the air, like a life rolling aside. He had majored in communications at UCLA, and gone into the Marine Corps with a commission. Somewhere he must have taken a wrong turn, a dead end. You cannot always tell from brief biographies. They do not

125

include unhappiness or error. Everyone seems so confident and straight ahead in *Current Biography*.

He had married the daughter of a Berkeley radical, Marge Bender. He worked for her father, writing for his magazines and editing a little. It didn't seem enough for someone with his ambition. Perhaps he loved Marge: they had a daughter. But he wrote a play, *Under the Christmas Tree*, about a marine on furlough who rampages in his old home and kills his unavailing parents. It was successful off-Broadway; it was done often in the sixties, bought for the movies, but never heard of. When I read it, I could not credit its thrill at dreadful cruelty. You understand, I do not say such things cannot happen. We all know of massacres. But how can anyone treat them lightly?

I wrote to Converse's publisher; the letter never came back and never produced an answer. I would have let him go out of sheer inability: I do not know how one becomes an indefatigable inquirer. I grow tired waiting for chance's lead. No Marlowe.

Then three months after my day at the dentist's, I saw in the paper that John Converse would be lecturing at the university in Lincoln on "Conscience and Reporting." It was open and free to the public.

He was a tall man, thin and slack. As he lectured, the light fell on the bald peak of his head. His voice was languid and inexpressive, except when it tensed against giggling as he made a sarcastic remark. He talked about his "crisis" in Vietnam, and the call he had heard to write "not from the several, bogusly intelligent points of view of war's leaders, but in the impacted fear and degradation of those in the way of a war." As if real writing could be so bereft.

He spoke for an hour, with desultory questions for another fifteen minutes, and then there was cheese and wine in the Faculty Lounge. I sipped a cold claret, looking at the heartbreaking Wilson Keyes of a wild garden in Laurel Canyon. I waited for Converse to autograph his book, and to satisfy fawning, hushed questions. One young woman was possessively attentive, but he slid her aside when he realized I was waiting and would not go away.

"I wondered if we might have dinner," I asked him.

"Oh, dinner." His gaze drifted away to the young woman.

"I am Mo Cutter's uncle," I told him.

"Really?" Surprise made him stupid, until he grinned, and it was insolent. "Well, I never."

"I would like a chance to talk with you."

"Would you? Why?"

"I am so much in the dark over her death."

"I could do breakfast, I suppose."

"Tomorrow?"

"I have a ten a.m. flight. Can you come to the Holiday Inn?"

"Eight?"

"Eight-thirty, say."

I stayed in Lincoln, in a motel. Those places have not changed. I wondered if it might be the last time I ever tried to sleep in a motel. I cannot have many motel chronicles left, I trust. Yet I would linger on in the drab cubes a year if it meant another day of life.

He was late the next day and he had cut himself shaving. A year later he was made editor of *Newsweek*, but that morning he was soiled and hungover from the girl in his room.

"Old Mo then," he sighed, as he drank coffee with Tylenol.

"I know about your friendship," I said, to save time, I thought.

"You do? You think you do?"

"She wrote to me. She sent your picture. I don't mean to blame you."

"You're old Uncle George, aren't you? The sly one."

"Sly?"

"Took her to the movies."

"Yes, sometimes."

He looked at me and he forked hot cake in syrup. "Felt her up in the dark."

"I did not." I hated myself for blushing.

"She said so."

"It's not true." He had made me disavow her.

"Ah. . . . Well, Mo wasn't always too straight, was she? She did make things up. And then, once she'd started on heroin—"

"She took drugs?"

"An addict. Scag addict."

"When did you see her last?"

"What?" He began laughing, as if my ignorance had only just dawned on me. "That night!"

"The night she died?"

"Of course. I . . . fucked her. Excuse me. You know."

"I thought Richard Bone . . ."

"After him. I saw him leave. But it wasn't either of us."

"Wasn't what?"

He searched for a way of saying something he normally left unsaid.

"That made her do it—if she did it. Or maybe Cord had the house burned down. Cutter was after him. Had this crackpot theory that

Cord had murdered some girl he was involved with. Nonsense, of course. People don't do that."

At everything he said I felt the ground around me less certain. I wanted to be utterly deaf. He was so familiar with such black subtleties between people, and so indifferent.

There was a silence. "I made that up about you in the dark."

"Why?"

"She never said that. She said something about you—something pleasant, I think—but I don't remember. Why do you care?"

"I think about her. Isn't that enough?"

"No, not really. At least, I shouldn't think so. Look, I have to go. But supposing I was the last to see her alive—I may have been. There was nothing I noticed. Nothing. She didn't need other people, or wrongs, to do a thing like that. It was in her, that's all."

"But noticing depends on kindness."

Have you ever seen a younger man study something old, then wipe it from his mind, knowing he will live longer?

"Those who notice most are often good at hiding," said Converse. He got up and went away, leaving me to pay for his half-eaten breakfast.

JACK TORRANCE

Jack Nicholson in The Shining, *1980,*
directed by Stanley Kubrick

Born on October 4, 1938, in Bedford Falls, Nebraska. I should know. He went away from there in 1954, east, to the great cities, calling himself Jack Torrance. He would do nothing except the most menial and humiliating jobs, for he had made up his mind to be an artist. Every night of his life he spent in movie houses. Then he went home to his room and watched more films on television until he fell asleep on their copycat plots. Then he got up and went to his work. He had no friends and he never made contact with his family. People vanish in this manner every day.

By the time he was thirty, Torrance had decided to write. When he went to work, he took with him a black briefcase that contained the manuscript of all his writing. He was so unwilling to risk losing it. In time, he went back and forth from his job, operating copying machines, with two suitcases and a briefcase filled with paper. He had never shown any of his work to another human being.

Then in 1973, he met and married a woman named Wendy. "What you got in the bags, hon?" she wondered. "Oh," he said, rolling shyness and pride around in his smile, "just my books, my works." "Can I see, hon?" It was an innocent enough request—it would have been unkind not to ask. "Why no, my sweet, certainly not," said Torrance, smiling again at her crestfallen face. She looked like a little boy who had, all along, been pretending to be a grown woman.

But as this married life went on—Jack hardly knew how—Wendy grew large with child. "Maybe you should get a better job, hon." She had a way of almost talking to herself. "Now that we'll soon be three. Why, you could teach, dear, knowing as much as you know. Wouldn't you think?" And he simply watched her, letting his inner groan climb silently to where the gods of *belles lettres* could smile at it.

He found a job in a private school in Vermont teaching English, and their son, Danny, was born there in the middle of a blizzard so severe that it delayed the arrival of the midwife, thereby allowing the death of Danny's twin brother. "What do we call him, beloved? The better to distinguish him, I mean." "Who, hon?" asked Wendy from her bed of convalescence. "The boy, the other one." "I don't know. Do we call him anything?" "Ah," sighed Torrance, "shall we say Tony, then? I think it would make everything a little more meaningful." "Sure, hon," said Wendy, sucked at by Danny and overawed by Torrance.

Vermont was not good, not with six months of winter, then mud and sticky heat for the rest of the year. Moreover, Torrance had begun to send his works to publishers, magazines and literati. They all came back, with a speed shown by the postal service on no other occasions. He was drinking. In one bourbon temper he had seized Danny and made to demonstrate a Luis Tiant curveball with him, only for the boy's shoulder to be dislocated. In Dickensian contrition, Jack gave up drink, pouring eleven bottles of the amber out into the snow (keeping only a snifter for an emergency).

To smooth over the ugly incident, they all moved to Boulder, Colorado. There Jack would settle to write his masterwork. But awkward realities intruded—the friendliness of neighbors, the humdrum need to make ends meet, Torrance's own extraordinary laziness and the little chatter all day long between Danny and the imaginary being who lived in his mouth, Tony.

Therefore Jack answered an advertisement requiring a winter caretaker for the Overlook Hotel, deep, deep in the mountains. It was a large, old-fashioned luxury hotel, attractive and salubrious in the summer, but inaccessible from October to May. The management needed someone to be there, to answer the radio, maintain the heating and so on. It was an ideal job for a writer, and yes, of course there was room for Wendy and Danny, too. Room? Why there were 237 rooms, not to mention the variety of bars, restaurants, games rooms, solaria, ballrooms and hideaways.

Torrance bundled his work and his family into their yellow Volkswagen and headed into the mountains in the first somber chilliness of October. They arrived as the last of the summer staff were leaving the Overlook, including the black cook, Hallorann, who took a special shine to Danny. Torrance was reminded by those departing of how an earlier caretaker—named Grady—had been so weighed upon by the isolation and the eerie serenity of the Overlook that he had chopped up his wife and two children, in small pieces, as if preparing a ragout.

Life went on in the Overlook, Danny going up and down the monstrous corridors in his pedal car, Wendy making breakfast for three in a kitchen equipped for three hundred, and Jack in the privacy of an abandoned sun lounge conjuring up the mood and creatures of his fiction. He became a little more dreadful—I say this, and who could be more reluctant to admit it? He was churlish to his family, even while he was imagining going into one of the hotel's empty bedrooms to find a tall, Nordic nude (a woman) arising from the bath to give him a wet embrace. But even in his dream he hated himself. For this siren changed into a hag whose ulcerous sores set him screaming. "Don't whistle through your teeth, hon, puts my nerves on edge." "Does it, dunghill?" And so on.

What was he writing all the time, in those empty, sun-blanched rooms where the timbers creaked and the outer brightness of snow rose like a tide against the glass? All those years of solitary movie-going, a pastime that left him forever pale, had degenerated into a vast, God-forsaken novel (albeit masquerading as a work of reference) involving the characters from those movies, their lives enlarged beyond the scope of the films. A mad book, a unique book, but not his own book. And like all thieves, he went in dire terror of being stolen from. That was why he left a top-sheet on this pile becoming a book, covered with the dittos of one line, "All work and no play makes Jack a dull boy."

In his mania, Jack was meeting Lloyd, a barman, in the Gold Room, and coming back from those imaginary conversations drunk. He had encountered a butler, Grady, in the crimson-and-white gentlemen's bathroom, who had advised him to "correct" his family.

Far away in Florida, Hallorann picked up a telepathic call for help from Danny, and set out for the Overlook. Torrance became violent, and Wendy had to homer him with a baseball bat, a Carl Yastrzemski, as it happens. She shut him up in the food store, but someone let him out—was it Grady? could a ghost open a door? Hallorann arrived only to have Jack bury an axe in his panting parka! Wendy and Danny fled for their lives, out into the moonlit snow. In a maze without a center, Jack chases his child, driven back into boyhood, until he stops, numb and weary, the steam of his sweat turns to frost and the last grimace of Torrance becomes an ice entrance to his dead mystery.

Wendy and Danny make it away in the snowmobile that Hallorann has arrived in—that's why he was needed. And in the hotel, the aimless eye of patience, with months to go before the thaw, sees a group photograph on the wall, with a young Jack there, Jacko even, and the date: July 4, 1921—it's a holiday picnic, and isn't that Evelyn Cross in a burning white frock, and. . . ?

But no human eye saw that picture, and in the May that came, Jack's stiff corpse was dropped in the earth, a bone for it, and Wendy was notified by letter.

Ah, you say, what happened to that work-in-progress?

> *I have a special fondness for Jack. He taught me that I might be mad, instead of just unhappy—quite a striking addition to my role. And then he sprang to life, so real a character that he chose to steal the half of the book already written and make off down the beanstalk. I had to give chase, of course, but through tears of love for him for seeing such promise in the story so far.*

VIVIAN STERNWOOD

Lauren Bacall in The Big Sleep, *1946,*
directed by Howard Hawks

Born in 1907, in the Sternwood mansion on Beacon Hill in Boston, Vivian was the first child of Colonel, later General, Guy Sternwood (1869–1941) and his new wife, Millicent Webster, a great-grand-daughter of Daniel Webster. Vivian's father was one of his country's most respected soldiers. He had fought in the Philippines against Aguinaldo, and although trained as a cavalryman he had written a short book, *An End to Horse Power* (1904), that predicted many of the military developments realized in the First World War.

During Vivian's childhood, the Colonel fought in Mexico with Pershing, and then in 1917 he went to Europe. He was instrumental in directing the strategy of the 1918 Meuse-Argonne offensive, one of the few decisive attacks of the entire war. However, in October 1918, he was seriously wounded when a shell hit his car. Both legs were broken and there was extensive damage to his hips. He endured seven operations, and managed to walk a little until 1922. But, thereafter, he was confined to a wheelchair. Rather than suffer the New England winters, the Sternwoods moved to Los Angeles, to 3765 Alta Brea Crescent, a property purchased for the General by Noah Cross, an old colleague from the cavalry.

Guy Sternwood's last great defiance of his disability was to have another child, a second daughter, Carmen, born in 1920. She was thirteen years younger than Vivian, who came to fill many of the roles of a mother to Carmen when Millicent Sternwood died in 1925. With the General incapacitated, and looked after by John Norris, his orderly from the Western front, the two sisters resembled mother and child. Yet there was no affection between them. Vivian was tall, sophisticated and ruthless when she had to be. Carmen was a gamine, a child-woman, helplessly cunning. The sisters disliked each other, and kept company as a way of practicing their malice.

Vivian's own life centered on her friendship with Evelyn Cross, the daughter of the Sternwoods' benefactor, and a truer sister than Carmen. When Evelyn suffered her teenage breakdown, and had to go away to a family property in the redwood country, Vivian went as her companion. General Sternwood was happy that his family could repay the debt to the Crosses, but he was perplexed that Vivian would not tolerate the least mention of Noah Cross.

In 1928, Vivian married Esteban Hernandez, an actor brought up from Mexico by B. P. Schulberg in the vogue for "Latin lovers" that followed the death of Valentino. Hernandez made a few films, with some success, especially *Swords of Toril* (with Barbara La Marr), but his accent was too heavy for sound pictures. Vivian had met him in 1926, at the Hearst ranch. She enjoyed his cheerful indifference to his own career and his stamina in bed. But, out of work and money, Hernandez went back to Mexico, to Agua Caliente, in 1930. He kept in touch with Vivian, but he knew she did not want to live south of the border, and he was developing business interests that kept him occupied. Simple divorce proceedings took place in 1931.

By then, Vivian was keeping company with C. C. Julian, the Canadian entrepreneur whose fraudulent oil company had caused a scandal in Los Angeles in 1927. Divorced by his first wife, Julian was promoting mail-order schemes. He and Vivian were secretly married in 1932—for Julian had hopes of using her as a contact to the Cross fortune. A year later, Julian fled the country because of mail-fraud charges. Both Vivian and the thirteen-year-old Carmen went with him, by boat to Hawaii and then to Shanghai. Their revels came to an end in that city: Julian killed himself after a riotous party at the Astor Hotel. It was all Vivian could do to disguise Carmen's part in the orgy and to put blame on "an allegedly nineteen-year-old secretary," from Chifu, not seen again. Shanghai was Carmen's coming of age. After that, she assumed any man wanted her, and she asked strangers if they knew how the Chinese screwed.

Back in California, Vivian sent Carmen to the Rutledge School up in Mendocino. But no school could hold Carmen. She seduced those appointed to guard her, and then escaped while they slept. She came home on a truck she had picked up in Oakland and led out of its way by a day's journey. The driver was pale and anxious to be rid of his passenger. Vivian had Carmen examined by a specialist. He said she was calculating, not mad. A nymphomaniac? No, merely a wanton, without inhibition.

So Vivian got on with life and in 1936 she met Sean Regan. He was an Irishman, always spouting bits of Gaelic, an officer in the IRA, in America illegally, doing what exactly? Raising money, some said. But Regan was not energetic. He sat around, telling stories and drinking. He appreciated General Sternwood and he helped bring Vivian and her father closer together; she could be kind to her father when Sean was there. So she married him in a rush of gratitude. That was in 1937, a year when Vivian needed strong liquor or a man with the same effect. Evelyn had been killed on the streets, and nothing anyone could say altered the general opinion that she had been wayward and deranged, a discredit to her long-suffering and public-spirited father. We are in the hands of those who survive us.

It was a year of betrayals. When Carmen met Regan she asked him to go to bed with her, just like that, in front of Vivian, the General and Norris. "Not just now, sweetheart," Sean had said, and Carmen broke into peals of laughter as if they were all to take it as humor.

But later that summer, Carmen found Regan out in the garden doing a little target-shooting with a pistol. She asked him to teach her. So he showed her this and that and gave her the gun. She held it in her small white hand, the fingernails dipped in red.

"Will you now?" she wondered.

"Will I what?"

"What I asked."

He considered and he said, "You're too determined, Carmen."

So she turned the gun on him and shot him in the stomach. He died at her feet, raving idiotically at her composure, so she kicked at his wound with her bare feet until the toes were crimson too.

Vivian buried the body in an oil sump. She told Carmen never to tell their father, and the wide-eyed killer agreed. It was said that Regan had just gone away, as unexpectedly as he'd appeared. Vivian lived somewhere between widowhood and desertion. But then, in 1939, Carmen got into trouble again. A bookseller, Arthur Gwynn Geiger, sent the General several IOUs signed by Carmen. So the General hired a detective, a man named Marlowe, to clear it up.

Marlowe wanted it all out—how Regan had been killed, how Carmen had posed for Geiger in pornographic pictures, and so on. Vivian waited, until 1941, when her father died. Then she went to Noah Cross, told him what she knew and what she guessed, and asked him if he could get Carmen into an asylum and make sure she stayed there.

"At my discretion?" asked Cross, and Vivian was left to wonder what he might do, or have done, to establish Carmen's insanity.

"She's not to be hurt," she told him, and he sighed and smiled and said he'd never hurt a soul. Five weeks later, Carmen entered a hospital in Oregon. Noah Cross took care of the bills and arranged to have her watched night and day.

Vivian was the last Sternwood left alive and free. She was rich and nowhere near old yet. She lived in a strenuous active way, drinking too much and not taking enough care over whom she met. She was reputed to have helped back Bugsy Siegel in his Flamingo Hotel, the beginning of modern Las Vegas. She was said to be the mistress of Jonathan Shields, the movie producer. She was a close friend of Samson DeBrier, and a hostess at some of his gatherings.

Otherwise, she remained tall, illustrious and determined to get what she wanted. It was only that she wanted less, and was readier to seek the oblivion of drink, amusing company or sleeping in the sun. She died in 1972, of cancer. Her will and that of Noah Cross left provision for unending vigilance with Carmen.

L. B. JEFFRIES

James Stewart in Rear Window, *1954,*
directed by Alfred Hitchcock

It was the turning point in Jeff's life, and in the end nothing about it displeased him as much as that. He didn't believe in turning points happening to him. He had photographed plenty of them: a tidal wave shattering a building, a figure lifted off the ground by the bullet that was killing it, a racing car stuck in midair, life-and-death instants. But he had been the cool recorder of them all, and he lived by the principle of never getting into the picture himself. Now there he was on all the front pages, both legs in plaster, with a plan of the courtyard. He had even posed for one idiot, holding the telephoto lens up to his face. And the paper had gotten a picture of Thorwald and put it on the lens. "Peeping-Tom Pix Man Snaps Murder," was the headline, as if he were the only voyeur in New York, a city of windows and vantage points.

Was this what forty-two years of acquired craft had been leading to? He felt trapped, not just by another eight weeks in plaster—if there were no complications, and the surgeon had told him about what to expect at his age—but by the media, the phone and Lisa. Lisa Carol Fremont, a dame with class, turning on a light with each name. He had to marry her now. It was the will of the city and its newsprint love for a hero and a heroine. She could tell him she had proved herself in action, wriggling her hand at him to show him Mrs. Thorwald's wedding ring on *her* finger. Giving *him* the finger and letting Thorwald work out the dotted line across the courtyard to where Peeper Pix Man was sitting and waiting.

Lionel Bartleby Jeffries, born in La Crosse, Wisconsin, 1912. Graduated with honors in English/journalism from the University of Wisconsin in 1934, the first student to get photo projects accepted for credit. He'd stayed in the Midwest for two years working on papers, getting quicker, building his portfolio. He never did atmosphere or portraits, just hard news stuff. He got a jewelry-store robbery on the Loop in Chicago, and he sold those pictures in New York and Europe—with old ladies scattering, and the bag in one jittery thief's hand spilling open, pearls in midair like drops of milk. He was getting known.

In 1937, he went to New York, freelancing. An old La Crosse contact led him to Joe Losey, who was making documentaries for the Rockefeller Foundation. He hired Jeff and it was good work, but Joe had been full of political angles; he liked emotional pictures of poor people. But they got along, arguing all the while, and on the side Jeff had taken a series of pictures of the Mississippi in flood: houses floating, with people perched on the roofs, rowboats full of chickens, that kind of thing. *Life* had bought three of them—it was his first time in the magazine.

He banked on the war. He had no family ties, he'd go anywhere, and this was going to be the first war really photographed in action. Not just rows of Brady corpses and the generals smoking pipes under the trees, but the moments of action. He got *Life* to send him to London in 1940 to cover the Blitz. While he was there, he met some RAF boys who talked about photoreconnaissance. They took him up on a couple of the early bombing raids and he learned about the special cameras.

So he got into the air corps and was promoted and assigned to help set up the photorec. teams. That's how he met Tom Doyle, the best unblinking, blue-eyed pilot he ever knew, the man who was flying when Jeff got the D-Day stuff, the Arnhem pictures and the Dresden night-raid spread. All the while he was flying Jeff was selling pictures to magazines too. *Life* kept hold of him throughout the war, and just assumed he'd be on staff afterward. It was a pinnacle for Jeff, and he realized later that he should have had some other goals so he could keep moving.

From 1946 onward, it was one trouble spot after another: the fighting in India, the Berlin airlift, Trieste, Vienna, Perón in Argentina, Malaya, Korea, sweating with fever, freezing your butt off. Traveling, living in hotels, eating when he could, knowing every journalist in the world but having hardly any friends, except for Doyle, who'd become a New York City detective. No long relationships with women, but the political reporter in London, a translator in Buenos Aires, the hotel manager in Singapore. Women who were there when he passed through, women who didn't want explanations.

Then, in 1953, he'd met L. C. Fremont. She worked for a fashion house and she'd had this idea to pose six models in silk nightdresses up in the Bronx, and she'd wanted a "gritty, realistic" look to it, so she'd asked for Jeff, and as luck would have it, bad luck he told her, he'd been between planes. So he took those weird shots, and there'd been that secretive smile on Lisa's face, and the pictures were sensations. People were that foolish. He got a lot of the credit for them. They were exhibited in museums and later on Susan Sontag had written a piece about them in the *New York Review of Books*—which never had photographs anyway!

Lisa was after him. Not just for more assignments—she said they had to keep on with that "adventure"—but marriage. He liked her. But she was perfect, and he wasn't used to career women, not as people to know or go to bed with. If she came over to his place, she had her calls forwarded and tied up the phone. He wasn't the settling type, not even at forty-two. He'd be active for years yet.

Then the racing car hit him. In the picture it stayed stuck in midair, but in life a wheel had broken his leg. So, just as Lisa wanted, he was laid up, at her mercy. But he *was* lucky, or so it seemed to Jeff. For out in his own backyard something started to happen. The guy at 125 West Twelfth, Lars Thorwald, murdered his wife. Jeff saw it, or enough bits of it to piece the story together.

But that was what got *him* in the papers, and it killed his nerve. It had never happened before, but when Lisa was in the apartment over the way, and Thorwald found her and started in on her, Jeff didn't want to look. He wanted to go to the window and shout out to Thorwald, "Stop! I can see you!" But he hadn't done that. He'd covered his eyes, and then looked through his own fingers. He'd lost his confidence, and gotten a wife instead.

It changed his life. Everything else, up to the day he was killed in the Tet offensive of 1968, had come from that. He married her, and he stayed in New York. The fall had been bad. One leg was never as good again. He wasn't as mobile. Lisa said it was all for the best. She helped him open a studio in Manhattan. He did a lot of fashion work. She got him to call himself Lionel Jeffries, which he hated until LBJ came along and Jeff saw some remote benefit in it.

They got divorced in 1962, when he had an affair with a model. Damn it, how could you look at those broads all day without screwing them? Then when Vietnam got hotter, he came to a decision. He left his studio to his assistant and he went out there as a freelance. But he was fifty-six, and he limped, and the war he'd known before had fronts, fixed targets, things to photograph. In Nam, he was slow and the war was water running all around you. One day he got caught. He started to take a picture of a woman trying to stop the bleeding from her leg, but the woman took out a pistol and shot him. Jeff's last picture showed the flash of her gun, caught in midair. But the flash came all the way and got him.

LARS THORWALD

Raymond Burr in Rear Window, *1954,*
directed by Alfred Hitchcock

He was the son of Swedish dairy farmers who had come to Minnesota on their honeymoon with an intention of staying never divulged to parents back in Sweden until the young couple had their homestead and their first cattle. Lars, their oldest child, never met his grandparents, but he lived with their pictures on the wall, honoring them, and writing to them once a month until they died. He was born on the farm in 1902.

As a boy, home from school, he would go out to the fields and count the cows as they lumbered in heavy with milk. He learned to milk them himself and he walked among them when he was very small, his head no higher than their sad, bashful eyes. Lars liked the simplicity of those creatures, he liked the smell of their dung and the warmth of their milk. He gave the cows names, and he knew them all, so that he grieved if one of them died.

At sixteen, he left school and, without thinking about it, started to work for his father on the farm. He was twenty, when he went to St. Cloud and met Gunnel Strand, the daughter of another farmer, people who had come to America a year after his parents. He courted her and they were married in 1923. He and his father built another room onto the Thorwald farmhouse so that Lars and Gunnel could live there. As the oldest son, it was taken for granted that Lars would have the farm one day. He and Gunnel tried to have a child of their own, but although their love filled their resting hours, no child came.

Then, in 1928, on a winter night, Lars was driving Gunnel home from St. Cloud in a snowstorm. He would blame himself later for one glass of beer too many. But there was ice on the road. The car locked in a skid and the passenger's side struck a tree. Gunnel was killed by the force of the impact, and Lars had to walk the rest of the way home carrying her body.

He never recovered from that loss, he might have stayed happy all his life if Gunnel had lived. He had been brought up to live in slow, calm steadfastness, for good or ill. He remained on the farm until 1932, but then he left. Times were so much harder, the farm could not support as many people. His younger brother, Gunnar, was married with children of his own, so Lars left and wished him luck.

He went first to Chicago (who knows if he and L. B. Jeffries didn't look at each other from opposite sides of the street?), and he worked as a guard at the Art Institute, slowly putting on weight as he sat for so much of the day. Then, in 1939, he decided he would go to New York. He had a second cousin there who worked at Macy's and got Lars a job: a store detective. But it only lasted a year: Lars was not observant enough.

In 1943, he answered an advertisement for a traveling costume jewelry salesman. His beat covered lower Manhattan and Staten Island. With a suitcase of samples, he went on foot, calling at stores and those houses where previous customers had lived. It was a wearying job, but he reckoned he couldn't be choosy. He got used to it, he learned a little about the cheap costume jewelry he carried, about how to get a sale from being stubbornly boring. He learned shortcuts, he worked out the best places to eat, he passed the time of day with Moe Williams and bought a tie or two from her. And he picked up Anna Bryant as a customer.

She was a widow who lived near Willow Brush Park on Staten Island. He met her in 1948, when she bought a brooch in the shape of a rose. She was quite a handsome woman, he thought, and so talkative that his reticence didn't show as much. They went on a date, to see *Sorry, Wrong Number*, and when she had finished explaining its plot to him over their supper, she said, "You know, *we* could get married. We might do that. We both need someone to look after us."

He consented; he could think of nothing else to say. They married

139

and moved into an apartment on West Twelfth Street. It was a little expensive, but he was ready to walk rather faster and she said she could probably get a job. But her health was not good. Not that doctors could put a finger on what was wrong, but Anna spent more and more time in bed. Lars would make dinner for her when he came home, yet she scolded him for being late.

Lars did all he could to interest or divert her. He told her stories about his day, but she said they were too mundane. He read cookbooks to make the dinners more appealing. He said he had heard that L. B. Jeffries, the famous photographer, had moved in across the way. And he used to sit in the dark smoking cheap cigars watching the life in the courtyard. There was a dazzling woman (she reminded him of Gunnel) living in the apartment above Jeffries. Lars decided to kill his wife. It was worth a try and he never appreciated that the whole world thinks of it.

Later, a lot later, when he was on death row in Sing Sing, Jeffries came to visit him. They were surprised to discover that they had been born within three hundred miles of each other. Jeffries had known several Swedes in his youth. He took some photographs of Thorwald and, before he died, Lars saw them printed in a magazine. He had not realized how heavyset and forbidding a man he was. No wonder Jeff had been suspicious.

> *This Thorwald is the best example I know of an unexceptional, downtrodden man, one of the quietly desperate, sucked into a drama against his will, and never acquiring the confidence or panache it requires. It was as if a mistake had been made.*

ALICIA HUBERMAN

Ingrid Bergman in Notorious, *1946, directed by Alfred Hitchcock*

Only children cannot help but see themselves as central figures in what is going on—even if they are outcasts. This is not to charge them with vanity. They may be passive observers or helpless victims, hubs of numbness, a vacancy around which all things revolve. Equally, the contest in large families may spur on remarkable self-centeredness in children. But the one among many *is* in competition. No matter how narcissistic, he or she regards life as a group performance, an ensemble. The only child has an intimation that he or she is the only person alive. His and her portrait of the world is an illusion that regularly taunts the solitary consciousness. Is it possible that the only child finds it harder to believe in things? Does he see all life as a mystery only he has noticed? And what of an only child born to an only parent?

Alicia Huberman was born in Vienna in 1919. She was the daughter of Reinhold Huberman (1889–1950), the physicist, and of his wife, Charlotte, who died when Alicia was two weeks old, of blood poisoning incurred in giving birth. Disappointed by the city, Professor Huberman left Vienna with his child and took up a position at the University of Göttingen. While there, he contributed to the experiments of Gustav Hertz and James Franck, involving the electron bombardment of gases to stimulate light emission. This won them both a Nobel prize for physics in 1925, from which Huberman's exclusion always rankled.

The professor doted on his daughter and was sufficiently alarmed by vulnerabilities in her health to take her to a doctor for a checkup every three months. No serious maladies were found, but the close scrutiny kept Alicia wary of her own constitution. She grew up timid, diligent and successful at school, yet threatened by the way her father, her everyday housemate, the god of her needs, assured her that his work was too complicated to talk about.

In 1934, when Alicia was fifteen, her father told her they were going on a trip to America. She asked why, and he said times were changing in Germany, several other scientists were departing, so why not? After all, he could probably get a respectable position in America. They might be glad to have him there. Alicia did not argue or think of the loss of friends. Her father had been her closest companion. She intensified her study of English and worried about the voyage and the chance of seasickness.

It was as her father had said; it always was, like being told a story. Soon after arriving in America, he was invited to join the faculty of Georgetown University, and they were helped in finding a pleasant apartment close to the campus. In due course, the professor told her, she would become a student at the university. Alicia's English developed very well; it made her more conscious of German being spoken in the house. Her father had colleagues in. They would shut themselves in his study and talk till the early hours of the morning, eating a cake she had made.

In 1938, Alicia entered Georgetown. Her father was still teaching there, and he surprised her by forbidding her to take any of his classes—she was not drawn to them, the subject seemed beyond her—and not to acknowledge him if their paths crossed on the campus. They were to behave "professionally." It seemed like a game, to ignore her father, and it perplexed Alicia. She had a dream in which he no longer spoke to her at home and then one morning asked her, politely, "Who are you, young woman, and why are you living in my home?"

It was in 1942 that Professor Huberman went away. She was not to be alarmed, but he could not tell her where. They could write to each other, of course, but not directly. There was an address in Washington they were to use as a clearinghouse. Alicia had the apartment to herself, and several of her friends from Georgetown made use of it as a place for parties. Sometimes they talked about her father, and one of them guessed that he must be in Los Alamos, New Mexico, the hush-hush research place in the desert. Alicia wrote to the professor asking if this was so, but he ignored the question. Then, when he came home for Christmas in 1943, he was more suntanned than she had ever known him to be. His health was garish.

In 1945, a man called on her with news. He said her father had been arrested as an enemy agent. A random watch on his movements had amassed much incriminating evidence. He would be tried secretly, and was already in detention in Washington. But they would arrange for Alicia to see him. She went, and her father was impenetrable. He talked of the old days in Vienna and what she would do with her life now. He never discussed the accusation, and she lacked the courage to refer to it.

A friend said Alicia shouldn't mope. Parties were arranged, and she learned to drink whiskey. In a few weeks, she was a drunk. Her apartment was one long party. Her father was given a ninety-nine-year sentence. She saw him the same day, and he said it was not unreasonable. She was not to be concerned. Her old fears about this sole relationship being lost were realized. One day a dark man, aloof and cold, was at her party. His name was Devlin. His air of anonymity seemed sultry to her. She let him make love to her. He didn't like her, she knew; so she fell for him.

He asked how she felt about her father. She didn't know the answer. He thought it was a shame and said she could help America. The government needed to know her father's contacts. There was a man in Rio de Janeiro, Alexander Sebastian, whom they suspected. As far as they could ascertain, she had met him once when she was a child. Would Alicia gain his confidence? Was that too much to ask?

They went to Rio together. Devlin would kiss her and then, between kisses, urge her to get closer to Sebastian. She felt like an instrument, without a will of her own. To please Dev she would do it. And Sebastian was kind. He asked her about things, and gave small, attentive laughs if she tried a joke. She relaxed in his company. She began to trust him. Then she remembered he was an accomplished deceiver like her father, someone who could do one thing but not refer to it, just like Dev in their contorted embraces. Then Sebastian asked her to marry him.

She reported this to Devlin, assuming he would overrule it. But he stayed professional, and said why not? To Alicia, it was not horrifying to marry Sebastian: he was entertaining and considerate. It was worse to betray what she felt herself. A spy had to be promiscuous, and she could not manage that. She didn't have the energy to lie. Her health began to deteriorate, and she hated the gloating way Sebastian's mother said, "My dear Alicia"—such a hiss there—"marriage seems to agree with you." The old woman, the authentic Mrs. Sebastian, made "agree" sound like the effort to gulp down something unpleasant.

Alicia had Devlin invited to a big party at the Sebastian home, and that's when he found the earth in the wine bottle. But to deflect discovery of his real search, Dev let Sebastian see him kissing Alicia. Every kiss was calculated. Of course, Sebastian was not fooled. He and his mother began to poison her, very slowly, at the frightful evening coffee rituals. She had claustrophobia. She felt sicker as the slow days passed. She could neither sleep nor concentrate. Something in the lethargy of the poison seemed to suit her fallen state. She accepted it.

Then Devlin came to the house one night, while Sebastian was in conference with the other Nazis. He went up to her room, picked her up and carried her down the stairs. Her weakness let her feel like a leaf swept forward by the wind. To be rescued, we need an inkling of death wish. In Alicia it was now a chain inkling. She went mad—she was not saved—and Devlin was able to go back to business thinking love was a pill.

ALEXANDER SEBASTIAN

Claude Rains in Notorious, *1946,*
directed by Alfred Hitchcock

The parents of Alexander Sebastian planned to meet on the island of Madeira, at Reid's Hotel, for the birth of their child. The mother, Grazina, went there three months ahead of her time to be in the best health. The father, Lorenzo Sebastian ("The Coffee King"), on business in Europe, set out from Lisbon in ample time. But his schooner foundered, with the loss of Sebastian and the crew of six. So Alexander was born in 1893 to a mother actually just widowed, yet unaware of the loss.

The mother moved her son to a home on Lake Geneva, where Alexander grew up. In those years, she handled the affairs of Sebastian Inc. with more astuteness than her husband had managed. She saw to it that their coffee penetrated the market of the United States, all the more significant when European sales were interrupted by the Great War. As a child, Alex had private tutors. In 1911, he entered Christchurch College, Oxford, to read Classics.

During the war, he lived in Switzerland, Brazil, America and England, conducting business under the tutelage of Mrs. Sebastian. He also made himself available to British Intelligence as a source of information picked up on his visits to Berlin. For Alex had secured contracts for delivery of coffee to the German Army. It was galling to mother and son that similar deliveries to France and England were made difficult because of the hostilities. As Alex said at the time, "War should not hinder the flow of necessaries, coffee or information. Only humorless puritanism impedes them."

After the war, Alex took increasing control of the business, and in 1918, aged twenty-five, he acquired the monies left by his father and prudently reinvested by Mrs. Sebastian. There was time for pleasure, too. Alex was a gourmet and a devotee of sophisticated company. He spoke five languages (French, German, English, Portuguese and Italian), and moved easily in and out of the great estates of Europe, bending to all politics, consistent in his charm and his faith in trade. In the early twenties, he was a close friend of King Carl II of Rumania and a go-between for him with his mistress, Magda Lupescu. When that couple was forced into exile, they found a home in the Sebastian mansion in Geneva.

Always interested in novelty, Alex went to Vienna in hopes of being accepted as a patient by Sigmund Freud. He was turned away because there were so many young women ahead of him on the waiting list, and because Freud quickly detected "the balance of a born yachtsman" in Alex. However, Alex liked the city and spent a good deal of time there over the next few years. Among many others, he made the acquaintance of Professor Reinhold Huberman, and one Sunday afternoon he taught croquet to the professor's exquisite but rather fragile daughter, Alicia.

It was in 1928 that Alex had an intense weekend of conversation with his mother. She estimated that Europe was in flux, that a new Germany would be born again soon, destined to engage in conflict with the Reds. Its natural ally in the crusade would be America, the land of capitalism and technology. England and France were finished. The allegiances that had been sensible in the Great War should be reassessed. It was up to Alex to identify the emerging forces in Germany and make contact with them. "I suppose so," he said wistfully, for he could never quite fathom such far-reaching motives, even if intrigue delighted him.

So Alexander Sebastian drew nearer than he felt was tasteful to the leader of the National Socialist Movement. He also devised a plan whereby, in the scuttle of prominent Jews to get out of the new Germany, a few spies might be passed along too. In particular, he advised Professor Huberman on getting to America, establishing a career there which who knows . . . ? "And Alicia will have so much more fun there, won't she?"

By 1937, Alex and his mother had shifted their base to Rio de Janeiro. This was not his inclination. Rio offered less than Europe in the way of society. But his mother pointed out that in an extensive and wide-ranging war it was imperative to be close to one's raw materials. Moreover, South America lay there on the modern globe, a monster asleep, so unknown that it had to become more important.

During the war, the coffee trade was a cover for a courier system that brought information down to Rio out of the U.S. and thence across the Atlantic. It was through Alex's small, adept hands that some of the atomic secrets passed. He did not understand what he was conveying, but he regarded espionage as part of a useful sharing. "In an age of such power as this, secrecy will only lead to undue advantage and precipitate action."

But in the middle of the war—torpid days in Rio, with guilt and shortages pressing on the neutrality—his mother fell ill. It had never happened before. So it was food for his curiosity that he felt neither anxiety nor pity. He cared for her, in the usual ways, but he was indifferent to her fate.

He examined his own life: he was fifty, fit, prosperous, not cast down by the world's war, not spoiled by his advantages. He deserved better. He would make sure he got it. This ambition took precedence over Sebastian Inc. and the future of National Socialism. It survived his mother's recovery. He had at last picked up a proper sense of his own soul. It soared above Germany's possible defeat in the war. Who lost wars anymore? The victors would be obliged to prop up the vanquished.

In this blithe mood, his life welcomed back Alicia Huberman. He recalled the awkward child on a Viennese lawn, perplexed by the narrowness of hoops. He had made a joke about "Miss Hoop-erman" that had kept her laughing for ten minutes. What bliss that she should appear in Rio now a lovely woman. His mother warned him, but he was not deterred by the difference in age. He married Alicia and he was happy for five months.

Then his mother demonstrated how Alicia was an agent of the enemy. Nor did she shirk that task. She explained to Alex that he had put them both in jeopardy. She whispered that Alicia had used him, that she was nothing but Devlin's pawn. He slid back into middle age and he permitted the arsenic to put gradual rings of smoke around Alicia's sad eyes. They gave it to her every night, a drop in her coffee.

Alex had to keep the story from the others. His wife would succumb to her illness. Any other solution might point to the error he had made. And so when that suave thug Devlin came in and carried Alicia away, as if she were a rag doll, he had nothing to do but compose his parched face, go back into the house and admit failure. The silent, thrilled disbelief was his death sentence.

Alexander Sebastian passed away in 1946, in Rio de Janeiro, of a wasting illness that accomplished its end in eight weeks, the invalid meekly sipping coffee every night, watched over by his mother.

WALKER

Lee Marvin in Point Blank, *1967, directed by John Boorman*

He would be Walker still. Though he lay in an empty cell on Alcatraz, shot more times than he could count, looking up at the dahlia stain of rust and time in the corner of the wall and ceiling, he would fear no demise. He would survive, Walker still. There was a power of imagination that could melt away bullets and heal their wounds, as if the film of him being shot could be run in reverse, the bullets breaking out of skin which closed behind them, the slugs rushing backward to their guns and making the exact insertions no matter that the gun kicked just before they arrived or that a flare was sucked back into the gun just before the bullets.

In 1967, at the age of forty-five, with his wife, Lynne, and a wartime buddy, Mal Reese, he had carried out the biggest job of his career, of his life, on a Wells Fargo office. Afterward, they had gone by helicopter to the abandoned prison of Alcatraz, in San Francisco Bay. But instead of dividing up the money, as agreed, Reese had shot Walker, and Lynne, he realized, was party to the betrayal, not simply the beautiful young wife he had met on the waterfront on a rainy day, with the wet making her silk blouse cling to her body, with drops of water hanging on the lobes of her ears, with her brown hair sticking to her brow, but a liar, a traitor, a whore for jovial Mal Reese.

Lying in the open cell, crumpled in one corner, gazing up at the stain in the other, Walker estimated that they had cheated him of a ninety-three-thousand-dollar share. The sum was as odd, round and appealing as his dreams of vengeance. He would get them and count off the ninety-three thousand even if every dollar had to be a leaf of their fine skin. He would go after them. He would be Walker, thumping down however many corridors it took until they trembled at the sound of his coming. As he felt his blood knocking in his head, he heard his own hard shoes on the corridor, walking toward his victims.

He would raise himself from out of the corner and out of the cell, and he would go down staircases and corridors out onto the small island of rocks and brambles to what passed for a beach, and there he would let himself be carried out on the cold currents of water in the Bay. When Alcatraz had been a prison, it was said that no escapees had ever made that swim. But the prison had had central heating and large meals, so that flabby, tender inmates became too soft for the water. The broken Walker was still hard and cunning. He would make no swim; he would let the current of desire carry him to shore.

He would survive. The bullets would be removed or his muscular insides would chew and digest them. They would be lodged there like knots in his wood. He would recover, and as his strength came back he would begin to look around for Reese. And one day he would be on a pleasure boat in the Bay, listening to the loudspeaker describe the impossible waters, when a man would approach him, a man who knew what had happened, a man who would tell him Reese had done what he did with the compliance of the Organization. But Walker could go after him if he listened to the man's advice. This man would be called Fairfax.

Walker would find Lynne, alone, abandoned by Mal Reese, awash on a sea of narcotics and melancholy. She would kill herself the night he came to her, as if she knew that was a traitor's only duty. And Walker then could go after Lynne's sister, Chris, a woman he had always liked, but he had met Lynne first and been lost in her rain-soaked attraction. He would find Chris, and she would agree to help him. There would be no need for explanations. Like two sleepwalkers they would share their dreams.

He would trace them and track them down one by one, the members of the Organization who had welcomed Mal in. There was Stegman, the car dealer. Walker would go to meet him, to try out a car. He would take Stegman on the trial drive, battering the car against walls and concrete posts until the story spilled out of Stegman. And there would be Carter. He would go to Carter's office, and push the man around past one Venetian blind after another, the plastic slivers rippling as the man's body went through them. And he would meet Carter in an L.A. storm drain, but a rifleman would pick off Carter, and Walker would find a parcel of ninety-three thousand cutout pieces of paper, not the money, and only a ribbon of credit cards in Carter's pockets, like an umbilical cord between him and the system.

And Chris would be bait for Mal. She would send word to him that she had always wanted him. And the bodyguards would pass Chris up to the penthouse in the outside glass elevator. Walker would watch her rise. And while Mal was slowly undressing Chris, he would come up too, overpower the guards, until he found Chris and Mal both naked. And he would lead the timorous Mal by a sheet wound round his nakedness to the edge of the roof and then, in panic, Mal would move. The sheet would unwind and his pale nude body would drop to the street. Avenged, but still minus ninety-three thousand dollars.

He would go on, as far as Brewster, the head of the Organization, the one man who could authorize his money. With Chris, he would go to Brewster's L.A. house, lie in wait for him and terrorize him. The flustered Brewster would say all right, all right, you know you're a very bad man, Walker, and Walker might smile to himself. No one would see. But the arrangements would be made, for a drop-off of ninety-three thousand dollars, on Alcatraz again.

And Walker would be there in the sepulchral galleries. He would watch Brewster in the spotlight in the courtyard as the helicopter came down with the package. And Brewster would call out to Walker to come and get his money. But Walker wouldn't go. Then a shot would ring out and Brewster would be dead. And Fairfax and the rifleman would walk down to the courtyard, like a couple of golfers coming up to the green. And Fairfax would say his plan had worked. He would have used Walker to clear a way to the top of the Organization. Then Fairfax would say that Walker could come down now. It would be safe now. Fairfax would open the package to show him the color of money.

But Walker would never go down. He would stay transfixed by the way the dried-out puddle in the courtyard had left a stain like a flower.

CHRIS ROSE

Angie Dickinson in Point Blank, *1967,*
directed by John Boorman

She might have been so many things. This is a country made for pretenders, with an art that tempts hope. She lost count of how many times people told her, "You could be a model, did you ever think of that?" And she made herself available. Born in San Diego in 1942, she moved up to Los Angeles when she was seventeen and tried to be noticed. She had boyfriends who knew people in pictures. And once she went for a weekend on Catalina with a photographer. He did a few poses of her, but he was more taken with the fog. She had been to some studio parties. Once an associate producer took her to dinner and a hotel afterward. He asked if she would fellate him, and she agreed if he would test her. "Shit, no," he said, plaintively, "this is personal." So she walked out. She had decided to be practical and she knew that someone who might become a star could still end up a hooker.

So she told herself pictures were corrupt. She ate health foods, she jogged, she went with a schoolteacher and she looked better than ever until a lifeguard at Venice stopped her and said, "You in pictures?" So she went with him and he was nothing but it was the best sex. It was a limited kind of paradise with him, but Chris was empty because what might have been still appealed to her more.

She had an older sister, Lynne, the wild one, who had gone to Alaska as a waitress and married Walker. Some people called him a psychopath, and Lynne regarded him with fear sometimes. But Chris liked him. Behind that craggy look, she thought, was a weird human who had decided achievement was foolish. They had odd talks in which she went with his silences. "Suppose you think you're good-looking?" he said once. Chris blushed and Walker studied the fire. "It's not worth much," he said. "Won't last."

"I know that."

"Yeah, but it's something," sighed Walker, as if he had thought about it a lot and come away with respect for transience. Chris looked at his sleepy face. He wasn't noticing her, but she felt a tugging at her spirit, as if he were imagining her.

Then one day her mother called from San Diego to say Lynne had phoned and apparently Walker had disappeared.

"What did she mean?" asked Chris.

"You know. Gone off. For good, I think. I think it's for good."

Chris called Lynne but there was only an answering machine. Four months later she bumped into Lynne at a Mexican restaurant on Fairfax. She was tanned and happy, and with another guy, Mal Reese. She told Chris they had been to Acapulco for a break.

"What's the matter?" said Chris.

"I'm doing cocaine," Lynne told her.

"What about Walker?"

Her sister's mood dropped. "What's it to you?"

"I don't know."

"You look good, Chris," resentfully.

"I do?"

"Yeah, bitch. You know it." They laughed and it was over.

That was the last time Chris saw Lynne. Lynne was found dead in her house two weeks later. She'd taken a whole bottle of antidepressants and she'd choked on her gray vomit. Two days later Mal Reese called her.

"Is that Chris?"

"This is she."

"I wanted to say this that time we met, you're a very lovely lady."

"Did you know Lynne died?"

"God no, I didn't know that."

"Tuesday."

"Jesus. Is that right? Are you free tonight?"

She didn't answer.

"We must get together so you can tell me about it."

So they had dinner, and then Mal suggested taking her back to his penthouse apartment for a brandy. He said he knew a man in casting at NBC. Chris went along with it; it held off the isolation. They hardly mentioned Lynne, and when Chris once talked about Walker Mal shut up completely. She went to bed with him, and in the night, as he rolled over on her for a third time, she felt a breeze in the room and she had a brief, untrusted vision of Walker coming to rescue her with a part in a picture. But nothing came except the morning.

> *The happiest man, the most settled and assured,*
> *is flawed if he cannot sleep. And the one to be*
> *tortured and shot the next day has mercy if he*
> *does not have to stay awake.*

MA JARRETT

Margaret Wycherly in White Heat, *1949,*
directed by Raoul Walsh

Born in 1881, in Telluride, Colorado, the daughter of a brothel-keeper, Kitty Reilly, she was named Lucy Gray. Her mother already had offspring—Alvin Brown, Sukie Black, Pence White—and gray was the next color in line. Unacquainted with her father, yet guessing he might still live in the vicinity of the silver-mining town, Lucy developed a forthright questioning manner; every man felt she had her suspicions about him. From the age of seven, she would trudge through the snow, the mud and the summer dust with a six-gun knocking on her slender hip. No one knew whether it was loaded until that day, in 1892, when two fellows held up the Sheridan Hotel and backed out onto the street. "Varmints!" Lucy cried out, to turn them, for she would not shoot a man in the back. Her first shot took one of the bandits in the kneecap, the second went through an onlooker's beard, and the third struck the manager of the hotel, coming in pursuit, between the eyes.

This was not good for the brothel business, already disrupted by Lucy's habit of wandering in and out of rooms looking for her mice. So Kitty, not without a tear, sent her daughter away. The pretext was the child's alarming cough. Common sense put it down to the cigars, but Kitty reckoned it was the altitude. So Lucy was sent to live with a cousin of Kitty's in McCook, Nebraska. She learned to ride there and worked at ranching. But she excelled in shooting competitions, and she was known for her way of aiming while smoking a stogie.

At seventeen, she met William Jarrett in Cheyenne, Wyoming, as Buffalo Bill Cody's Wild West Show played the town. Jarrett was assistant business manager to Colonel Cody, a scrupulous mathematician with a flair for the show business. Sixteen years older than Lucy, he was smitten by her spunk—they met when a mouthful of tobacco juice she had directed at a spittoon (nine feet away) landed on the shiny toe of his shoe. "Were you aiming at it, young lady?" he wanted to know.

"What's it to you, pisspot?" she gave back, not promising a love match, but William could smell out a tender heart, and he bought her a buffalo dinner straightaway. When he learned she was a shootist, he asked for a demonstration: Lucy was part of the Wild West Show before she'd finished buffalo farting. But it was hard for her because Annie Oakley—old souse—was the shooting star, except that she was often too drunk to hit a wall. Lucy was employed to do the real shooting that Oakley had once been capable of. A wagon would come into the arena with Annie up front blasting away on nothing, and Lucy under the canvas plonking the targets. It did not foster friendly feelings between the girls.

Lucy and Jarrett were married in 1898, and a son was born the next year—Cody, after their buckskin boss—in Casper, Wyoming, as the show toured. For the first five years of the child's life, they stayed with the show, roaming the West. But in 1904, they built a homestead in the part of South Dakota near Custer. It was a wild place, with Indians around, and Ma kept the child in one arm and a gun in the other.

Away from the show, William Jarrett was hardly able to chop a cord of wood, much less skin bears or make decent whiskey. So Ma took to doing a little holdup work in small banks in Nebraska. She would sometimes take Cody along, originally for luck, but once he cottoned on, he was cover for her. Ma had taught Cody to shoot as soon as she'd given him a pipe.

Ma never was sure about the death of her husband, on a camping trip with Cody. But there were things between men you shouldn t inquire into. William had been a worrier, and he was holding her and Cody back. They could get a gang together now. The automobile had put a fresh face on the holdup business, and while Ma had had to go into spectacles, so that her shooting slowed a touch, she was a merciless driver, so long as you had a strong car.

All through the 1920s, the Jarrett gang kept active. There was the bank in Chillicothe, Missouri (1922), the railroad holdup outside North Platte, Nebraska (1925), and the Wells Fargo job in Topeka, Kansas (1927). It happened that I was riding on the train they stopped near North Platte. I was fourteen then, and I had been visiting my grandmother. The train stopped and I could hear a lot of laughter and whooping down the line. I was able to watch out of the window, and I have never forgotten the jaunty wave Ma gave me as she strode around in boots and a cotton dress. She went on, then stopped, came back and handed me a chocolate bar out of her pocket. "There, son." She smiled. Her hand was small and bony; her nails were cracked. The back of her hand was dotted with freckles and she wore a thin gold wedding ring. There was a six-gun in the other hand; it seemed as big as a man's finger in a baby's fist. I kept that chocolate bar for years, till it was hard and black. It was the best story I ever had for my children—that and the one about Johann Tickle. I think Harry threw the chocolate bar in the fire.

Then, in 1928, outside Aberdeen, South Dakota, the gang was trapped in a motor court and Cody set off so as to let Ma get away. Cody was taken and, with a lot of bribing of witnesses and barefaced lies, they were able to get him fifteen years in the state penitentiary.

He was out in ten, but it was a bad time for the family and Ma was never quite the same again without her boy. She was reduced to typing envelopes and baking pies while he was away. What's more, Cody's headaches got a lot worse in prison. That was one of the reasons he was released in 1939, because the doctors suspected he had a brain tumor or something and didn't have a long way to go anyway.

Ma and Cody decided to head further west, and so they moved on into Idaho and Oregon, but it was cold and high there, and somehow Ma had gotten superstitious about living at altitude. She was sure it hurt Cody's head. They did a few jobs, but they lived simply and many a night in front of the fire they'd read Charles Dickens to each other. Actually, that was the period when Ma really mastered reading—and shot an owl to celebrate!

It was in 1942 Cody met the other woman—Verna, yellow-haired tramp. She was from Chico and said they'd love it in the south where it was warm. She got her hooks into Cody—always parading in her underwear and pouting at him—and they got married, damn it! Then in no time Ed Somers was coming by, an "old, old friend" of hers, full of ideas for a new gang. Ma could see Verna had the hots for Ed—greaseball hunk, he was—and she could tell that Cody didn't always catch on. He needed looking after still.

So, anyway, in 1945, the new Jarrett gang held up a train in the Sierras. Then all hell broke loose. Cops were out after them, and Cody said he'd had enough. He turned himself in on a smaller job (three-year sentence, he thought) just to get the heat off. But they gave him another fifteen in Folsom, so he knew he had to crash out. Ma looked after the so-called "gang": most of the time it was telling Ed and Verna to stop using themselves as mirrors. She went to see Cody in prison, and she'd heard that there'd been an attempt on his life there. Hell! If you had to be in prison, you expected security. So she told Cody she'd settle Ed—it had to have been his idea. But Ma was sixty-eight, and Ed worked out with weights. It was a real fight, but in the end Verna put a bullet in the back of her head to shut her up.

CODY JARRETT

James Cagney in White Heat, *1949,*
directed by Raoul Walsh

The headaches had begun as his trick, like a fingertip of grease put on a fastball so that it fell off the table as it neared the plate—a certain additive, a definite effect, illegal but winning. Whenever Cody Jarrett wanted his mother, and didn't want his father around in their precious air, he would curl up, with his hands between his legs, shudder and whisper, "Head hurts." Whatever she was doing, Ma would order his father away, she'd pull the drapes together so that the house became darker and more auspicious, and she'd come to his side, smelling of flour, tobacco and gunpowder.

"Head hurts, Ma," he'd say.

"I know it," she told him.

"You're with me."

"It'll pass, by and by."

As he lay there, letting her gnarled hand stroke the back of his neck, he was dizzy at the lack of pain and his own guile. But as the years went by, and he acted his heart out to hold on to Ma, he noticed that the strain of his belief in the play had begun to make his head throb. Then, once, in amazement, he realized that he was having a headache, unbidden, not ordered. It had stolen up on him, a pain imprisoned in his brow, so that he didn't dare move or open his eyes. "Ma!" he cried in a voice of such fear and agony that it startled the seventeen-year-old Cody and made him afraid of the force in himself. Ma came, and his father came too, two faces looking down into the cradle of migraine.

His father said that Cody was moping in the house. They should go off into the hills, get some fresh air and exercise. "That wood stove," his father explained, "makes the air go stale, and you spend all your time indoors reading comic books." So father and son packed a tent and put on boots. Ma watched them depart, and she told William to come back and get a gun in case of mountain lions. He took the pistol and a box of bullets and put them in the backpack. Cody stood watching, his shoulders hunched, a tense look on his face.

They didn't converse in the hills. His father cooked a meal the first night while Cody gathered wood. He watched his father at work and pretended to be a hostile tracking the white man. He thought how easily he could pick off his father.

"Hey, dreamer!" yelled William Jarrett. "What'd I ask?"

"All right, Pa." Ma would be baking now with a pot of milk and moonshine warming on the stove.

Three days later, Cody came back down the same path toward the house. He was carrying the pack and the same anxious expression.

"Howdy," said Ma, and then an hour later, "Pa coming?"

"No Ma, he's not."

"What's he doing?"

"Got hisself killed."

"How'd he do that?"

"Fell right off a cliff. Body landed in rushing rapids. Swept away."

"Damn it!" said Ma.

"I know," said her son in a heartfelt way.

It passed off.

But Cody had the headaches now like the color of his hair. It went from brown to gray but the headaches didn't grow older or weaker. Ma saw she should never let him off on his own.

It was while he was in prison the first time that Cody got teased by other men about Ma. These guys were always talking about the sex thing and they had pictures of cuties in bathing suits. When he came out of prison, Cody had worked it out that he ought to get himself that kind of woman so he'd be less odd. Verna looked exactly like the pictures, so Cody said he'd marry her. She laughed at him, but then he slugged her good and she got that wicked-bitch afraid look in her eyes. Ma couldn't understand about Verna. She said the girl wasn't good for him. But that wasn't the point. Just keep her around for appearance.

The new Jarrett gang did a lovely train as it came out of a tunnel in the mountains. But one of the gang used his name, Cody, and the driver heard. So Cody gave him one in the gut and the guy tipped over on a lever, and the engine gave off white steam right in the face of one of the gang. He was a goner—blind and helpless.

Back in the cabin, Cody got his worst headache yet; maybe it was Verna's powder-puff scent. Ma took him into another room. "Don't let them see you," she said as he curled in her lap. "Might give 'em ideas." Then she passed him a drink: "Top o' the world, son." That was saying it.

So Cody took a rap on a small job and in the prison he meets this Vic Pardoe, and they get along. One day at lunch someone whispers in his ear that Ma is dead. The head starts to burst. Cody Jarrett gets up ranting and roaring, Cody can see him, and he staggers along the top of the tables before four guards restrain him and carry him out. That guy's nuts, thinks Cody.

The doc is for putting Cody in an insane asylum. But he gets a gun and breaks out with Vic. Goes straight for the old house; it's night when he gets there. Cody gets to Verna; she's so scared she's wetting herself. But all she can do is set up Ed, and Cody plugs him at the top of the stairs so he goes tumbling down. What are stairs for?

Then the gang plans a new job, just to prove Cody's his old self.

Night before it, Cody meets Vic outside the house and they have a regular talk. Vic wants to get into L.A. to see his wife. "You're lonesome, like me," says Cody. "All I ever had was Ma. I was just talking with her. Always trying to put me on top, she was. . . . Maybe I am nuts."

But "Vic" was a cop, it turned out. Liar. Traitor. Knife in the back. Couldn't trust anyone. Cody ended up on top of the gas tank and one of the shots set it off, a column of fire and heat with Cody laughing in it. His headache had finally exploded the world.

BRIGID O'SHAUGHNESSY

Mary Astor in The Maltese Falcon,
1941, directed by John Huston

Everything visible was real: the long legs, her high breasts, the swimming-pool-blue eyes, and the waves of what we call red hair. But redness in hair covers a range of hues all unlike the smart red in a box of paints—there's rust, whiskey, dried blood, paprika and ginger, iron-strong earth, a claret where it meets the glass, one of the russets you find in a Cox's Orange Pippin (an English variety of apple), copperiness, a thin bitter red that could be sour or poisonous, a noble faded red like the red of Raphael. The red of red hair goes on forever, and you've never quite pinned it down. I always wanted a red-haired child, but Mary Frances and I were brown and brown, so it might have been strange and worrying.

Brigid O'Shaughnessy had the unequivocal body of a fine creature. But she was a frightful liar. If you asked her the time, and she looked at her little watch, with a face the size of a dime, instead of telling you it was 8:56 (and you had a train at nine), she'd say, "Oh, it's early yet, just after a quarter to" or, "Heavens, it's nearly ten past. You'll have to stay the night." She had a set of names for herself in the way con men keep a wallet full of cards—she could be Arlene Wonderly, or Stella Leblanc, Hope Middlewhich, Hermione Heigho, Winifred Wadman, Gwendolen Torrance—I don't know what!

She was born in Annamoe, Co. Wicklow, Ireland, the child of a professor of literature at Harvard who was teaching that year at Trinity College, Dublin, and was having a weekend walking in

Wicklow with his wife when—the rain falling—she said, "Horace, I would like us to hurry."

"How so, my love?" he enquired.

"I'm pregnant," she said.

"You didn't tell me," he complained.

Enough of that. There are childhoods so flat you can put a reader to sleep with a faithful account. If I was to tell you how thoroughly and religiously Brigid was brought up, you'd only say, "Well, how is it she turned out an incorrigible liar?"

Cut to when she's eighteen, with a shock of pimento hair only fierce brushing could tame. Straightaway, she carved up men with her falsehoods. She had a beguiling trick of dropping her eyes, lowering her voice and drawing muskily close to a man—all in the spirit of intimate confession—to say, "Dear heart, I have to say something. . . ."

The he in question was like a cork in a vortex. He listened and was moved a mile by her sad tale. Then time passed and he cottoned on that this revelation had been mist. He mentioned it, "I say, my dear . . ." And wham, her eyes were pools of remorse, the blush was raspberry and she came closer still, so that if he'd looked he might have seen the rising of her nipples beneath her blouse. "That *was* a fib, dearest, a half-truth really. I want now to tell you the hard facts. . . ." And so on, a little closer, a little more hushed and momentous, a better show every time.

To cut it all short, we come to 1930 and there she is—red head at morning, sailor's warning—in hot pursuit of the Maltese Falcon, a statuette stuffed with gemstones and a history harder to believe than it is to tell, and anyway who's seen the bird in the last century?

But we all need something to be looking for, and the falcon made a pretty trail by way of Constantinople to Hong Kong and San Francisco. It picked up colorful characters as it traveled: Casper Gutman, Floyd Thursby and Joel Cairo for starters, with Pacific voyages on boats called *La Paloma*—everything a romancer could wish for.

But then in San Francisco, looking for help, she'd gone to Spade & Archer, and in that alley off Bush Street, above the Stockton Tunnel, as Miles Archer came closer to swallow the next sotto voce untruth, she had put a bullet inside him. And later, Spade had worked it out, despite her holding her trembly body against his with that threat of ultimate coming clean in her eye. Imagine a milk-white body with that Titian hair, imagine that, Sam, you were saying to him without opening your mouth except to breathe and let him see the cooked lobster of your tongue.

It could have gone on forever, this farrago of lies and a falcon too heavy to fly. Yet Spade called it quits. Not that he wasn't impressed by the lies or the liar. But he came up with a stuffy quote about what's expected of a detective, how if your partner's bumped off and you know who did it why it's "bad business" to let the killer go. And, anyway, he knew enough to know he shouldn't trust her. He had seven or eight reasons for turning her in and, against them, only the vision of that hair on top of that pale body. So he turned her in, the sap. You know a man like that's a depressive and that one day he's going to come to a full stop, the end of his alley, and never say or write another civil word.

Spade didn't know if they'd hang her or give her life. He never bothered to find out. He was the sort who had read about Lot's wife. Well, they made it life, and who can say it wasn't because, there in the court, she gave the judge the impression of edging closer and looking up at him with the unadorned, woeful truth? "Your Honor . . ." did she begin?

She went to prison, and no one ever knew how, but after two years there, they suddenly realized she was nine months pregnant. She was delivered of a boy baby, named Sergius, but she agreed he should go to an orphanage and not know the glum truth about his real mother—unless she ever found herself in a position to reveal it. He did well, too, in the air force and Hollywood. But that's too much to get into here.

CASPER GUTMAN

Sydney Greenstreet in The Maltese Falcon, *1941, directed by John Huston*

THE BABY EATS HERE! said the sign, in bold red with the exclamation mark like a flame. The sign was attached to a playpen in the window of the best bakery in Mitcham. Mr. and Mrs. Gutman did cakes, pies and puddings, as well as a range of loaves. And they took no less care with those offerings than they did with their rotund infant, Casper, who sat, large, pink and glowing, in the playpen as an advertisement. He had been born in 1879, a thirteen-pound baby. The exertions of the delivery were such that his mother had to be kept on a diet of lard cakes for a year.

Casper's parents were German, and they had come to London fifteen years before his birth. I don't know why. I can't know everything. Look into your own family trees and try to account for all those jagged changes in direction.

As a boy, Casper kneaded the dough. He could crawl into the oven itself to retrieve loaves. He was the delivery boy, and he was always on show at fetes and fairs with a sampling of the family eats. Still, it was his large, contented presence that spoke loudest. To look at Casper was to wonder whether one didn't have room left for just one more turnover, or another slice of crusty farmhouse.

He was spared most of the burden of formal education. Eating or urging others to do so took up much of his time. Yet, by the age of eighteen and at 270 pounds he had amassed a body of diverse knowledge. Without any central preoccupation, he had an archipelago of hobbies and subjects. They included card games, the Great Western Railway, Levantine history, the comic novel, horse racing, the grammar of Latin languages, food (of course), mental arithmetic, the Hanseatic League, bizarre murders, shaggy-dog stories, the life of Sterne, cricketing statistics, papal anecdotes, fire irons, Chinese tortures, the campaigns of Wallenstein, miniature gardens of the Japanese type, the history of puppets, culinary aphrodisiacs and those vagaries of fact that are often lumped together under the title "Believe It or Not."

He managed to be active without ever really doing anything, ubiquitous yet not there when a crucial question arose. His declared profession was stage conjurer, and he did manage the company that included Walter Little. He was sometimes quoted in the popular press, and he sold a few jokes to music-hall comedians of the second rank.

It was soon after 1920 that he became caught up in the quest for the Falcon. The object had first drawn his attention in the coincidence of two of his interests—Levantine history and papal anecdotes. The death of his father (from a surfeit of éclairs) enabled him to sell the bakery to an emerging conglomerate, lodge his mother in a nursing home in Middlesbrough and be off, around the world, following the savage-claw trail of the Falcon. "Ah yes, sir, the Falcon!" he would sigh, the comment coming out of him like a sweet zephyr.

Late in the 1920s, the search grew apace, crowded with competitors, not least Mr. Joel Cairo and Miss Arlene Wonderly. The lady was not anyone he knew, but Cairo and he had crossed paths before: a bridge problem that Gutman sold to the *Daily Mail* for a guinea had been solved by this same Cairo, writing from Tiflis. The trio had their meeting eventually in San Francisco in 1930.

"We begin well, sir and madam," said Gutman. "There is, as far as I can see, no trace of the ordinary among us."

Miss Wonderly began to tell the truth, and Joel Cairo said a modest "when" as Gutman poured jiggers of Wild Turkey.

"Ah, sir," creaked Gutman, "I trust a man who says 'when.' For isn't timing the essence of polite behavior and a good kill?"

Miss Wonderly again, blushing plum, begged to get something off her chest, but Gutman had spied a copy of *Tristram Shandy* in Cairo's morocco briefcase. There followed a digression on the book and its author. For this was one passion that united Gutman and Cairo. They to-ed and fro-ed about Eliza, my Uncle Toby and so forth, their voices making an exquisite harmony: Cairo soft, snakelike and begging; Gutman as boomy as far-off thunder.

A little put out, Miss Wonderly said, "I am afraid I do not know the book or its author." Like gentlemen, they turned the discourse to her and, among other pretty confessions, learned that she had first seen the light in a small Irish town, Annamoe.

"Oh, that is most remarkable," thrilled Cairo.

"Indeed," said Gutman, "for you will be delighted to hear that Sterne as a child fell into the millstream at Annamoe."

Miss Wonderly went ruby with pride and consternation: "Of course, you gentlemen must understand that I had nothing to do with it."

Their laughter had scarcely died away when the San Francisco episode drew to its close. But Gutman and Cairo were well met, and not inclined to trust one another to continue the search alone. Put it another way, the Falcon was probably a pretext. They became a team, doing their best to endure the thirties and the war in travels through Asia Minor, the Orient and South America. When Gutman's funds ran out, in Macao in 1945, he and Cairo took to bridge professionally. There and then, they whipped Bannister and Grisby in a challenge match for $3,000.

As they grew older, they did not think of the Falcon for weeks at a time. The sedentary satisfaction of bridge became more appealing. They made seven spades, doubled, on the Q♣ lead in this hand at Caracas in 1949:

Coata

♠K
♥J32
♦KJ862
♣KJ83

Gutman

♠Q109752
♥KQ86
♦—
♣965

N

W   E

S

Cairo

♠AJ43
♥A109754
♦Q
♣A7

Sternberg

♠86
♥—
♦A1097543
♣Q1042

Their last recorded hand was in 1951, in Marienbad. After that they fade away. But I am confident they went on to campfire soirées in the Matto Grosso, reading a little Sterne to one another, or yarning about the Falcon. It is possible that, independently, they had both reached the conclusion that the bird was too rare ever to be seen, let alone caught or plucked. Yet as I think of them, they would not have admitted that ultimate impossibility to each other. And so they would have gone to sleep blissful in their partnership, tricksters to the world but loyal to the game.

> *I wish I had time to write a dozen Gutman and Cairo stories, all bravado and vulnerability. They might be a great success—erudite, rather inefficient villains. There is no warmer myth than that of ill-matched friendships that go on forever, so moved by their dream that transport becomes their nature. Such creatures might be no longer sure whether they were huntsmen or quarries.*

VICTOR LASZLO

Paul Henreid in Casablanca, *1942,*
directed by Michael Curtiz

Why does no one attempt a life of Victor Laszlo? Did he intimidate actors? He was a liar, of course, and a liar in life may be a bore to deal with. A sad abandoned bore. Every dishonesty betrays the fabric of discourse. We trust the cloth less, and perhaps we speak less when we remember lying. But put a liar in a framework that includes the pressures pushing him into falsehood, and he can become a whimsical hero. There is something redemptive in the honest portrait of a liar, and of why he tricked and cheated. His wretchedness falls away. As for being boring—he may reappear in magical hues.

The life would have scenes in Eastern Europe and on the eastern edge of the U.S.; it would insist on romance taking priority over politics; and it would have the consummate fraud being taken seriously, but declining to fall for the world's earnestness. It would be a black comedy and—as a now elderly but experienced moviegoer—I would like to see Robert De Niro and his freezing smile in the part.

There is no way of telling when or where Victor Laszlo was born, nor whether that is the name he was born with. 1909 to 1911 probably covers the moment itself. As for place, there are Hungarians who claim their nationality not by birth or parentage, but in cast of mind. We know Laszlo was in Budapest in 1919, a child in a suburban orphanage, the star inside forward of their soccer team—all this from a group photograph and one action shot of Victor, billowing shorts below his knees, taking a ball on his tiny instep where it seems as heavy as a cannonball.

By 1930, Laszlo was on his own in Horthyist Hungary, a land suspended in time, busy with its café life, with novels, gossip and theater, torn between old Hapsburg allegiances and the approaching Nazi blight. Laszlo had several occupations. He was an injury-dogged soccer player, written off as a sloucher in the sports pages, but as precious to some fans as Len Shackleton or Tommy Harmer, a man of languid brilliance and inspired passages. He was a cartoonist, a domestic ironist, his men having to balance harridans with gold rings against blondes in short skirts. He was an actor: small parts, handsome but unsound, seductive in the right role but not always audible.

163

And so the 1930s passed, leaving Laszlo a little puffier, a smoker and the husband of Magda Meszaros. He was content at first. Granted regular surprises in his life, he was not deep or demanding. He never disliked Magda. But he could not stop falling for any other woman he noticed. There were affairs, lies about having to see a man about a car, wrong numbers, and sick cousins in the country. This wore him down. The indignity of so many furtive ploys nagged at him. He needed a nobler part and great lines.

So, one day in 1939, he let Magda sniff out details of a liaison with Ivy Horvath, a journalist.

"It is as I suspected," said Magda. She always opened a conversation with drums.

"Do not be hasty," Victor advised her. He felt better already.

"What do you mean, swine?" Oh yes, this was the ticket.

"Have you noticed the state of the world?"

"Cabbage is very dear."

"And why?"

"There is a war coming?"

"And what happens then?"

"What?"

"Spying."

"With that Horvath tramp?" He felt like a comic with a new routine.

"She is a German agent—can't you tell?"

It struck home. "She *is* very jolly."

"I have been asked to see her. Required, really."

"For the country?"

"The Admiral himself requested it."

"You have a letter from him?"

"Would he put such things down on paper?"

His wife went quiet. Who can say she fell for it? She may have swallowed hard and eaten poison. She was dead a year later. But that last year may have been the happier because she credited Victor with a high duty. He sang when he washed up.

Wretched Hungary, leaned on by Germany. Unlucky Laszlo. For his wife could not keep quiet about his secret life. She was so proud, she talked, and talk spread as far as the Resistance. They reckoned this Laszlo must be an agent from another branch of the clandestine tree. So they employed him too, and had him run fearsome risks that he could hardly protest. The only benefit of this ironic plight was that fresh ladies flocked to him, all considerate of his "other" life.

Early in 1941, the "movement" instructed him to make his way southwest, out of Hungary on a long quest for America. It was that or a concentration camp. And so he made his way to Casablanca with Ilsa Lund, fond of her but infatuated with his story.

He arrived in America, and he spoke in large halls about the camps and the darkness in Europe. He went into antifascist raptures; he spoke with reverence about socialism. He thought this play would run forever, and wondered if one day he might be on a stamp. But after the war, he was ostracized. America was all fashion. In the late 1940s, the FBI came to him and said it would be easier if he talked of his own accord. If only they had known! Nothing now could stop his torrent. Still, the actor in him agreed to be reluctant. He let the perspiring government agents trap him in inconsistencies. He could make a cheek muscle flutter in panic. He was patient, letting them coach him into remorse and coming clean. Doctors told him he was ill, but Laszlo shone with the rapture of confession. He went before the House Un-American Activities Committee in a brilliant rendering of pierced shiftiness, correcting his deaf inquisitors on the spelling of names he was making up. Three years later, in 1952, he passed away, leaving as many mysteries as unpaid bills.

> *We are as pleased to see a sham swing through*
> *life in a book or a film as we are ready to enjoy*
> *the screen's smashing to pieces of one car after*
> *another. The wish to keep free from bumps and*
> *fibs in life is so nerve-wracking, do we need to*
> *let the forbidden force have a fling?*

RICHARD BLAINE

Humphrey Bogart in Casablanca, *1942,*
directed by Michael Curtiz

We used to tell stories about Rick. He was only ten or so years older than this writer, but can't you remember the luster that ten years has for a kid? Growing up near Omaha, I used to see him around the city. He seemed tall and unshaven, a wild fellow. But I find now that he never grew above five feet eight. In the few pictures I have of him later in life he seems to be making an effort to look dapper and impressive. In those early days, you heard stories about Rick "borrowing" someone's car for a night drive and outrunning the cops. He had girls hanging around him a lot of the time. He looked bored with them, but he'd let them kiss him sometimes. It was a privilege to catch the dime he tossed through the sunlight and hear the "Hey, kid, get me a Nehi, will you?" I did that twice, and the second time he grinned at me. I thought I felt the sun beaming. Yet I saw Rick's crooked teeth when his mouth bared.

He had been born in Omaha in 1900, the son of a pharmacist. (Later, I know, he said he was younger, and from big tough New York; forgive him—no one in this book has managed without a few lies.) If I remember him as a kid out of school, the figure in the best adventures, older-seeming than his peers, a boy's man, it wasn't that he neglected his studies. It surprised me, on going into it, that his grades were steady and high. He had an A– average, and he kept on working, trying to be better. The more I look at his record now, the more clearly I see a short, diligent man, whose amiability and natural bravery must have furnished his legend. Or was the legend just something I and others like me required? Was he only the conscientious boy who had to act up to it? When you think about how he turned out, you have to wonder whether his disillusion had something to do with that early feeling of inadequacy. Maybe I helped urge heroism on him and it became his curse. But was I supposed to look at the world and not use my imagination?

Richard Blaine went to Lincoln, to the university, in 1918. He majored in history, and he was especially interested in economics. He was one of the group that owed so much to Professor Wilson Keyes, though he and Keyes had heated arguments in class. Rick was already affected by radical ideas, and Keyes was a tough conservative who could never see past the sacrifices imposed in Russia in the name of communism. But that's how Rick grew in our eyes. He was quarterback on the football team his junior and senior years—which was a big thing in Nebraska then and now. But he had a reputation, too, as a red-hot debater and a guy who tried to read Lenin in Russian.

All the same, in those days he still helped out in his dad's pharmacy on Ames. He was generally ready to do a good turn for the old folks. He was best friends with Ralph Hunt, and he was godfather to Ralph's second daughter, Laura, born in 1920. Here's a picture of him outside the church, holding the baby. And Ralph's next to him, holding Mary

Frances's hand. She's gazing up at her younger sister with that fretful look on her face. So young, so worried. Rick looks as proud as can be.

It surprised everyone when he went to Detroit to work in the Ford factory. Rick could have been in management, I'm sure, but he stayed on the assembly line because he said he wanted to get to know the working man. He was there for three years, and he came back a lot harder and a sight less cheerful.

He lived in a room in Omaha then, full of books and Mitzi Glass. They had gone together a little at Lincoln, and she was the best-known radical in town. Because of her great red hair, and her severe looks, people used to call her "Red Mitzi." Now, I'm sure there were some who hated what she believed in, or were afraid of it, but I think a lot of people were fond of her really. Rick loved her. They never got married because they said it was an irrelevance, and that made for a gulf between Rick and Ralph. But Omaha could take him then, without spitting him out. There was never any of the outrage that got talked up later.

Anyway, in those years, Mitzi was organizing farm labor and Rick helped her; he was writing his novel about the automobile industry—*Drums of Steel*—and he was drinking. No one ever denied that. I know some people who'd admired him once gave up on him. They called him a layabout and a lush, and no one much liked his book: it's awkward and high-minded, but the stuff in the factories is good, I think. It was what happened to Mitzi that moved Rick on. In 1930, there was a strike up near Bassett. Strikebreakers came in and Mitzi got hit on the head with a fence post. It took her five months to die but she never regained consciousness. The word was that Rick went into the hospital one night and smothered her. If so, it was merciful.

He went out to California then and he did a lot of organizing with fruit workers. That was hard. The labor was poor, Spanish most of it, and itinerant, and the bosses were rough on union men. Rick stuck to it and that's the period when he joined the Party. But he got pneumonia in 'thirty-three, a bad case. He was always weaker afterward, and drinking still. Then in 1935 he went on a trip to Moscow. It was for students mainly, but Rick managed to go on it and he was there two months. From all I can gather, he came back redder than ever. But he returned by way of Africa, having gone on from Moscow to Abyssinia on some sort of mission.

It was no surprise in 1936 that he started speaking for Spain and the Republic and early the following year he was over there with the

Abraham Lincoln Brigade. He fought all through the war, at Madrid and then in Barcelona. He was a captain, and his health was finally shot by the experience. Worse than that, I think, he was disenchanted. That war, he thought, could have been won. He despaired not so much at the free countries staying neutral, but at the dissension in Spain itself among the various branches of the anarchists and the Communists. In addition, he didn't like anything he heard about the trials going on in Moscow. By the end of the war, he had given up the Party and he was looking for a different life.

Rick was in Paris for a time doing not much, except trading on the black market and carrying on with Ilsa Lund. He was regarded as a cynic by then. The drinking was constant, and not even Sam, a guy who had come out of Spain with him, could keep him cheerful. The affair with Ilsa was hopeless; she had all these causes, perhaps Rick used her to remind himself of all he'd lost. He wanted it to fail, he was dependent now on self-pity. So when the Germans came in, Rick got out. As I heard it from Sam, Rick was going anyway but later he persuaded himself that Ilsa had let him down.

He got to Casablanca and he opened the Café Americain, where anything was possible. You could buy or sell whatever you wanted —jewels, drugs, papers, lives—it was a rat-race of a market. There were people of all nationalities and persuasions. The war was held down by money, greed and fear. It was an ugly place, and the movie they made romanticized it and Rick. He was as vicious as he had to be by then, just taking his cut on whatever happened, OK-ing every kind of deal and arrangement.

The big new thing in his life was Louis Renault (1891–1964), the head of the Vichy police in Casablanca. Apparently he took one long look at Rick and knew he was homosexual underneath all the brooding and the sneers about women. He could see Rick was dying too, and he was decent enough to do what he could for him. After Strasser was killed and the weird but wonderful Victor Laszlo got away, Rick and Louis slipped off into the fog together. They went south, to Marrakech, and they lived there after the war, until Rick died in 1949. I can see him sitting out in the sun, slipping a coin in an Arab boy's hand in return for one of those sweet cordials. Louis took the best care of him, and at the very end they were laughing together over reports of the red scare in America.

ELSA BANNISTER

Rita Hayworth in The Lady from Shanghai, *1948,
directed by Orson Welles*

"You need more than luck in Shanghai," did she say? And more than one man to give you a name anyone would remember?

Is evil an unequivocal current in the world, a primary color in human nature? Is it useful or necessary to preserve the word? Was Hitler evil, was Noah Cross, was Elsa Bannister? Or should we rescue them a little and say they were disturbed, in the hope that actions such as theirs are automatically demented, quite outside ordinary human nature? If they were mad, then was all the harm they did meant in the hope of some larger good, and did madness blind them to the truth? Or were they just as deliberate and careful as an author, inventing a bad character, and then letting themselves slip into it, enjoying the wickedness as any child might? Is evil just a notion we share, a word in common, or is it a box that all of us must look into once at least?

I met Noah Cross once, in Omaha, at a party for Potter when he was ninety. Well, not quite met, I suppose. Saw him, asked him a question and got an answer. We say we have met the famous when they are unaware of us. We treat them like sites and wonders, and come away with snapshots. I knew some of the things he had done, and I think I regarded him as someone who just lost control. Not mad but weak, weak in a way that seemed to him like strength. But he proved a witty man, a man in control, capable of fine discrimination in cutting and eating a broiled sea bass, in recollecting a hand of bridge, or in describing the talk at San Simeon and judging whether Louise Brooks was to be trusted. He spoke in elegant sentences; his eyes twinkled over nice points, as if he were teaching them to good students; he declared himself a devotee of doubt and moderation. He seemed neither mad nor compulsive. He said to me, confidentially, "You see, Mr. . . . Bewley, most people never have to face the fact that at the right time and right place, why, they're capable of anything." It was a dark, brazen estimate, but he made it sound encouraging. I suppose we did meet, even if he fudged my name and offered that motto to any local building-and-loan man—dry sticks who deserved a shiver.

So Elsa was born in Chifu, in China, in 1918. Born in what was called a house of joy at that time and in that place, the child of a whore named Poppy Munson, a Eurasian of a rare kind, I gather, with Oriental features and fair hair. "Blue, blue eyes, but slanted in their secret way," said Cross. He had been in the East at that time, and he declared—in a spirit of generosity—that he was the father of Elsa. I doubt that anyone could know that for sure. Poppy Munson had too many Caucasian clients. But Cross believed enough in doubt to use it.

Elsa Munson was brought up in her mother's trade, and she was famous as a child prostitute. Sailors told stories about her. We cannot say what she thought of this, whether she was hurt or complacent, whether the ordeal unbalanced her or seemed matter-of-fact. Whatever, she was a party to the orgy at the Astor Hotel in Shanghai in 1933 terminated by the suicide of C. C. Julian. Yet two healthy adolescent girls could surely tip a drunk out of a low-silled window if they felt the urge. If they were bored, horrified or out of their minds. If they were evil, or curious about evil's reputation.

Cross sent money for the girl to be brought to America. He put her in a boarding school in Connecticut, had her taught English, go to dancing classes, eminent doctors and fashionable priests, turned out a polished woman. Then he sent her one of his lawyers to arrange her adult affairs. This was in 1939, when she was twenty-one. The lawyer was Arthur Bannister, a lurching figure on two sticks, a crippled frog without the power to jump for himself.

Elsa married him, to get out of her finishing-school prison. Of course, he looked at her askance as any hobbling lawyer nearing fifty would wonder at a beautiful young woman picking him. But a lawyer is no novice with iniquity or compromise. He could see the liberty that Elsa was winning, as well as the sly jokes that would play to his back. But he would abide by the uncertainty and the jealousy. And if he ever felt shame, then he could contemplate the times when Elsa, like a dainty cat, would have to roam over his broken body at his instruction. A kind of usefulness held them together.

Bannister was transformed as a lawyer. He relished his ghastly lame-spider walk from table to witness. He extended it, sucking in attention. His strategies became bolder. An exhibitionist had always been masked by his crippled condition. Aroused by Elsa, he came into the open. His reputation and his income increased. He was talked about, and always the young, blonde, baleful-eyed wife was alluded to as the secret in his career.

Bannister took a partner, George Grisby, a brilliant, unstable man whose trial tactics were notorious. Their practice was based in San Francisco, on Montgomery Street, and their fame spread on a series of bizarre murders and society divorces. Elsa presided over one of the big houses on Washington Street, near the Presidio, keeping small dogs and romantic poets around the place, an icy hostess at dinners for other lawyers, a woman who seemed old already—never quite young or hopeful, never exactly American, never flawed by a single rash dream. Evil in idleness, perhaps, a lazy evil, too indolent to strike, bored evil, a variety that can float on unmotivated cruelty.

In New York on a summer night, she was riding in a horse-drawn carriage when hoodlums tried to rob her. A strolling passerby, Michael O'Hara, rescued her and drove her back to her hotel, yarning about China, Macao and sundry haunts. He had a half-caste look himself, high cheeks and narrow almond eyes full of self-love. He had a drugged face, and he was so large, so garrulous, so very innocent that Elsa thought to take hold of him like a balloon and make him squeak. She got Bannister to hire him as bosun on their yacht. Wasn't Michael a sailor, reeling along on dry land as if riding a swell?

Their yacht, the *Circe*, was headed down to the Caribbean, and then by way of the canal and back to San Francisco. It was the Bannisters' vacation, and Grisby was brought along to keep them amused. Elsa could see that Michael adored her; anyone could guess why she had had him hired. It inflamed him all the more that Elsa took their love for granted instead of letting him win her in his slow, romancing way. But she let Michael see Bannister humiliate her, and she was breathless with excitement the night Michael compared them all to a sea of sharks drunk on blood. It was like the stink of an orgy. Did she think she might destroy them all? Surely she never believed in going off with Michael to a house on a high cliff, called Nepenthe, where they would be happy. Happiness was not her thought. She was irked by existence, and wanted it to burn with the heat of the sun. Elsa was captivated by pictures of the new atomic explosions, a death by light.

The *Circe* sailed through fermenting seas, they picnicked on islands, dived from rocks and canoed on rivers filled with snakes, alligators and flamingos. In San Francisco, there were two killings and a trial where Bannister cross-examined himself. Elsa smiled at his mockery of the law. Finally, a bewildered Michael—a baby bull—ran away from the court. Elsa found him in a Chinese theater on Grant. There in the dark his hand felt the gun in her silk bag. "I was taught to think about love in Chinese," she whispered to him, her mind set on the Chinese show; but he had guessed the truth from the hard shape.

It all ended in the fun house with her and Bannister shooting at images of one another until all the mirrors were gone and only the real bodies stood up. And so they killed each other amid all the broken glass. Was she evil? Was she to blame, or did those early influences explain her malice? Is destruction an energy that takes us all at some time or another? Or is a woman as dark as that because so many men fear the way she provokes them? Elsa Bannister, dead at thirty. Evil's such a grand word, good's such a towering thought. I rule them out in favor of another pair—bored or hopeful, fatigue or life. As Bannister said himself in the fun house, "Of course, killing you is killing myself. But I'm pretty tired of both of us." That thing called "evil" has been through disappointment first. It thinks itself betrayed by life and wants revenge.

ADELINE LOGGINS

Tatum O'Neal in Paper Moon, *1973,
directed by Peter Bogdanovich*

In Bogue, Kansas, on a July day in 1936, they were burying Rose Loggins. Just the preacher, Rose's nine-year-old daughter, Addie, and a scattering of Bogue people including the man driving the car when Rose was killed, and his brother, for moral strength. Moses Pray came by as they were tossing in the earth. The noise of it gave him start number one. Number two was finding it was supple Rose turning stiff as the boards.

Moses was known a little in Bogue, but only a little because if you are in the business of selling Bibles to widows you have to keep moving; when customers see you it should be for the first and only time. So much acquainted with widowhood, Moses was especially sad to come upon a recently deceased lady, and a lady alone, for Rose Loggins had never obtained, or sought, benefit of clergy.

He had scarcely had time to put his hat back on at the close of the simple ceremony when those neighbors charged by Bogue with delivering Addie to her Aunt Billie in St. Joseph, Missouri, dumped the kid on him. He had a car and he had let on, while still distraught and before they had hinted at the child's destiny, that he was going in that direction. This Addie was a blunt little nut who looked like a boy and turned fiercer than a girl if you made that mistake. There was also the uncalled-for suggestion from those Bogue hicks that since Moses and Addie had such a resemblance . . . How in the world anyone saw *that* Moses did not know; he could barely recollect now, all those years later, whether he and Rose had ever, even once, partaken in a way that would bring even the *chance* of truth to those coy, sidelong looks.

So Moses just took the dour child, with her belongings, to the Bogue depot to put her on a train. That was reasonable since he had, so to speak, been presented with $200 by the car driver's brother on account of the accident. Whatever was left from that after the one-way to St. Jo would be compensation enough to Moses for the good deed.

However, at the depot, Addie pipes up with the idea that the $200 is rightly hers since the brother had meant it for Rose's surviving child, and now Moses was stealing it. Furthermore, she was herself suspicious that she might be Moses's kid. You have to be so careful what you say in front of the young. Just to avoid an ugly scene, Moses sold back the train ticket and put the brat in his car.

So Moses set out for St. Jo reckoning to play the Bible game along the way and deposit the girl with as much of the $200 as she could count before he was off. The Bible game was very simple. You bought a paper with all the death notices. You saw that Pearl Morgan, say, had lost her hubby. You found where she lived, got over there and picked out a nice Bible in red or blue leather and you quick-printed on the front, "For Pearl." Then knock on the door and, "Good day, ma'am, I'm just delivering the Bible Mr. Morgan ordered. . . . Oh, no! He's dead? . . . Well, I am devastated. . . . Yes, that's right, ma'am. . . . 'For Pearl' it says. . . . Oh, *you*'re Pearl. . . . Now, you don't have to take it. . . . Well, it is $6.77." Whereupon Addie interrupted and said, "Oh no, Daddy, remember, this is the $9.54 edition." Just like that!

One way and another Addie got herself into the act. He didn't know where she'd learned some of her tricks, like the twenty-dollar-bill routine. She even outlived Trixie Delight, a vaudeville artiste Moses picked up in Cawker City. At first Moses had just thought Addie was downright jealous, but he took a better view of her when she alerted him to how Trixie was taking a little bit on the side from Floyd, the desk clerk at their hotel. After that it was just Moses and Addie getting on with the father-and-daughter show, though Moses was always careful to insist they were not kin.

The last bit of Kansas they took in a rush because some sheriff was after them: they had sold his own whiskey to a bootlegger who happened to be the sheriff's twin, yet more fraternal than identical. But they made it over the river into Missouri and thought they were safe in St. Jo when the sheriff turned up and just beat Moses black and blue. Moses took Addie to her Aunt Billie's and the child resigned herself to the new home. But in two minutes she knew how dull it was going to be, and before three she was running down the road after Mose. On those Midwest roads you can see in your rearview a mile behind you.

That settled the partnership; they got along very well for the next few years, without ever having to discuss whether it was business or sentiment that kept them together. We come to 1942, with Addie now fifteen, and a forward fifteen, showing just what can be done with good bone structure and a young woman with lipstick. They were in their hotel room in Ponca City, Oklahoma, when this conversation ensued.

"Mose?"

"Hmm."

"Mose."

"What is it, honey?"

"You're absolutely certain, are you, that you're not my father?"

"How many times do I have to tell you?"

"Hmm."

"Anyway, I'm only thirty-three, hardly old enough to be your father."

"No?"

"No."

"You'd have been seventeen. Couldn't you do it then?"

"Well, who knows? I wasn't doing arithmetic. I didn't do it, that's all that counts."

"Hmm. I think that's an excellent thing."

"Certainly is."

"Excellent."

"How's that?"

"Well, Mose, the way I'm beginning to feel about you, it'd be a shithouse if we were kin."

"What?"

"Oh come on, slowpoke."

"Button that up!"

"Mose!"

"What do you think you're doing?"

"Cuddling."

174

"Cuddling!"

"Seeing as we're not father and daughter, I think we should take advantage of all these shared hotel rooms."

The very next day Moses Pray joined the army and got off to war. It was one duty taking priority over another. The country was vulnerable, and he knew that Addie would get by.

JAY LANDESMAN GATSBY

Alan Ladd in The Great Gatsby, *1949,*
directed by Elliott Nugent; and Robert Redford, 1974,
directed by Jack Clayton

So much of it comes back to the mystery of being a Midwesterner. But in attempting to describe that, you must be able to say where the area is. There was a man once who said, without a flicker of irony, that San Francisco was the part of the Midwest he hailed from. Earlier today, doing a crossword, Mary Frances asked if Pennsylvania was ever considered to be in the Midwest.

Why not? The Midwest could be that mathematical center, a pinhole, or it could be all "the dark fields of the republic" between two narrow coastal strips, like the body inside its skin. Then there's that *New Yorker* cartoon, like the surrealist map of the world, warped by feeling, with desert prairie beginning on the other side of the Hudson, and stretching as far as the Pacific. When Americans use the term don't they think of a space of tranquillity or absence in the heart of the country, in the heart's heart? The ruffled dun-colored carpet across which coast-to-coast flights must pass, the uneventful land below while the movie plays at thirty-seven thousand feet?

I'm looking now at the Rand-McNally; it's one of my favorite books on America. I'm studying the two-page spread on Nebraska. That's Midwest to most people. It's a state determined by straight edges, except in the east, where the crinkle of the Missouri breaks the rectangle. And it's geometrical-looking inside the boundaries, with straight-line roads, the tidy blocks of counties, and so much white space to make the lines look bolder and more confident. Lines can go frantic there, the way taut wire curls up when it snaps. Up in the northwest of the state, there's Cherry County, "where the hay is so

fine,'' said Willa Cather, ''and the coyotes can scratch down to water.''
As far as I can tell, the county is ninety-five miles by sixty-two miles,
that's 5,890 square miles. Yet, really, on the map it's a picture of
nothing. There's a row of small towns in the north, along 20, and two
roads going north-south, 61 and 83, with hardly a notch on them.
There are a few lakes, the threads of rivers and the McKelvie National
Forest. But it's bare, flat and empty. Maybe the most interesting
thing in the county is the place where Mountain Time meets Central
Time, out there in the nothing, with an hour in a single stride.

There's so few people in Cherry County, and so few who'd want to
be there. If Nebraska means dullness in Manhattan or on Russian
Hill, then Cherry County is what Nebraskans regard as the back of
beyond. And in all the high-pressure places in America—where books
are published, movies produced, the country governed, the money
counted, TV generated—the Midwest stands for that sleepy space and
the anonymous audience. ''The dark fields of the republic''—extensive, conservative, unenlightened, pastoral. A place where, if you
stay, you are seemingly content to be lumped in with the average, the
quiet and the normal. A part of the nation where all the writers on the
fringes imagine exists an archetypal uncomplaining Americana, like
Bedford Falls.

As if there isn't strangeness in Nebraska. As if the wind coming
across all that flat warm earth couldn't make a person feel the terror of
being fifteen hundred miles from sea in any direction, choking in the
dry aroma of wheat and dirt, until your head feels full of chaff. As if
the straight roads didn't have sudden, inexplicable kinks in them, like
the barbs in wire. The Midwest is taken for granted. It is not
glamorous or romantic; it is not noticed because the movie is playing
then, and because from that height there is so little to see. But don't
think the Midwest doesn't long to be in the movie. Let me tell you:
Marlon Brando, Montgomery Clift and Fred Astaire, all born in
Omaha; Robert Taylor in Filley, and Henry Fonda in Grand Island.
No, there's great acting and dreaming here, like barbed wire in our
heads.

James Landesman Gatz was born in Kulm, North Dakota, in 1890.
He was the son of poor farming people. Not much interested him
except the thought of getting away, improving himself, being popular
and successful. As a teenager, he set himself a schedule of exercise,
work, reading and elocution. He resolved to keep out of saloons, take a
bath every other day, save money and so on. He reckoned he could be
a hero and a famous man. He saw his task as having to find his

happiness and live with it. In America, the poor and the unknowns, some of them, quiver with impatience and humiliation.

When he was seventeen, he went off to St. Olaf's College in southern Minnesota, but it didn't work out and he took to beachcombing along the shore of Lake Superior. One day he saw a yacht at anchor, close to the land. The *Tuolomee*, it was called; its polished wood shone in the sun. There was a man on deck who saw Jim watching. He called out to him across the water, "What's your name?"

"Jay Gatsby," said Jim, just like that. He hadn't known he would say it, but it was all his hoping. The man on the yacht was Dan Cody. He owned it. He was rich from the gold rush and he called Jay on board and asked him to stay.

From 1907 till 1912, Jay lived with Cody, sailing to the West Indies and the Barbary Coast, working the boat and talking to Cody. He learned about the world, because Cody had had it by the tail for years. Jay got off the boat another man, smooth if not quite sophisticated, knowledgeable, graceful, and inwardly as empty as an actor has to be.

He made his way and he joined the army, so in 1917 he was training at Camp Taylor, near Louisville. The officers could meet the best young ladies of the town, and so it was that Gatsby and Daisy Fay fell in love, in the acutely romantic way that suited a man with his hopes for himself and the world, and which occupied her intensely for the moment. But he went off to the war. He brought great honor to himself in the Argonne offensive. He won medals and was made a major. After the war, he took the opportunity, offered to officers, to study at Oxford. He was at Trinity College only five months, but it was in that time he learned Daisy had married Tom Buchanan.

When he came back in 1919, he got a job with Meyer Wolfsheim, the gambler, in New York. Why a gambler and a racketeer? Gatsby was nearly thirty. He had to put away his uniform and his medals, and he had lost Daisy. If he wasn't to give up on his hopes he had to move fast. So he worked for Wolfsheim and happened to join him in the same year as Prohibition. In as hopeful and desirous a country as this there's always profit in short supply.

Gatsby got rich and famous, but he stayed mysterious. That's an actor's way, for if everyone hails his Hamlet he doesn't want to let on that only hours before "a little more than kin, a little less than kind" he was riding the subway to the theater. Gatsby bought a house in West Egg. From his terrace, he could look across the water at the green light on the dock of the Buchanan property.

He met Daisy again. He was sure they were still in love and she had been waiting to be reclaimed. A poor Midwestern boy who has waited that hard and long reckons the princess will be bound to recognize him. But Daisy was a coward. She couldn't quite make the break, and she couldn't own up that she had been driving Gatsby's car when it hit and killed Myrtle Wilson. So Gatsby took the blame, and the East slapped him in the face with its cold, hard hand. For the one and only time in that summer of 1926 he tried floating on the air mattress in his pool at West Egg. That's how George Wilson found him and shot him dead. Jim's father came to the funeral, but that was about all. The great crowd from his fabulous parties had melted away, the poor son of a bitch.

NORMAN BATES

Anthony Perkins in Psycho, *1960,*
directed by Alfred Hitchcock

This place where he lived was not a desert or a busy town. It was a small place, where at church, on Sunday, most of what had happened during the week was passed around. Life became plainer because of these dry accounts. People knew one another with the rather clinging loyalty of a community aggrieved by the building of a new highway. In its sudden obscurity, the place stuck together.

But it took ten years for anyone to realize that Norman Bates, out at the motel, had kept a version of the mother they had buried in reverent distaste, or that a few people who stopped at the motel, and the somewhat fewer still who went on up the road, had seen her, a prim silhouette in the window, sitting in the glow of a lamp, asleep or thinking. When it all came out they recollected how little they had seen of Norman in those years. He had come into town twice a month, maybe, for provisions. Otherwise he had stayed with mother, running the deserted motel, and the community had thought of him as a crooked tree, always there whenever you passed. No one thought to marry him, or cheer him up; he was a closed-off man, circumscribed by the tragedy. They never dreamed anyone so unobtrusive, so courteous, could have been fermenting in such a passionately crazy existence, and still reply with his boyish uncertainty when spoken to.

Everyone thought him straightforward and limited; then, afterward, they were merciless about his wickedness and dishonesty. Yet not to be open is not always lying; it can be no more or less than closed.

This was in Stanislaus County, east of where Route 5 now blasts along the San Joaquin Valley before it comes to Tracy, and the road goes right to Sacramento and left to Oakland or San Francisco. Modesto is the big city in Stanislaus County, but that's in the east. The west is just the Stone Hills and the northern end of that valley, an irrigated furnace where so much of the country's fruit and vegetables are grown. A mile or so to the east of 5 is the old 33, an important road in its day, but neglected now. Fairvale is maybe twenty miles from Crows Landing, and the Bates Motel was twelve miles from the town.

It's strange country, flat but rumpled like an unmade bed, where orgy or listlessness have an equal chance. It is a small town of itinerant workers, mistrusted by the natives. It is the "Golden West," yet so far still from San Francisco and the real flourish. There's suspicion there and resentment, a lot of isolated houses built on elevated ground, as if the owners wanted to see anyone coming. Henry Bates put up his house in the late 1890s. He was a builder, and his own place was meant as his advertisement. It was an imposing two-story wooden house with attic rooms above, like hooded eyes, and a deep fruit cellar. It was on a knoll with steps leading up to it from the path that stopped at the wide verandah. There were bushes around the house and a tree at one rear corner, but it stood out against the sky like a mask watching the land.

Henry Bates took a wife in 1930. By that time he was fifty-four, and his wife, Norma Ray, from Turlock, was only twenty-eight. She moved into the house and, they say, made it brighter and more agreeable. In 1932, they had a son, Norman. The house was large enough for a big family; maybe that's what Henry intended. But it had picked up an empty atmosphere from being the house of a single man, and not even the three of them could dispel the feeling of rattling in too spacious a box. The wide, steep staircases and the high-ceilinged rooms made Norman an anxious child, always on the edge of panic if out of sight of his mother.

In 1940, Henry built the motel. Twelve cabins on the flat ground between the house and the road. There was more and more touring then, but the war cut it back and Henry became depressed. He died in 1943 at the age of sixty-seven. The son was miserable, and it drew him and his mother even closer together. She often took him into her bed at night because he was nervous; she bought him records of the

Beethoven symphonies to play in the evenings when the wind was beating against the exposed house.

Norman grew lean and tall, like his mother, a woman of nearly six feet. He helped a lot around the motel, because after 1945 its business picked up. Weekends they had all of the cabins taken sometimes, and Norman had charge of the laundry and the linen. He loved to help his mother; he hoped he was eclipsing the failure his father felt at the end. Norman got to be fifteen and sixteen, and sometimes his mother invited young people over to the house for a party. All the lights blazed and there was dance music on the phonograph. There were games of hide-and-seek, from the fruit cellar to the attic rooms, and post office on the dark stairs. But Norman never got fixed up, and after the parties he wanted to dance with his mother until she was tired. Norman sometimes watched her when she thought she was alone—in her bathroom, dressing, combing her long black hair. It's not that strange in an out-of-the-way place, and maybe if no one knows or is hurt, then it's not even so bad. But fathers push themselves on daughters and sons fall in calf-love with their mothers. Loneliness and need are the reasons and climate for it; and they are too strong to be denied. But sometimes they are forced into unexpected, alarming directions.

Then, in 1950, the work started on the new highway. A lot of men came into the area as labor, and there was a foreman, Juan Padilla, head of the Mexican crew, who used to call on Norma. He was younger than she, but he wanted an American woman. Norma was still handsome; perhaps romantic freshness had been kept alive by Norman's fondness. Padilla lived in a trailer on the site, but he would visit and stay late and he got into the habit of sleeping over. He scarcely spoke to Norman, but he grinned at him and made little kissing noises when they were alone together. Norma didn't seem to notice. Norman felt he was losing her just as the motel was losing its traffic.

So one night he got a bottle of cheap red wine for Padilla, and he put strychnine in it. His mother never touched liquor, so he thought it would be safe. Padilla would drink and she would stay sober. But he misjudged the strength of their love, and her wish to do foolish things for the Mexican. Padilla teased her, sang to her, and cajoled; he told her she would be crazy with love if she took some of the wine. So he taught her to drink and they both died, side by side in the old bed with the satin coverlet.

Norman wrote out a letter in the red pencil that Padilla used on his work dockets, telling Norma he didn't want her anymore. He was thoughtful enough to add misspellings that might help identify the Mexican. But Norman was helpless with tears at the same time; he could not understand the overlap of cunning and disintegration in himself. When Sheriff Chambers got there Norman was incoherent. The sheriff had never had a case like it, but he worked it out that Norma had killed Padilla and then killed herself in what he regarded as the torment of a spurned lover. Looking at the naked Mexican's corpse, Chambers easily imagined melodrama. He felt a great pity for Norman, who had probably never in his life spent a night out of that house. He was really not fit to look after himself, least of all in that house. But he was eighteen, and it would be up to him.

For a time, Sheriff Chambers and his wife would call on Norman, but he seemed happier on his own. He stayed on the desolate premises; he went on changing the sheets on the motel beds and he cleaned the house so thoroughly that Mrs. Chambers always knew it by that sweet carbolicky odor. "What cleanser do you use, Norman?" she asked him, but he smiled and said, "Lord, I don't know," just like a man who didn't consider housework seriously.

What he had done, he had gone to the mortician's the night before the mother's funeral, and taken away the body in its periwinkle blue dress. He'd put rocks in the coffin, rocks and pillows so there was no rattling. That's what they buried. He'd kept the body at home and he'd done what he learned from a book on taxidermy to pump chemicals into it to preserve it. He invented a hobby for himself, stuffing birds, to explain the packages of chemicals he received from Toledo. Now, he was self-trained, and no book on preserving advises about human bodies. The corpse lingered; its perishing was too slow for Norman to notice. In love with someone, seeing them every day, you do not notice them growing older. And Norman talked to his mother as if she were alive still; as these monologues went on so, in his solitude, her answers crept into his head. Over the years, he became her: that's what the psychiatrist said later. But he had loved his mother so much that, once he had re-created her, she became stronger. There were times when the mother was more real than Norman, for instance on November 28, her birthday, when he celebrated the anniversary, alone, with Beethoven and an ordinary Californian wine.

And if those times of feminine arousal ever coincided with a single young woman staying at the motel, and thinking, Well, there's a kind man, so that she smiled at Norman's hollow, empty-eyed charm,

Mother's eyes saw and they came back later with a kitchen knife. A woman knows where her sharpest tools are kept.

Life can feel the same day after day, so monotonous it could crush you. Yet life, truly, is inoffensive; we feel ourselves collapsing. So people must make it different, if they are not to be depressed. Sometimes those who dread the steady state pick on death as a way out, and the deaths can be as unusual as the most unlikely murders in history. It's never too wise to linger with those humdrum smilers in country places. They give you the shivers, and they can be stranger than any city, professional crazy, without a hair out of place or a blown bulb in a motel sign, so that it still burns VACANCIES on stormy nights when the family that owns the place has had a row and would be best left alone.

> *Haven't you thought of murder, looked at the kitchen knives or the power sockets and wondered how you could inveigle your dearest to try them? It is one invention to think of murder, and another—far larger—to find a stranger for it. So we murder those we know, and justify our laziness with the purgatory it is to live with those we never quite reach, wondering who will die first if nature has its way, and which fool will be stranded.*

BRUNO ANTHONY

Robert Walker in Strangers on a Train, *1951, directed by Alfred Hitchcock*

What is that Tolstoy saying about families? I think it's the opening to one of his novels. Something about all happy families being alike, but every unhappy family finds a misery of its own. It always sounds so true; it's like the echo of a fatal shot at the start of a novel. An aphorism needs that air of encompassing wisdom in a few words, and the respectful silence that comes after a gunshot. But once, I remember, Mary Frances misquoted it, all askew in her helpless fury. It was in one of those day-long arguments, all over the house and on into the evening, desultory but still hunting for a way to wound. It was the way of our Sundays. She said—or rather she announced, letting the line spiral down from the top of the stairs, her voice so fine, quiet but penetrating, a voice in keeping with the day's gloom: "Happy families all go their own way, always valuable and personal; no one else could understand their pleasure. But unhappy families all act out the same tragedy."

Her error was poignant. It stilled all the bitter talk. I did not dare correct her; she would have lashed at me for pettiness, for always being right. And after all, she was right; there *is* that script in acrimony, that habit of walking in wounded steps. Then I thought about what she had said and it seemed just as true as Tolstoy's opposite conclusion. Was that just the resonance of an orderly sentence, or the grave voice of a former actress who has kept tragedy for home use?

I have another motto: all families seek to give the same image of health to the outside world, and yet all of them, alone in their own houses, exist in intimate, unspoken competition that would look like frenzy to outsiders. The Anthonys were once held up to the world as an example. There was a picture of the four of them in a 1933 *Vanity Fair*: Jonathan and Marion, and their two children, Bruno and Julia, nine and seven then. They were in the garden of the East Hampton house, enjoying a picnic, a god and his goddess, with two attendant fairies. There was a white tablecloth spread on the grass, with bowls of strawberries and champagne, and four thrilled smiles, the same defiant gaiety breaking out where four mouths opened to say "cheese."

In *Vanity Fair* it was a way of keeping faith with the idea of blissful summer, even in 1933. At the Anthony Agency, the company Jonathan had founded, one of his young managers saw the picture and said, why not? it has such real warmth, it's the very illustration we want for the life-insurance campaign. And so, for three full years, that lawn brimming with happiness was the emblem of prudent coverage for life, home and assets.

But in those same years, if you had come unannounced into their house on a Sunday morning—of course, this was scarcely possible to any invaders except readers, for they had solicitous servants—you might have found Marion in the drawing room sobbing incontinently over a painting she was unable to finish, Jonathan in his darkened room, stunned by his depression, Bruno spying on the servants, trying to lure them into his intricate booby traps, and Julia writhing and frothing on the stairs in a fit no one cared to notice.

There was a crack in the genetic structure of the Anthonys. Jonathan's father had killed himself, drowning in his own bath, sinking under the weight of despair. Jonathan had lived all his life under the same load. Marion had had seizures in her childhood that her parents had denied. It had been no more than childish excitement, they said. But Julia was an epileptic with fits once a week. Bruno did not show any such symptoms. But he survived in this household only by an obsessive attention to his own malicious plans. It was his way of not noticing the sister he loved. In a large house, he told himself, it is easy to miss those eruptions and instead find your sister so still and drained that she must be comforted. "Julia is not strong, like the rest of us," said Bruno.

Bruno in his teens seethed with clever ways to destroy the entire family. His own devout trait of speculation and the family's wretchedness came together in his mind as a subject for mass murder. He wondered how to arrange the four deaths so that the legend of the Anthonys' perfection would not be dented. He considered the car, with all of them in it, going over a cliff; he could see the front-page picture of the wreckage, and four overlapping bodies. Or a poisonous vapor to choke all of them in their separate bedrooms. Or lightning that hit the choppy blue surface of their pool while all of them were engaged in water polo.

But as the boy became the young man, such ideal dramas fractured in his head like the pieces of a broken plate, glued for a while, but then quietly freeing themselves in the hot washing-up water. Bruno was twenty and Julia seventeen: this was 1944, a year for invasion and liberation. Like prisoners, the two children had fallen into a pact against their parents in which their love for each other became confused with loathing of the elders. They did things to aid both causes. They would kiss and cuddle, sitting on the stairs, when their parents passed by—to be caught, to make their parents' lives and their own impossible. Every illicit caress was a stroke upon a genie's lamp called murder. They held their breath in the delicious, red-handed peak of danger and arousal.

Julia was sent off to an asylum. Her father said that her fits put her in peril. They were accelerating in frequency and delirium. She needed professional care. Bruno was not permitted to visit her. But he learned where the asylum was, from his father's canceled checks, and he could get there in a day's journey. He would howl outside the barred windows, like a wolf. Julia was moved to Arizona.

And so Bruno decided that he should kill his father. No need to touch his mother. She was so bereft he could handle her. But his father had taken away his most precious companion. With Jonathan dead, Bruno could assume control of the family affairs and have Julia released. The two of them could live together and play all the games they chose.

He had to discover a way of disposing of his father, and here Bruno's delicate genius—always derided by the father—came into its own. He dreamed up the principle of exchanged murders: two people, strangers, meet and offer to commit each other's murders. They will have an alibi on the crucial occasions. The police will see their motive, only to be confounded by the immovable explanations that on that night they were at dinner with the Carstairs in Connecticut or flying to Minneapolis. So long as the two parties stayed strangers, the arrangement would work. Bruno loved the simplicity of the plan.

Guy Haines was the ideal other, a semi-famous man, an athlete, such a good guy. Bruno hated him, and he could tell that Guy flinched whenever he touched him. No one would suspect them. So he followed Guy's cantankerous wife, Miriam, to the funfair, spirited her away from her hick beaux, took her on a boat ride to an island of love and strangled her there, squeezing until the fussy spectacles fell off her face. It was so easy. She thought he was a gentleman and was quite ready to be abused.

But Guy proved stuffy. He pretended to be horrified at the news, then he delayed over his part of the bargain. Bruno gave him a plan to the East Hampton house with his father's bedroom clearly indicated. But he could read Guy's lazy mind, and it was Bruno there in the bed (in one of his father's robes) the night Guy came to the house to warn Mr. Anthony. Oh, the foolish look on the idiot's face.

A little pressure was in order. So Bruno went back to the funfair to leave Guy's lighter there: it had crossed tennis rackets on it, ideal as a clue. He made the journey and stayed overnight in a not very prepossessing hotel to give Guy time to catch up. Best of all would be if the cops could nab Guy and the lighter in one swoop, with his guilty hand reaching out for the rackets. While he waited, he sent a postcard to Julia in Tempe: "Flying to you shortly, love. The world is slowly working itself out. There is a very loud amusement park right in front of my present lodgings."

Guy did follow Bruno. They met up on a carousel and as it whirled round, faster and faster, the calliope racing, the enameled plaster horses plunging up and down in their effort to get away, Bruno wondered if Julia's fits were like this. He was thinking of her, and of how soon he would be with her, in arid zona, when the whirlpool of noise, fun and happiness cracked and he became a dead man with the lighter there in his open hand. If the police noticed it, they would realize what he was trying to imply. Guy would *have* to kill his father, and everything would be all right. He would go all the way to Arizona and carry Julia out of her prison. Perhaps she wouldn't know him now. If it was madness, why, madness must have its advantages. In which case he would marry her.

DOLLY SCHILLER

Sue Lyon in Lolita, *1962, directed by Stanley Kubrick*

"Husband at home?" he croaked, fists in the pockets.

Thus reunion, not in the Indian Ocean and not a waltz into darkness, but at grimy Coalmont, the last house on Hunter Road, all dump and ditch, on September 23, 1952, he near the end of his journey, she frankly and hugely pregnant and exhaling "We-e-ell!" at the sight of him. HH meets Dolly Schiller, after all these years. She, the seventeen-year-old, had married Richard "Dick" Schiller, gotten pregnant and wanted to pay off their debts so they could move to Alaska, where he had been promised an opening in his very specialized corner of the mechanical field. It was the last time Lo and HH clapped eyes on each other. He gave her four thousand dollars to ease the way, he elicited the lowdown (it had been dramatist Clare on the QT who'd had his way with her), and then he drove off through the drizzle of the dying day noticing that the windshield wipers could not keep the moisture from his eyes. She was dead three months and two days later, during childbirth, on Christmas Day, up in Gray Star in Alaska, where not all facilities matched Dick's mechanical field. HH was dead too, of coronary thrombosis, in legal captivity just before the start of his trial for the murder of Clare Quilty. So the three of them were wiped off the board, without issue, in three months.

Dolores Haze was the daughter of Charlotte (née Becker) and Harold Haze, conceived on a 1934 honeymoon trip to Vera Cruz,

Mexico, and born on January 1, 1935 (what a chance alighting on holidays) in Pisky, itself in a corn, coal and hog-producing area. At that time, HH was twenty-five, Paris-born and Lo-bound, still not quite married to Valeria Zborovski. How astonishing it is to look back on your life, busy and vital at the time, it seemed, and to realize you were still twelve years away from your date with destiny, and might as well have stayed in bed as gone to the wedding.

HH came to the U.S., after being divorced by Valeria, in early 1940. He wrote a history of French lit. for English students, he went on an Arctic expedition and he was in and out of asylums. It was in 1945 that the widow Haze and her Dolores moved to Ramsdale, New Hampshire. HH was then hot out of an asylum where he had contrived his own recovery by games of wordplay, dream-scheming and general storytelling (rather of the lo-and-behold variety). He too came to Ramsdale, looking for a summer's quiet concentration. He would have lodged with the McCoos, but their house burned down, and so, at a loss, he was sent to 342 Lawn Street, where Charlotte and her Lo resided. Who says there is not some omniscient author dealing out the hands? Where are we if those two do not meet? And what caprice is it that can say, "Why not in Ramsdale, New Hampshire?" with a straight face?

HH first saw her there, on May 30, 1947, feeling like the fairy-tale nurse to a lost princess, for she was the spitting image, the look-alike, of his childhood sweetheart, Annabel—hence HH's love of the moment of truth in a twelve-year-old girl.

Well, things moved fast, and so they must, for a nymphet's prime does not last long enough for a slow coach. On June 21, they had a tussle on the sofa, or—as it were—by just touching her HH set all paradise loose and let a happy hand slide up her sunny leg until she rolled off the sofa. Then Charlotte packed her off to camp and on the same day accepted HH's distracted proposal of marriage—legalized in a few days while Dolores was still away. Six weeks after that—talk about "Days of Our Lives"—Charlotte found the journal in which HH had been penning up a storm for Lo and ran outside in tumult, meeting a suitably swerving car. Kaput. The howl of brakes, the soft bump, and the renewal of summer's whispering silence.

So, on August 15, HH goes to collect Lo from camp. He takes her that night to a hotel in Parkington, The Enchanted Hunters, where daughter and stepdad share a room (342!) and the stark act of love, adding their names to a register that included Marie Samuels, Georges Beaulieu, Carl Proffer, Clare Quilty, and P. H. Vazak, among so many others—such are the summery delights of Parkington.

They spent a year then exploring America, a year of motels—ideal places for slumber, argument, reconciliation and insatiable, illicit love that has no home—and travel among the wondrous places and place-names of the country, without a worry about the Mann Act. It was a year of Little Iceberg Lake, Hell's Canyon, Death Valley, Hot Coffee, the Grand Tetons, Mission Dolores, Milner Pass, Scotty's Castle, Goose Necks, Poker Flat, Phoenix, Arizona or Alex, Mississippi. They were insects, the two of them, endeavoring to crawl in and out of every tiny, exotic place, the happy-bored patrons of an endless drive-in, they always in the car, and it, the changing scene, dissolving in and out on the wraparound white screen. A movie tour, with all the setting suns and painted deserts bloody as fruit salad in the best flicks of 1947–48—*Duel in the Sun, Pursued, Out of the Past, Body and Soul, Lured, Kiss of Death, I Know Where I'm Going, Brute Force, Ramrod, They Won't Believe Me, Dark Passage, Red River, Force of Evil, State of the Union, A Double Life, Sleep, My Love, I Remember Mama, Unfaithfully Yours, A Foreign Affair, No Minor Vices* (I can't go on . . .).

Later: and so in the dying summer of 1948, Dolores Haze enters Beardsley College for Girls, where she is cast in the play *The Hunted Enchanters* by Clare Q——y. HH sniffs a rival, maybe the driver of the Aztec Red pursuer so much in the corner of his eye. He aims for a second transcontinental idyll (always HH's dream) with Lo. And on July 4, 1949, as epochal as a bomb test on Bikini, CQ makes off with Lo. Thus start the sad years of HH, the looking and the waiting, the searching and the hoping, until on September 22, 1952, he receives the Hello, Dad letter from Dolly Schiller in Coalmont.

I am not put off or shocked just because an older man, far older, should see and want to touch the firm, innocent beauty of a rosebud. No, and not surprised either that after bloom the rosebud falls away and there is as little left as there is on the blank page at the end of a book or the pale screen after a show.

BERNSTEIN

Everett Sloane in Citizen Kane, *1941,
directed by Orson Welles*

He had a law degree, the result of night school and toiling at his books till two a.m., then getting up at six to be at the factory by seven. It was a relentless routine for seven years, for Nathan Bernstein was far from brilliant. It took the edge off his youth, and made him seem ten or fifteen years older than his real age. But he never let himself be resentful. He didn't practice the law he worked so hard to master; he never turned into a smart Jewish lawyer. But he felt better for having the law degree, a little more worthy and safer if anything ever happened. And studying law had taught him to talk. The studies took away any social life; but he never complained, not even to himself. There are men who would as soon push themselves near death as risk the horror of being laughed at by a lady. Perhaps Bernstein looked at all the doubt and anxiety in courting, and gave it up for work. But a man like that, a man so caught up in business that he did not notice growing old, could harbor private visions of romance that never faded.

He was born in Hoboken in 1859, in sight of Manhattan but outside its privileged aura. He scanned the city's surface so many early mornings, the columns black but burnished by the sun rising behind them. Then, at the end of the day, the setting sun threw a low platinum light back on the city, which gave it depth and warmth. Its grays became mauve and the browns turned gold and ginger. Throughout the day and during his lifetime, Manhattan came to look more magical and exalted from New Jersey, more like an illusion. The increasing row of monuments loomed over the ragged Jersey shore, like civilization on the edge of swamp and wilderness.

Bernstein's parents were Austrian; his mother spoke no English; his father was a pawnbroker. Yet Bernstein became chairman of the board of Kane Enterprises, sitting in solitary splendor on top of the Inquirer Building after Kane had gone. Kane's will left instructions for Bernstein to keep the use of the office and the title for as long as necessary. The tycoon had always trusted loyalty; it was the surest kind of friendship. And Bernstein had never once picked up the cynicism to think badly of Mr. Kane, or regard him in less than the light in which Kane saw himself. Even when the boss lied or manipulated, Bernstein kept his eyes on the glorious career requiring the deceit. He loved Kane, and Kane knew it; but neither man ever spoke of it.

Bernstein was twenty-eight when he answered the advertisement in the *New York Chronicle*:

> Gentleman newly arrived from the West, possessing funds and ideas, requires general manager who will be tireless but amusing when tired.

The interview that followed a month later, when Kane returned from Lisbon, was not prolonged:

"Mr. Bernstein. . . ."

"Yes, Mr. Kane?"

"Ah . . . I was thinking. Have we met?"

"I answered the advertisement."

"Exactly, Mr. Bernstein. This . . . newspaper."

"Yes, Mr. Kane?"

"Think it might be fun to run a paper?"

"Well. . . ."

"Could you manage a paper, Mr. Bernstein?"

"I believe I could."

"Could you manage me?"

"Not if you noticed it."

"Mr. Bernstein, I believe we are going to be fine friends."

Nathan Bernstein was Kane's general manager when they took over the *Inquirer* in 1890. That meant he hired and fired people, handled contracts and parties, and generally oversaw the affairs of a man who reckoned he might, if he had to, lose one million dollars a year for sixty years.

In 1896, when he was thirty-seven, Bernstein was going over to Jersey on the ferry. It was a Sunday afternoon, but he had spent his morning at the office. It was a hot afternoon, and he felt sticky in his business clothes; not that he owned much else. He saw the other ferry coming in as his pulled out—two slow boats clanking and honking as they passed—and he saw a girl standing by its rail, all in white, carrying a white parasol, excited to be in the city for the rest of the day. Perhaps she was going to meet a boyfriend; she didn't look more than twenty. Bernstein didn't speak to her, and she never noticed him. For years afterward, he looked for her on the ferry, but he never found her. And he never forgot the smile on her face, a smile for the day, the old ferryboats, or a rendezvous twenty minutes away. In that moment, he had seen the years of his empty future stretched ahead of him, and he smiled with the sadness of a fulfilled man.

Nathan Bernstein died in his office in 1945, days after the news of victory in Japan. The obituary in the Kane papers misspelled his name.

SUSAN ALEXANDER KANE

Dorothy Comingore in Citizen Kane, *1941,
directed by Orson Welles*

At eight o'clock in the evening, on West Seventy-fourth Street in New York, sometime in 1915. . . . It had rained hard an hour earlier, and the streets were still empty of people. There is all the poised tension of a trap in the air. Charles Foster Kane was on one of his nocturnal walks to the Western Manhattan Warehouse, going down to the waterfront with only a cane as company—perhaps he never intended getting there. But he set out on that walk often; it might have been established that he used Seventy-fourth Street. Then it would only need a fresh, muddy puddle, a passing carriage, and Susan Alexander, half-moaning with the pain of a toothache, half-laughing.

It sounds contrived, the kind of chance meeting to make a man of power suspicious. Did Jim Gettys construct the scene, guessing that it could grow into a "love nest," to destroy his best opponent's best chance? Or was there some more mysterious director of fate at work? It is not that Kane was a philanderer, likely sooner or later to get caught in an affair. He seems so timid with love, sex or women; they are all like statues he bought in Greece but never bothered to unwrap. No, he needed a special kind of sentimental occasion: the atmosphere of his mother and the presence of a novice; someone who would be entertained by his amateur magic without knowing who he was; someone with a career he could fashion. The arrangement is so astute. If Gettys was this clever, lucky New York to have such a boss. Only a great and important man would know how open he was to a nobody, a cross-section of the American public.

Alexander was not her name. It was the strong but romantic name she took for herself when both her parents were dead. She had the choice down to Alexander, Mallory or Rivers, all more musical than Stock. The Stocks were of German descent, born New Yorkers, who had been able to move up from the Lower East Side to Seventy-fourth Street. Susan was born there in 1894. But by the age of eighteen, she was on her own in the world, employed in the sheet-music department of Seligman's. She did not quite read music, but she had hopes of being a singer and it was a comfort to her to be in the music business.

Then, that wet night in 1915, she went down to the drugstore to get something for her toothache, and she met this large man dabbing at the mud thrown up on his face by a carriage. She offered him hot water and took him home; there was nothing seductive about that, not until her tender imagination asked to leave the door to her apartment open. That small ajar was like an idea occurring to the dirtied man. And because she had laughed—without any malice, women laughing do not have to be fearsome—he took it into his head to entertain her. He could waggle both of his ears at the same time; it was something he had learned at Harvard from a Venezuelan. He put his hands together and made shadow silhouettes of animals on the wall. Before long she sang for him, in that small salon voice, pretty, brittle and afraid of any larger hall.

A year later, the gubernatorial race was on, and Kane could not visit Susan as often as he wanted. If he had won the election, in all that euphoria and busyness, he might have dropped her—not without a generous gift, but still dropped her. Gettys could not let it go. He divined that all Kane needed to finish himself was a challenge; there was a ruinous need in the newspaperman for politics to be glorious, touched by honor and drama. He would be a terrible governor when the job bored him; it was a rare act of public spirit in Gettys to ensure that the state was spared Kane. He sent a simple note to Mrs. Kane, and on the night of the great oration at Madison Square Garden she invited her husband to go up to West Seventy-fourth Street with her.

The grim confrontation urged Kane to the abyss. All chance of doubt was sucked away in the roasting air of melodrama. He defied Gettys and Emily, he ignored the qualms in Susan. Let the loving people decide. Susan knew then and there that he would marry her, that she would be powerless, and that the marriage would be a disaster. She could see an avenue of pillared unhappiness ahead of her.

They married on the run in Trenton in 1917, and the honeymoon yielded place to singing lessons. Kane missed his son. He tried to squeeze love out of his life to reduce the pain. He treated Susan like a property that had to pay off. Even Matisti, her singing teacher, felt for her, the most forlorn student he had ever had. Matisti recognized her ordeal and fell in love with her, despite her strangled voice. Amid the horrors of the Chicago opening, he made bravura, restorative love to her; it was almost a teacher's duty. But Kane blamed him for her failure; Matisti was sent away. The mortifying tour of *Salammbo* continued and in 1920 Susan sought to kill herself.

Then, he relented, and in a matter of weeks it was as if opera had never existed. He removed her from it and put her down elsewhere, as the hostess of the growing Xanadu. So she lived in Florida, too pale-skinned for suntan, in a house too large for contentment. She became an expert on jigsaw puzzles, a listless center of picnics, a half-forgotten companion to a man who no longer thought of being funny. She left him in 1932, walking out on all of it with just a couple of suitcases.

She became a chanteuse, singing in small, smoky lounges, talking to an audience who had come to see notoriety and who were ready to needle her into gossip. For a few years she managed, and in 1938 she put her money into the El Rancho in Atlantic City. She sang there, but she was the show. She'd drink with the customers, or on her own. She was there in 1940 when Kane died, and there drunk when Thompson, the reporter, came to interview her.

It was easier after he died, like the light coming back at dawn after a sleepless night. She gave up singing and decided to make a success of the place in Atlantic City. She changed her name again, got rid of it all. Over the years she won respect on the East Coast, and she enjoyed hiring other, younger singers and running a clean house. She never married again. There were other men, but after Kane she did not trust real feelings. She could only wonder whether she wasn't just a figure in someone else's great drama. So she said who needs it? She died in 1978, in Atlantic City, an old lady known for her tough kindness.

RAYMOND

Paul Stewart in Citizen Kane, *1941,*
directed by Orson Welles

Anyone who ever went to Xanadu between 1927 and 1940 knew him. Sometimes guests passed their weekend there, or their week, without ever seeing Kane. But it was Raymond who greeted them, who made sure they were comfortable, and who saw to it that their car was ready and waxed when they left. They all knew Raymond's number on the house phone. It was Raymond who happened by in the rose garden to name all the varieties, he organized the menus for the picnics, and he personally put the catsup with the silver on the dining table. He was all-knowing, and he was discreet; he could hide a drunk or supply some cocaine. He ran the place. It was his kingdom. He even gave himself to rumor, chuckling if someone asked whether he was really a Cajun. "Just cagy," he answered, and the smile flattered the questioner. Far more than Kane, Raymond knew that Xanadu was a hothouse of unconfirmed possibilities.

But no one was sure if Raymond was his first or his last name, or whether he was Ray Raymond, or Ramon Ramone. Was he American or Italo-American? His accent slid and his complexion fluctuated, like a movie with replacement footage. He disappeared not long after the deal giving Xanadu to the nation. No one knew where he went, but who remembered where he had come from?

He had been hired personally by Mr. Kane. Yet no service contract was ever found. No one was sure how Raymond had been paid. His small room was stripped bare before he quit. The one personal trace left was the tidy circle of grease on the wall where he had sat up in bed doing whatever he did. He had handled all the petty-cash arrangements and he could have taken a small fortune out of the several household accounts without anyone knowing.

Afterward, people wondered. Had Raymond been a spy? Was he the plant of the government, the FBI, organized crime—or all of them? If someone really knew where the bodies were buried at Xanadu, wouldn't all those interests (and others) value a piece of his time? After all, everyone went to Xanadu; it was where show people sought privacy. That couldn't fail to make the world wonder and worry. Moreover, it had been palpable all along: Raymond ran the place. He was the one who said, "It was Rosebud," wasn't he? It was Raymond who presided over the burning of so much.

MARY KANE

Agnes Moorehead in Citizen Kane, *1941,*
directed by Orson Welles

There are mothers in a quiet stir of dementia because of the family's ruin, mothers moldy with decay propped erect at an upstairs window; there are mothers whose deaths allow the real story to grow; there are mothers waiting in breathless anticipation to know whether their lover is their son. An only child is a matter of choice or fate, but an only mother is an inevitability. The mother has this advantage over wives for any man—his way of selecting a wife makes him doubt the dream that there is a one and only true wife for him; yet maternity gives him that assurance with the first heartbeats of consciousness, or like the three beats on a stage before the play starts. We could marry anyone, but mothers are as fatal as character.

This is the most perplexing mother of them all, the mother who does not just explain a story but whose existence shows the need for story. We tell stories to clear away the darkness of family history and influence, things in life we are not brave or intelligent enough to explore. Every narrative utters the secret pain of family.

Mary Clay was born in 1832, in England. She came to America when she was eight, her own mother dying on the voyage. With her father, she went by wagon to St. Joseph, Missouri. They lived there for several years, during which he worked as a sign painter. In 1856, when she was twenty-four, Mary traveled to Denver, Colorado, to take up a position as housekeeper. In that city, she met James Kane, a saloonkeeper, and in 1858 they were married.

Since they both had some experience in running establishments, it seemed sensible for them to open a boardinghouse in New Salem, Colorado, in 1859. It was in the mining country and there was demand for a clean house where God-fearing miners and their relatives might stay, secure in the knowledge that the premises were not also a brothel. To that extent, the boardinghouse reflected the dominance of Mary in the marriage. There were those who saw Jim less as her husband than as the odd-job man she employed.

Fred Graves was such an observer. He came to New Salem in 1864, a year after the birth of the Kanes' son, Charlie. Graves was an attractive young man, limping away from the war, a jack-of-all-trades but a prospector for the moment, just bursting to shout "Eureka!" He had a room at the Kane boardinghouse, and he talked to Mary a good deal in the long winters. Graves may have been simply her companion, but there were suspicions in Jim's mind. He knew he was a disappointment to his wife.

Graves went farther west in 1868, worn out by mining and the hope of being lucky. He owed six months' rent at that time, and he had no money after he had bought his ticket to San Francisco. But Mary let him go and only half an hour before he left Graves thought to give her the deeds to his fruitless mine. He scribbled out the deed of sale and hurried away, jaunty with the prospect of change. Always change.

Once or twice Jim Kane went to look at the old mine. He kept his liquor in the shaft. And once, in 1870, Mary took young Charles to show it to him. They walked into the cold tunnel, hand in hand, talking about ghosts from the old Indian burial ground. They had a lantern and they saw the way blocked ahead of them. There had been a fall, recently it seemed. Charles asked his mother about the flickers he could see in the rock from the lamplight. She guessed it was nothing, but she came back later to look more closely. She carved out one piece of rock veined with glitter, put it in a bag and took it down to the assay office.

The Colorado Lode would be known by 1900 as the earth's third richest gold mine. Mary hired a geologist to examine it, and then in 1871, when she knew, she closed it down.

"What are you doing?" said a bewildered Jim. He thought the mine had been blessed by his booze.

She wrote a letter to Walter P. Thatcher on Wall Street and he wrote back saying he thought it could be managed. Mary Kane had proposed that a trust be set up by Thatcher to run the gold mine and hold it and its profits until Charlie's twenty-fifth birthday. At that time, the whole thing would be his, the capital and all the reinvested money. As part of the deal, Thatcher was to take Charles away to Chicago, to be his guardian, and to ensure that he had an education and upbringing that befitted a rich young American.

The boy would not see his parents, but he would only appreciate that absence gradually. In return, the Thatcher Trust would pay Mary and Jim Kane fifty thousand dollars a year until they were both dead. Jim argued it, but Mary was adamantine. Why, oh why?

The mine was hers. Jim was a waster. Maybe he loved Charlie, but he was a bad influence. Yet he was a weak man, and his son was strong enough to handle him. Mary might have left Jim fat-rich, drunk and happy in Colorado. She could have gone east with Charles. She could have guided his education. She could have lived with him and seen him. Did she think she would hinder him or make him ashamed? Or was Mary Kane not truly interested in her son? Did she prefer the freedom and the fifty thousand dollars for herself? Was there that dreadful loneliness in her of being mystified by family expectations? Couldn't she pretend for the boy?

She never saw Charles again. Jim didn't stay in Colorado. He went the way of Graves to California, and he was dead by 1874. Mary had bargained with him. He could have all the fifty thousand dollars of the first year and his liberty in return for leaving and abandoning his claim to all future moneys. It was so immediate a bounty, Jim could not resist it.

Mary Kane remained in Colorado, stayed on in New Salem. She did not appear to use or understand her own freedom. People said she was cold and miserable, but she may have wanted just to be alone. She did not look for a new man or change her ways. She died in 1888, having used her money to build a large hotel, the Overlook, on the site of the old boardinghouse. It would become a fine establishment in its day, a hotel fit for dreams.

All of Mary Kane's things were shipped east when she died, to a warehouse in New York—her clothes, her glass and chinaware, the wood stove and the sled her father had made for her with the painted rosebud on it still pink and fresh.

SALLY BAILEY

Susan Sarandon in Atlantic City, *1980,*
directed by Louis Malle

Not quite Miss America, maybe, but as lovely as you'd want to see, living in a shabby apartment, getting in at one in the morning, weary and afraid that she smells of the oysters she spends the night serving. This young woman has gone east out of an inexplicable desperation, or one that she has never paused or troubled to convey to those left behind. It was assumed, and so no one could deal with it; hopes are dreams, but so are camouflage and evasion.

She was born in what she thinks of as an unsophisticated fastness of the Midwest; she prefers to forget it now, and seldom owns up to it. I have heard she tells the story of being from Saskatchewan. No one says she has run away, or is missing. Her parents understand approximately where she is, and she assumes they have that rough idea. She counts on them not to ask questions. There's nothing to report to the police; nothing to hire a private detective for. But just suppose the father went after her, not chasing—just wanting to know, then she'd do anything to get away, go wild, run from her apartment leaving clothes, a hot iron and snapshots behind her.

When she gets home at night, she turns on one muted lamp—as if it were a signal, as well as tender golden illumination for what she has to do. She takes off her shirt and throws it on the floor. She has done that all her life, and she lives for the ideal of a new shirt every day. The old ones are shameful, tossed in the trash. Then she arranges herself in the mirror and slides the chemise off her shoulders, off her breasts. There, in Atlantic City, six nights a week, she cuts open a lemon and squeezes its juice on her arms, on her breasts, rubbing the juice between them, in her armpits and absentmindedly on her nipples. So as not to smell of fish, thinking that the place she comes from was so far from the sea.

Does she know the instant when the man across the way, Lou Guarini, an elderly dandy with silver-plate hair and a cautious walk, looks up from his dark to watch this young woman at her toilet? He is old enough . . . old enough, anyway. What a strange, circuitous route it is that she went so far away and yet is now willing to have an old man spy on her in this intimate situation, a lover if he was twenty feet closer. The shy are always exhibitionists in another part of their lives.

She was twenty-eight when she got to Atlantic City, not less than young but a little battered in her innocence, with startled eyes that had seen more than she could ever admit. She had hopes of becoming a croupier, wearing black and white and arbitrating fortune. There was a school of instruction at one of the casinos—the Alexander—with a genuine Frenchman imported to teach the talk, the ease and the sublime acceptance of chance. Sally met the old woman who ran the casino, not long before she died, and the raddled blonde looked her up and down.

"How old did you say you were?"

"I didn't say," said Sally.

"I didn't think you did. If you had, I wouldn't have asked you again because I'd have remembered."

"Twenty-five."

"You're old already."

"I want to learn."

"Yeah? What are you running away from?"

"Nothing."

"Like hell it's nothing."

"My mother. My mother, my father."

"Where?"

"Nebraska."

"Speak French?"

"Sure."

She had a few sentences rehearsed which came out fine, and the old woman grinned and told her okay. So Sally took the course, and she worked in the fishbar in the evenings to pay the rent. Then her sister, Chrissie, arrived, pregnant from Sally's ex-boyfriend, Dave. Somehow Dave had gotten hold of this cocaine, but the Mob came after him and they killed him. At least Chrissie's kid wouldn't have to bother with a father!

Sally didn't know how to handle the funeral and that's when this Lou character stepped in, Mr. Practical, Mr. Experience. But he had a lover's look in his old pink eyes, and he confessed to Sally how he studied her at night. She didn't know whether to be shocked or wise, so she reacted as if it were nothing much. She made love with Lou that night, and she knew enough to be kind and to enjoy her generosity. It was slow and then quick, but he was gentle and very eloquent. She felt safer with him than she had in ten years.

A couple of hoods humiliated him the next day in front of her, and she saw how old he really was. She wanted him to be able to melt away, he was so close to tears. But there was something about him, or about what she had done for him. A few nights later, he shot the two gangsters like someone in a movie. It turned out he had been dealing in Dave's cocaine. In a matter of a few days, magic had reached down and touched him, turning tarnish to true silver. He was rich, and he had won the love and respect of a young honey.

They went off together, saying they were going to Florida for a good time. The first night they stopped at a motel and they made love again. The next morning, while Lou was in the bathroom, she took some of his money. Did she mean him to see her? Kindness repaid kindness. It was his greatest pleasure just to watch her. This was the way of not saying outright she had to go her way. He declined to notice the theft. He let her take his car and he hitched back to Atlantic City.

Sally drove to Baltimore, she traded the car and she got a plane to Paris and then to Nice. She knew that was near Monte Carlo, and she was wondering how she'd look in a black croupier's suit with a white silk shirt, a fresh one every night.

Chrissie, Christina, she's still in Atlantic City. She writes often, long, placid letters on lined paper, telling me everything she's been doing (nothing much), and how my grandchild is (Albert). My eye flies through the letters. They are too detailed and calm for me, I suppose. She is a good girl, good but undemanding. That's what I want to say. She tells me her life is working itself out, and that she is full of great hopes. That's all very well. She has her own business, faith healing. Apparently she hears from the others, off and on. It seems she is our center now, poor thing. She says I must come to Atlantic City, and bring Mary Frances. But I flinch at the prospect of all the arrangements.

GILDA FARRELL

Rita Hayworth in Gilda, *1946,*
directed by Charles Vidor

For something like twenty years, men she had just met were always telling Gilda, "You should have been in pictures. I mean that sincerely."

They were speaking their truth, but they were ill at ease because they knew the world took that line for a lie—being the sort of men they were. So they felt badly about themselves, and sometimes they went away thinking Gilda was a coquette who'd led them into it. But they weren't just telling Gilda she was sexy or beautiful. They felt something else—it might be the way the light picked up the back of her head, or her trick of looking past people, so that they felt unnoticed, like a movie camera. Or perhaps it was because with Gilda there was always what you heard—reputation—and her intense, impatient amusement when she was there with you, her presence.

People in movies have a sensational *now* about them and a mysterious past. That's what acting is: when Miss Julie first appears you have to hold your breath because of this sweaty, barefoot young woman wanting to dance *now*, on midsummer's night, with castanets in her nervous hand; but you have to see all the way back down an uncertain corridor to her past. Gilda was like that, as sexy as a photograph: she made you notice and left you wondering.

She laughed and tossed her strawberry-blond hair when men wondered why she hadn't been in movies. And she never let on that she could have been. That was too much like boasting, and Gilda wanted presence to speak for her past. Explaining was so unglamorous. But one day in 1938, she could have been in a picture. Gilda was born in Santa Monica in 1921, and she was a girl who used to hang around the studios. She got noticed. One day a fellow asked her if she could dance, and was she old enough. "Sure," she said straightaway, never liking to be seen thinking. They were making *Strike Up the Band* at Metro and she was in the chorus if she wanted for the "Do the Conga" number, with Busby Berkeley as the choreographer.

And Gilda was there, waiting for wardrobe, when this other guy came by.

"Hi, doll," he said. "You sing a little?"

"Sure."

"One look and I knew it. Want to work?"

"I'm working here."

"Days, right? I mean a position."

"What sort of position?"

"I got a boat. Offshore. Nice class of people we have. I run a show and it's quality stuff. You know Errol Hill?"

"No."

"He produces for us."

"Singing and dancing?"

"Exactly."

"What would I make?"

"Why don't we talk on the way?"

The guy was Tony Cornero and he had worked out how you could get outside legal city limits off the Santa Monica beaches. So he had a big boat out there, the *Rex*, as a pleasure palace with gambling, and he had a ferry service—water taxis—going from the pier. It was a lot of fun while it lasted, and Cornero was soft on Gilda, which suited her. She did a couple of numbers every night, and then she'd circulate, talking to the customers. Tony was a very faithful guy. He never went with anyone else, and Gilda respected that. So she flirted, but she kept herself for him.

Well, Earl Warren, the California attorney general, got after the boat and when he busted them, Cornero took Gilda to Las Vegas. They stayed there for a few years, and in 1945 they went to Havana. But Tony had the notion to start up the gambling boat again after the war, and he went back to California. Gilda remained in Cuba because of Ballin Mundson. He was an older man, gray-haired with a scar on his face and a dangerous gentleman act. He had a casino in Argentina but he came to Havana several times a year for a "holiday." He spent a lot of his time there, with the Germans living on the island. In 1945, Mundson asked Gilda to marry him. He told her he would overlook her checkered past, hold no grudges or suspicions, and take her as she was. She never thought she was anything she shouldn't be. This tolerance was like iced water on your tummy as you soaked in the tub. It frightened her. But Mundson was attractive: the more condescending he was the more she wanted him. She wanted to be in bed with him so she could examine his scar.

They married and he took her to Buenos Aires. Mundson had a manager at the casino, Johnny Farrell, and Gilda could tell that he was jealous of her. He thought she had disturbed the nice arrangement he had with Mundson. At first she wondered if Johnny was in love with Ballin, but she never saw any evidence, so she decided it was just a money and power thing. She got used to Farrell being frosty with her; she enjoyed it. In return, she let Johnny see her talking to other men so he'd have to decide whether to tell Mundson or not. He got this constipated face and held his silence.

Ballin Mundson had a secret deal with the Germans in South America. Except that Ballin was cheating them, so some of them came to Buenos Aires to settle with him. He killed one of them and got away in a small plane, but the plane crashed in the sea and everyone assumed he was dead.

Johnny took over the club, and Gilda started to like him. He was more relaxed without Ballin and his swordstick. Gilda was always drawn to men who didn't like her; it made her feel the more seductive. But Johnny was angry with her, told her he was guarding her for Mundson. Keeping me prisoner? asked Gilda. Just to irritate Johnny, she did an act in the floorshow, "Put the Blame on Mame," with a striptease that made him stiff with embarrassment. If Johnny wanted her, Gilda thought, why lie to himself?

Mundson wasn't dead, he was in Rio. He came back one night, and he just took it for granted that Johnny and Gilda were lovers. People always had their minds made up about her, as if she were their invention. But old Uncle Pio shot Mundson when he went after her. People she hardly thought of were often waiting to rescue her. This time Mundson was really dead.

"We should get away," Gilda told Johnny.

"The two of us?"

"Sure."

"Why should I trust you?"

"Don't, if you don't want to."

"Do you love me?"

"Sure."

"How do I know?"

"Ballin knew."

They went to Miami, and Johnny ended up working for Santos Trafficante. He and Gilda were married. But nothing worked out well for Johnny. The more he mistrusted her, the more she provoked him. And the Mob didn't appreciate a man who couldn't keep his wife under control. Johnny was found dead in the harbor in 1961. Gilda moved around. She had been Hyman Roth's mistress for a while in the 1950s, and she was with Fredo Corleone for a time. These men liked her because she had been with Tony Cornero. They loved her out of loyalty to the code.

Today, she's in a home in Pasadena. She has bad arthritis and needs constant nursing. A check for her bills comes in the first of every month from a Florida bank. That's why the nurses still gossip about her. They tell stories that awful gangsters are paying for her because of all she did for them. They've assumed that her disability is a reward for being so bad. So they chatter away in the gap between this sad old lady and her shady past.

HANK QUINLAN

Orson Welles in Touch of Evil, *1958,*
directed by Welles

On October 4, 1957, his sixtieth birthday, Hank Quinlan would be obliged to retire as police chief of Los Robles. How could that Libra keep calm at such a prospect? It was just as Tanya had told him, across the border, when he asked her to read his fortune: "You haven't got any. Your fortune is all used up." Quinlan knew that. He was clear in his mind that he would die anyway, from candy bars and corn chips, in his stinking house, if he didn't have to pull his terrible weight around on police business. So he acted accordingly. It had always been a likely conclusion.

He had been born in 1897 in San Diego, the son of an Irish-American stoker in the navy and a Mexican woman. He was a half-breed when the type was rare and the name damning. As a child, he had thought it was too much bad luck, and contemplated an adult life in which he moved away and opted for one race or the other. His name was American, and he could pass for white, but in his feelings he suspected he was more Mexican. He believed in horror, in the Church and in fortune-telling; he hadn't much faith in making money or being a success. Occasionally it occurred to him that there was a dark fate contained in his misfortune. For he had a mind that dealt in logic and intuition simultaneously, guessing a thing and working out how it might be so.

When he was seventeen, he married a girl, the only girl who didn't sneer at his mixed blood. She was a Danish blonde, Eva Anderson, and he was proud of her. He joined the city police force and enjoyed wearing the uniform. In 1916, Eva was murdered. She was strangled in their own home. There was blood in her blond hair. There were a few things stolen and there were words in Spanish daubed on the wall in her blood. So the stupid detectives worked it out that Mexican thieves had done it. But Quinlan had a hunch it was another Dane who had been after Eva before Hank came along. He talked with the detectives. He even said, "Look, I'm half Mex. I think I know." But they told him he was distraught and he should leave the case to them. Everyone in the San Diego police felt good when they got a couple of Mexican kids and charged them. The two were executed, but Quinlan knew they were innocent.

Next year, the Dane enlisted in the army, so Quinlan followed him. They went to the same training camp, the same regiment, the same troop ship. Quinlan never talked to the Dane, never gave a hint of knowing who he was, and the Dane avoided him. But he watched Quinlan. Except that if you're fighting an enemy, it is hard to watch out for one of your own, too. One day in a Belgian trench, the Dane got it, a bullet in the forehead just below his helmet. Not in the back, that might have been noticed. Quinlan called to him, so the guy would turn around, the only time he ever spoke to the man.

When Quinlan returned from the war, he moved to Los Angeles and he was promoted to detective. He was on the William Desmond Taylor case, and he got to question Mabel Normand one sweltering afternoon in her bungalow at Sennett. He had another of his hunches, but then the word came down to go vague on the case. That sickened him. He didn't like the big cities and having to work with other cops and the D.A.'s office. Quinlan couldn't abide being denied when he was right; he looked for a smaller setup, one he could arrange in his own way.

So in 1925 he moved to Los Robles. He was an assistant at first, but he could see that in a few years he would make chief, and the place suited him. Los Robles was two small towns split by the border. Los Robles was American, and Robles was Mexican. It was the one place Quinlan had known where his own mixed blood felt natural. He spoke good Spanish, so he made useful contacts on the Mexican side. With that, he became an even better cop than just hunches and hard work could manage. From 1929 onward, he was chief and he ran things the way he wanted. There was action in a border town, of course—knifings, immigration matters, some gambling and whoring, a little drugs. The Grandis controlled most of it, and they came to an understanding with Quinlan. They kept things tidy, they stayed in business and he got the "license fee" every year. It happened everywhere, and there were no outsiders and no undue violence. The wrong people never got hurt or upset. Los Robles got a good reputation, and it became a favorite honeymoon spot. The town managers appreciated Quinlan, even if they didn't invite him to banquets. They gave him every latitude and kept out of his way.

There were two murders in Quinlan's time, and for one of them there was no evidence. Hank knew who the killer was, so he told his deputy, Pete Menzies, to keep riding the guy until his nerve cracked. One day in 1935 they went to call on the suspect, and he came out at them headlong with a gun. Menzies was dreaming. He slipped in surprise and Quinlan had to protect him. The guy fired his gun; Hank was hit in the leg. Menzies shot the killer dead. But Quinlan had a limp ever afterward, and he put on a lot of weight. Menzies was full of guilt and gratitude for Hank, and he swore he'd never desert him.

Quinlan didn't marry again. He was the recipient of pity; ladies in Los Robles baked pies for him and invited him to Sunday dinner. But, in truth, he hadn't enjoyed marriage much. Eva had always wanted to talk and Hank was a more reflective person; his hunches came out of being quiet and peaceful. Living alone didn't trouble him. Whenever he felt horny, he'd just stroll over the border and spend the night at Tanya's. She never talked when he didn't want it, and she could always guess what he was hoping for without him having to tell her. The two of them trusted instinct.

From 1950 onward, Quinlan saw retirement coming up. There was a deal of time still, sure, but he knew what he would have to do. He waited for the right kind of case. By 1957, he was restless because nothing had come along in his damned settled town. Hank had done what he could to stir things up. He'd spread talk that had Joe Grandi worried; Joe kept on coming to him with wild versions of his own rumors. Hank had told that Mexican shoe clerk, Sanchez, that Marcia Linnekar had the hots for him.

That did it. Just over the border, and on his side too, Rudy Linnekar's automobile was blown up. With Rudy driving and his latest girl friend on the blue leather bench seat beside him. What was left of the girl they could strain through a sieve, but they found one of Rudy's shoes on Main Street—with his foot still in it. Much too much dynamite had been used, an extravagant amount, suggesting spice and passion.

Quinlan knew that Sanchez had done it, just as he knew Rudy would warn a Mexican off seeing his daughter while Marcia would welcome sex with color. Hank planned to frame him as he'd done before with thieves, and then let Pete Menzies realize how he'd rigged the case. If that didn't quite work—because Pete might stay loyal— here was a bonus for fortune: a solemn Mexican narcotics man, Mike Vargas, who had just happened to be near the car when it blew, just about to kiss his new blonde American wife. Hank couldn't see how Mexicans were getting away with stuff like that with white women, even if this one was a thick armed tramp and Vargas too much a fool to see it.

Vargas tried to interfere. He thought Sanchez must be innocent, because the kid had appealed to him as a fellow Mexican. Vargas had seen the shoebox empty in Sanchez's house where later Hank had "found" the sticks of explosive. So Quinlan just tweaked his Mexican tail. He got a gang to go over to the motel where Mrs. Vargas was staying and they raped her some and shot heroin into her so she was a wreck. Of course, Vargas could never have worked it all out: he had lousy instincts. But Pete was around to help him and Hank let the trap close in like a warm sleep.

He knew Pete had a recorder on him, he was so jumpy but so awkward; he moved as if he had a boil under his arm. Quinlan let the whole story spill out down by the filthy river, and there was Vargas lumbering along behind them so dumb he couldn't even keep the reverb down on the player. In the very end, it was Menzies who shot Quinlan. But Hank plugged Pete, too, and the two old friends went within minutes of each other. Hank had a hunch that way they could be on the same troopship to wherever they were going. There was never any reason why a cop who could think for himself had to submit to retirement.

RAMON MIGUEL VARGAS

Charlton Heston in Touch of Evil, *1958,
directed by Orson Welles*

He was "Miguel" in Mexico and "Mike" in the U.S., a man of twin allegiances, a Mexican citizen, an investigator of unworldly talent and distinction, but someone not entirely trusted. It was said of him that Vargas could never turn a blind eye. It made him a liability, an earnest man in a land of necessary compromise.

Ramon Miguel was born in Mexico City in 1926, the son of Escobar Vargas, a teacher and writer of adventure stories, and Jane Shannon, an American woman of considerable private fortune who had come to Mexico to buy Aztec treasures for her father's museum. At their level of society, a mixed marriage was a mark of originality, so long as the couple lived south of the border. Miguel was born and raised in a lovely house in the mountains, with servants, horses and an extensive library. He spoke English and Spanish, he learned American manners and jokes, and his parents looked forward to him having an illustrious career.

In 1944, he entered the University of Mexico, where he studied history, captained the polo team and was a convivial member of a conservative dining club. Upon his graduation, he was awarded a scholarship so that he could attend UCLA for two years to study American government. While there, he wrote a thesis, *The Serpent and the Eagle: The Mexican-American Relationship*, which was subsequently published in both countries and reviewed by William F. Buckley as "political science waving the flag of Ouida . . . yet sound for all that."

Vargas returned to Mexico City in 1950 and was made an inspector in the Security Division of the police. In 1953, he was transferred to the Narcotics Division, and in the succeeding years he was prominent in a number of arrests and seizures along the border. By then, he had a reputation for diligence and probity not easily escaped; it made the government very content to confine him to the detection of drugs. It was in 1957 that he met and fell in love with a young American woman, Susan Benyon, who was working as a courier in the area of El Paso and Ciudad Juárez.

When their marriage was announced, a government official spoke to Miguel's father, intimating that possibly Susan was a risky consort to so promising a career. The official could not speak unequivocally, but Susan's father was under suspicion for involvement in drug trafficking, and there were unquenchable rumors that Susan herself transported drugs and might even have insinuated herself with Miguel to facilitate that work. Miguel was outraged by this devious manifestation of racial prejudice, but in view of the concern he did agree to marry discreetly and honeymoon in Los Robles. "It'll be perfect," promised the brave Susan.

The day before the nuptials, he dozed serenely after he and Susan had made siesta love. When he awoke, there was his betrothed, smiling at him, and showing him a fresh plaster cast on her arm.

"Michael, my dear one, guess what?"

"What?" Impeccable in English, but not supple.

"I broke my arm."

"As we made love?"

"No, you silly. I slipped out of bed and I fell on the bathroom floor. I actually heard the crack—I was afraid it might have woken you."

"I never stirred."

"No, I know. You had excelled. So I simply ran over to the hospital and they set me—all in an hour. Wasn't that splendidly efficient?"

"Perhaps you will not be fit enough for the honeymoon."

"Don't you dare to even think that!"

So they were married, with the train on Susan's dress draped very artfully across her fat arm in all the photographs. They made their way to Los Robles and got caught up in all the troubles of the Linnekar killing. Mike was so solicitous, he sent Susan off to a motel while he consulted on the case with the horrible, fat police chief who smelled of refried beans. How was Mike to know that the motel in question was out in the middle of nowhere, with a hopped-up jitterbug as the only authority in sight? It wasn't his fault that the gang of greasers had come by, with a boss woman who sounded like the Devil, and done such unspeakable things to her. No, she didn't want to talk about it, or care to remember the look in their bloodshot eyes.

At last they were reunited. Mike was vindicated. Susan's heroin addiction could be controlled. The honeymoon could resume. But then Vargas suddenly noticed the difference.

"Susie. What happened to your plaster?"

"Oh Mike . . . they took everything."

"They cut the plaster off your arm?"

"They must have."

"Such animals!"

"I know, dear, I know."

"But doesn't it hurt?"

"Not as much as I expected. It must be mending."

"We must immediately go to another hospital and have you replastered."

"I suppose you're right."

It was years before the whisper reached as far as Miguel's ears that the "plaster" had contained four kilos of cocaine that Susan had been smuggling across the border. By then, it was too foolish to discuss, and too ridiculous to have investigated.

Miguel Vargas has been for many years the senior official in that branch of the Mexican government in touch with the U.S. Immigration and Naturalization Service. He is experienced in all matters of the border and he has collaborated with Professor David Gregory in preparing briefs for new legislation. He is kept very busy and has probably not yet heard the reports that his wife is having an adulterous lunchtime liaison with a man close to the American ambassador in Mexico.

JEFF BAILEY

Robert Mitchum in Out of the Past, *1947,*
directed by Jacques Tourneur

When he was just a little boy in Bedford Falls, Jeff said, "I like the bad guys." We were alone, at the far end of the yard. The last clumps of old snow were still on the ground, gray and hard. I think he was hoping I would explain it to him. Jeff was the youngest of the three of us. It was only later that someone told me how, when I went into the water to rescue Harry, the brother in the middle, Jeff had just watched from the shore. He never moved. But he was only seven. Still, he went dull afterward with me the hero and Harry the lucky survivor. There was no role for Jeff. Maybe the watcher had begun to ask himself why he only watched.

I asked him, "How's that?"

"I don't know." He kicked a stone and it hit the watering can, a dead shot, twenty feet away. He stared at his own skill, without pleasure.

"You don't like what they do, do you?"

"I s'pose not."

"Suppose, Jeff."

"Oh, George!"

"I'm only helping you."

"Maybe it's because they're so alone."

"The bad guys?"

"Yeah. I feel sorry for them. I mean, everyone's against them."

"I know," I said. "You have to wonder about them."

"Right, you wonder why they're bad. You think it's because they're lonely. And things."

"What things?"

"Well, don't you ever wonder what it would be like to do a bad thing?" I was thinking how to answer him; he must have looked up at me. "No, I s'pose you don't, Georgie." The sneer made me angry. My hand came up and hit him on the back of the head. It made him stagger, and I saw tears he couldn't squeeze back.

We always ended up laughing about it, but he kept that dark, thoughtful expression. I never felt I'd shaken the idea out of his head. It wasn't loose in there, it was part of the way he saw things. Mary Frances was afraid of Jeff; she never knew whether he was laughing at her or waiting for her to make a mistake. "He's too quiet," she said. "And too smart. I get frightened watching him think. He's gloomy, George." Was she trying to signal me about her frailty when faced with that mood?

Jeff never said he'd been warning me, but I think it was what we both thought of before he left town. He had some feeling that I was too good to be true, too noble for my own sake, that I was stuffy, solemn, a dead weight. He never apologized or explained. He never said he'd loved Mary Frances, or hated me. I don't believe either would have been quite true, and Jeff never bothered to say anything for conversation or kindness. He was attracted to her, I'm sure—that wasn't hard—but it was more that he had glimpsed the outline of a trap and was too proud or too black to walk away from it.

It was almost as if I'd set it up by meeting Mary Frances and marrying her. Neither he nor she ever bothered with justification. It was not something put down to my being so lousy depressed and such a pain to be with. They didn't say anything. Jeff just told me to forget about it, it was nothing, and Mary Frances said, "Don't let's mention it." She stayed with me, and he went away—so action settled it, if you weren't disposed to go on thinking about where he was and whether they were communicating. It makes me feel helpless to remember it this way, like a train rumbling along and we're all passengers who get on and off, and the train never knows or notices. That's what Jeff was like. But he was wrong if he thought I was only good, or that good is not difficult too.

So in 1937, Jeff went away, when he was twenty-two. He went to New York, the city, and I'll bet he was in his element there. The cities are made for watching and not talking, so you pass through the crowds untouched by all the stories you see and hear. You have to be unmoved in cities; you have to be able to look at the bums and the hopeless cases and say, "So?" to yourself. Jeff could do that.

He became a private detective and he called himself Jeff Markham. I don't know why he picked that name, but I can guess why he wanted a change. In the city you are free to be whomever you want, a hundred people a day. It's like picking a name for a character. You make yourself up; you decide on this raincoat and that hat. So he was Jeff Markham, with a partner named Fisher.

They had a fair business, and Jeff lived in Brooklyn. Then in 1943 they were hired by Whit Sterling. He was a businessman of some kind, but it was crooked, even if you didn't know how. Fisher said to leave him out of it, but Jeff said no need, the case was just personal.

211

Sterling had had this woman, Kathy Moffat, and they'd lived together for a time. Then one day she had shot Sterling and vanished with $40,000 of his money.

"Why'd she do that?" said Jeff.

He grinned. "I don't know. I still don't know."

"What do you want back, her or the money?"

"I want it all."

Fisher told Jeff it was his case, and so Jeff started tracing her. He was good at it, I think, and not everyone is. If I look for someone, I don't know how to start. Jeff knew the system and he tracked her down inside three months. She was in Acapulco and he found her one day when she walked into the bar where he was waiting. Perhaps it was one of those moments when he looked at her and said, "I can't help it," to himself. Fate. He could pass by the bums, and harden himself to wrecks dying on doorsteps, but then there was a providence he couldn't resist.

So Jeff and Kathy started a love affair. I don't know what it meant to her. Jeff was handsome. Maybe she loved him. Or maybe she had the same kind of irresistible impulse. Maybe they were both people who trusted the smell of their own weakness, who felt temptation more than anything. They stayed down in Mexico. He told her about Whit Sterling and his assignment. She said that Sterling was a monster. She had shot him because he was so bad to her—yet from the way she said it, he could have sold her mother to a glue factory or just failed to notice her new earrings. That cool way of talking blurs all iniquities. But, no, she'd taken no money. That was her lie, the moment when coolness fell away and the eyes ached with sincerity.

They moved on to San Francisco, afraid that someone would be coming after them. It was Fisher who came, tickled to be dogging his own partner. Sterling had called on him and Fisher was upset that he'd not heard from Jeff. He saw Jeff at the races and he followed him back to a cabin up in Marin where he and Kathy were living. When he realized what had happened, Fisher asked for some money to keep him quiet. The two men fought, and from somewhere Kathy had a gun and she shot Fisher dead. Then she got in their car and drove off, leaving Jeff to get home on his own. The gun was one surprise. The other was finding a bankbook and seeing that Kathy had a while before deposited $40,000. There's always some $40,000 or other, as solid as a gun.

So Jeff buried Fisher up in the forest, and he moved away. He didn't want to go on being a detective, and he decided he didn't enjoy cities anymore. So he went to a place called Bridgeport, in California, up in the Sierras, and he opened a filling station there. He kept to himself, but he made a couple of friends: Dickie, a mute kid who helped at the station, and Ann Ferguson, the dentist's daughter.

She didn't have what Kathy had had—not the danger or the duplicity—but he might have married her. Then one day in 1947, a fellow named Joe Stefanos stopped off at Jeff's place. You don't have to be looking for someone to find him. Stefanos was an associate of Sterling's and he remembered Jeff. So he told Sterling, and soon Jeff got a call to come on up to Tahoe for a talk.

Sterling was all smiles. No problems, he said. "It's all in the past, and anyway, I got Kathy back. What else do I care? She's in the next room." She was, too, the same as ever, lovely but slinky, with eyes like beads you couldn't pick up. And Jeff was still hooked. So he went along with Sterling's suggestion that he work for him again, especially after a quiet moment together when Kathy tells him that she still loves him, that she only came back to Whit out of fear. That's when a man has to see there's nothing so stupid he wouldn't do it. There might be a last intelligence in recognizing that compulsion, when desire triumphs over all reason and honor, when it banishes the fear of wickedness or shame.

So Jeff got involved, and it gets worse, with him ready to wipe out strangers for a chance of holding her cold hand. A lawyer is killed in San Francisco, and he is blamed for it. He's on the run, and Ann is helping him but she knows he's still fixed on Kathy and he can't see what she's giving up to be with him. All that desperation. By now, Jeff has guessed Kathy's behind it all—he wants it like that—even if he can't always admit it. She has to be other than ordinary. He could have been something decent and valuable—a doctor, a teacher or a man who gave his life to the building-and-loan business, so that he had nothing for himself.

He went back to Tahoe at night and found Kathy had killed Whit. He never knew or bothered to ask why. Reasons and explanations were like aging; they would dull Kathy's shine. She told him they must go off together again, to Mexico, and it would be like it was before. Day after day, if he wanted, she'd come strolling into that first bar and it could start again. Jeff may have agreed. But as she packed he called the police. When the two of them set out, they drove into a roadblock. Kathy knew what it meant. She shot Jeff and the police shot her; the first shot condones all the others. The police pour in fire these days, they're so edgy. The chief there wrote me a well-meant

213

letter. He said that Jeff had gotten in with the wrong kind. For he had left a diary, with a clear, unbiased account and a note with my address and what the finder was to do in the event of his demise.

> *I could never believe a life like this in our family, only a few years away from me. I roughhoused Jeff and I could handle him then. But when I write about him I see the self-destructiveness we shared—he in Mexico, on the road, in the lap of a tramp; and I safe and sound in Nebraska, a little deaf and going to waste. Maybe he knew more and opted for quickness. I found Travis once pretending to be his Uncle Jeff, and Mary Frances vomiting with fear.*

BREE DANIELS

Jane Fonda in Klute, *1971, directed by Alan J. Pakula*

Those murders were bottomless holes they tried to walk around, always with a dread of falling. Yet the murders were also incidental to the uneasiness between the two of them. So, as they inched their way through the night they watched out for the murderer, but they waited for each other. There were moments when she lost sight of the two threats, the two men who wanted her, when Bree Daniels was not certain she could tell them apart in the dark with only sound, smell and touch to rely on.

She had been born in Los Angeles in 1941, the daughter of a doctor whose Camden Drive practice included several show-business luminaries. Bree grew up with an uncertain sense (for her father was proud but discreet) of movie stars having small holes or imperfections in their glowing looks, too humiliating to discuss in public, but attended to by her father. When Bree was a little girl, she sometimes woke up in the middle of the night, crying for help. She had a flaring appendix, a detached retina, a bone disease, a migraine, and so on. Her father came to her room to deal with her. The first few times, he carried the old stethoscope he kept at home and put the cold metal disc on the troubled parts of her body. Playing the game, he said to himself.

But he became bored with having his sleep disturbed. "You have hypochondria," he told her one night. "What's that?" asked Bree, hushed by fear. "Is it serious?"

"Who knows?" said her father. "It's when imagination makes up illnesses to get attention. Go to sleep."

It sank in slowly on Bree, only just before sleep; her father believed she was lying. But she woke up every time with the true throb of pain or worry. She could not believe she was acting. It *was* pain, something wrong, and her father's presence did ease it, as if that cold metal disc sucked the hurt out of her. But her father stopped coming. He shouted out in the dark house, "Stop it, Bree." And she lay there in terror that she was dying, forbidding sleep.

When she grew older she realized that many of her father's best patients had imaginary complaints too. He took them at their word, and he would not be her doctor. Bree broke her foot in basketball when she was thirteen. She limped home and her father said it was bruising, without touching the foot. In the middle of the night her mother had to rush her to the hospital. Her father never mentioned it afterward.

She went to UCLA in 1959, a theater arts major, and she fell in with a group of young film-makers that included Francis Coppola, Carroll Ballard and, the most original and interesting of them all, Dennis Jakob. He asked Bree to act in a film he was making. It was about a young woman who pretends to be a ghost every once in a while, goes out in the night, and finds some young man to haunt.

They shot the film late in the fall of 1962, during the Cuban missile crisis. As they worked, often at night, in a deserted house on Sunset, in Topanga Canyon, on the beach and by the Sepulveda reservoir, the student crew had a radio bringing in bulletins of impending war. Bree felt this might be the last film ever made, and she put the force of her life into it, exhilarated and emboldened by the crisis. She loved doing it, having the crew so quiet you could hear small creatures ticking in the undergrowth, having the passwords—Camera . . . Speed . . . Action—and then partaking of her passionate reverie, a mood of ghostliness or materiality, while the camera sucked on her. She felt as if she had had sex after every take. She looked at the camera, awed by its desire and the implacable composure marking it.

The film didn't work. It didn't all cut together; the transitions were jagged; people said Bree was riveting, but why was so much of the other acting stilted? Don't all actors inhabit the same story? Dennis told her she should use the footage to get real work in pictures.

She called on agents. Her father gave her one name—just one, to satisfy her mother. She carried around the sixteen-millimeter film. Some people looked at it, or said they had; they said it was interesting, or they could not recall the big scenes. But it was hard to have the picture synchronized in double system so that they could hear her breathy silences conspiring with the night. There were promises made, odd, strained meetings; she was invited to some parties, and to Mexico. She was asked to read a few times, but nothing transpired. She made it as clear as she could that she would go to bed if necessary. They said, "Oh no," with a smile. "What do you think we are?" Integrity smothered her every wile.

As she waited for calls, a friend asked her to be in a play. It was *A Doll's House*, a cold Norway Christmas done in the Valley in July, sweating in the flannel costumes, but loving to have the audience under her spell. It filled two months of her life, as good as the film, but she had not been paid for either. Then another company asked her to take a small part in *The Mousetrap*, and they would pay her. For a few years in California she was in theater. Everyone said she should try New York: her hard edge would go down well there.

She moved east in 1966, and she had to start again. She got a few parts, but people told her to go for modeling jobs as protection. They said she had a new look, California Kennedy. Another model, Arlyn Page, asked her one day if she wanted to make a hundred dollars. Arlyn had a job on Long Island and it clashed with a "date" set up in the city. "A hundred dollars for a date?" said Bree, and Arlyn answered, "Sure, you know." The date was a teacher from upstate New York in for a conference. He gave her five old twenties and all she had to do was fuck him once and stay the night. He was a sad optimist and it was easy making him feel better.

It got to be that it was always there if nothing else came along. There was no need to be poor. And if there wasn't an audience or a camera to command, then she could soak up the authority of providing fulfillment for some timid, inexperienced man. It was acting for an audience of one. After a few months, she realized she was good at it; people were asking for her. She had calls in a way she never had from producers or agents. She was something like a star, and she got a service. There were some bad times. Tricks who wanted her to stand on them and pee on them, one man who had beaten her up—but he'd paid her and paid her extra when he cut her. Apparently, there was a rate he knew for such mishaps. There were others who admired her, and told her she was magnificent. There was one gentle old man who just liked to meet her somewhere and watch her undress in as slow and thoughtful a way as she could manage. He told her she was a goddess, and he murmured to her in a language she did not know.

Then in 1971 she turned thirty, and there were more tricks than parts. One day a man came to her apartment, a John Klute from a small town in Pennsylvania. He was a cop, or an ex-cop, and he was investigating the disappearance of a friend. One of the things this man had left behind was a pornographic letter, never posted, but written to Bree Daniels. Had she known him well?

Bree told Klute to get lost; he had helpless, still eyes that frightened her. He was so passive it got on her nerves. But he stayed around. He got a room in the same building, and he started to watch her. Bree felt there was someone out there spying. One night she knew there was someone trying to make as little noise as possible on the roof. She screamed, and suddenly Klute appeared from nowhere to protect her. The tread on the roof was still there. Two people had been watching her, Klute and the other.

Klute said that his friend must have been murdered, and that the killer was sure Bree was a clue. It didn't help that she had no idea how. So Klute looked after her. Sometimes she thought he was as creepy as any killer could be. But it was better than nothing having him there at night when the house creaked and the water pipes groaned.

It came to a head. Arlyn Page was murdered; she had been involved, too. Bree became more frightened; whatever Klute expected seemed to occur, but still he looked hurt, helpless and out of it. She said he should see a doctor; it seemed ridiculous in the middle of a crisis, but he took the idea seriously. He told her never to take chances. But Bree was desperate to end the suspense. One day she had to go to the old man's garment factory. He called for her, he said some pleading words in his strange tongue over the phone. When Bree got there, after dark, there was no one in the place. She waited and she heard sounds. Then the killer arrived and told her he would kill her too now. Bree stifled a laugh. Amid the danger and the terror, she could not shut out the naughty glee that she might be imagining this.

*Is there any crisis or epiphany now that we can
take on its own terms? Or do we sidle through*

> life like private eyes, noting the echoes and the
> similarities, saying, "How like that story this
> is," chuckling and comparing, even if it is our
> death.

JOHN KLUTE

Donald Sutherland in Klute, 1971,
directed by Alan J. Pakula

"You want to go off on your own on the case?" the chief had said.

"Yes, sir," said Klute.

"Where?" It was always tiring talking to Klute.

"New York City."

"On your vacation?"

"No, sir. As long as it takes."

"John, listen. You're a fine cop. You have problems with some of the other men, but you do good work. Outstanding. I know you like to work on your own. I know you and Tom Gruneman were friends. I appreciate that. But he's missing, John. He's not murdered, not that we know. And he's been missing five months. Some people prefer to be missing. You with me?"

"Yes, sir."

"I can't afford to send you off on a missing persons until we know more. Now, the family could hire a private operative."

"They've done that."

"And nothing?"

"No, sir."

"Well, that's how it is. Do you know how many missing people there are, John, in all the U.S.?"

"No, sir."

"It's a lot. Plenty. Anyway, John, I can't let you go."

"Then I resign, sir."

"Goddamn, John. . . . I'm sorry."

So he traveled to New York City, thirty-two, a psych.-soc. major out of Penn State, a year in the military, eight years a detective, single, independent. He had always wanted to be a private eye; when this case came up he hankered from the start to go it alone. And he wanted to meet the woman to whom Tom Gruneman had written that dirty letter. Klute had never had a secure relationship with a woman, but he was frightened of hookers. On this case he would have to meet one. He could tell himself he had no choice.

The city horrified him, but he would not let that show. He kept looking straight ahead, he studied maps and guidebooks in his hotel, and he never asked for help. Like everyone else in the city, he thought, he began to be enclosed in his own intense purposes.

He called on Bree Daniels. She struck him as danger straightaway; it was like running across open ground under fire being with her. Her whole look seemed naked, like a young breast, taut and fragrant. But the danger attracted him. He did not so much want to touch her as watch her being touched.

Klute took a room in her building. He could see her window from his. He sat there in the dark and watched her come home, put on the amber light and change her clothes. He followed her around the city. The crowds and the straight streets were ideal for pursuit. He wondered if everyone in New York was following someone. She never knew he was tailing her. He watched her go to several clients; he saw her waiting at an advertising agency, in a row of younger women with more amenable faces. He saw her come home, alone, and he noticed another dark shape on the flat roof above her apartment.

He guessed that she was bait he could take advantage of. Suppose somehow the killer knew that he, John Klute, had come to the city with no other design than to find him, the killer. Then he might realize that Klute was following Bree Daniels—a woman the killer had known? That the killer might have introduced to the killed? She knew many men by their numbers. She might have a book of accounts.

Klute had seen Bree disrobe for the old man with the clothing factory. He had watched the garments fall away silently and the body, pale and distant in the lamplight. Anyone could have looked at that window at that moment; she and the old man were oblivious in their remote idyll. So he was familiar with the factory, and he knew where to be hiding when the willful Bree ignored his flat advice. The killer's name was Cable, a partner in Tom Gruneman's old business, so obvious a possibility Klute had dismissed him long ago, had even discussed the case with him. Klute came in just as Cable was about to murder Bree. He timed it perfectly, like a climax, but he felt no excitement, for he could see that the uneasy relationship with Bree might be over now. She lay there, drained by the imminence of her death, her fierce face looking up at him, trying to work out the story.

219

He took Bree back to Pennsylvania, away from the scabrous city where men had her number. They were married for four years, from 1972 till 1976. Klute rejoined the force, and Bree prowled the home. She became restless in the marriage. She could never find a way of being in the country town. She tried to see the other cops' wives, but she was harsh to their small talk, and they began to be disconcerted by her. Nor could she shift the cold stare from John Klute's face. He smiled, he laughed, he looked down on her with the intensity of a lover, but the chilly gaze came back when he imagined her infinite experience. She noticed him watching her. One afternoon she went for a walk through the town, without shopping, plan or an errand, and she realized he was tracking her, his police car creeping along on its mission.

She left him, and went back to the city. At thirty-four, there was no further illusion about acting or modeling. She became a whore again, and she had to prove that she was tough and competent enough to make business in the twelve or so years left to her.

John Klute quit the force again; he returned to New York. Out of money, he lived on the streets. It was a small step down; how easily his plainness became derelict. We are only inches from the gutter; its smell will come as no surprise. He watched Bree as well as he could, but he was losing his quickness. He knows where she lives. He has seen her laughing at a restaurant table, while the flambée flared. He has seen her at the fights in Madison Square Garden, restless in a cheap fur coat as her escort talked with other men. And once, as she slipped from a limousine, he held the car door and got a quarter from the old man in a mohair coat who whisked her into his building. Her perfume stayed behind her on the winter night. But she never noticed the wreck he had become. Bree has given up watching, and lives for the moment.

> *Sherlock Holmes would occasionally spring out of the disguise of a street tramp to catch a thief, or goose Watson. It had the added effect of seeming to suggest that every bum was in disguise. I have thought of trying it, in a stained coat, with stubble on my face, booze in the eyes and a sack tied up with string, coming to the back door to see if Mary Frances has any old memories to spare. She might ask me in and*

say, absentmindedly, "My husband seems to
have gone away." I could wear his old clothes,
shave with his cutthroat, revive his crushed
wife. . . .

MARY ANN SIMPSON

Kathleen Turner in Body Heat, *1981,
directed by Lawrence Kasdan*

He was the one in the band not sweating. She chose him for that
and for his isolation from the others. She could see he was Latin, but
she counted on a minimal exchange over this delicate request. And it
might be a perverse talent to determine not to sweat. Something thin
and lethal in the trombone player made her guess it was his act of will.
The way he held the trombone she could see it as a rifle or her own legs
draped over his shoulder. On hot nights in Florida she did not stop
imagining bodies touching. She craved the breezes of an island.

"Sometime while you're playing," she explained, "a man will
come out of that bar over there. He will stop to listen."

"He likes this sugar shit?" His English was correct but the slang
sounded stilted.

"He is sentimental."

"What's he look like? There are guys all over."

"He's tall, fair, with a mustache. His hair is combed back,
like a . . ."

"Like a Latin."

"Why not?"

"And all I do is signal you?"

"That's all."

"Come up with the slide?"

She nodded. It was too hot for more assent.

He laughed. "Like it has a hard-on."

"You can manage that?"

"I try, señora." Now he sounded like a Cuban hustler from Miami,
imitating Speedy Gonzalez to be cute.

She dropped the limp twenty into the bell of his trombone. It rose
to swallow, like a fish.

"So much?" he said, but then, "Maybe so little?"

She took her place, six rows from the front on the end chair. In her white skirt and her white blouse the trombone player couldn't miss her. Mary Ann had learned that if you were very noticeable people never saw anything else about you. So she sat in her own steamy damp listening to one swing classic after another while Ned Racine assembled his frail will to go out in the hot night. To master patience, she recited her other name, Matty, over and over again, under her breath. The old man next to her looked up, as if his worn-out life depended on it. She smiled modestly, to confess that this half-uttered, half-felt Matty was her best beau. But the old man looked stricken because he had revealed himself. Even at the end of their tether, men lost their heads over her.

The music pushed aside the thick vapor of the Florida night. She felt her brow—hot as a saucepan beneath the skim of perspiration.

"You what?" Matty had drooled at Wheaton, the first time they met, freshman roommates in the fall of 1965. She knew then and there that Matty had a cavernous weakness: she had to be liked. Whatever she said, there was always that need in it: "Oh, please like me. I'll do anything for that." If she told a story it was so her telling would be pleasing. When she asked, "You what?," whiny-eyed and defenseless, it was an offer of servitude.

"My temperature runs high," Mary Ann had told her. "A hundred is normal."

Matty Tyler came from Santa Barbara. She had been sent to Wheaton because her mother had gone there. Matty had led a gentle life. She said how spoiling it had been and how much less virtuous than Mary Ann's harder time in Joliet, the southwest end of Joliet, near the canal. Mary Ann was at Wheaton on a scholarship because she was intelligent and because her father was in prison after he had been caught embezzling from the bank where he worked. He had found God in prison, and Mary Ann had stopped visiting him since it was all he ever talked about.

Matty and Mary Ann were inseparable: Mary Ann let the light-weight Californian stick to her, and let her pick up the checks. In return, Mary Ann figured the tip, as soon as she saw the total, without the tax; she never tipped on the tax. Matty was bothered by all calculations, preferring to pay with a flourish. "All set then?" she'd ask. And every time Mary Ann overrode the sly wish to answer, "No, bitch, just sit there until I say so."

Mary Ann had carried Matty through Wheaton. She had rewritten her papers, told her what to think and guided her into a lady's B. She had the time. Mary Ann had straight A's until her junior year, when she realized she was too obtrusive. So she worked for a B and a C. It was hard for her. The comparative religion teacher, a wistful campus guru named Rosenthal, watched her sink, suspiciously. He called her to his office one day and said he couldn't understand what was wrong. On the spur of the moment Mary Ann said it was because she was in love with him. Then and there she gave him an expert blow-job. He was demoralized at having allowed it—he had been like a man looking at an X-ray of himself—so he gave her a grim, castigating C and moved on to higher things.

Afraid to lose her, Wheaton hired Mary Ann as a West Coast fundraiser. She went to California with Matty, and she took an office for the job in Santa Barbara. They kept in touch as much as possible while Matty helped her mother plan parties. At one of those affairs, Mary Ann met J. J. Cord. He owned parts of Santa Barbara, and he sorted things and people into those he possessed and those that belonged to others. It was simple and direct, the way California had been carved up a hundred years before. He made Mary Ann his mistress. He got her an apartment near the water, visiting her two evenings a week, parking one of his old, dowdy cars in the alley. Mary Ann watched how he dithered over her body, happier to look and own than become enmeshed.

"What does the name Noah Cross mean to you?" he asked one night.

"I've heard of him."

"How would you like to be at his hundredth birthday party?"

"When?" she said, wrinkling her nose at the prospect of a hundred.

"He'll surprise you," said Cord, his voice like a banker's speaking of a great ballplayer.

"That'll be nice," she agreed, twirling Cord's soft, sticky rope around her finger.

"Careful, sweetie, with your nails."

"Sweetie!" She reproached herself, dipped her head and kissed it better in the fall of her auburn hair.

The party was in Ireland, at Noah Cross's estate, with chestnut horses in the meadow in front of the gray-stone house. Black limousines went between the house and Shannon all weekend, carrying pretty celebrities—Adolph Zukor, Picasso, Jacqueline Onassis, Norman Mailer, Barbara Hutton, Hugh Harkness, old European monarchs, Cher, Pélé and Bricktop, whores, dukes and poets,

223

Giancanas, Gores and Windsors, with their entourages, all expedited by Michael O'Hara, Cross's ebullient majordomo.

Cross was borne around the house by two rugby-playing farmers, sitting on a carved Indonesian throne, sipping champagne and conversation and then nodding suddenly asleep, only to wake and be as quick as a boy for two or three minutes. Gifts rolled off him like wrong answers. He dismissed them all, searching for the rare thing a man of one hundred might want or taste.

In the early hours of the next day, Mary Ann explored the house. She walked into a drawing room awash with moonlight, like a room in a black-and-white movie. She took off her shoes and pit-patted across a marble floor toward the French windows. They eased open at her touch, and she stepped onto the warm stone terrace. There was an odor of jasmine in the mild air and horses snuffling in the dark. She caught the whiff of hot hay where the sun had beaten on a field; a half-cooked grassiness was hanging in the night air. Then Mary Ann smelled man, ancient, close and musky.

"Well now, Mary Ann," the voice creaked. He had picked up every name that entered his house. "Mary Ann?—that's a smaller girl's name."

She did not answer; it was heaven to have him prowl around her with talk.

"Sit here on the stone." She did as Cross told her, leaning her back against his sparse legs.

"I fancy I've worked it out."

There was no need to prompt him or ask for his walnut hand to play in her hair. She felt like a treasured great-granddaughter.

"Cord did not come with a gift?"

She shook her head; it tangled his hand.

"Yet Cord is not, would you say, inclined to forget?"

"Oh no." Cord would know what was expected, and what would be a golden treat.

"I'm sure of that. Can you see the horses?"

She could. The longer she looked, the easier it was to pick out the phantoms strolling in the night, like Stubbs horses slowly composing themselves.

"So I have decided," said Noah Cross. "You must be my present."

She guessed this man had been prepared to die for eighty years or so. He had nothing left but life and candid pleasure. There had been little else for years. People were afraid of him but she was attracted to the tranquil practicality.

He wore a white suit of Indian linen. It picked up every drop of moonlight and was easy to unbutton. She let the top of her dress fall down and she pressed her breasts against his soft dick. Neither of them spoke. Perhaps an hour passed, an hour of the gentlest caressing, before it rose as far as it would go and pushed out its thin but still wicked juice on her breasts.

"Excellent," said the old man, and the respect in his voice fell on her like a cloak.

"I love you, Mr. Cross," she said, so wanting to convince him. She bent down with her mouth so that his thing would not disappear in the night. She kissed it and put it back to bed.

Mary Ann remained in Ireland. She rode horses and walked the dogs. She could telephone wherever she wanted and read any of the books. She picked raspberries and gooseberries in the garden, and blackberries in the hedgerows. For an hour every afternoon, she and Noah Cross took tea and he taught her his principles of triumph.

"Not to have done a thing you've thought of—that will mortify you," he told her. "You will be dead soon. How can you contemplate that and not *do* things?" He told her how they might be done. He urged her to make life her stage. They were as engrossed as children in a game, two people as bad as I have ever heard of. But the evil have their tenderness, and the virtuous cannot keep schemes of destruction out of their heads.

Cross suggested that she have a friend over, so she called Matty. Cross inspected the two of them together. "Like twins trying to be strangers," he noticed. Matty was flattered: she wanted others to see the resemblances. Mary Ann saw Matty relax, as if free of a lifetime's constipation. But what had Cross meant in it for her? She looked at him and saw only eyes painted with the enjoyment of an afternoon and two pretty girls.

"Isn't he a dear?" said Matty when Cross went in for his nap. "And he can't be too demanding. That's nice for you."

Mary Ann smiled through Matty and thought, I will have to kill you, dear heart, I will really have to.

For two years she lived in Ireland, sleeping with Noah in the bed as large as a ship, with two setters stretched across the end beyond their feet. Until one morning in June 1972, with sunrise searing the windows so the dogs looked like blood. He was awake before her, as always, watching her young struggles not to give up sleep.

"Would you, my darling?" he asked her, putting the words into her like eggs in poaching water.

They were both naked: summer was coming. One setter woke and grumbled when she tossed the sheets back and knelt beside him. It was an old, sweet twig in her mouth, but warm and supple. The phone rang.

"Ruination."

She drew breath. "Let it."

"I am."

But it rang on, and a last duty to importance drew Noah away. He went to the table, naked and gaunt, his old body and the older penis upright. As he talked, he beckoned to Mary Ann; she went nimbly across the carpet. She was never so expert that kindness deserted her. As Noah Cross heard the stupid news from Washington, he came in her hot mouth, a hundred and two, and gasped at the freedom in his collapsing chest. She looked up and saw his face being abandoned. Noah tumbled down, dead. Mary Ann swallowed as she felt for his pulse and heard the petulant voice on the phone still asking for Noah. . . .

The band started to play "That Old Feeling." Mary Ann looked down at herself. Her breasts pressed against the silk from thinking about him. When she looked up, the Latin trombone was lifting like a gun aiming at a duck. The guy winked at her. She stood, turned and strolled in a bored way up the aisle. She left an elderly man behind her, a sentimentalist, vanquished that she would not listen to the music.

There was Racine, dripping, silly and indolent. She saw him see her and she watched his mouth open. His moustache was like the embossed scar for a wound he had not yet suffered.

It would take time, she knew, so it was agreeable that he was attractive in a defeated way. But it would work. Seven years of planning would not be denied. When Cross died, she had used the press's hounding of her as a way of persuading Matty Tyler to change identities with her. Matty was only too happy. And once it had started, it was awkward to go back because the new Matty had met Edmund Walker, who was disposed to marry her. What would a big real-estate man think if his fiancée had an assumed name? "Go on," urged the new Mary Ann. "I want you to be happy. And the name suits you."

For five years Walker grew richer, more explanatory and more tedious, and then in Miami, where they lived, Matty heard of Ned Racine, this less than rigorous lawyer who had made a mistake on a will. She knew the bar where he went, the music he liked, the old

226

movie talk he hoarded, and how vulnerable he was to femmes fatales. So she strolled up the aisle and let him examine her and she reckoned six months before she could make the change in Edmund's will, get Racine to murder him, let the investigation gather, have Ned take the fall and let "Mary Ann" do her one last best friend's turn, and then follow the money to Sulaco.

She had always wanted to be rich and live in an exotic land, and Noah Cross had helped her believe in it. In Sulaco, by the shore, she would write mystery stories and see if her spirit lapsed in the hothouse of luxury.

I have had only a glimpse of her there: a postcard, with a looming cliff behind her and a gigolo reflected in her dark glasses. She looked trapped and ill, despite her tan. She never had the love of life that let Noah Cross last so long. She will be back, driven to intrigue, and she will know where to stand for the moonlight to catch her ivory silk and for "I love you" to linger in the scents and stew of the night.

But perhaps she will come back better, too, more able to notice that the half-deaf elderly man next to her heard, "Daddy, Daddy," and looked up ready to be transformed. Just as some children suppose themselves foundlings, so there are parents hoping to be claimed, undeterred by a toothache frown of evil in the young.

Do the deaf make mistakes, or do they lip-read
the story?

JOHN FERGUSON

James Stewart in Vertigo, *1958,*
directed by Alfred Hitchcock

Is there some construction or do we live in unshaped turmoil? Is the mass of human creatures just random contiguousness, an impossible tottering pile, or is there an elegant cellular pattern in human association, so that the numb crowd is inspired by eternal forms of feeling and relationship—love, jealousy, curiosity, vengeance, desire, incest, ambition and fear of falling—flexing and pulsing through time and space, like the brain waves of sleep? Can the whole show be held together, or is it a collection of stories in which only stupid coincidence tempts the patternmaker? And similar concerns . . . etc. etc.

John Ferguson was a captain of detectives. He had flown in bombers in World War II from the flat eastern edge of England to the medieval cities of Germany. He had been the navigator of the leading plane in the formation, which is to say the pathfinder, surrounded by maps, calculations and the toilet-roll trail of the way to the target, which he unwound during a flight. Then he would slip down beside the bombardier and look through the blast of the open hatch to the scars and dimples of the ground below. He matched these with the lines and clusters on the map and told the bombardier when to let the bombs go. The dead weight fell away from the plane; it lifted like a mother free of pregnancy. And soon the land flared and blinked with golden markers of destruction.

Later, when he examined photographs of Dresden, he told himself they were the aftermath of other raids, for the ruined city in no way conformed with the descriptive rigor of the maps. Like all men in the service he was told that he might expect reaction, exhaustion and remorse after the war. For ordinary men, decent people, had been made destroyers of the world. But Scottie, as they called him, never faltered. It had been a just war, one that had to be fought.

So he returned to San Francisco, the city where he had been born in 1915, the place where his father had died, falling from the top of one of the towers on the Golden Gate Bridge as it was built in the 1930s. Scottie joined the police. He had not thought of that before the war. He had wanted to be an architect; his degree from Stanford was in that subject. But the war taught him the pleasures of maps, routing and calculation, of search and destroy. It seemed to him that police work would employ these preoccupations, for what was it but the wish to bring order to the map of San Francisco, so that its grid could function?

In that city more than most, the smooth regularity of the map is affected by higgledy-piggledy ground. The cloth of the map is draped over a hard and arrested upheaval. Thus, one night in 1957, John Ferguson was engaged in a rooftop chase; they never found out whether it was a cat burglar or a Peeping Tom. With another detective, Scottie went up and down over the roofs of Pacific Heights after the dark shape. But Ferguson slipped: the roof was slimy from the fog. He slid down the tiles and was left dangling from gutter no more secure than sleep after five a.m. The other detective came back to help him. But in reaching down he tipped over to his death. Ferguson was left hanging, too nauseous to look at the zooming ground and the ragged body lying there.

He developed chronic vertigo. He could not stand on a stool to realign a picture or change a light bulb. Whenever he looked down he swooned; if any kind of desire filled him he might faint. He had to give up the police force and dramatic excitements. There was nothing else to do but go into a private line of detective work. It was the only way he saw of conforming to his illness.

Not long after this decision, he got a call from an old Stanford friend, Gavin Elster, who owned a shipping line in the city. They met, and Gavin asked him about his vertigo and his life in general. "You never married?" asked Elster. "No," said Scottie. "Not that. I don't think I'm suited to it."

"You like women, though?"

"Oh, very much. Very much."

Then Elster told him about his own wife, Madeleine, and why he was worried about her. She was beautiful, she was wealthy in her own right. They had a happy marriage. But Madeleine harbored some inner anxiety that Gavin could neither pin down nor dissolve. She had become obsessed with an ancestor who lived in the Bay Area a hundred years before, a woman named Carlotta, who had killed herself.

"Doesn't your wife need a doctor?" said Scottie.

"She refuses. You know how it is. I want you to keep an eye on her. Tell me what she does. Don't let her know, but follow her and be close—just in case."

Elster said he could afford the open-ended inquiry. He was sure that Madeleine's mood was temporary. It would pass, but until then. . . .

Ferguson began to follow Madeleine Elster. She was a blonde who wore gray and lilac. He got used to looking for her colors; they led him on like a motif, or some instinctive déjà vu. She was not hard to follow. She went in obvious and apparent ways, like an actress in a play whose feet have learned the chalk marks of rehearsal. And she did not look around her much; she did not look behind her in even a casual way. Rapt in her own thoughts, she went straight ahead and seemed more beguiling because of this certainty.

It was just as Elster had said. Scottie saw her first at Ernie's, dining with Gavin. The two men had arranged this. She stood close to him that night, while Gavin paid, so he was able to take in her aura. Then in the morning he waited for her outside the Brocklebank Building, on Nob Hill, where the Elsters lived. She went to a flower shop on Grant Avenue, and took the flowers to the grave of Carlotta Valdes, 1831–1857, at the Mission Dolores. He watched her misty-morning reverence there, and then followed her to the Palace of the Legion of Honor in Lincoln Park, where she sat in front of a painting of a woman which Scottie found out was called *Portrait of Carlotta*.

Then she went to the corner of Eddy and Gough, to the McKittrick Hotel, where she had rented the upstairs front room, which was the last place Carlotta lived before she killed herself. And then—all this time Ferguson followed her by car, parking in a dream of available space—on by way of Presidio Boulevard to Fort Point, the foot of the Golden Gate Bridge. There, while he watched her, the gray-suited woman slipped into the fast, cold ocean: Scottie went in after her and pulled her out, water falling from her dark gray suit like the feeling of apartness. He was holding her, heavy, unconscious, but sentient.

He fell in love with saving her. He took her back to his apartment at Lombard and Jones. He took off the gray clothes while she was still unconscious. Or was she sleeping, dreaming of a romance? They talked; they became friends. Madeleine told him about her feeling that Carlotta lived on in her, urging her to replay an earlier life.

The next day he drove with her, out to see the redwoods in Marin. There was a tree trunk cut open, with the rings of age marked off in a concentric calendar of history. Madeleine found the place in the tree where Carlotta had been born and died, no thicker than veneer. That night, she dreamed of a tower in a Spanish village, with an intimation of falling. Scottie heard her story and remembered there was a place just as she had described, at San Juan Bautista. He decided to take Madeleine there to make a complete exorcism of this haunting nineteenth-century tale.

But when they got there, as Madeleine discovered the further real details of her story, she became agitated. She ran away from Scottie and started up the staircase inside the tower. The detective ran after her, as fast as penmanship in an author who sees the conclusion for his story and wants to get there before its twist slips his mind. But as Ferguson began to climb the stairs, his vertigo returned. He was in an agony of nausea, from giddiness and the fear of what Madeleine might do. He was halfway up the tower when he heard a scream above him and then saw a dark shape, a bundle rushing downward, fall past the window at his level. He looked down and saw the gray-suited, blonde-haired body spread-eagled and still on the Spanish tiles below.

In mystery stories, in film noir, the spirit of the story has a secret pact with the villain. It has to be, for the construction of the narrative is like the ingenuity of the plot. Is that why Jeff felt drawn to the bad, because they are authors, because the atmosphere of intrigue must always honor its design?

JUDY BARTON

Kim Novak in Vertigo, *1958, directed by Alfred Hitchcock*

No one knows what a stripper looks like. He had seen her "dance" a few times before this sank in. Peeling to the lethargic beat of tumescent music, she wore vivid makeup, glitter in her hair and crystalline clothes, all hooks, straps, sequins and secret snappers. The stripper's art needs special garments made to tear away like the husk of a pomegranate. So you do not notice the woman as she is, because you are looking for fulfilment of the mind's eye. You are examining an idea—depravity or pleasure, or their perilous symbiosis. The woman is playing a character. Her self stays garbed. Gavin Elster realized this when he saw Judy Barton leaving the club in Oakland where she worked. For he did not notice her. She slipped past him. He was still searching for the odalisque in the green spotlight. The real woman was so edgy and unimpressive, such a mess.

But the area between her brow and her chin, and between her ears—the stamp of her face—was so like Madeleine's. He had realized this in the club, under the lights; that stare was imprinted on the wall of his mind already. Seven years of reproachful, frigid Madeleine had put it there. This Judy had the same insecurity, but she was coarser, more carnal, a copperhead, not the ash blond of Madeleine.

So he came back another night, to the dark part of Oakland, and he spoke to her. She thought it was another pickup. His car, his clothes, his voice alarmed her: how easily wealth seems sinister. How foolish of the world not to understand that he was broke, that he depended on Madeleine's money. Gradually he seduced her. He knew enough of her anxiety to woo her with insights. More than that, he was himself

231

seduced by his wife's features so transformed by sensuality. A whore had taken over the chapel called Madeleine. He thought of his abstinent wife with vengeful disdain now that he rode on Judy's body and he could look down on the same face, unrestrained and heaving.

Judy believed this suave man loved her. She had never known such dulcet kindness, or such consideration. She appreciated that he could only meet her on the east side of the Bay; he understood her ambition to be a performer. He began to school her. They had bed games in which she was another person. He praised her ability to imagine herself as someone else, and he said they might marry if only Madeleine were dead. He was joking, of course, but the game might be fun.

He bought her outfits—gray suits, with mauve scarves. He had her dye her hair blond (it was becoming), and when it had grown longer he taught her how to put it up in a special twist like a vortex. Then he mentioned his plan. It was daring; it was becoming. It would require her total belief as an actress. It would win him for her.

She was to come over to San Francisco in her new look—so like Madeleine's that only Gavin would know the difference. Then she was to let herself be followed by a detective hired by Gavin because of concern that his wife was going mad. Judy would play the part of the wife, entranced by the sad history of a relative from the last century, Carlotta Valdes, whose melancholy drew her toward a solemn but well-shaped suicide.

"What if Madeleine, your wife, sees me?" asked Judy.

"She never goes out, she's so . . . depressed."

And so Judy began to be followed. It was hard not to notice her devoted shadow. But it was easier if she remembered the morbid gravity of Madeleine's daily ritual. She led the detective from clue to clue, establishing the story. Although she never looked at him, she began to feel the weight of tenderness in John Ferguson, like a bomb begging to fall or a love aching for a beloved. The intrigue worked; the plot turned into a narrative, even to the most risky moment of all, when she dropped into the Bay gambling that he would follow.

She kept her eyes closed as he rescued her, as he put her in the back seat of his car, as carefully as if she were a bouquet, and she remained in her imitation of sleep as he fastidiously took off her wet clothes. She wondered if he would recognize a stripper's body. But her embarrassment was eased away by the care she could feel in him. Once, his hand brushed against her skin, and she knew he had done it experimentally, out of temptation. She knew this man she had not yet seen was in love with her, and she felt his attention falling on her like dew.

Judy fell in love with him as they talked: he so longed to deter her from her scripted "death"—it was as if a character somehow knew that the duke, say, was destined to be shot in 1914, unless he could rewrite his story. It was easy to provoke the trip to San Juan Bautista because Scottie believed he could rid Madeleine of her curse. When they got there, Judy saw the signal at the top of the tower telling her that Gavin was ready.

She ran slowly to the tower, so Scottie could think of catching her, but because she had already lost the excitement of the play. Regret had taken over. She knew she was inflicting this conclusion on him. But there was nowhere to go but up to the top of the tower. Gavin was there with Madeleine's unconscious body. It was the first time Judy had seen her; she had not expected such likeness. They were identically dressed—Gavin had planned every detail—and Madeleine was draped in Gavin's arms, a stand-in for the death scene. There was even zest on his face as he looked from one gray-suited blonde to the other. Judy believed that for a moment he was not sure which one to throw away. The thought made her scream, and then Gavin released Madeleine's body to the ground. And put the same arms around her.

Gavin had guessed they could get away because Ferguson would have passed out. Such yearning cannot stay conscious.

They drove back. When Gavin returned to the city he had the grim news of his wife's suicide, and the pitiful guilt of the detective he had hired to guard her. Judy went . . . to Omaha, let's admit it. Gavin had told her to go away for at least a year, not to contact him, then to return and call him if she wanted to. He paid her off.

But she was not comfortable elsewhere, and she would not work as a stripper again. She was a typist for a bank, the Potter Bank. The shyness Scottie loved in Madeleine soaked into her. After six months she came back to the Bay Area, and she lived in the Empire Hotel on Sutter Street. She planned to spy on Scottie, watch him from afar. But before that could be accomplished, he saw her on the street. He was transfixed; Judy hardly knew how not to notice him. It felt like a mortal sin to be so unaware.

He approached her and talked to her. He had altered. He was more irritable, less gentle; self-hatred lived in him, eager for more victims. But he courted her, looking past her red hair into the small window of her eyes. He loomed over her with his suspicious love. He asked her to dye her hair blond, to wear clothes like Madeleine's. It hurt her. If only Scottie could fall in love with her, the unnoticed her, they could go away and forget Gavin Elster. But he saw Judy just as an actress who might revive Madeleine's role. She could not speak out. It would kill her to admit betrayal.

Judy came to Scottie in gray, as a blonde, as Madeleine. The man was moved to tears by the illusion. But Judy did not have to own up to all her lies. She had kept a necklace that Madeleine had worn, an heirloom of Carlotta's. Now she put it on and waited for Scottie to recognize it: it was an act of passive self-destruction, worthy of Carlotta.

She saw Scottie notice it and remember; then came his fury and the need for revenge. What would he do? She half-wanted him to kill her. She deserved it. But he drove them both to San Juan Bautista, to the mission tower. She was consenting but afraid, and though he had to drag her up the tower she was urging him on. When they reached the platform at the top, he looked at her, the image of his dead love, the dead love alive again, and disorder swept *him* off the roof to his death. God keep us from finding whatever we search for.

Judy Barton went away. She did not speak up. It was easy for the world to conclude that the tormented detective had killed himself, had succumbed to vertigo again as he relived his failure. Gavin Elster goes free to this day, a pillar of San Francisco society. I could correct that error, I suppose; I have worked the story out. But I have duties of my own before that.

Years later, I still wonder how good an actress Mary Frances was. When we say good do we mean a cool talent to pretend, or a helpless need not to be oneself? She was as good as I have seen, but I must have looked emotionally. Did I stop her acting, or save her from it? Or did she sink into her amateur play, loving it too much for only three hours a day? What was her role, then? Heroine or victim?

SMITH OHLRIG

Robert Ryan in Caught, 1949,
directed by Max Ophuls

Leonora appreciated the psychological imponderable in the state of his health. That must have been why she went to work for a doctor when she left Smith.

It was Smith Ohlrig's curse that he had everything—in a way, possibly, *was* everything. His cold bravado boasted of this, when he really wanted rescue. The illnesses, the fainting fits, the sudden onset of angina were not only frailties that he had willed in himself, the ultimate fruits of hypochondria. They were the way he had found of asking for love. But since he had everything, he was not supposed to need anything else. The bravado amounted to cruelty sometimes. Anyone with Smith suffered from it. But his uncertain health insisted that *he* suffered most, more mysteriously than others, and that he was beyond remedy or treatment. In a doctor's office, Leonora rediscovered the dull ways in which people can be helped.

Smith clung to ordinariness, or so it seemed. He could be charmingly offhand about his wealth, his companies, his influence. He alleged he had forgotten what he owned. His absentmindedness tried to erode the awesome legend. That's why he spelled his name for people, as if it weren't printed on two or three things in most homes. That's why he repaired his own cars and so often took over driving from his chauffeur. He had his humdrum doctrine in eating: at the best restaurants, he ignored the caviar and the French ways of preparing fish. He ordered a sandwich, and made a radical show of preferring it. He drank milk and Dr. Pepper, at the same time. It was meant to be endearing, but the bland tastes were so rigid that they became famous and forbidding. Instead of appearing ordinary, he resembled someone in the early stages of craziness.

He seldom kept up with business, but he was always reading the sports sections. He would become a devotee of some ball team, an unknown intimate of its players. "Kipper went two-for-four today," he'd say. If Kipper slumped and the team slipped, he'd make a big show of worrying over it, putting in calls when they were on the road to see how the game stood in the fourth or the seventh. Then he bought the team, just to put it out of his mind. For once he owned a

235

baseball team, he immediately developed a passion for tennis or horse racing. His new team went into a panic because he never called. They thought he was angry with them. Their game deteriorated and every player was certain he was being traded. They got presents at Christmas, but nothing else. He heard of their losses, on the field and at the bank, with a dry lack of interest. "They think I'm made of money?" he asked.

Childhood, romance and ambition—all those states of hope and desire—had been eclipsed in him just because of the money. He was no businessman; he was self-taught in a weird half-knowledge that no one liked to challenge. He was capricious, fickle and willfully uninformed. He was always doing several things to avoid one. If there was a crisis in any of his concerns, when its decision came to him (for he arranged everything to need his approval), he would announce that he was going to drive to Salt Lake City to break in a new car. Being always the person in charge may have impressed him as a measure of his concern—that common human touch persisting despite corporate hugeness. But it left the companies dangling on his whim. He always waited to be inspired, and he lost fortunes because of it. But there were more to make up the difference.

It was as if, being hailed as the richest and most powerful man in the world, he had to demonstrate his helplessness and his indifference to wealth—made of money, he never took it as nourishment. He had a vague longing, beyond his cracked reason, to mock money and its authority. He was an American; he wanted to be supreme but ordinary, a tycoon and a regular guy, an author and a reader.

It made him inaccessible. So full of oddities and eccentricities, he had no substance. People complained that there was no real man there, just an assortment of Smith Ohlrigs, ways of playing the part. He married Leonora, and then lost interest in her. She might have made a man of him only by refusing him. If she had declined becoming his possession, she could have had whatever she wanted and she might have organized his life. He was only aroused when she left him. For he hated himself and he was moved if anyone else could share that feeling. All his maladies aided his conviction that he did not deserve to live.

But he could not free himself, except by driving across the country alone, in search of a common American who had not heard of him. And so when Leonora left him, he went in upon himself and he made a firebreak around his last position. He ordered sterile chambers in the secure penthouse floors of hotels. He surrounded himself with cleanliness, and often that took the form of nothingness. He sat still for days on end, alienated from himself, a moldering wreck preserved in a vacuum, the ghost of a madman who might be driving across some nocturnal desert, uncertain whether he was a dreamer or being dreamed. The more nothing prevailed, the more legendary he became. Unseen, he was imagined. Nonexistent, he was omniscient. Dead, or inert, he could be everywhere. He made a rare journey: uncomfortable as an author, he became a character for everyone, like the bogeyman or Santa Claus.

HOWARD

Jason Robards in Melvin and Howard, *1980,*
directed by Jonathan Demme

He was driving in his blue Chevrolet Caprice from Gabbs, Nevada, to Cypress, California, one night in January 1968. His name was Melvin Dummar. He worked in a magnesium mine in Gabbs and he was going to Cypress to see his daughter, Darcy, who lived there with his estranged wife, Lynda. He was on 95, somewhere between Tonopah and Beatty, when he pulled off the highway looking for a place to take a leak. He was driving on a dirt road when he saw a man lying on the ground. Melvin stopped and got out of the car. He helped the man to his feet. The guy was over sixty, tall, thin, bleeding from an ear. He wore sneakers, pants and a shirt, and his hair was ragged. He told Melvin he had been out riding his motorcycle and he had crashed.

So the man asked Melvin if he would take him to Las Vegas. They drove on together, and the man said he was Howard Hughes. Melvin got him to sing a song, and when they entered Las Vegas "Howard" asked if he could be dropped off at the back entrance to the Sands Hotel. Melvin gave him a quarter and they parted.

Melvin Dummar never said the man had *been* Howard Hughes, only that that is what he had claimed. Eight years later, an envelope was found on the desk of a public-relations officer on the twenty-fifth floor of the Church of Jesus Christ of Latter-Day Saints Building in Salt Lake City. Inside it there was a second sealed envelope that contained a three-page document handwritten on yellow legal paper.

It purported to be the will of Howard R. Hughes, "being of sound and disposing mind and memory." It was signed and dated March 19, 1968.

There were sixteen spelling errors in the 261-word will. To describe the Hercules flying boat, the will used the popular term "Spruce Goose," no matter that Hughes himself hated it. The handwriting resembled that of Hughes and the will left his estate as follows: a quarter to the Hughes Medical Institute, an eighth to be shared among the University of Texas, the University of Nevada, the University of California and the Rice Institute of Technology, a sixteenth to the Church of Jesus Christ of Latter-Day Saints, a sixteenth to set up a home for orphans, a sixteenth to the Boy Scouts of America, a sixteenth to be divided between Jean Peters and Ella Rice (the two wives of Howard Hughes), a sixteenth to William Lummis (a cousin), a sixteenth for a school scholarship fund, a sixteenth for his personal aides, and a sixteenth for Melvin R. Dummar (spelled DuMar). The remainder—an eighth—was to be shared among the key men of the companies he owned. Noah Dietrich, a longtime associate of Hughes, fired by him in 1957, and by then eighty-seven, was appointed executor. Dietrich said, "It's the real thing." Some smart handwriting experts said the will was genuine, but others declared it a fake. Eventually, the courts decided that it was not the true will of Howard Hughes.

Dummar later admitted he had put the envelope on the desk on the twenty-fifth floor in Salt Lake City. He said a man had given it to him at the filling station he then had in Willard, Utah. Yet Dummar still said he had had nothing to do with the writing of the will. He maintained that in 1968 he had picked up a man who said he was Howard Hughes.

As if authenticity counted in this country. We have all pretended we are Howard Hughes, and it was surely a game that could have occurred to him. After all, he loved to make movies: he made a film about Al Capone, but called the character Tony Camonte; and he made love to the breasts of Jane Russell with a camera in a way worthy of an imagination that could never meet or talk to the real Jane.

Driving across the desert at night, not that far from Beatty, I have pretended to myself that I was Howard Robard Hughes to keep myself awake. I have allotted the portions of my estate, I have recalled the great thrill of the air, and the line of dark-haired actresses that I knew . . . and my head has been filled with glory, hope, absurdity and violence. And when I looked out of the window at the night desert rushing by, I have seen old men, hermits and unfound Crusoes, waiting to be discovered, loping along with the jackals. In the desert, fancy soars and a wondrous resolution of all ills comes to mind. The car roars with my excitement.

EVELYN CROSS MULWRAY

Faye Dunaway in Chinatown, *1974,
directed by Roman Polanski*

Even in a book, I have kept them as far apart as possible. There are only darker stories still between here and the end. And no matter that the Cross always stuck in her, Evelyn Mulwray was never simply guilty. There were those who remembered her as a radiant woman, an emblem of Los Angeles in its best days, the 1930s. Some people sigh and say that anyone who saw that in her did not know the real woman. I am not sure. She was a terrible victim, if you like, a spoiled soul. But was the sin, or the mistake—the rape—was that central, or was it something she learned to accommodate? Those who knew her (so few) and those who have fed on the scandal since (so many) took it for granted as the critical incident of her life, the worst thing. I am not sure. It may be the thing of which her father was most ashamed; it may be what made him a monster. But Evelyn could have feared other things more.

Her first fourteen years are flawless, in the way some lives started just before the Great War strike us as being passed in the last poignant light of a confidence that would soon end. That is sentimental: the Cross family had made its assurance and its home from the best official brand of piracy the world has known—free-enterprise venture capitalism. But the same fraudulent fondness may have worked for that very generation. In 1919, Evelyn Cross, nursing her mother in the influenza epidemic, was old and young enough to know the damage done to the world and to look at photographs of family picnics in the Santa Monica hills when she was seven and eight and nine, a white iris in her picnic dress, and feel the recent, unrepeatable bliss. Her innocence coincided with the world's weary sinking into suicide. She was not sucked down, but she whirled around like a flower on top of the water.

lying on a sofa, reading?

At twelve, she had said goodbye to a dozen young men often around the Doheny house, not so much older, but Galahads to the "up-to-date" young lady. Eight of them never came back; only one of the others was not wounded, and he had a nervous deafness from which he never recovered. In the brief American war—nineteen months—California had not lost its weather or its charm. It was a small city then, Los Angeles, conscious of all its countryside. People rode and walked on the paths in the hills. There were painting classes at Malibu, and nature rambles on Cahuenga. This was not southern England, where you could hear the bombardments. America was so removed from the war whose peace it would direct, and California was four days away from Washington or New York. It was the last paradise in the modern world, and Californians still live in a state of loss.

Her mother died, despite her father's assurance that that would not happen. He had been talking to himself, I think. Noah Cross had a great fear of being alone. He loved a full house; he had wanted many more children. He may not have loved his wife, not once that first physical desire had been met, and he took that with him wherever he went, like a gun to be fired. So Evelyn's mother must have known about some infidelities; there was a whiff of sexual gunpowder to Noah Cross. He was a rogue, a user, a robber baron—all of that. But I'm not sure if his energy had been malicious before 1919. Quite literally, he did not know the damage he did. Afterward, he knew; and he acted with what had to be regarded as aim and accuracy.

Noah went to pieces when his wife died. He could not be bluff, sweeping, jocular and commanding. He wept, he could not drag himself out of bed for days at a time; he lapsed into the self-pity of a child. And he had only a teenage daughter to help him recover. What happened? The law says she was raped; she was too young to have a mind in the matter for it to have been anything else, under the law. And what pedantry it is to speculate whether a fifteen-year-old was willing with her father. Isn't it? But I am not sure that Noah Cross could have done it if his daughter had not, even secretly, been consenting. Suppose, out of some mixture of mercy and curiosity, she offered it? She would not have said anything, not have known how to be seductive; but suppose she merely elected not to get up some afternoon when her sad father came dangerously into the room where she was lying on a sofa, reading?

Evelyn Cross loved her father. She admired his flourish, his laughter, his ways of riding, eating and telling stories, his appetite for doing all at the same time. She was his spellbound audience, reluctant to go to bed because it meant giving him up, like a storybook. She wanted to ask him to stop, so she wouldn't lose her place. She loved him physically. He smelled of horses, tobacco and that sourness that clings to a man's body and which a lap-child follows like a trail. She loves and shudders at it as much as at her own excrement. It is normal for girls to love their fathers, and normal again for that love to be erotic at least for a moment as they grow up. For Evelyn that moment coincided with her mother's death and her father's crisis. But he should not have let it happen. He could have angered her, hurt her, by saying no. But he was a weak man, as well as a titan; he could not bear to show her his fear.

Perhaps her kindness settled it. Perhaps she drew her troubled father down to her, held his head against her small bosom, felt the quickening, heard him go silent and then knew her inner thigh was being felt by his warm hand. She would not know what to do. He did it. But so often the man thinks he does it, and blame was not in anyone's thoughts that afternoon. It was just a meeting of need and kindness, of ignorant wonder and weakness. He may have been more gentle and tender than he had ever been in love. He may have christened her, welcoming and guiding her, praising her startled excitement, telling her she was wonderful and beautiful. They may have slept in the deepest contentment of their lives. No one ever heard Evelyn hate the moment or the way it was done. Yet it may have been snatched, brutal and selfish; and he could have prevented it.

It was luck that her moment should be so dramatic, and luck or passion's forgetting that it made her pregnant. But bad luck or good luck? If bad, then it must have been good that Hollis Mulwray was around, willing and able to marry Evelyn and take her north for the birth of the baby, Katherine. But Hollis assumed that Evelyn meant to be sheltered from her father. Perhaps the two of them should really have talked more to each other, not less; and perhaps pain and guilt were their most likely starting points.

Hollis's generosity must have implied to Evelyn the guilt and horror she was expected to feel. It could not be missing if he loved her as he did. And being in love with Hollis was the best thing in Evelyn's life. He was older than she; he was not handsome, and next to her father he struck no one as brilliant. But he was discerning and kind, and I am trying to suggest that kindness was vital to Evelyn. They told Katherine as she grew up that she was Hollis's child by an earlier liaison. Evelyn looked after her like an older sister. Hollis made a good father. Seeing him with Katherine, Evelyn realized the ways her own father had failed her.

So she felt as much reproach as horror. As Katherine grew older, it became harder for Evelyn to consider a clean sweep of honesty. That's what Vivian Sternwood, her closest friend, urged on her; that's what Jake Gittes wanted, but he wanted to marry her too, while all she found in him was single-minded physical satisfaction, too blunt for his soft heart. But by the time Gittes came on the scene, Hollis was dead. Evelyn never had doubts about the murderer. There were business reasons for Noah Cross killing Hollis. They had made Los Angeles between them, in such a theft that they never trusted each other. But that wasn't reason enough. No, Noah was jealous of Hollis; he longed to be seen as the father of Katherine, fifteen in 1936, that precious age. By then, Noah Cross had come to terms with his badness. He almost boasted about the courage it took. It made him feel greater than other men. Just as it did when Evelyn shot him and he did not even fall from the wound. And he felt true power when the police shot Evelyn, right through her imperfect eye, and he knew only relief as he held on to Katherine.

Someone told me that the thing you want to know about people is what most frightens them. It is advice that could come from a writer or a secret policeman. I don't think incest frightened Evelyn Mulwray, at least not the hot act, not the part of it called rape. She had done it, and known the excitement. She may have engineered it out of a curiosity that would not be refused. She could not reject it out of hand when Katherine was such a happiness for her. So she hated her father—well, most people seem to need to do that, sooner or later.

No, what Evelyn Cross Mulwray feared most was telling Katherine, talking about it to her child. There is a part of us, so deep down and buried, that could sleep with our own children. But the soul, or whatever, then has to describe the act in language; and then the body writhes away from hearing in the worst tortures. The animal is on a leash to the mind that will not let it forget or use the excuse of vagueness or exaltation. Evelyn and Noah were alike in this: they could let action do the thing, but when the word had to be uttered they fell back in dread.

> *I can never get Noah Cross out of my head. He is a demon, utterly unlike the man I have wanted to be. But I am greedy for details about*

a dark room in his life

> him. He monopolizes me. Some part of me I do
> not know must want to be a man of action
> striding across the world, laughing at the
> wreckage he leaves. Am I depressed because I
> will not allow Cross in my life?

HARRY MOSEBY

Gene Hackman in Night Moves, *1975,*
directed by Arthur Penn

Named Harry for my brother, and Moseby for the ancestor who fought at Antietam and the Wilderness. We had the Civil War sword; it is in the attic, still, somewhere. He was born Harry Moseby Bailey in 1940, our first child. But he dropped the Bailey, to obliterate or forget the family he came from. It was an unexpected evasion in a censorious boy, always going on about "getting to the bottom of things." Wherever he is now, I fear he rants to himself and others about control, "having one's shit together," reading his fortune when he stands up to assess what he has left in the toilet. I'm sure it's a sturdy python: he would eat sensibly and look after his body. But there's a dark room in his life that would turn his bowels to water if he admitted it. He keeps me in that dark room. He walks around it, never solving it or counting the weariness of walking so far.

His first two years he turned us into lovers, Mary Frances and me, asleep in a cot next to our inspired bed. He was happy until he was seven, growing up in Bedford Falls to news of the war. Harry kept the letters from his Uncle Harry; he was as conscientious about the war as only a child could be. One day he sat on my knee—this was 'forty-four, that June, with pictures in the paper of the beaches, one named after his favorite Omaha, bringing sea to our landlocked state—and he asked me whether my ear was adequate reason not to be there. I felt guilty, his manner was so demanding. I explained it again. Mary Frances came in and said, "We're both lucky to have him," a benediction over my head, so so serene. Then she altered. "Can't you get that into your stupid head?," and I knew she was going. From one phrase to the next, she could jump the tracks. Harry just stared at her in that little boy's way; she moaned and went away teary with

243

another failure. The moan, high and small, like a dying cat, stayed in the room. "There, Daddy," said Harry, to comfort me.

Nineteen forty-six and 1947 were the bad years for him, and for all of us: years of anxiety and smothered feeling with nothing to be sure of: his parents were frantic, eager and fearful, all at once. But it was a few years before we understood it was more than Harry could take. His younger brother was born in 1945. As soon as that happened I knew we had waited too long, let him be an only child imagining the world should be that way. Then in 'forty-six there was the problem of the bank, when it seemed that we would founder and close, and what everyone kindly agreed to call my "breakdown." God! and all the rest of it. Mary Frances out of her mind at my depression: I had guarded *her*. And then the trip I took to New York and all that followed from that. Mark's visit. Harry was too young to comprehend, so we told him nothing; we could not bear the thought of children picking up our dismay and anger. But he lived in his mother's moods as much as anyone. They were climatic, the air in the house vibrated with her frustration and I was a cellar of unhappiness. He heard his Uncle Mark shouting in the house, and he must have heard his mother scream, such a hideous cry and such a relic of the actress she had buried. Then later, when she visited, he saw how beautiful Aunt Laura's face had been spoiled. After that, she stopped coming. He adored her, too. Harry knew that the fabric around him had been torn in several places past repair. He hated disorder and, since I was the head of his household, he made me culpable. Did my deafness stop me hearing the first ripping sound in our family?

When he was fourteen, he asked to be sent to the military academy—to get away and to reproach me. I knew I had lost him, and I never said it was more than I deserved. But I feared for him. He was a boy still, despite being tall and strong, and having to shave; I wondered how he would deal with the rupture. Sometimes you can see a look in a tense face that says, "This is my tragedy, it will destroy me, but I will never give it up"—like someone who can't swim, clutching someone else, ready to drag them down.

He came home once again in 1958, before he went to USC. That was all. He didn't pack up his things; there was not that much warning. He simply left his childhood, an untidiness for us to clear up. It was a large family, and I still don't understand what bursting energy it had that so many of us flew away from it, like the pieces of an explosion.

I watched his life from afar; I wasn't told that he did write two or three times a year to his mother. He majored in psychology at USC, but his greatest achievement there was being free safety three years on the football team. He was a first-round draft choice in 1962, taken by the Detroit Lions, and he was All-Pro in 1964, 1965 and 1966. I saw him on television, but it's not a game of faces. It's all helmets and the huddled strategy. But he was good. You felt he had a passion about keeping his end zone intact. He was only 180 pounds, but he could stop much larger men inside the five-yard line when they were going at full speed. He absorbed their velocity, forced their momentum upward and crashed them down on their backs. It took the strength out of him. He retired in 1968, looking older than his real age.

He had met a woman in the Lions' business office, Ellen Pressmann, and they moved out to Los Angeles. Harry set up a practice as an investigator: it was his old, self-appointed role as the sorter-out of truth, a free safety who stopped the attacks. So much of what happened was his own fault, taking care of things, and looking away from those truths he could not settle. Harry was a problems man, but only for problems he could solve. The others he ignored.

By 1974, his marriage was coming apart. Ellen was seeing another man, Martin Heller. Harry went to challenge him. Heller was a cripple—from Vietnam, I think—and not much use to a woman, or not in the ways Harry was most afraid of.

"What does she want from you?" he asked Heller.

"Someone to talk to."

"Talk! Talk about what?"

"You mostly," said Heller. "She doesn't understand you."

"There's no mystery about me," Harry must have roared—the old horror.

About that time, he got a call from a woman named Arlene Iverson. She'd been in some pictures in the forties—she was a femme fatale in a few *films noirs*. She had a teenage daughter, named Delly, who had run away; would Harry find her? He always said he could find anyone—but only if he decided to look, of course—he never found me, though he used to tell maudlin stories about trying to see me.

Harry discovered that Delly had known a group of movie stuntmen. One of them, Quentin, had been her boyfriend. He told Harry she'd gone off with Marv Ellman, another stuntman. The leader of that group, a stunt designer and an agent for others, was Joey Ziegler, and he suggested that Harry look for Delly in Florida. Delly had a stepfather, Tom Iverson, an ex of Arlene's, and he ran a diving school down in the Keys.

He flew to Miami, and then he drove down to the Iverson place, between Long Key and Marathon. Delly was there with Iverson and his new wife, Paula, a tall, dark-red-haired woman who attracted Harry. It wasn't a very savory setup: as far as Harry could tell, Iverson was sleeping on and off with both the women, and no one was disposed to protest about it. There was a defeated air to the house, of freedoms turning to poison.

Harry tried to persuade Delly to go back home to Los Angeles; I doubt if he caught the irony in "home." He had a searching gaze, but he was always so sure he knew what he was looking for. Delly told him no, but Harry stayed around. One night he went out on a boat with Paula and Delly. He and Paula started arguing, the sort of fight when one person wants to be gentle but is afraid of seeming weak, and the other meets attack with counterattack. It reminded Delly of every parental row she'd ever heard, so she dived overboard to get away from it. Harry threw a searchlight on the water. Then Delly came up crying because she'd seen a dead man in a crashed plane on the seabed. She was overwhelmed, a child again. When they got back, Iverson assumed that his sleeping with her would be sufficient comfort. But Paula disallowed it at last.

In the middle of the night, Harry was awakened by Paula coming into his room. She wore her nightgown, old-fashioned and darned.

"How's Delly?" he whispered.

"Sleeping. You?"

"Thinking. What in hell is that kid supposed to do with this world?"

Paula crept into bed with him. They talked a little and then they made love. They slept and Harry woke when he heard Delly screaming; in his dream it was the cry of all lost children, but it was Harry himself who had been screaming. When he woke his mouth was stretched open, but his voice was strangled. The girl was screaming for him.

He went into Delly's room and he soothed her. He asked if she was sick. He told her he'd go with her back to her mother. He said he'd take her to a football game if she liked. The girl was calmed by his quiet voice and by his hand stroking her back. Then Harry looked up, and he saw Paula standing in the doorway. There was an expression of inexplicable distress on her face.

"You're a football player?" she wanted to know. "You were?"

Harry took Delly back to Arlene, and he wondered about his own marriage: Paula's warmth had shifted him away from Ellen. He was thinking of escape and a new life. Then he learned that Delly had been killed, in a car crash, with Joey Ziegler driving. He was suspicious, and he felt responsible for Delly. He met Quentin, and the young man told him it had been Marv Ellman dead in the plane off the Keys.

Harry flew back there. He discovered that the coast guard didn't know about the crash, though Iverson had promised to report it. At the Iverson place, he realized that Tom had killed Quentin too. Harry took Paula out in a launch and he forced her to explain. She said that there had been a gang—Iverson, Quentin, Ellman, Ziegler—flying stolen archaeological treasures in from the Yucatan. Harry said he was going to sort it all out, and would she marry him then?

"No, never," said Paula. "Do you know what I did? The night I made love with you? I did that to keep you occupied while Tom went to dive for the plane. There's a Mayan fertility statue on board, its belly is filled with heroin."

They reached the marker buoy, and Paula dived herself. She came up with the female statue Tom Iverson had never found. There was a ragged hole in the woman's abdomen—as if she had had a Caesarean—and there was nothing inside.

"Abortion," Paula shouted from the water. Then they both looked up at the sound of an aircraft. It dropped down toward them and a shot rang out. Harry was hit in the leg. As he fell over in the boat, he told Paula to dive to save herself. But the head of dark wet red hair just watched the small plane come back again, inviting it, and the brilliant pilot knocked it off, as if shooting a cabbage. But the impact shook the plane out of trim, and a wing tore the water. The plane cartwheeled; it snapped in two; Harry saw Joey Ziegler drowning in the cockpit, clinging to the last angle of air. The fine spray of Paula's head and hair blurred the sun.

I cannot write this in one night. It takes every night there is. So I have to leave it open in the day by the window, where anyone could see it. And I do that: I take that chance with Mary Frances. Not for me some top-sheet about work and play to divert prying eyes from knowing who's in bed with Jack. No, she has day after day to go through it all, finding and imagining references to herself. Leaving it there is my bravery, wondering if she can act every evening as if she has not read it or whether I will come

> back and find the table bare and smoke rising
> from the chimney. But she can act, of course; so
> well, I am her fan as well as her fool.

PAULA IVERSON

Jennifer Warren in Night Moves, *1975,*
directed by Arthur Penn

Two people do not remember all they shared, even if they were together one still summer night. There are several strands of talk in their memories, more and less than they really said, things they have tried to forget, and things they only said in their imaginations. There is what one meant and the other understood. Harry Moseby remembered lovemaking: it was the peak he had hoped for as soon as he saw Paula Iverson; so his mind smoothed away the slope of what led up to it. Paula had another version; it need not be correct, or his wrong. There are conflicting conversations in every dialogue. But it helps explain why she did not dive away from a plane intending to skim the surface of the water.

"Where were you when they shot Kennedy?" she asked him.

He knew instantly. "We were starting the afternoon training session. Karras was missing, and then he came out on the field. No one would believe him. He was crying."

"I was in L.A. It was my senior year in high school."

"What were you doing?"

"In bed with a boy. My first time."

Harry said nothing, and nothing is a part of talk.

"He kept the TV on and they interrupted the program. It was the morning still there."

"We won the game. Baltimore."

"You think it was Oswald?"

"Had to have been."

"Only Oswald?"

"Twelve years ago. We've had all the reports and do you think there hasn't been a thought in every journalist's head and every private eye's that if there's more to it he's going to find it out? Twelve years and what do we have as an alternative? Nothing, that's what we have. That and all the doubt."

248

"Yeah, that's what we got."

They lay side by side, touching slowly, their bodies were so suspicious.

"So you won in Baltimore?" she smiled.

"Right. I was supposed to meet my father there."

"Yeah?"

"I hadn't seen him for . . . five years. Haven't seen him since."

"Why not?"

"Family, you know."

"Same old thing."

"He was supposed to meet me, or we were going to meet. After the game. That was the plan. But I expect the Kennedy stuff . . . changed his mind."

"You call him?"

"Don't think so. He just didn't turn up."

"You waited?"

"Right."

"He lived in Baltimore?"

"No. This was at a hotel. He's from the Midwest."

"He never showed?"

"Suppose not."

"Did you ask at the hotel?"

"Can't recall."

"You should."

"You know . . . I was scared."

"Maybe he was there."

"Maybe."

They heard the cicadas, giving the night a serrated edge.

"You crying?"

"No sir!"

"You are."

They made love, touching each other as lightly as possible, for it seemed prudent not to make noise. She had only once before, at college, had to let her orgasm out in silent cries. She felt that she was dumb, or deaf. But she could hear the water lapping against the dock. Perhaps it was Tom paddling out into the stream. The crickets had stopped to listen.

Later, she woke suddenly, disturbed by his alarm. She heard the last of a cry from another room; in the dream, it had been the vagrant sound of her pleasure, looking for a home. She followed Harry into Delly's room and watched him talk to her. He was tender with her.

That gruff military air fell away; he seemed relaxed, as if he should have had a daughter. Then Paula heard him tell Delly that he had been a football player, and she knew she was going to be sick.

"You're a football player," she accused in horror.

"Oh, once upon a time," he grinned.

"What happened to your father?"

"He's alive still."

"You know?"

"He's fit. Has a deafness in one ear."

Paula turned away to look at the rims of light on the tide. Tears would not come; she did not deserve them. It was like the moment when fear finds its need, knowing there is a prowler outside, longing for him to show himself and end the suspense.

"Poor old man," she said, and went back to her room, her mouth full of vomit. I hope she said that.

I was her uncle; he was my son. But none of us saw each other anymore. She was the daughter of Laura and Mark McPherson, born in 1946 in New York. But her father left her and her mother when she was an infant over a drama she might have seen, but without understanding. Still, as she grew into childhood, she would talk to an imaginary friend.

"Who's that?" her mother asked.

"My little sister," said Paula.

"Nonsense," said Laura, laughing.

"No, Mother," said Paula with a firmness beyond her years.

She went to school, in New York, and then in Los Angeles. She was used to hearing nothing from her father, and she endured her mother's futile second marriage to Shelby. She disliked being an only child. She nagged her mother to tell her about her relations in Nebraska, but she did not dream of seeing them. They were not much more real for her than that imagined little sister.

Paula went to Smith in 1964, and she rode across country on the train. It went through Omaha in the middle of the night and she kept herself awake to look at the lights of the city. But the train did not stop. She studied English at Smith, and she wrote a good deal. Her final project was a research paper on Sylvia Plath, a Smith girl herself once, and a recent suicide. Paula herself was depressed at Smith. She found a psychiatrist and she was given drugs. The man said there were so many dark corners in her personal history. She should find her father, he thought. Nothing found could be as bad as not knowing.

She didn't tell her mother. In 1969 she took the job at ICM that her mother had arranged for her, and she did well there. Her script reports became famous for their prescience. She was given clients of her own. She packaged two successful movies—*Memory Street* and *Woken by Bleeding*—and she was not yet thirty. She might have gone far. She went out twice with Warren Beatty.

But she preferred Tom Iverson. He was a figure of imprecise power and wealth, on the fringes of the industry. He had been a stuntman and that loose coterie of individualists admired him. He had contacts high up in the Teamsters. He had been married before and he had been in jail once, for six months, for fraud. He was nearly twenty years older than Paula, but she planned to marry him and go to Florida, where he had a business.

Laura scolded her irresponsibility. All the planning would be wasted. Tom Iverson was no good; trust her opinion, she had seen that type before.

"My father?" said Paula.

"If you like."

"Where is he? I want to meet him."

"I don't know."

"You must know."

"I give you my word."

"I'll look for him."

"You mustn't."

"Why? Why?"

There must have been a lifetime's longing in that question, an awful vulnerability to the doubt. Laura made up her mind. It was the truth, she didn't know where Paula's father was, or whether he had changed his name. But her father had gone off with another child when he left.

"My sister?"

"Your half-sister," said Laura. "So I think."

It went on all night, the daughter preying on the mother's secrecy, the mother losing all the armor of her life. They both knew it was their last talk. A few months later, Laura killed herself. Paula had to take care of the funeral.

She married Iverson, and she went to Florida. It was hateful, he was loathsome. But she preferred it to Los Angeles. She liked the water and the colors at either end of the day. The racket was miserable. Every month she meant to leave, but then Delly arrived and Paula looked at her as a waif she might help. Harry Moseby came next. She never knew why he attracted her, for she didn't like him. It was something deeper and more helpless. She betrayed him and seduced him; she thought that might help remove the mystery. And then she found the reason for her feelings.

Maybe a small madness overtook her. She was not pregnant. She imagined it, if you will, and took savage comfort in the cracked open womb in a Mexican stone goddess. She would have watched the airplane all the way into her head. How did we think we were safe from chance, when it was all that had brought us together once before?

TRAVIS BICKLE

Robert De Niro in Taxi Driver, *1976,*
directed by Martin Scorsese

I received it in June 1974, a postcard from New York City, a picture of Forty-second Street at night. The gaudy, not exactly registered colors show neon bubbles of pink and amber, the glaring marquees like flesh beginning to rot, and a sleek brimstone cab passing by. On the back, there was a stamp of the American flag, my name and address, and this poem, written in jagged black ink:

> here comes a little fellow riding his bi-sickle
> and all his inside thoughts are in an outsize pickle
> now, father of the family, please don't be fickle
> or else I'll come and tickle
> you—at least give a nickle
> to stout-hearted Travis Bickle

The Bickle was written in red.

It was the first we had heard from him since 1971 and the letter from the Marines announcing that, after forty-seven days' captivity under the forces of North Vietnam, Pvt. Travis Bailey had escaped and rejoined his unit. I wondered why the Marines wrote—out of strict duty? to help the letter-writers who had so many notices of death to convey? or because the corps knew that so many of their men no longer wrote to their parents? *Semper Fidelis.*

And I wondered how to read the verse. I realized I did not know my son's mind well enough to judge whether this was affected childishness, hostility, irony, scorn, disturbance or his true voice. Did he need money? Was that the point of the "nickle"? And why would he think I might be fickle? Had his name really changed? What was his outsize pickle? The grim chant to the verse jangled in my head, and I always saw his wolfish white grin. It was only later that I understood the picture was part of the poem: the city and the cab, like Sodom and Gomorrah and their approaching thunderbolt.

This was our second child, born on August 6, 1945, the day we dropped the atom bomb on Hiroshima. Yet he was a source of peace. I still remember the day in 1946 when he lay in his cot, twitching in a patch of sunlight, when I knew I could not leave him, and would stay with Mary Frances and Nebraska because of that. My decision was made above him, but he slept on, his small fists clenching and unclenching at his dreams. I wondered if my deliberation was just the drama of his sleep. I stayed. But in time the child left.

Travis was nine when Harry went off to military school. It was a severe loss for him, for he revered his older brother—not Harry simply, but the force of example in a brother bigger and stronger. Harry guarded Travis in boys' battles. He told him stories about armies and fighting. He showed him the difference between the ways Joe Louis and Marciano fought. It made Travis grow up on the alert for older models and advisors. Perhaps it persuaded him about God and all his duties.

As Travis developed, anyone could see the gulf between his need for conviction and his fear of uncertainty. He wanted to be a hero, but he needed someone to design the role for him. He had tantrums when he failed his own hopes, inaccessible bouts of recrimination in which he abused himself. There were early signs of violence. Once, in an argument over nothing, he hit a boy two years older and broke his jaw. He implored other kids to be his friends, but he alarmed them with his ugly need. Girls laughed at him, and he laughed back stupidly. There were occasions when I found him in the yard or on a street corner, alone and still laughing, but deserted by the objects of his mirth.

In 1961, when he was sixteen, he found God. The first discovery came at the church where we went at Christmas, and where Mary Frances sometimes spent hours at a time, sitting alone, muttering. But Travis gave up on the Church. He said it was hypocritical and out-of-date. There was a small temple in Wahoo—a cult, it would be called now. Its members lived in a commune. I picked up fragments of their doctrine. They believed in missionary work: Travis was sent all over the West, hitching and preaching. They insisted on peace, celibacy and poverty as the ideal states and Travis became a disciple of them all—learned but a crank, ragged, lonely and belligerent. He was arrested in a demonstration at Offutt Air Force Base in 1964, protesting some of the early troop movements to Vietnam.

The worst thing was the convert he made of his mother, her forlorn attempts to show him her faith, and his rejection of her. The last thing he wanted was company in his faith. It had to be alien to us. But his mother's woeful instability heard his passion and thought it could aid her. He laughed at her visions, beating her off. She looked at him as if he had struck her. I only have plain words to tell you what happened. But we lived in a madhouse, all of us unhealing wounds for each other.

Then in 1968 he joined the Marines. For all I know, it was at the instruction of his temple, the action was so contradictory to what he stood for. He must have lied about Offutt to get in. He was sent to Vietnam a year later. I don't know much about his time there: he is like the unknown soldier. But he patrolled in the mud and the jungle, and I imagine he shot some of the slim native people when he did not know whose side they were on. Perhaps he preached to his fellows; perhaps the bizarre faith failed him. He was captured. He must have been tortured and degraded. But he escaped.

He left the Marines late in 1971 and then there was nothing until that card in 1974 from New York. I don't know where he went or what he did. He may have rested, traveled or settled somewhere; he may have done all of those things. The temple denied knowledge of him. He became the creature of my imagining. But when I received the card, I knew he had altered in the empty years.

He became a cab driver. The rest is nearly famous. As he went from Harlem to the Village, from Sutton Place to the piers, from Wall Street to the Bronx, he began to loathe the city. He was looking for a pretext, I think. He was in training again, buying guns, eating bread soaked in brandy, testing himself in the flame, writing a journal to himself, and becoming two men—the hard physique and the interior monologue.

Then one day a child got in his taxi, a girl of twelve, only to be half-pulled, half-seduced away by a man. He could not forget her age, her high voice, and the debauched costume she wore. As he drove, he searched for her. We may have hunted for a lost female child, he and I, at much the same time.

Her name was Iris. He did find her again: it is the role of whores to be predictable, to use the same streets. She thought he wanted to buy her, like anyone else. He could not let her see that he needed to save her. But the more he talked to her the clearer he made it that she was in great danger. At about the same time, she decided that he was right, but mad. Simultaneously, she recognized her own predicament and the absurdity of his as a rescuer.

He prepared himself for the assault. He killed her pimp, the man who rented the room to her, and two of her clients. Four deaths, and he was shot himself, sitting in blood when the police arrived. The pictures were everywhere, with diagrams of the house and one paragraph saying that Travis Bickle, once a Marine, came from the Midwest and had been a religious fanatic.

I never understood why he was not confined for the rest of his life. But he went free. He had slaughtered known criminals, all of them armed; he had acted in self-defense, coming to the aid of a minor—no matter that he was himself heavy with guns and knives. He was a kind of hero, as frightening as those he had killed. They let him go. It was as if he had passed into a movie in which fact yielded to his fantasies, and the law became a pillow to his unhindered, unrestrained desire.

FREDERICK MANION

Ben Gazzara in Anatomy of a Murder, *1959,
directed by Otto Preminger*

In the beginning, I had supposed I would somehow find myself an Al, one of those reliable, businesslike, career killers, men who keep to themselves, looking like hundreds of others, men who render an uncommon service at competitive rates and then return to the crowd. Do you remember Al? He shot Pete Lunn in Brentwood, New Jersey, in 1946; and when he was shot himself he happened to be a man who had gone out that day without any identification. Was he the last of a dying breed? The last freelance killer? Was his profession co-opted by corporations and syndicates, taking all of the Als out of the way of private contracts? There must be many who, some time or other, want a sure killer all to themselves. An Al could be addictive, a permanent hiring. And Als might be a little less grim with health insurance and a company pension at sixty.

So I made up my mind to set out without an Al. I would wait for something to turn up. It was a strange, cheerful mood in which I believe I must always have been prepared to do it myself. But I knew I was too emotionally involved. I would bungle it, shoot an innocent bystander—if any such remained.

I set out from Los Angeles the day after the funeral, after a breakfast at the Chateau Marmont (another youthful ambition realized), where I read the trade-press paragraph on the funeral, with Paula's macabre tribute. I saw no reason to rush; I am never that confident driving a rented car, so I went patiently, giving myself the time to look at country that had been only names on the map. I had never been to Las Vegas, and I thought, Why not? I stopped there the first night, but I got in before dark, coming across the desert, seeing the fever of neon in the lapsing rouge daylight. It looked like a town painted in blood. I was intimidated by the big hotels, and I didn't have money to burn. How long might this business take? So I found myself a motel on Paradise Road called the Showdown, but I did visit the Sands that night just to look at the gambling.

There's no indication of night or day in those places, just the tables, with the croupiers in black and white, and people sitting or waiting for seats and the air of digestion that you get in a crowded cafeteria. I made one bet at blackjack, and I won. I felt perplexed at the omen and got up and went away, stepping carefully between the cowboys and the old ladies, suspicious of pickpockets.

The next day, I kept going northeast on 15, clipping the corner of Arizona. Around midmorning I got lost, and found myself in a haunted little town surrounded by dirt roads, but with made-up roads at its center: Colorado City, a place of many children in long dresses and shirts buttoned at the wrists, all with milky faces and a starched look in their eyes. It seemed to be the isolated home of a cult. I stopped at a store to ask the way and there were kids in silent clusters watching me. I drove on quickly, my back pounding from their eyes, afraid of breaking down. There are pockets in this country, laws to themselves, where anything could happen.

So on and on: to Grand Junction, Colorado, that night and a Best Western. The names change but the motels are alike: they have the same shape to their rooms, the same bed, the same pictures on the walls and TV sets showing the same old movies—*Night and the City* I saw there, falling asleep in *The Dark Corner*.

Going on 70 and 76 I was in Nebraska the next day. It was late October, and the sky grew darker. There was snow in the mountains and the familiar hiss of cold stretching through the state. I didn't go home, though I could have made it. I went close, but somehow I felt safer not being known: Beaver Crossing, the Rendezvous motel, *They Live by Night* and *Farewell, My Lovely* on TV, stuff I can watch till the end of time.

In the morning, I drove through Lincoln and Omaha on 80, on to Des Moines, and then on 35 around Minneapolis, getting into Duluth after dark, stopping at the Detour motel. It was too cold for my constitutional, and *He Walked by Night*—which you don't see that much—was preempted for football, Green Bay versus Detroit. A dull game, the Lions have lost a lot.

And so it was the day after, the first Tuesday in November, that I got to Thunder Bay itself. The water of Lake Superior was the color of an old iron frying pan, and the sky was that scraped white when the wind has blown all day. You can feel the Arctic there. I could only think of bars and hotels as places to ask. It was a day and a night before I went in to an older inn, catering to sportsmen, and the man behind the bar gave me a beer—I was woozy from all of them—looked at the picture, turned away to scoop the head off my glass, looked again and said, "Older than that? Gray hair?"

"Very likely," I said.

"About fifty-five?" I love the way Canadians say "about." "Barney something or other. Used to work here. Moved down to Marquette, I heard."

About a year ago, he thought. I know, I know, you're wondering about Frederick Manion. Be patient. I was wondering too, wondering how such a man might materialize.

The next day, I drove back into America, along the Superior shore, through all the flat towns, hunched against the wind, and came to Marquette. As I drove in, I saw the lights of the Thunder Bay Inn, and I felt like Barney whatever coming to the place, and being struck by the coincidence.

I went into the inn: large, crowded, a lot of soldiers with noisy women. I sat at the bar and waited for the man to get to me. He had an embroidered name on his vest: "Alphonse, call me Al," it said.

"Thank you, Al," I said when the beer came.

He looked at me knowingly, the way barmen are always ready to say they remember you, and he grinned defensively.

"Barney around?" I asked casually.

"Mr. Quill? No, he's bowling tonight. Mary's here, though—in back." He nodded his head. I looked through the doorway at the end of the bar. It was open, and I could see into an office. A woman of maybe twenty-five was sitting there with a ledger and a calculating machine. I knew that face as well as I knew the name. I couldn't stay there, so moved but content with a beer. I left my drink and walked out into the blast of the night.

I had to work out how to do it. For all I knew, Barney Quill was someone else. I had to make certain. But the young woman . . . if there was no trace of him here in Marquette, how could I explain the way I felt I knew Mary's hunted look, the way she seemed to be staring at herself?

I moved into the Twilight motel, with a waterbed and *You Only Live Once* on the late movie, about a good man (Henry Fonda, no less) who becomes a killer. I enjoyed it again, along with the local ads—the car dealers peering at cue cards, the discount-furniture store with the owner in a Halloween mask (an old ad held over) and here, one for an inn, the Thunder Bay Inn, with its smug boss, Barney Quill, behind the bar, chatting to the camera about his range of beers and bar specials. It was him, Mark McPherson, gray now, but still dark and menacing. If I hadn't seen him, I would have known the voice and the slick, insolent way he had with the camera. I went to sleep happy at having found the man I wanted in this board game of motels.

The next night I went to the Thunder Bay Inn. It was crowded and I sat in an ill-lit corner. I was sure he wouldn't recognize me—it had been nearly thirty years, and we had met only once. The bar was full of soldiers again, and there was one man, a lieutenant, who caught my attention. He was in his late thirties, maybe, with very dark hair and sardonic eyes. His table included a younger woman, a flirt, touching all the men except the lieutenant. He watched her and the other men with a fixed, silky smile on his face. The more I studied it, the more I thought that man could be a killer. He was apparently sociable and amiable, but I felt the distance he was keeping between himself and his silly gang. The woman stood up and I heard some remark about the little girls' room. She walked away so that everyone could get a good look at her bottom. Everyone watched her go except the lieutenant.

Then he stood up and strolled over to a cigarette machine, collecting coins from the pocket of his uniform. I followed him, trembling with excitement and apprehension. Would I actually talk to him? What could I say? I saw his name tab: Lt. F. Manion. He pushed quarters into the machine, got a pack, opened it and put a cigarette in his white ivory holder: it was a sinister affectation. Then he realized I was standing beside him.

"Your turn, Pop," he said.

"Oh, thank you," I muttered, and he had gone.

I was mortified by my own feebleness. I had been speechless, helpless, a coward, sure the man would laugh at me or still the din and repeat what I had said, incredulous at my nerve. And what would I say? "I wonder if I can interest you in killing someone."

Back in the motel, I wept as I watched *On Dangerous Ground*. I had come so far, and promised this vengeance to myself for so long. Yet now I could not grasp it. I thought of going to a gun store, equipping myself, striding in tomorrow and killing him behind his own bar. But I have always abhorred violence; and always known that I would need an instrument. Yes, I have seen so many killings on film, but it is a fallacy that the viewer becomes more prone to use a gun himself.

One more night, I returned to the inn, resolved that it would be my last. Lieutenant Manion was nowhere to be seen. But Quill, or Quilty—whatever—was there again, applying liquor and bonhomie. The woman from Manion's party was there too. She was wearing a tight sweater and pants. When she danced with other soldiers near the jukebox, you could see she had no bra on. And you could see the outline of her panties through the sheer, synthetic material of the pants.

Then the woman left, and only a few minutes later Quill went out too, leaving Al to manage the busy bar. I had the impression that Quill followed her.

An hour passed. The crowd was lessening. I was blue and tipsy, sure I had failed, when Quill came back. I was sitting near the door that night, and I was no more than twelve feet away from him. He was an old man too, I could see, and he seemed out of breath. He went back behind the bar, whispered to Al, and I could hear Al's giggling above the talk and music of the bar.

I finished my last drink and got up. I took a final look at Quill. In stupid bravado, I waved to him. He paused, looked through the smoke and waved back: a tavern owner has to "know" everyone. I moved to open the door, but it was pulled away from me as Lieutenant Manion came in.

"Good evening," I said, but the man never saw me. There were tears in his eyes, and, I realized, a gun in his hand. He walked up to the bar and he put five bullets in Barney Quill, leaning over the bar and reaching down to make sure the job was done. My delirious laughter was the only sound in the raw silence of shock.

MARK McPHERSON

Dana Andrews in Laura, *1944,*
directed by Otto Preminger

I walked out into the starry night jubilant. The breath of my song turned into mist in front of me. I stomped down to the water, thinking to crush the shingle with my amazed liberation. He was dead, and I had not had to lift a hand. Just as my weakness had sent me away, it seemed that the world had felt my desire and responded by sending forth a killer, driven by his own furious reasons—whatever they were—but I had seen tears springing in eyes that had been heartless the night before. Now I, the hopeful killer, found myself in tears that a miracle had lifted away the guilt I had not been brave enough to accept. It was as if a secret author had designed everything and let my despair and its mercy cross on the threshold of the Thunder Bay Inn. There on the narrow shore, I looked out at the steel glaze of Lake Superior in the moonlight and I howled at the moon.

"My dear fellow," said an elderly voice; I felt a gentle hand on my shoulder. I turned. It was a man of about my age, white-haired; I could smell whiskey, like sauce on the ice-cream night. "What's the trouble?"

I made an effort to control my laughter and my tears. The tension of the last week had made a wreck of me.

"A man was just killed in the inn," I explained.

"Good Lord," he said under his breath, looking at the inn's bright windows. "Was it murder?"

"A soldier," I said. "He shot the owner of the place. He seemed to be in a trance."

"You're shocked," he said. "You should take a little brandy. It's so cold tonight."

With that, he gripped my arm and I let him guide me to another tavern, quieter and still unaware of the sensation up the street. He sat me down and called for two brandies. He introduced himself as Parnell Emmett McCarthy. I said I was spending the night in town, on my way from Montreal to International Falls. Mr. McCarthy waited for me to calm myself, and then he extracted the whole story from me with a skill that belied my feeling that he was not far short of drunk.

I went back to my motel a young man again. I could not sleep, but stayed awake for *The Asphalt Jungle* and *Where the Sidewalk Ends*. As dawn broke, I went to my case and took out the letter given to me at the funeral by Paula:

> Dearest George,
>
>   I have heard he is in Thunder Bay. This news is not fresh. He may have moved on.
>
>   The other girl is or was with him. My dear, I do not think she was Mark's. I let Mark take her because he promised then to leave us alone. I have never forgiven myself, but I think the child was yours. Remember me.
>
>   All my love,
>
>   Laura.

The trial never knew of him as anything but Barney Quill, the deceased. The corpse has no history; it is enough that its violent coming into being initiates the trial. His whole shady past was covered by the revelation that Mary Palant was his daughter. There were lascivious gasps all over the courtroom: Marquette had thought she was Quill's mistress. Even now, they couldn't quite separate the old idea that he had been sleeping with her from the hot flash that he was her father. Suppose I had said she was not his, but mine, those gasps would have started tittering. The credulousness of that kind of audience can only be teased so far. Revelation is always close to the ridiculous.

The woman who had seemed like an army slut was actually a Laura, Laura Manion, the lieutenant's wife. They had been married a few years, since a time in Georgia when his and her first marriages had been broken apart by their affair. It was the contention of the defense, ably conducted by a Mr. Paul Biegler, backed up by none other than Parnell Emmett McCarthy, that earlier on the fateful night Laura Manion had left the inn. That Quill had pursued her and offered to drive her back to the trailer she lived in with Manion.

But he had driven off the highway into some woods—the place was found and avidly splashed in the local papers. He had hit Mrs. Manion, pulled off her pants, ripped away her panties and raped her. The abused woman had staggered home and told her husband. In his rage, he had gone straight to the inn and, under what Biegler called "an irresistible impulse," shot the innkeeper.

The state's case, conducted by a smart lawyer from Lansing, was that Laura Manion had been as willing to go with Barney Quill as she seemed happy to dance with anyone. They said that Manion knew his wife's looseness, and that it was murder plain and simple. For his part, the lieutenant remembered only a daze. I sat in the court (I could not miss it), tickled to think that a cloud of unknowing had met my need.

The case hinged on the evidence of Mary Palant. For the young woman had found a pair of torn panties upstairs in the inn, and put them aside. She had heard evidence in court and been reminded of them. They came into court, a tattered white flag of nylon, but with a label—the Smart Shop in Phoenix—that confirmed Mrs. Manion's memory of their purchase.

I looked at the two women, Laura and Mary. It still seemed hard to think of Laura Manion being raped. But if I thought that, why surely I would have to query all rapes—it is an old male humbug that women always want it. Mary Palant's face was more stricken. She had honestly given evidence that helped save a man for his wife. But it gave credence to the gossip that her father was a wolf. Her father? She had had to admit it in court: how Quill years ago had had an affair with a waitress in Blind River, Ontario, never married, then welcomed Mary when her mother died in a flood. But the constraint in Mary's face made me think she had lost not only a father, but her good opinion of him.

When the trial was over, I went to call on her. Yet again, I realized I was tongue-tied, weighed down with an awesome question too great to be asked. She was running the inn now, with the help of Al; it was the best way to fill the days.

I introduced myself; she was polite. I told her that I had talked to her father a few times before the shooting; that I had liked him, had been horrified by what happened, and a little curious to know more about him than had emerged in the trial.

"I felt he was a more private person," I told her.

"Yes," she said. "I think so."

The child has to trust what parents say about its origins. Suppose that waitress in Canada had been paid to look after Mary. Suppose Quill sometimes called on them. Suppose the little girl had wondered if he was her father, and claimed as much in her most ardent dreams. Then the mother had died. I grant the flood (I looked that up), but I wondered if Mark had not held the waitress under. She had no other kin; that is how Quill took the child. I checked: he had adopted her.

"Was he really your father?" I asked her, and I could not tell what answer I wanted.

"I thought so once," she replied, "but later . . ."

I might have prodded her. But I had reached the point of wanting to leave things alone, and there were tears in her eyes at least as honest as those I had seen on Lieutenant Manion's face.

"You have a fine inn here," I said, to change the subject.

"It is," she said, and I knew as if pierced that she and I had the same fondness for out-of-the-way places.

GEORGE BAILEY

James Stewart in It's a Wonderful Life, *1946, directed by Frank Capra*

I was born in 1910: I will be seventy-five this coming February, and I will make it so that I can go to Marquette again in the summer. I was born in Bedford Falls, Nebraska, and I have lived there all my life. Nor do I have any intention of leaving the place; those hopes and fears have all gone. I was born conservative and local, and such a man can hardly deal with experience, take pleasure or accept tragedy, unless he abides by his nature. I have been away from Bedford Falls a very few times—I mean traveled away. But in my mind I have always ranged farther afield—not just to the West, or back to New York—but into possibilities, stories, other lives that I could not have. All my life, I have loved the movies, and they have a legion of slaves, pale, overweight and shy, but fantastic journeyers, of which I am one. We all of us have to be somewhere every moment: it is our dull duty, whether it's in Bedford Falls or the Pierre Hotel in New York. But the screen is like a map for our dreams on which we may always travel, without ticket, tiredness or pain. It is our greatest frontier, like a magic mirror.

Perhaps I am absurdly proud of Bedford Falls. I know when I was young I had a tendency to make myself sentimentally cozy about certain things: it was immaturity, I daresay, and I had to get as far as thirty-six before I learned anything different. Some days I see Bedford Falls as a nondescript town, a flat land with flat lives, small and small-minded, cautious, critical and piously inhibited. It may be so. Yet once I regarded it as ideal, like the small towns on Christmas

263

cards, held together by the light of the star, by its own fellowship and by satisfied isolation from all the rest of the world.

Well, today Bedford Falls is nearly a suburb of restless Omaha. There are strategic bombers in our sky, trucks half a mile away, going east and west, carrying goods, and there are cars in every drive. When I was a child, Omaha was a treat, apparently a day away on a bus that went twice a day. If you went, you had to wait by the stop amid cornfields, alone in a mass of silent growth, feeding America. Today our grain goes to Russia, along with the threat of the bombers. In those days, people walked and stopped to talk: the town was content with itself. It seems like a moment of grace—but maybe it was rancid then, and America is just a story of its men and women going from happiness to stoicism.

I had two brothers, Harry and Jeffrey, and there were only five years covering our ages. They made me a father figure, because Pa was so busy, and so weary, from running the Bailey Building & Loan. I saw so much of my life in his, but I was pleased to be led then. It was a childhood of perfection, I still think: modest in means, rich in feeling. But I cannot tell now whether that is true to the time and the place, or just a measure of my young optimism.

There were dangers and disasters, but they were averted. When Harry fell through the ice, I went in and rescued him: it was the natural thing to do, and I never felt bitter that my hearing went in the one ear because of the cold water. And I saved Mr. Gower from accidentally putting poison in a prescription. Who wouldn't have done that, if they'd known? The town made me a kind of hero. I should have been all the more confident, but it left me anxious. I never trusted ice or the obvious again. It was the start of my suspiciousness, and when I found myself as a worried, worrying man, depressive, alarmist and fearing the worst, why, I was deaf too to go with it, the perfect physical accompaniment.

It was in 1927 that I first saw Mary Frances Hunt. There was a fair in Omaha that summer, and a gang of us went over for a weekend. There were parties and picnics, and that's how I met her. She was ten and I was seventeen; it's a matter of fact that I fell in love first with a child, a girl in a white frock. At that time, I don't think I was aware of what was happening. A seventeen-year-old does not own up to being smitten by a kid, least of all to himself. But my mind knew. It started to compose itself for the patience I would need; perhaps my fear of going away seized on Mary Frances as a reason for choosing safety. In any event, when Pa died the next year and I was faced with going to

Lincoln to the university or running the company, I stayed in Bedford Falls. People said I was swell for letting Harry go two years later, but I was a coward too.

The 1930s were so hard. The Building & Loan went from trouble to trouble during the Depression. I was never home early. I could see people's pity at the haste with which I was aging. Faster than Mary Frances was growing up. I found reasons to be in Omaha, and I watched the Hunt girls, Mary Frances and Laura, attracting more and more attention. I was nearly a comic figure to the young set at their picnics. If Mary Frances did like me, it was because my image of premature failure interested her dramatic instincts. She was a fine actress. I couldn't deny it, but I was frightened by all the urging that she go on the stage. Not just because I would lose her then, but because I thought her parts acted on her like an illness. She had the nature of an actress—repressed in life, alive on the stage—but when she went back into life she was inflamed by what she had felt in the play. She was no longer satisfied or calm. With every play she became a little more disturbed as a person. Only I seemed to see this; but I loved her, and that made the difference.

Her mother had spells of melancholy or worse. There was some weakness in the family line, like an angle to the nose or a color in the eyes. There was the year when Mary Frances and her mother sank into crisis simultaneously. It was hot and windy and Mr. Jed Harris came by, proposing to make Mary Frances a famous actress. It jostled her terribly. For three days she had to be tied to her bed. Laura and I took care of it. Their mother was in another room, groaning so steadily that it got on your nerves.

Laura told me there would always be times like these, but I married Mary Frances in 1938 and took her to Bedford Falls. She cheered up a lot. We had Harry in 1940 and Bedford Falls had maybe its last great age during the war, dedicated to the soldiers far away and to self-sacrifice at home. I looked forward to the peace. I wanted to do my bit in ensuring that warriors coming home could have a house and a life to justify the fighting. But being left out of the war made me gloomy, and I had been a little influenced already by the dark holes of despair that overtook Mary Frances once or twice a year. We had another son, Travis, in 1945, but I could tell that Mary was near her brink.

The crisis came in 1946. Uncle Billy—my right-hand problem at the Building & Loan—lost a packet of money. It looked like ruin, prison and an end to everything. I was out of my mind. I thought of killing myself, and it taught me how troubled my head was already that there was no real stamina for life there to sustain me. I would have done something, and left Mary Frances, Harry and Travis. I could not trust or believe in myself. It was a dreadful discovery, worse than the loss of the money and the prospect of exposure.

Just before Christmas I went away for a few days to New York. It was subsequently called "the episode with the angel." That was Mary Frances's way of explaining it, the first sign of her refuge in religion. I went to see Laura, who had been in New York for several years. She was successful, it seemed, and I had a notion that she might loan me some money. I had never met her husband, Mark, before, and I was taken aback by the animosity between them. They had a daughter, Paula, but Mark paid no attention to her. He deliberately spoke of the ugliness he encountered as a policeman, and he brought unaccountably strange men to the house for beer and cards.

Laura wanted to help me. She had developed so much and so well, it made me suspicious of Bedford Falls. I did wonder whether Mary Frances might have dazzled Broadway if she had been able to accelerate as Laura had. Laura looked like a film star; she looked like a magical Mary Frances, the woman my wife could have become but for me, our town and her illness. But I had to consider whether the last might not be aggravated by the first two.

It was the last weekend before Christmas. Laura was buying presents, making arrangements, working at Bullitt's, and trying to get some money together for me. She knew Mark would forbid it if he found out, and most of her money, at her own early insistence, was in a joint account. There were secret meetings and complicated plans. She and I met at the Pierre Hotel and she gave me an envelope full of money. I could hardly speak, but when I looked up she was weeping.

"So you'll be going now," she said.

There was so much gathered but untouched sentiment in us—the dark clouds of Mark and Mary Frances—the air brimming with Christmas and the way in which Laura resembled the wife I had wanted. There were a few hours before my train. We never discussed it. Laura went away and came back with a key. We went up to a primrose-yellow room and made love in the winter light. Then we left. I went to the station, and Laura to her apartment, the two of us due at our family Christmases.

The Building & Loan was saved. Bedford Falls went on. We heard that Laura was pregnant again. Then in the spring of 1947, Mark McPherson came to town. He drove in, without warning. It all happened while I was at the office. He introduced himself to Mary

Frances, admired Harry and Travis, sent Harry out into the yard, and raped my wife, as quickly and brutally as he could.

I never saw him. Harry came to the office. He said, "Mommy's ill," very quietly, and took me home. Mary Frances was in the bathroom, naked, washing herself repeatedly. I never knew what Mark had told her, but she knew what he had done to her was for a reason, a rebuke. Harry may have understood more than she did, even if he was only seven. Travis was asleep in his cot. Mary Frances was demented, and an actress playing dementia. I have never known which for sure. The bad times come and go. She is like a character in a high-strung movie, like Olivia de Havilland as twins in *The Dark Mirror*.

What else would you want to know? I am seventy-four and Mary Frances is sixty-seven. We live in the same house; the crises now have more room to hide in. I sold the Building & Loan to the Potter Corporation, and I am what is called comfortable now. I have a video recorder and a library of films. In addition I have two sons who have changed their names from Bailey and who will not see me, a daughter in Atlantic City and another in the south of France. Among the four of them, my children have been in on the killing of over a dozen Americans. They all have their own nightmares.

I will go to Marquette again for a week in the summer, to the Thunder Bay Inn. I enjoy the lake, and the walks. There is a good library in the town and the people at the inn know me. Mary is married to Alphonse Poquette—Al, he prefers to be called—and they have two children, Tracy and Craig. Al is a little brusque. He finds me tedious, I think. Why not? I do not enjoy myself. But Mary invites me in to their part of the inn for tea sometimes. We talk, sitting there in the warm lounge, me with my uncertainty about who she is, never to be disturbed, she with her consistent, shallow friendliness, and both of us sitting beneath the glow of the lifesize painting of Laura that she inherited from her father.

A version of my early life is played on television every Christmas, but my country rumbles on in the darker pattern of my years since then, torn between Santa Claus and the bogeyman.

*   *   *

I sleep less and less. With so little to do now, why should I be given more time?

It was no longer night when I awoke, but there was still nothing but dark. The lights on our street go off at one in the morning. There is no sense of threat here. The night is a complete rest, or absence. So at five I can tell the several steps by which degrees of black are being withdrawn from the night. It is dark still, but a dark that has felt the first intimations of something else.

I lay in bed another half hour. It was not unusual that George was not there beside me. When I saw the first streaks of reflection in the oval mirror I got up and put on the scarlet dressing gown he bought me in New York, his one time there. It is threadbare, but it was a Christmas present and I will not give it up. He has told me that I look like Santa Claus in it. I am tall still, for a woman, and I have white hair above the red gown. Anyone without his glasses might make the same eager mistake.

Did he see that figure come down the stairs, stepping over those that creak, so the movement might look menacing, like a limp? I expected him to be asleep. I meant to shut the window and put a blanket round his shoulders. I have learned to do all that without ever waking him.

But he was sitting as if thrust back in his chair, his head twisted so that it was turned to look at the staircase and at me. Did he see me? Was he so wrapped in what he was writing that he wondered if he saw a specter on the stairs and had his heart quiver, just once, and stop? Did George die, frightened, seeing me, looking like a figure in a play come to rescue or rebuke him? The look on his face matched either prospect. The wanting to know and see was frozen, his mouth open and the last run of dribble was like a snail's trail on his chin. I saw the details, as if he had written me to be his discoverer.

His book, this book, lay on the table in front of him. The pages looked like stones in the coming light. They have lived on the table for years, defending it against polish. Perhaps I can save the table now, if I pack up the pages.

The book goes on and on about the actress I might have been, and the tragic player I became in this house instead. I have never understood such a waste of hope and worrying. I had none of the need to be an actress. I was only a girl with a certain cautious talent, and too much shyness in social situations. I acted, I daresay, to find a husband. It was the only way I knew of showing I was ardent and attractive. I found George, but he could never overcome the guilt that he had stopped me being an actress. It was one of his ways of ensuring unhappiness.

When truly he was the one of us who should have left. He had a chronic aptitude for the far-fetched stories of the movies. He was always seeing fatal nymphs in Tennessee towns, or hearing the engraved conversations that carry haunted lovers up to the screen, their faces torn by suspense. He could not look at anything without suspecting its capacity for story.

But he was afraid of that world, and so he remained here in Bedford Falls, saying he was deaf, needed, too prosaic, too ordinary to travel, a man with an unsound heart. But he traveled all the time in his mind. For years on end he was in the exciting motion of pictures, carried away, leaving his body in the chair by the window, but not noticing that real people growing up and growing sad were waiting for him.

The light now is pigeon gray. I will have to call the doctor, the mortician and the children, one after the other. There will be a quiet funeral in Nebraska, its plain loss not alleviated by long-lost daughters or the first rising notes of a rescue theme. We are all real here, and we have to bury the bodies when they have been abandoned.

Mary Frances Bailey
November 1984

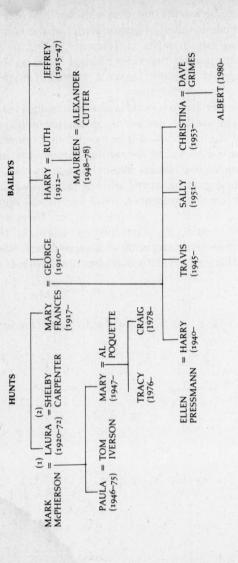

HUNTS

BAILEYS

MARK McPHERSON
= (1) LAURA (1920–72)
= (2) SHELBY CARPENTER

MARY FRANCES (1917–

GEORGE (1910–

HARRY (1912– = RUTH

JEFFREY (1915–47)

MAUREEN (1948–78) = ALEXANDER CUTTER

PAULA (1946–75) = TOM IVERSON

MARY (1947– = AL POQUETTE

TRACY (1976–

CRAIG (1978–

ELLEN PRESSMANN = HARRY (1940–

TRAVIS (1945–

SALLY (1951–

CHRISTINA (1953– = DAVE GRIMES

ALBERT (1980–

FILMOGRAPHY

American Gigolo (1980), written and directed by Paul Schrader.

Anatomy of a Murder (1959), directed by Otto Preminger; screenplay by Wendell Mayes, based on the novel by Robert Traver.

Atlantic City (1980), directed by Louis Malle; screenplay by John Guare.

Badlands (1973), written and directed by Terrence Malick.

Beat the Devil (1954), directed by John Huston; screenplay by Huston and Truman Capote, from the novel by James Helvick.

The Big Heat (1953), directed by Fritz Lang; screenplay by Sidney Boehm, from the novel by William P. McGivern.

The Big Sleep (1946), directed by Howard Hawks; screenplay by William Faulkner, Leigh Brackett and Jules Furthman, from the novel by Raymond Chandler.

Body Heat (1981), written and directed by Lawrence Kasdan.

Casablanca (1942), directed by Michael Curtiz; screenplay by Julius J. Epstein, Philip G. Epstein and Howard Koch, from the play *Everybody Goes to Rick's* by Murray Burnett and Joan Alison.

Caught (1949), directed by Max Ophuls; screenplay by Arthur Laurents, from the novel *Wild Calendar* by Libbie Block.

Chinatown (1974), directed by Roman Polanski; screenplay by Robert Towne.

Citizen Kane (1941), directed by Orson Welles; screenplay by Welles and Herman J. Mankiewicz.

Cutter's Way (1981), directed by Ivan Passer; screenplay by Jeffrey Alan Fiskin, from the novel *Cutter and Bone* by Newton Thornburg.

Double Indemnity (1944), directed by Billy Wilder; screenplay by Wilder and Raymond Chandler, from the novel by James M. Cain.

The Gambler (1974), directed by Karel Reisz; screenplay by James Toback.

Gilda (1946), directed by Charles Vidor; screenplay by Marion Parsonnet, from Jo Eisinger's adaptation of a story by E. A. Ellington.

The Godfather (1971), directed by Francis Ford Coppola; screenplay by Coppola and Mario Puzo, from the novel by Puzo.

The Godfather Part II (1974), directed by Francis Ford Coppola; screenplay by Coppola and Mario Puzo, from the novel by Puzo.

The Great Gatsby (1949), directed by Elliott Nugent; screenplay by Cyril Hume and Richard Maibaum, from the novel by F. Scott Fitzgerald.

The Great Gatsby (1974), directed by Jack Clayton; screenplay by Francis Ford Coppola, from the novel by Fitzgerald.

High Sierra (1941), directed by Raoul Walsh; screenplay by John Huston and W. R. Burnett, from the novel by Burnett.

I Walk the Line (1970), directed by John Frankenheimer; screenplay by Alvin Sargent, from the novel *An Exile* by Madison Jones.

In a Lonely Place (1949), directed by Nicholas Ray; screenplay by Andrew Solt, from an adaptation by Edmund H. North of the novel by Dorothy B. Hughes.

It's a Wonderful Life (1946), directed by Frank Capra; screenplay by Frances Goodrich, Albert Hackett and Capra, additional scenes by Jo Swerling, based on a story "The Greatest Gift" by Philip Van Doren Stern.

The Killers (1946), directed by Robert Siodmak; screenplay by Anthony Veiller, from the story by Ernest Hemingway.

The Killing (1956), directed by Stanley Kubrick; screenplay by Kubrick, from the novel *Clean Break* by Lionel White, additional dialogue by Jim Thompson.

The King of Marvin Gardens (1972), directed by Bob Rafelson; screenplay by Jacob Brackman.

Klute (1971), directed by Alan J. Pakula; screenplay by Andy K. Lewis and Dave Lewis.

The Lady from Shanghai (1948), directed by Orson Welles; screenplay by Welles, from the novel *If I Die Before I Wake* by Sherwood King.

Laura (1944), directed by Otto Preminger; screenplay by Jay Dratler, Samuel Hoffenstein and Betty Reinhardt, from the novel by Vera Caspary.

The Long Goodbye (1973), directed by Robert Altman; screenplay by Leigh Brackett, from the novel by Raymond Chandler.

Lolita (1962), directed by Stanley Kubrick; screenplay by Vladimir Nabokov, from his own novel.

The Maltese Falcon (1941), written and directed by John Huston, from the novel by Dashiell Hammett.

Melvin and Howard (1980), directed by Jonathan Demme; screenplay by Bo Goldman.

Morocco (1930), directed by Josef von Sternberg; screenplay by Jules Furthman, from the play *Amy Jolly* by Benno Vigny.

New York, New York (1977), directed by Martin Scorsese; screenplay by Earl MacRauch and Mardik Martin, from a story by MacRauch.

Night Moves (1975), directed by Arthur Penn; screenplay by Alan Sharp.

No Man of Her Own (1950), directed by Mitchell Leisen; screenplay by Sally Benson, Catherine Turney and Leisen, from the novel *I Married a Dead Man* by Cornell Woolrich.

Notorious (1946), directed by Alfred Hitchcock; screenplay by Ben Hecht.

Out of the Past (1947), directed by Jacques Tourneur; screenplay by Geoffrey Homes (Daniel Mainwaring), from his own novel *Build My Gallows High*.

Paper Moon (1973), directed by Peter Bogdanovich; screenplay by Alvin Sargent, from the novel *Addie Pray* by Joe David Brown.

The Passenger (1975), directed by Michelangelo Antonioni; screenplay by Mark Peploe, Peter Wollen and Antonioni, from a story by Peploe.

Pickup on South Street (1953), directed by Samuel Fuller; screenplay by Fuller, from a story by Dwight Taylor.

Point Blank (1967), directed by John Boorman; screenplay by Alexander Jacobs, David Newhouse and Rafe Newhouse, from the novel *The Hunter* by Richard Stark.

The Postman Always Rings Twice (1946), directed by Tay Garnett; screenplay by Niven Busch and Harry Reskin, from the novel by James M. Cain.

The Postman Always Rings Twice (1981), directed by Bob Rafelson; screenplay by David Mamet, from the novel by James M. Cain.

Psycho (1960), directed by Alfred Hitchcock; screenplay by Joseph Stefano, from the novel by Robert Bloch.

Rear Window (1954), directed by Alfred Hitchcock; screenplay by John Michael Hayes, from a story by Cornell Woolrich.

Rebel Without a Cause (1955), directed by Nicholas Ray; screenplay by Stewart Stern, adapted by Irving Shulman from a story by Ray.

The Shining (1980), directed by Stanley Kubrick; screenplay by Kubrick and Diane Johnson, from the novel by Stephen King.

Strangers on a Train (1951), directed by Alfred Hitchcock; screenplay by Raymond Chandler and Czenzi Ormonde, from the novel by Patricia Highsmith.

Sunset Boulevard (1950), directed by Billy Wilder; screenplay by Wilder and Charles Brackett.

Taxi Driver (1976), directed by Martin Scorsese; screenplay by Paul Schrader.

The Third Man (1949), directed by Carol Reed; screenplay and original story by Graham Greene.

Touch of Evil (1958), written and directed by Orson Welles, from the novel *Badge of Evil* by Whit Masterson.

Vertigo (1958), directed by Alfred Hitchcock; screenplay by Alec Coppel and Samuel Taylor, from the novel *D'Entre les Morts* by Pierre Boileau and Thomas Narcejac.

White Heat (1949), directed by Raoul Walsh; screenplay by Ivan Goff and Ben Roberts, from a story by Virginia Kellogg.

Who'll Stop the Rain (1978), directed by Karel Reisz; screenplay by Judith Rascoe and Robert Stone, from the novel *Dog Soldiers* by Stone.